PRAISE FOR

THE ONE THAT GOT AWAY

"Bethany Chase is utterly charming and writes about
loss with wisdom and heart."

—Allie Larkin,
author of *Why Can't I Be You*

"Don't let this one get away: Chase's debut is fun,
romantic, steamy, and populated with heartfelt
characters—not-to-miss delicious escapism!"

—L. Alison Heller,
author of *The Never Never Sisters*

"We fell in love with *The One That Got Away* from
the very first page. In her charming debut novel,
Bethany Chase reminds us about the one that got
away, and makes us wonder what would have
happened if he hadn't."

—Liz Fenton and Lisa Steinke,
co-authors of *Your Perfect Life*

"*The One That Got Away* is juicy, steamy, witty, and
real. Bethany Chase kept me laughing out loud as I
quickly turned the pages. With a love story perfectly
balanced between sexy and sweet and settings so
vivid and hip they feel like a literary Pinterest board,
Chase will have you swooning."

—Taylor Jenkins Reid,
author of *After I Do*

THE ONE THAT GOT AWAY

THE ONE THAT GOT AWAY

A Novel

BETHANY CHASE

BALLANTINE BOOKS

NEW YORK

A Ballantine Books Trade Paperback Original

Copyright © 2015 by Bethany Chase
Reading group guide copyright © 2015 by Random House LLC
Excerpt from untitled novel copyright © 2015 by Bethany Chase

Published in the United States by Ballantine Books, an imprint of Random House, a division of Random House LLC, a Penguin Random House Company, New York.

BALLANTINE and the HOUSE colophon
are registered trademarks of Random House LLC.
RANDOM HOUSE READER'S CIRCLE & Design
is a registered trademark of Random House LLC.

This book contains an excerpt from an untitled novel by Bethany Chase. This excerpt has been set for this edition only and may not reflect the final content of the forthcoming edition.

Library of Congress Cataloging-in-Publication Data
Chase, Bethany.
The one that got away: a novel / Bethany Chase.
p. cm
ISBN 978-0-8041-7942-3
eBook ISBN 978-0-8041-7943-0
1. Women architect—Fiction. 2. Men and women relationships—
Fiction. I. Title.
PS3603.H37923O64 2015
813'.6—dc23 2014035768

Printed in the United States of America on acid-free paper

www.randomhousereaderscircle.com

2 4 6 8 9 7 5 3 1

Book design by Diane Hobbing

For Ginny, who I miss every day. For Wynne,
who claimed me as hers. And for Rosie,
who loved all three of us

THE ONE THAT GOT AWAY

1

Every woman has one. That name you Google at two o'clock in the morning. That intoxicating connection that somehow never solidified into anything real; that particular memory you still visit every now and then, for that guaranteed hit of pure, sugar-packed dopamine. It's that story that starts with "There was this one time" and ends, reluctantly, with "but I guess . . ."

Tonight, I'm going to see Eamon Roy again, for the first time in more than seven years. My one and only one night stand; the lone exception in thirteen years of not-on-the-first-date sex. It's not that I put a lot of stock in rules when it comes to dating; I just don't find it appealing to sleep with a guy until I know I like the idea of waking up next to him. I liked waking up next to Eamon. I liked it a lot. And every other guy I've been with has felt the same way about me—including, notably, the man I'm planning to marry. But Eamon was different. Eamon was a first and last in several categories.

"Sarina! Penis straws or penis shot glasses?"

Oh, my good holy lord. They're back to the party favors again.

My roommate, Danny, perches his pointy elbows on the edge of the restaurant table, swinging one long, loafer-clad foot expectantly. He's serving as Best Gay, a Technicolor hybrid of best man/maid of honor/wedding planner/emcee, for his business partner, Jay, and Jay's fiancé, Dominic, who are getting married this fall up in Palm Springs. Tonight, his self-appointed mission has been to convince the reluctant couple to throw a raunchy double-bachelor party here in Austin a few weeks before the wedding.

I glance at Jay for guidance, but all I receive is a bug-eyed headshake. Clearly Jay wants neither straws nor shot glasses. Too bad for Jay.

"How about penis pops?" I suggest, relishing Jay's gape of horror.

"Genius!" crows Danny, clapping his hands so loudly that more than a few heads swivel toward us.

"They had them at this bachelorette party I went to a few months ago," I continue, straining to be heard above the din of the crowd filling the back courtyard of the restaurant. "Cherry-flavored. Lots of anatomical detail. I'm talking veins and everything."

Jay grabs one of the leather-backed drink menus stacked on the table and swats my shoulder with it. "Danny, we are *not* having penis pops, for the love of god."

Danny raises a peremptory hand. "Yes we are. You ceded control when you put me in charge of this whole thing."

"Well, then we have to have it somewhere other than Albion," says Jay. "I'm not giving our staff a photo op of me with a red candy penis in my mouth."

"Nope, it's happening here. Though it's cute you think they take you seriously as it is."

Jay, who treasures his status as the enforcer of their managerial duo, starts to protest, but Danny quells him and the conversation moves on to other details of the party. My work here is done—the back office at the restaurant will be festooned with high-fructose genitals for weeks.

While they talk, I study the teeming courtyard, savoring the perks of ownership: free drinks and food, a permanent spot on the cushy banquette in the corner, and guaranteed proximity to one of the heat lamps that help take the edge off the cool March night. Austin is in the midst of the South By Southwest music festival, and every place that can scratch out enough floor space for a drum kit and a couple of guitars has morphed overnight into a music venue. We're packed to the rafters with the young and the painfully hip: it's a national convention of stovepipe jeans. The person I'm looking for is nowhere in sight, though. And somehow, I don't think he's going to be rolling up in stovepipes.

After a moment, the small figure-eight shape of my friend Nicole pinches into view, tacking her way between hipsters, a glass of Chardonnay clutched in each hand like a priceless relic. Nic is my fellow POW, who staggered with me through the five sleepless years of drafting, models, and presentations that was RISD architecture school. She's also the link that brought me into this circle: when I moved to Austin almost eight years ago she introduced me to Danny, her best friend from high school, and we immediately got on like a house on fire. "Literally, *flaming,*" Danny likes to say when we explain this to people, with accompanying fluttering movements of his hands.

"I brought you another glass of vino," she says, plunking down beside me as she hands it over. She takes a lingering sip of her own wine and sighs. "God, that's good. It was almost worth missing out on alcohol for nine months, just to be able to have it again."

"Should I remind you of that next time?" I say.

Her free hand drops to her soft little belly, which she still refers to by Danny's title, the War Zone. "Don't say 'next time' yet! Let me get through a year with the first one before you sign me up for another."

"How is the little dribbler?" I ask. "Does he like those alphabet blocks I brought him from Argentina?"

"Yes! I meant to tell you. He's obsessed with them."

"Oh, good! Noah will be so pleased. You should have seen him in that store, examining all the toys to make sure they were all safe, and handmade . . . no plastic factory-made crap for Gabe."

"Aw, you guys are sweet. Though I think Gabe's taste is hardly as discriminating as Noah's."

"No one's could be. He's going to be the most high-maintenance parent on earth."

The effect on her is like pumping the gas pedal on a Mustang. Nicole has been referring to Noah as my future husband since our third date.

"Whoa!" she yelps, and slaps my knee with her drink-free hand. "Did he finally get you to talk about timing for getting married?"

"No, you didn't miss anything. We have to get through this separation before we can think about that for real." Noah, who's a partner at an international finance law firm, is two months into a yearlong rotation with the firm's office in Buenos Aires. He's working on some huge corporate merger about which my information is strictly need-to-know.

"I don't see why," she says. "It's not like it's a mystery that it's going to happen. And actually, the masterstroke would be to get the whole shebang planned out while he's not around to split hairs over color schemes and song lists. Voice of experience here," she adds, waggling her hand in the air like an overeager student.

"He's not that bad. The only thing he's going to care about is the menu."

She takes a measured sip of Chardonnay. "How many minutes did you say it took him to decide on one acceptable toy for my four-month-old son?"

Balls. "You do, as usual, have a point."

"It's a gift," she says, breezily brushing her apricot-colored curls back over one shoulder. "So have you thought about it at all?"

"Thought about what?"

"Wedding details. Or even a general idea of when you might let the man make an honest woman out of you."

I wipe the condensation from my glass in one neat stripe after another. "Nope. Seems premature until we're actually engaged. But when that occurs, I promise you my inner wedding planner will come roaring to life." I dart another look over her shoulder, hoping she won't notice.

"I saw that," she says. I should have known she would bust me; it's what she does. "What time was he supposed to be here?"

"I have no idea."

"Well, whether he makes it or not, you look hot. Which is completely by accident." She takes another deep sip of wine but slides me an elaborately nonchalant high five.

"Absolutely," I say, slapping her outstretched palm. She knows I painstakingly assembled the perfect sexy-without-trying outfit before coming out tonight: my favorite leather cuff bracelet, black Frye boots, a fitted black V-neck T-shirt, and—with a tiny pinch of guilt—the jeans Noah swears make my ass look like the answer to world peace.

In fact, she expressly commanded me to wear the jeans. "Noah may have touching rights, but he doesn't get to be the only guy who notices you have a sweet ass. Let the stupid bastard get a look at what he missed." It doesn't matter to her that Eamon's rejection of me is seven years in the past; Nicole's Don Corleone loyalty means no slight is ever forgiven.

She's also the only friend who ever knew how much I'd liked him, and understood how crushed I was when I heard he was seeing somebody, a couple months after we slept together. My sense of connection to him had just been so immediate and effortless that I couldn't comprehend his not feeling the same way. Even though it became unmistakably obvious—once I had run out of the excuses you make for guys when you're in your early twenties—that he didn't. The sting was so sharp that even after I finally shook it off, I still maintained a perfect record of avoiding him every time he came back to Austin to visit Danny and his other friends. Even after I was in my own relationship, in love and deeply happy. It just seemed easier that way.

Until this time, when I suddenly decided that enough was enough—I was thirty-one years old, our fling was ancient history, and instead of forgoing a Friday night at Albion during SXSW because Eamon was in town, I was just going to fucking grow a pair.

A male voice bellows out Danny's name from across the courtyard. We all turn to look for the source, then Danny shouts a delighted "Ame!" and launches himself off the banquette. And there he is in the doorway to the courtyard, looking past Danny, finding my eyes and smiling right at me.

2

It's funny how, when you only get to spend a very finite amount of time with someone you wanted to know better, you find that certain details have cut deeper tracks in your memory than others—something about the way they looked, or one particular comment that made you laugh, out of hundreds of sentences. The image of Eamon that flits into my mind at that moment is of him, sprawled half on top of me in my bed, swearing as he struggled with the zipper on my favorite jean skirt. Laughing into my eyes, his smile so beautiful it could stop a bullet. The same smile he's giving me right now.

The thing is, it's not as if I haven't seen him between then and now. I just haven't seen him in person. In the two years after we met, he went from a talented NCAA star to one of the marquee swimmers on the American national team. So after living with former top-ranked—and still fanatical—Texas Longhorn swimmer Danny through two rounds of Olympics, I have seen a lot of Eamon Roy on TV. Culminating in a stellar performance at last summer's Olympics, less than two years after a brutal car crash almost killed him. But I haven't actually spoken to him since he kissed me goodbye that morning all those years ago.

I stare as he and Danny collide in a back-thumping embrace,

then begin picking their way across the courtyard to our table. The Eamon I remember was twenty-one, with the lanky beauty of a colt, still growing into his young athlete's body. He looks the same in all the basic ways: same yield-sign torso, defined jawline, and unfairly long-lashed brown eyes, though his dark hair is cut shorter than I remember. His face still has that openness that invites you to slide a chair next to him and tell him all the stories even your best friends don't know.

But whether it has to do with the hell he must have lived through as he recovered from his injuries, or it's as simple as a college kid growing into a man, there's a gracefulness about him, a completeness, that wasn't there before. I had been hoping that, with the perspective of the intervening years, I wouldn't be able to understand what I thought was so special about him in the first place. Especially after almost four years of basking in all of the countless things that amaze me about Noah. But as I watch him walk toward me now, attraction whomps me in the chest, and I realize, to my irritation, that my previous policy of avoidance was more sensible than I had given myself credit for.

Beside me, Nicole is peering at him like Gollum at the Ring. "God damn," she hisses in my ear. "He got even hotter. I can't believe you hit that, you lucky bitch."

"If you mention that, I will shank you and leave your child motherless." I wipe my damp palms on my jeans as Danny and Eamon reach our table.

"And you remember these two," Danny says, gesturing to me and Nicole. "Also known as Trouble and Hell on Wheels."

"Which one is which?" Eamon's smile is like sunshine.

I extend my hand to him, but he pulls me in for an easy hug, and kisses my cheek affectionately. I inhale his scent: a mellow mix of shampoo, laundry detergent, and a faint whiff of chlorine. He must still train regularly—hard habit to break, I guess.

"Hey, Sarina. It's been way too long since I've seen you."

And whose fault is that? "I feel like I just saw *you*," I say. "Danny's had our DVR backlogged with your race footage since the summer."

"Oh, so his manners haven't improved since *I* lived with him," he says, flicking Danny on the back of the head.

"Whatever; all she watches is *House Hunters: Outer Space* or some shit," mutters Danny.

"No, you were amazing," I tell Eamon, and I mean it. "The whole team was."

He tips his head graciously. "Thank you. It's been a relief to let things get back to normal, though, believe me."

Danny flags down one of our many musician–slash–cocktail waitresses, who double-times to our corner when she catches sight of Eamon, and we order a round of drinks. Conversation quickly turns to the merry-go-round of traveling and appearances that Eamon has been doing since retiring from swimming.

"I'm sorry," Danny snits at one point, "but can't they come up with a better term than *retire*? It makes me think of my grandparents in Boca."

"That's just the way it is," says Eamon. "As far as the competition is concerned, I'm over the hill. Maybe I could have stuck it out for a couple more years, but I wasn't interested in hearing Bob Costas reminisce about how great I *used* to be, once I started getting my ass handed to me by nineteen-year-olds."

"Yes, because twenty-eight makes you ancient. Somebody get this man some Depends," drawls Danny.

There is a pause as the waitress returns with our drinks, bending her torso unnecessarily low as she hands Eamon his—a Lone Star beer. Awareness flashes over me at the sight of that red-and-white logo. Did he order that because they don't have it in California and he misses it? Or was it because he remembers?

"So what brings you to Austin?" asks Jay. "Just wanted to check out South By?"

"He's moving back!" yells Danny, with a deliberately dorky raise-the-roof gesture. Under the table, Nicole's heavily platformed foot makes abrupt contact with my shin.

"Nice! You gonna be coaching for UT?" asks Jay.

Eamon laughs. "Hell, no. Tony Parsons would nail my balls to the deck if I tried. No, USA Swimming brought me on as an ambassador to promote the sport. It's going to be a lot of traveling, so I got to choose my home base. And I love it here—I always wanted to come back once I stopped competing."

"You make it sound like it was their idea," says Danny. Turning to the rest of us, he continues. "Eamon scheduled a meeting with the director of USA Swimming two weeks after he finished the Olympics, and pitched her a point-by-point proposal for ways he could increase popularity and visibility of the sport. And of course, she green-lighted it all."

I try not to look impressed, but suspect that I am failing. Nicole certainly is.

"So when you heading back this way, then?" she asks. On my unspoken behalf.

Eamon takes a swallow of his Lone Star before he answers, and when he raises the bottle to his mouth I notice it: peeking out from the sleeve of his shirt, a tattoo of the Olympic rings along the inside of his right wrist. I'm not generally much of a tattoo girl, but that, on him, is mind-bendingly attractive. "I've got a few things to wrap up in Berkeley, but I should be done around the end of the month. I need to find a temporary place to rent while I'm here this weekend. Then as soon as I get back for good, I start house hunting."

My eyes water as Nicole nails me with her foot again. I will have to notify her later that causing me sudden physical pain is a poor way to remind me to look nonchalant about a piece of disconcerting news.

"You looking to buy?" asks Danny, and Eamon nods.

Shit. I know exactly where this is about to go. And I do not want it to go there. But before I can think of a way to stop him, Danny goes leaping into the breach. "Well, if you need an architect, there's your woman," he says, jerking his chin toward me.

Eamon turns to me, eyebrows hiked. "That's right—you did the renovation on Danny's house, didn't you? I'd forgotten that."

Ah. Well, then. If he'd forgotten I designed Danny's house, then he certainly didn't remember about the Lone Star. I should not feel surprised and I absolutely, *definitely,* should not feel sad.

"And she designed this place," Danny continues, "and our new bar, Clementine. *And* she designed that new spa, Balm, that just opened down on Cesar Chavez. You're looking at a rising architectural star, my friend."

"So is Nicole," I point out.

"Sure," she says slowly. "In the field of institutional health care design."

"Wow. You did an amazing job, Sarina—this place is beautiful. I had no idea it was your work," Eamon says, looking around at his surroundings: the sandy concrete courtyard, oiled teak furniture, sculptural desert plantings, and the amber glow of the main bar beyond. "God knows I could use your help with whatever I buy."

And god also knows the last thing I need is a time-sucking microproject for an obsessive perfectionist. Especially one who will probably expect me to work for him as a favor because he deigned to sleep with me back at the dawn of time. No, thank you.

"Oh yeah?" I say, offering only polite interest. "What sort of help?"

"Depends on the house. But I've always liked the idea of picking up a fixer and redoing it exactly the way I want."

In spite of myself, my attention is caught. I love fixers. It's easy to design a great building from the ground up, but to coax a modern, functional space out of an outdated pile of bricks—now that's a challenge.

"Well, that's the way to do it," I tell him. "You should be able to find a good deal if you're willing to put the time and money into a renovation—especially if you buy the one dump on a great street and turn it into a gem. That should be a solid investment."

I know without looking that Nicole is giving me crazy eyes. The more so because I have folded my legs safely underneath me. But giving the guy ten seconds of advice is a far cry from getting involved in his project.

"That's the plan," he says. "That, and I promised myself one day I'd have a shower where I wouldn't have to bend my knees to wash my hair."

"You could get a jump on house hunting while you're here," suggests Danny. "Since you're going to be looking for a rental anyway."

"That's a great idea," Eamon agrees. "I've got some neighborhoods where I want to look, but I haven't lived here in so long. Maybe I'll take a drive around and see what's there."

"We'll take you to do that, obvi," says Danny. "Ree can show you what neighborhoods are good to invest in."

"That would be awesome," Eamon says, already thanking me for something I had not possessed the slightest intention of volunteering to do.

"No problem," I say brightly, tasering Danny with my eyes. "I was planning to work tomorrow, so I'm not sure I could go on the drive, but I can give you some notes."

"Come on, Ree, it won't take long. Ame's only here for a couple of days. Pry yourself away from your laptop for two hours."

Aaaaand now I look like an asshole if I continue to demur. Too bad Danny is sitting out of Nicole's striking range. "Okay, fair enough."

Not content with the mischief wrought so far, he continues.

"And, Ame, cancel your stupid hotel room and stay with us. We graduated from air mattresses. We have a full-on guest room. It's almost like we're actual adults."

Oh goddamnit. Normally Danny's bottomless hospitality is one of my favorite things about him, but this particular guest I could live without. Not to mention this hell-born house-hunting escapade.

"Thanks, but I wouldn't want to impose," Eamon says, shaking his head.

Danny heaves a dramatic sigh. "It's not an imposition, you fool. Who stays in a hotel during South By?"

"Maybe it's not an imposition for you, but did you ask your roommate if she minds having a houseguest for a few days?"

"Of course I don't mind," I lie, "but I hope you're not allergic to cats. Mine likes to use the guest room as his nap space. There's fur everywhere."

"Doesn't bother me. All right, I'll take you up on it, if you're sure I won't be in your way."

"Oh, shut up—you're coming," says Danny, raising a palm to show the matter is closed.

—

We stay at Albion until nearly three, drinking and talking until, despite some baleful muttering from Danny to the effect that we are all losers with weak constitutions, we spill out onto the street for the requisite round of goodbyes. Once we get home, though, Danny sinks onto our big gray sofa to take his shoes off and promptly falls asleep, mouth open in an inelegant gape that would mortify him if he ever saw it. I briefly consider grabbing a picture of him but decide to give him a pass, just this once.

"The bastard," says Eamon. "After all that talk."

"Typical," I say through a yawn.

Eamon clearly doesn't share my scruples about Danny's privacy, as he calmly takes out his phone and snaps a photo of his sleeping friend, leaning in close for maximum detail.

"That's going to be spectacular blackmail material," I observe.

"I thought so too," he says. "For now I'll just use it as his caller ID photo."

A ripple of laughter escapes me. Danny would faint with shame if he knew. At the sound of voices, my cat, Newman, pads into the living room to investigate the newcomer.

"Hey, buddy." Eamon drops to his knees and extends his hand to Newman, who approaches and sniffs cautiously, then bumps his sleek black head against Eamon's knuckles. This is highly unusual; typically Newman regards strangers with the squint-eyed suspicion of his namesake.

"That's Newman," I explain.

Eamon looks up at me, eyes crinkled with humor. "From *Seinfeld*?"

"Of course."

"Hello, *Newman*," says Eamon. "He's a Manx?" he asks, clearly referring to the stubby nub that punctuates Newman's rear end where his tail ought to be.

"No, he lost it in a bar fight," I deadpan.

Eamon's crack of laughter causes Danny to stir briefly, but he doesn't wake. Danny could sleep through a hurricane. "Wish I could have seen the other guy," Eamon mutters.

This is how it was with us, I think suddenly.

I grin stupidly at him for a moment before I remember that I'm supposed to be playing hostess. "Let me show you where you're sleeping."

He follows me up the stairs, and oohs appreciatively when I open the door to the subdued gray and tan room. "Wow, you guys weren't kidding. I like this painting," he adds, moving closer to the big abstract piece that hangs over the bed, a study in taupe and gray shadows.

"Thanks. My mom painted that."

He shoots me a startled glance over his shoulder. "Seriously? She was really talented." His informed use of the past-tense verb is the first acknowledgment, all evening, of the fact that he and I have ever had any interaction more personal than a passing conversation at one of Danny's get-togethers.

The ache blooms, right below my rib cage, as it always does when I think of her. "Yes, she was. Well, I'm at the end of the hall if you need anything," I say, then feel heat creep up my throat as I realize that not only does he already know from personal experience exactly where my bedroom is, but it sounds as though I have just invited him there. All that was missing was a sexy lift of my eyebrows and a slow-motion lip-lick.

"But, um, you should be all set here," I add, stumbling over my embarrassment. "The bathroom's right through that door."

He smiles, politely ignoring my discomfort. "Thanks, Sarina. I'll see you in the morning."

"Sleep tight," I say, and pull his door shut behind me.

In my rush to enclose myself in the privacy of my bedroom, I trip over a pair of boots I'd left lying by the door. *"Chrrrrrist,"* I mutter, and belly flop onto my unmade bed. If Eamon really is moving back to town, he's good enough friends with Danny that I'm going to be seeing a fair amount of him, so I have got to quit with the staring and the blushing. *Especially* the blushing. Addressing it directly is out of the question—we have too little history together, and it's too long ago, for it to even merit a clearing-the-air conversation. Admitting that it's still on my mind would do more harm than simply continuing to stand on the carpet it's swept under. I'm over it—I just have to make sure from now on that I act like it.

3

Dread pulls me out of sleep the next morning like a kid tugging on my shirtsleeve. When my eyes snap open, I remember: I've got my one-night stand as a houseguest. And I am apparently supposed to spend the day Miss Daisying his ass all over Austin as a prelude to helping him renovate a house I have neither time nor inclination to work on.

I stack my hands under my head and trace my eyes along the wood beams traversing the ceiling of my bedroom. They were hidden under a grid of yellowed acoustical tile until Danny and I got our hands on the place. As I study them, I wonder how serious Eamon is about renovating. It's the kind of thing that sounds like fun to people unfamiliar with the process—you get to pick all kinds of cool stuff and totally customize your space to your own taste. But although he said he wants a fixer, the reality is that a young, single guy is much better suited to a place he can move right into.

It also occurs to me that, if he really does want an architect's help with the project, he could probably find a less awkward candidate than a woman he slept with once upon a time. Ancient history or not, there's no way around the fact that we've done things to each other's bodies that have no place whatsoever in a business relationship. Unless, of course, I'm the only one who remembers the details.

I wholeheartedly wish I *didn't* remember them.

—

When we met, I was new to Austin, having only been living with Danny in his tumbledown Barton Hills split-level for a few months. He would *not* shut up about his old roommate Eamon, God's gift to backstroke and butterfly ("Nobody can compete in both of those strokes, Sarina! Nobody!"), who was so cool, so funny, so talented, oh, and had he mentioned he was also hot like sun flare? This being before my forced indoctrination into the cult of swimming, I'd warned Danny that if I heard the name Eamon Roy one more time I would Sharpie it across his forehead while he slept.

Eamon was, I had been told no fewer than five times, coming to the demolition party we were throwing to celebrate the start of our renovation work on Danny's house (guests were welcome to bring hammers and chisels to join in the festivities). I was aware that I was supposed to be awaiting the event with the breathless anticipation befitting the arrival of a rock star, but I had already decided I couldn't stand him. Sight unseen. Rocketing down a snowy mountain at eighty miles an hour is cool. Lunging horizontally to dig a tennis ball out from six inches off the court is cool. Churning through chlorine at four miles an hour for a minute or two at a time is just not that cool. And besides, he was still in college, finishing up his senior year at UT; I was three years older and *way* too sophisticated to be impressed by college boys. I was into musicians.

When he arrived at the party, I was grudgingly forced to admit that he actually was as good-looking as he had been billed, but the gaggle of girls that immediately formed around him and his friends made me all the more determined to ignore him. I was in the kitchen, craning to reach a bottle of Cuervo from the top shelf of a cabinet, when he appeared next to me and grabbed it without lifting his heels off the ground.

"Here you go," he said, offering it to me along with a friendly smile. His voice matched the rich fudgy tone of his eyes.

"Thanks," I said, and started to move past him, but he stepped into my path.

"I'm Eamon, by the way."

"I've heard," I remember saying, which made him laugh. I liked the fact that his response to Danny's bragging was not false modesty, or entitlement, but amusement. In spite of myself, I was intrigued, and we started talking there in the kitchen. I'd always been a little baffled by the seeming closeness of Danny's friendship with Eamon, assuming the latter to be a chest-bumping meathead like most of the other athletes I'd met, but his intelligence and impish irreverence made it clear why Danny was so fond of him. After a long time, I set the tequila bottle down on the counter, having completely forgotten why I wanted it in the first place.

He cocked his head and studied it, frowning. "You know, that tequila's not looking so great."

"What do you mean?" Tequila is inherently toxic.

He lifted the bottle toward the bug-littered light fixture on the ceiling. "Just looks skunky. Cloudy, almost. I think you need a new bottle."

"But we just bought it. It's fine. Here, I'll pour you a shot to prove it." I took it from him and started unscrewing the cap, but he waved me off.

"Nah, I can't drink much when I'm training," he said, so

young but so serious about his swimming. "But I *can* drive you to the liquor store to get a new bottle of tequila." He cracked open the fridge door and peered inside. "You're low on beer, too. Wanna make a run?"

I couldn't understand how we could be low on beer when we'd been well stocked the last time I checked, but with the way he was smiling at me, I wasn't about to protest.

"Sure." I was still trying to play it cool, though I had stopped thinking he was nothing special about thirty-five minutes ago.

Of course, because it was 12:30 on a Saturday night, the liquor store nearest me was closed, as was the shady one a few streets over with the proprietor that Danny and I referred to as Cyclops. Eamon, who turned out to have surprisingly deep knowledge of liquor store locations for someone who wasn't allowed to drink for most of the year, chauffeured me around to three more possible locations near the UT campus while I car-danced to his *Rumours* CD. (College boy he might have been, but his possession of Fleetwood Mac's masterpiece attested to his credibility on the music front.) I was having so much fun with him that I didn't want to go back to the party, but after an hour of fruitless searching, we gave up on the tequila and decided just to head to a 7-Eleven for beer.

I was stacking six-packs of Lone Star into Eamon's arms when Danny called me to find out where the hell we were. He erupted with indignation when I explained about the beer.

"He's full of shit," he yelled over the noise of the party. "Why the hell did he say we were running low on beer? We have plenty. Get your asses back here, you're missing the party."

I hung up the phone and turned to Eamon in confusion. "Danny says we have plenty of beer. Tell me again what we're doing here?"

"Ahhh, I'm busted," he said. "I never thought you were low

on beer. I just wanted to hang out with you." And as I stood there, blinking in breathless surprise, he dipped his head and kissed me, right in the middle of the drink aisle with his arms full of the national beer of Texas.

—

It is still the best first kiss I've ever had. Better even, it pains me to admit, than Noah's, which transpired enthusiastically but somewhat drunkenly against the side of the pool table where he'd just spanked me three games in a row. And everything that came after it was just as good.

—

Grinning like fools, Eamon and I paid for our Lone Star and climbed back into his dirty old Jeep, where we kissed some more. He kissed me at every stoplight on the way back to the house. Including one time when we got too absorbed to notice the light had turned and broke apart, laughing, when the driver behind us leaned on his horn. "Worth it," Eamon muttered. He carried the misbegotten beer inside and kissed me again, in the kitchen. We kissed for a long time, and then, reluctantly, he pulled away.

"So, I gotta go home and sleep," he said, the wry tone of his voice indicating exactly how unsexy he thought that to be. When, actually, I loved that he took his training seriously, treating his body like the precision machine that it was. "But do you want to hang out next weekend?"

I didn't pretend to have other plans, the way my girlfriends would have advised me. The way I might have if it were anybody else. Instead I simply said yes, my heart banging inside me like the clapper of a bell.

—

I have over forty emails saved from the seven days between when we met and when we went on our first (and only) actual date. Playful, teasing, flirtatious emails. Emails that said, "I can't wait to see you" and "The only thing stopping me from driving over there right now is six A.M. practice" and "I spent my entire psychology lecture this morning thinking about you, instead of psychology." In the three or four months that it took me to process him out of my system, I must have reread the messages fifty times. Attempting to convince myself that I hadn't been a fool for believing our connection was something special, while trying to understand how someone who seemed to be so into me could have just evaporated into thin air. But there was no explanation.

For our date, he took me to the Alamo Drafthouse Cinema down on Sixth Street. He refused to tell me what movie we were seeing, or why we had to arrive at the theater half an hour early, but by the time we got there, there was already a crowd of people out front, chattering excitedly. The theater was located in an old brick building with a huge Art Deco sign out front announcing its name and a vintage neon marquee blaring light down on the sidewalk. The movie turned out to be *The Princess Bride,* a selection which delighted me, but the crowd seemed to view the familiarity of the movie as license to recite the lines along with the actors. After a few minutes I turned to him in frustration, expecting him to commiserate with me, but instead his eyes were creased with humor.

"It's a quote-along," he explained. "The louder the better." Then, to demonstrate, he cupped his hands to his mouth and bellowed, along with the entire theater, "Do you know what that sound is, Highness? Those are the *shrieking eels!*"

This crazy little jet of pure happiness bubbled up inside me at the perfection of it, the perfection of *him,* and I leaned over in my seat, so quickly I nearly upended my bottle of Dos Equis, and laid one on him. I didn't care that I tasted like fried pickles and beer, and neither, apparently, did he. The people behind us kicked our seats, yelling at us to get a room. But he was cute when, standing under the glare of the theater marquee an hour and a half later, he asked—pretending I hadn't just practically jumped him—whether I wanted to go track down an ice cream truck.

"Not really," I said, winding my fingers into his. Already wanting him so badly.

His smile promised me everything. "Well, come on, then."

The sex was unbelievable. More than in just the physical sense, although it was certainly that. There was just this sense of sweetness, almost innocence, to it that I hadn't experienced with anyone before, and haven't since. We stayed up until seven o'clock in the morning, talking when we weren't making love; I remember feeling a bizarre sense of pride that I was compelling enough to make him forgo his self-imposed Saturday night bedtime. I was positive that such lapses in discipline were extremely rare for him.

After discovering we were both originally from Virginia—he from the northern suburbs outside D.C., I from the far southwestern corner, pinched between North Carolina and West Virginia ("That accent is so cute I could listen to you read the federal tax code," he said)—we shared everything about our childhoods and our families, even the stuff you normally wait for a while before unloading. I told him that my mother had died of breast cancer two years before, and waited for him to either smother me in a big, sorrowful hug, eager to show me how sensitive he was, or stiffen with anxiety that I was about to start spewing forth a geyser of Feelings. Those were the two reactions that my personal tragedy had always elicited from guys in the past.

But he just rubbed my knuckles gently with his thumb, and asked me questions. How long had she been sick (ten years, going into remission twice). Had anyone else in my family had the disease (my grandmother, who died of it before I was born). Did I do the self-exams like I was supposed to (yes, with the unfailing consistency that other people reserve for prayer). They were the kinds of questions you would only ask if you actually cared about the answers.

The only sign, the entire time, that anything might possibly be less than perfect came at the very end, when I woke to the soft clink of his belt buckle as he quietly dressed.

"Why are you going?" I mumbled, reaching for him. "It's still early."

"It's almost ten," he said, pulling on his T-shirt. "I have a paper to finish up for tomorrow."

"Oh yeah . . . schoolwork," I teased. I had quickly come to enjoy ribbing him about the fact that I was older than he was. His smile was a little remote, but when he leaned over my bed to kiss me goodbye, his lips lingered on mine for so long that I slid my hands down to his hips, trying to pull him back into bed with me.

He gently dislodged them, whispering, "I really have to go. I'll talk to you later." I noticed that he was frowning slightly as he kissed me one last time—with irritation, guilt, or whatever else I'll never know—but at the time I just assumed he was thinking about the paper he still had to write. Either way, I wasn't concerned. I've never been the sort of person who can fall in love quickly, or easily, but as I sunk happily back into sleep that morning, I was most of the way there.

And he was . . . nowhere. I never heard from him again, not even a drunken late-night booty text. After a long, silent week had gone by, I cornered Danny and asked him—my pride around my ankles—if he knew anything. He shook his head, looking so sorry for me that I immediately regretted having asked.

"Is this the kind of thing he usually does?" I asked, trying to sound sardonically amused.

"No," said Danny. "Not at all."

He plainly didn't know whether the fact that his friend didn't *typically* treat women like disposable toys made his having done it to me better or worse, and neither did I. If it was such an aberration in character, what had I done to deserve the distinction? Danny offered to talk to him, but I refused to hear of it. It was bad enough that Eamon had blown me off; he didn't need to know that I'd actually been hurt by it. And he never said anything about the encounter to Danny, either, which I always thought was even stranger than his going AWOL on me. He'd slept with one of his best friend's roommates and never came up with so much as a "Hey, man, she's really cool and all, but it wasn't going to work out." It literally seemed to be as if the whole thing had never happened.

Eventually I stopped feeling that treacherous little leap of hope every time I checked my email, or my phone rang. I stopped "nonchalantly" asking Danny who he'd been hanging out with when he got home from a night out with friends. When SXSW rolled around, I let Nicole march me around to all the parties tarted out in biker boots and a miniskirt, because she promised the distraction would help me forget. So I hover-pissed in graffiti-covered toilet stalls at music venues all over the city. I dated guys who picked me up at them. Then, after what was supposed to be a cleansing break from the male of the species, I got entangled in a messy on-again, off-again relationship with a wildly talented— and even more wildly narcissistic—blues guitarist, which culminated a couple years later in a five-alarm screaming match under the streetlights outside the Continental Club.

And then I met Noah. Recovering from the aftershocks of that intense, unstable relationship, and the years of crappy judgment that had preceded it, I was wobbling like a vase somebody has jarred with their elbow. Then Noah reached out his hand to steady me. It was so blessedly effortless to be with him: he was seven years older, seven years kinder, and it was obvious from the moment I met him that he would never dream of accepting a greenroom blow job from a tongue-pierced backup singer named Des'rae. He would never dream of cheating on me at all. And by the time I let him inside my body for the first time, I was certain that when the sun rose on the next day, he'd want to spend it with me. And the next day, and the day after that, just like that sunrise, he'd always be there.

He made it so easy for me to fall in love with him. Somehow, his divorce a year earlier hadn't made him bitter, it had just made him lonely; he welcomed me into his life as if I were exactly what he'd been waiting for. I was wide-eyed at my good fortune. He had a ruggedness to him, which, mixed with his courtly Southern charm, reminded me of my stepfather, John, the best man I've ever known. I looked into his beautiful eyes, the color of oxidized copper—and I knew I was seeing my future.

—

A ping from my phone shakes me from my reverie. It's a photo, from Noah himself, who has taken a couple of rare days off work to hike the Perito Moreno glacier in Patagonia: against a backdrop of spiny blue ice, his feet are planted in the snow, arms flung wide into the glaring sunlight. His grin is as cheerful as his persimmon-orange ski coat, which he bought last year for our expedition to Iceland to chase down the northern lights. *This place is beyond cool,* says the text. *Can't wait to show it to you.*

Warmth glows in my chest. *Wish I were there now,* I write. *Until then . . .* I tug down my tank top and snap a photo of my cleavage. It's far from the world's most spectacular cleavage, but he sure likes it.

Never had a hard-on on a glacier before, he writes back. *First time for everything.*

As I dawdle in bed, trying to summon the motivation to get

up and go for a run, I catch a whiff of aroma in the air and sniff incredulously, but it's unmistakable—someone's brewing coffee. According to my clock it's only 9:14, which means Eamon must be up; Danny only wakes up before noon on weekends under threat of bodily injury or global apocalypse.

Crushing an impulse to hide until Danny gets up, I hoist myself out of bed and shuffle downstairs in my PJs. The kitchen is awash in sunshine, and the eat-at counter is neatly set with three places. Precisely folded paper napkins under all three forks waver in the breeze from the open window. Eamon is standing behind the counter, slicing up a green pepper, and greets me with a smile. I feel irritated that he has not somehow become uglier overnight.

"Hey! What's all this?" I ask, gesturing at the enticing array of eggs, ham, and veggies spread out on the steel counter in front of him.

"It's the least I can do for you guys, for putting me up for the weekend," he says. "Coffee?"

I stretch out both hands for the mug he passes me, and take a cautious sip. "Well thank you, but where did you get it all? Danny and I are lucky if we have an old withered apple in our fridge." I plunk down on one of the counter stools opposite him and steal a strip of pepper.

He realigns the pepper strips into a perfect row and begins dicing them with controlled little flicks of his wrist. "Actually it was one withered apple, three cartons of takeout, and a couple half-empty bottles of wine. I went out for a run and stopped at that corner market on my way back."

"You've already been out running? What time did you wake up?"

"Around six-thirty. Can't sleep later than that unless I'm sick or hungover. My body doesn't know how to sleep late—too many years of getting out of bed at four or five to go to practice."

"It must be weird not to be doing that anymore," I observe.

"It's weird as hell. It took a while to catch up with me, 'cause I was so busy with appearances and whatnot after the Olympics. But when I got back to Berkeley in September, I felt like I should be getting back into my normal routine, but instead it was like, okay, now what? I'm still working out every day, but it's the first time since I was a kid that I'm swimming without any particular goal. Other than trying not to get fat," he adds.

I snort. Danny has been whining about getting back to "competition weight" for the last seven years. "That's got to be disorienting."

"Yeah, it is. I can't say I don't miss it, but it was definitely time to move on to something different."

"Why not coaching?" I ask, reaching for more pepper.

He shoves the neatly diced pepper aside and reaches for a new one. "A lot of reasons. I wanted a break from the grind, but mostly I think I'm still too close to it. If I started coaching right now, I'd be jealous of my swimmers for still being able to compete. I don't want to live vicariously through other people."

While he talks, I watch him go to work on the second pepper, his hands deft and quick and precise. I've never seen anything like it. Of course he would have the right kind of muscle memory to excel at knife skills.

A memory bobs to the surface of my brain: lying on my side in my bed at five-thirty in the morning, Eamon stretched warm and satin-skinned against my back, my arm extended in midair. I had made the mistake of teasing him that swimming looked more like brute force than a microprecision sport, which had prompted a six-minute demonstration of the proper arm position for a freestyle catch. My self-conscious laughter faded as he patiently corrected me again and again, adjusting the angle of my wrist, massaging my tensed fingers until they relaxed. A quick kiss at my temple, then his soft voice: "Raise your elbow—tiny bit more—let your hand drop—more—yep. You've got it." Satisfied, he curled his arm around my waist and rested his cheek on mine.

I was enchanted. And now that infuriates me. Unwilling to look at him, I jump up from my stool and throw open the door to the fridge as if I urgently need to top off the milk in my coffee.

"And besides," he continues, oblivious, "I can always coach down the road, but the stuff I'm trying to do with USAS relies on people still having some idea who I am."

"Strike while the iron is damp," I mutter.

I settle back in my seat and reach again toward his little heap of diced pepper, but he swats my outstretched hand away. "Hey! Stop stealing that, or there won't be any left for the omelets."

I shake my bangs out of my face, unrepentant. "Whatever, just put less in Danny's."

"Why don't you make yourself useful and go kick him out of bed?"

I can't help returning his knowing grin. Danny requires food, caffeine, and at least sixty minutes of warm-up time in order to qualify as a human being after he wakes up in the morning. It's a testament to how much he loved swimming that he was able to tolerate the practice schedule for so many years.

My knock goes unanswered, so I poke my head around his door. "Hey, Danny boy, time to get your ass out of bed," I say to the long mound in the middle of his blankets.

The only response I receive is a short grunt of denial.

"Eamon's making omelets," I wheedle. "And there's coffee."

A long pause, then he rotates far enough to squint at me over his shoulder. His Popsicle-blue eyes are bleary, and all the parts of his elfin face look slightly misarranged. "What the hell is he making omelets with?"

"That was my question. He got a bunch of veggies at the corner market on his way back from a run. He's been up since six-thirty, being fit and productive."

Danny shudders. "Christ, he's inhuman. What time is it, anyway?"

"A little before ten. Come on, this whole house-hunting thing was your bright idea, anyway."

"Fine," he groans, peeling back his covers as if they were an especially stubborn onion skin.

"Look what I found," I call to Eamon as we enter the kitchen a few minutes later.

"Ugh, what is the matter with you?" moans Danny when he catches sight of Eamon, monitoring a bubbling omelet. "It's Saturday. Why are you up so early?"

"You know I can't sleep in," says Eamon. "And what happened to *you*? Back in the day, you used to be up at the ass crack every day too."

"I know, and then I quit swimming and got a life." Danny slumps disconsolately onto a stool and grasps the mug of coffee Eamon shoves at him.

"And now you're dissolute." Eamon ignores the baleful stare Danny shoots him over his coffee mug and flips the omelet. We all know the accusation is ridiculous; Danny's schedule might have shifted, but his work ethic is firmly in place.

"I'm a bar owner; it's in the contract. And besides, at least I'm not *retired*," Danny mutters into his mug.

—

Since Danny refuses to be seen driving his car—a scruffy Toyota that predates the Flood—any more than is absolutely necessary, that leaves my modest little Civic as the vehicle of choice for the driving tour of Austin. My car resembles a bomb site at the best of times, and I wince to see that today it is even worse than usual: the backseat and passenger side are strewn with an untidy potpourri of gas receipts, half-empty water bottles, material samples, and battered rolls of drawings. Danny attempts to secure shotgun on the grounds that he is older, but Eamon claims two additional inches of leg. I half-expect them to break into an arm-wrestling match at any moment.

"Oh, for god's sake," I say. "How *old* are you two? Danny, get back there. Pretend you have manners." He slumps into the back with a deep sigh. I crane around until I can see him. "And no kicking Eamon's seat, or I *will* turn the car around."

He gives a bark of laughter and settles back against his seat, arms crossed.

"He can't help himself," Eamon explains. "He's like the extra older brother I never needed. Speaking of which, how *are* your thirties treating you, Danny?"

Danny, who just celebrated his second straight thirtieth birthday, shoots him a nasty look.

"So, *anyway,* this is Barton Hills," I begin, gesturing out the window at the rows of tiny bungalows, interspersed with the occasional sixties-era ranch house, half-visible behind lush trees and landscaping.

"Only reason I could afford the house is that it needed so much work nobody else could be bothered with it," Danny volunteers from the backseat. "Ree here was the ace in the hole—she did the architectural planning in exchange for rent. We did most of the renovation work ourselves."

"The thought of you wielding power tools scares me," says Eamon.

"Oh, that was back when Danny was still into screwing things," I crack, and Eamon slaps a palm over his laughter. Danny is four months into a self-imposed dry spell inspired by a nasty breakup, and he's getting goddamn touchy about it.

"Ha-ha, Sarina," Danny says.

"This neighborhood is nice," Eamon observes, shooting me a wink. "Are all the lots about this size?"

"This size or smaller."

He makes a disappointed noise, and Danny pipes up. "Why, you need room for your six-car garage?"

"No. My pool."

"God help us," mutters Danny.

—

We spend the day driving all over Austin, from the posh neighborhoods in the hills to the west of the city, with their bloated mansions and scrupulous landscaping, to downtown, with its new high-rise apartment buildings like the one Noah lives in. He actually hates his place—he's been fantasizing about having a lawn to mow for as long as I've known him—but he agrees with me that an apartment is more practical until we're ready to buy a house together. Until then, he grows herbs and tomatoes on his little balcony that overlooks West Riverside. Every summer he kills them, but every spring, he tries.

To my surprise, Eamon seems eager to move ahead with buying a house—we've identified a few neighborhoods today where he is interested in looking at properties. And I think he is probably serious about hiring me to help him renovate whatever he finds. But I have to figure out the scope of the job before I can figure out how best to get out of doing it.

After a couple rowdy hours of live band karaoke at Danny and Jay's new hipster saloon, Clementine, I realize my webcam appointment with Noah is fast approaching, so I make an early exit. Eamon, yawning, elects to come with me. When we get back to the house, he asks if there is a printer he can use.

"I thought I'd take a look at some real estate listings to see if there's anything I want to check out while I'm in town." He pauses for a moment, then continues. "Actually, would it be too much to ask you to come with me tomorrow if I spot anything that's worth a visit? I'd love to get your opinion."

Balls. I had no intention of spending any more time with him, but real estate is like porn for me. "I've got muay thai class till eleven, but I could go after that."

His eyebrows shoot upward. "You do muay thai? Damn, you're badass!"

Just then, my cellphone rings—it's Noah, undoubtedly calling because he doesn't see me logged on to my computer. "Sorry, I need to get this, it's my boyfriend," I explain. Petty though it is, I feel a surge of satisfaction as I say this to him. "Help yourself to the printer—the wireless code is 'Newman.'" I turn away from his grin and hurry up the stairs to my room—and to Noah.

4

Once, a couple years ago, when Nicole and I were having a late-night, wine-fueled Deep Discussion about our respective partners, she asked me what my favorite thing was about Noah. My answer was instantaneous, because it was the first thing I noticed about him, and I have adored it ever since: his crow's-feet. Those tiny grooves that deepen at the corners of his eyes when he smiles. Nicole complained that a random physical characteristic shouldn't be my favorite thing about him, but I disagreed. Aside from how handsome they look on his face, the crow's-feet are a testament to the living that he's done. Playing outside all day long as a young kid in Mexico City, where his diplomatic family lived till he was eleven, getting brown as a dry leaf because nobody really cared about sunscreen then. Squinting into the equatorial sunlight of Panama, where he spent two years in the Peace Corps. And, of course, laughing. Of the two of us, I'm usually the person making the jokes, but he is always, always so happy to laugh.

When his blurry image appears on the screen of my laptop, I smile, like I always do. He has a fresh sunburn on his forehead and nose from all that sunlight bouncing off the glacier. If I were there with him, I'd be able to locate a few new freckles by tomorrow.

"Hey, Iceman! How was it?"

His face looms closer as he leans forward, elbows propped on either side of his keypad. "It was so awesome, kitten. Just phenomenal. I can't wait to take you."

"Tell me!"

"I've never seen anything like it. The ice always looks so blue in photos—I thought it must be some Photoshop trick or something. But that's how it really is. Something about the way the ice absorbs light. It's surreal. But you're going to have to leave the photos to me."

Noah is the photographer in our relationship. It amuses him that I, the supposedly artsy one, can't take a picture in focus to save my life. But the precisely measurable mechanics of shutter and aperture are right up his alley. "So did you just climb around all day?"

"We hiked for a while, then in the afternoon we came back and got on a boat that took us right up to the wall of the glacier. The face of it is all cracked and cragged, like some kind of rock. It was stunning."

"That sounds amazing."

"It's going to blow you away," he says, and taps his laptop screen in the spot where my nose must appear on his end. The best part about Noah's passion for travel is his generosity in sharing it with me. I can't always afford my share of the trips he suggests, but nothing makes him happier than to treat me. He says it wouldn't be fun without me there to share it. But still—someday I'll be able to pay exactly my half. "So what did *you* do today?" he asks.

"Actually, I wanted your opinion about that," I say. "Do you remember hearing about Danny's friend Eamon, the swimmer? He's moving back to Austin. He's visiting this weekend and he wants me to help him find a house and gut it." Noah does not know that Eamon and I slept together—and he will most definitely remain swaddled in his blanket of ignorance. Especially now that Eamon is moving back to town.

"Huh. Oh yeah, I remember. This is the guy that was in that car crash, or whatever? How does Danny know him?"

"From college. Danny used to be a really serious swimmer, remember? Texas has one of the best teams in the country. Eamon went to UT, too, a couple years behind Danny."

"I'll be damned." Noah is plainly stumped by the concept of Danny engaging in a notoriously demanding sport, let alone at a level high enough to have become friends with one of its top athletes. "So what's the question?"

"Well, assuming he does buy something that needs work, he's probably going to want me to at least put in a proposal. But I feel like either it's going to be such a small job that it'll be more hassle than it's worth, or it will be so big that I won't have time for it— especially with all the new work for Balm. I'm trying to figure out a way to get out of it without looking like an asshole."

Noah waves his palms in front of him. "Wait. Why are you trying to get out of accepting a job before the job even exists? Is the guy a jerk or something?"

I realize that I don't actually know the answer to this question. Sure, Eamon made me feel like crap back in the day, but he was twenty-one years old and I can't hold that up as proof of an immutable character flaw seven years later. There are much nastier things to do to somebody than sleep with them and never call them again.

"I don't think so," I say after a minute, "but I do think he's a handful. To get to that level, in that sport, you've got to be Type AAA. Somebody like that does not make an easy client."

"You can handle him," says Noah loyally. "It sounds like it could be interesting. I think you should at least see what happens."

"Really?"

"Truly. I'll be keeping fingers and toes crossed for you."

"All of them?"

"Every last one." He demonstrates, fingers snarled. "I'm going to be tied in knots until I hear what happens. Literally. It's going to make things tough for me over the next couple of days." He's trying to be deadpan, but, inevitably, his smile creeps into place. I can't believe it's going to be another two months before I get to be with him again. If the phone sex and blurry webcam calls are already starting to wear thin, I can't imagine how sick I'll be of both by the time he comes home.

Before I turn in, I decide to check on Eamon. I find him in the deserted living room, working on his laptop in boxers and a faded orange Texas Swimming & Diving T-shirt, with his long, muscular legs stretched out on the coffee table. A short, uneven scar tracks through the hair on one thigh—that must be from the compound fracture I remember hearing he'd suffered in the car crash. Absolutely incredible to be that seriously injured and recover to the top of his form.

"Sorry," he says with a smirk when he spots the direction of my eyes. "I thought you'd gone to bed."

"Eamon, believe it or not, I have seen a man's legs before," I say. As a matter of fact I have seen *his* legs before, though I have no desire to remind him of that. "Did you find anything good?"

"Yeah, I think I found a couple places that might be worth a phone call." He drives a hand through his hair. "I'm just not exactly sure what I'm looking for, in terms of the actual building."

I scoop up Newman, who is winding himself around my ankles, and plop down next to Eamon on the sofa. The blue light from the laptop throws his profile into relief against the darkness. He's got a slight bump at the bridge of his nose, and his upper lip sits just a little bit over his bottom one; the imperfections make his face sexier than just plain handsome. "Well, you tell me. You said you want to find a place to gut?"

"Yeah," he says, scratching Newman under the chin. "I want to rework it on the inside to make it mine. This is not something I'm selling in five years; this is going to be the house I live in forever." He shoots me a slightly sheepish look. "I've kept everything to the bare minimum till now, but I'm okay with throwing some money into this house."

I tent my fingers like Mr. Burns. "Consider me amply capable of assisting you with that." I push past the little pulse of pleasure at his laughter and continue. "Seriously, though, you need to know that a big renovation is a ton of work. It will probably take longer than you think it will, and it will *definitely* cost more. Especially with older buildings, the contractor will always uncover problems you didn't know existed until he opened up your walls."

"That makes sense," he says. "But I still want to do it."

"I'm going to remind you that you said that when you're six months in. So, do you have an idea of what sort of style you like?"

He gestures around him, at the slanted, wood-clad ceiling, open-plan living area, and huge, metal-framed windows. "Something like this. This place is fantastic. Still can't believe you guys built so much of it yourselves."

The familiar balloon of pride inflates in my chest. "Thanks. So, something mid-century then. About this size, too?"

"I need five bedrooms, or four bedrooms and an office. Nice outdoor space. A living area with lots of room to have people over. I want the house to feel comfortable, but not gigantic."

"Five bedrooms is a hell of a lot of space for one person, though."

He tips his head toward one shoulder. "I want a family, eventually. And in the meantime, I'll make my brothers and my parents come stay so I can show off," he says, grinning.

I wonder, not for the first time, what his brothers look like. Appears to be pretty solid genetic material they're operating with. "Works for me. Any other requirements?"

"Yeah. I need enough room for a short-course pool."

"Civvy, please. I do not speak Swimmer."

"Twenty-five meters long."

"You want an eighty-foot pool in your backyard?"

"Yyyyep." He folds his arms over his chest. "Oh, I'm sorry, did you think you were going to give me a little kidney pool? Concrete steps at the shallow end and some decorative tile around the edge?"

"Of course not, but eighty feet, that's . . ."

"The size I need," he says firmly.

"Okay, I can make that happen. Why does it have to be exactly twenty-five meters?"

"It's a standard size. Makes it easy to keep track of distance. And it's a frame of reference to judge my time," he explains. "So I can gauge exactly how slow I'm getting as I slide into middle age. Trust me when I tell you it's important to me; this is the one thing I'm going to be a dick about."

His frankness nudges a laugh out of me. "Well, would you *like* some decorative tile work around the edge?"

"As long as it's the right size, you can make it as pretty as you want."

"Eamon. I may not know the correct dimensions of competitive swimming pools, but I hope you don't actually think I would make your house *pretty*."

He grins mockingly. "Well, a girl architect, I figure there's a good chance—" He trails off, laughing at the expression on my face. "Come on, you left the door wide open."

"You might not want to antagonize the person who's responsible for making sure your house stays put over your head," I say.

We spend the next hour scrolling through the real estate listings. Every so often, he reaches across my lap to pet Newman, who is passed out on the couch next to me, feet splayed in the air. Every time Eamon touches him he purrs. I'm high on the rare pleasure of talking about buildings with someone who's as interested as I am. Eamon has a great eye and a quick mind—I can see him absorbing the terms and the information that I feed him, storing them away for later.

By the time we finally go to bed, I've got a pretty good idea of what he wants his house to feel like. And I've realized something else, too: a stylish renovation of a classic mid-century home, for a popular young athlete, is the perfect project to catch the attention of a magazine editor, and get me published. We have a promising list of places we want to check out, and I'm zinging with excitement to see them. Maybe having him back in Austin isn't going to be a *total* pain in the ass after all.

5

Since all available evidence suggests that there's a driving blizzard in hell when Eamon Roy fails to get his own way, I am unsurprised that, by the time I get back from muay thai the next morning, he's managed to charm a Realtor into giving up her Sunday afternoon for him. Danny declines to join us; he has a blind date with a friend of Jay's.

"For brunch? Sexy," Eamon observes.

"Tell me about it," says Danny. "This is what working nights does to your social life. You're lucky you don't have a real job."

Eamon shoots me a you-see-what-I-put-up-with look. "Well, let's hope you get laid—you need it."

"I might say the same of you," Danny mutters. "Weren't you leaving?"

"Have fun, Danny," I say over Eamon's long-suffering sigh, and push him toward the door. "Are you two always this obnoxious to each other?" I ask when we get outside, shielding my eyes against the sudden sunlight. "Or is this just the joy of reunion I'm witnessing?"

Eamon is grinning like a jack-o'-lantern behind his aviators. "Believe me, if Danny were polite to me, I'd be concerned about his health."

"You know, though," I say as we buckle our seat belts, "the night you got hurt, he wouldn't go to sleep until he got ahold of someone who knew what was going on. When I got up the next morning he was passed out on the couch with his phone on his chest. And after he finally heard you were going to be okay, it was free drinks for everybody in the bar, all night long."

"I didn't know that," Eamon says quietly.

"I probably wasn't supposed to tell you," I say with a sideways smile. "Might give you the impression that he actually likes you."

While we drive to the appointment, I give him a crash course on house hunting: what questions to ask, what questions to avoid answering, and the importance of never letting on how much he actually likes a place. He promises to be appropriately unimpressed. I am skeptical, though; his face is so expressive that he might not be able to help himself.

The Realtor, Joy, turns out to be a middle-aged blonde with long synthetic nails and assertive Texas Hair. Her first house, a desert-style recent build, is appealing, but we realize right away that the backyard is way too small for the pool. I insist on walking through the entire place anyway, wanting to watch Eamon for reactions to the space, light, and materials, but he's distracted and impatient, clearly wanting to move on to places that might be real possibilities. The second house has the right lot size, but the internal layout is so cramped and arbitrary that I can tell the cost of reconfiguring it would be far more than it's worth.

The third place Joy has to show us is a nondescript early sixties rancher just a few minutes' drive from the university. When we slow in front of the property, I can barely hold back a little hop of excitement—this is exactly the kind of thing I had in mind. The wide, low-slung house looks down on the road from a slight rise, across a lawn shaded by a beautiful old live oak; the tree's distinctive squiggly limbs are dark against the light filtering through its leaves. A deep porch extends almost the full width of the house's façade; it's currently adorned with a drab boxwood hedge, but it would be spectacular with a composition of native shrubs, loosely arranged to break up the rigid horizontal lines of the building. I try not to look excited as we park and approach the front door, but so far, so good.

The inside does not disappoint. The core of the house is a large, lofty great room with an exposed-beam cathedral ceiling and a row of gracious floor-to-ceiling windows along the wall that faces the road. Joy launches into an apologetic monologue regarding the rustic brick floors and the knotty pine paneling covering the walls, so I scrunch my nose distastefully. Eamon, however, is failing spectacularly at his poker face. His brown eyes are wide with interest, and he's sliding a hand over the paneling as if imagining how it will look with a coat of paint obscuring the ugly wood grain. Joy, scenting a possible sale in the air, suddenly becomes much more animated, giggling at him like a smitten SMU sorority girl. There goes his shot at getting it below asking.

She leads us through a good-size kitchen and dining room, then back toward the private wing, where four smallish bedrooms are clumped awkwardly around a single bathroom featuring a sink, tub, and toilet in avocado green ("They're original to the house!" tinkles Joy). The rooms are cramped now, but if we blew out the back wall of the house, it would be a piece of cake to add a couple more bathrooms and reconfigure the walls so the whole section is more spacious. Throughout, the ceilings are high, the windows large and well proportioned—the raw material is excellent. My skin buzzes with the familiar excitement of looking at a space that's just crying out to be brought up to its full potential.

We finish the tour in the backyard. There's no terrace, but it would be easy to add one, and there's more than enough room for the sacred pool. Cedars and live oaks line the property on every side, providing screening privacy, but, here and there, breaks in the foliage offer glimpses of the hills surrounding Mount Bonnell, about half a mile away. Late-afternoon sunlight glazes the grass and leaves with amber, and the tang of cedar brightens the air. It's beautiful, restful. As we stand there, listening to the wind rustling in the tree branches, Eamon picks a twig from the ground and snaps it between his long fingers.

"I'll take it," he tells Joy. "My attorney will contact you first thing tomorrow to work out the details of the contract."

Her chest puffs with surprise, but she rallies quickly. "Excellent news! I know the sellers are eager to close, so we should be able to get the paperwork settled quickly." She pauses, her smile sneaking sideways. "And may I be the first to say, welcome back to Austin, Mr. Roy."

—

On the way back to the car, I start to tell him it might be better to wait, see a few more places, at least *sleep* on it, but he is radiant with excitement and I can tell there is no deterring him. After eighteen years of unrelenting discipline, it must be intoxicating to be able to be impetuous for once in his life. And besides, it's not as if I think he's making a mistake. The place is perfect: solid construction, excellent bones, bargain price. If he really wants to commit to a fixer, then this is his house.

The whole drive home, I keep catching myself speeding. Eamon and I are tossing ideas back and forth rapid-fire, interrupting each other in our eagerness to get them out. I have no idea how I am going to find the time to handle this project, but there's no longer any question about taking it. Since my work until now, both at the firm I used to work for and on my solo projects, has been primarily hospitality-oriented, this will put me firmly on the map in the lucrative residential sector.

But even more than that, it's the challenge. That house has

the potential to be spectacular, and I *have* to be the one to get it there. I just hope Eamon will be able to visualize spaces based only on floor plans—I know my ideas are right, but I have to hook him right now, while he's in the mood to make decisions. And in the mood to spend money. There's a pretty shocking price tag attached to this much work.

As soon as we get home, I print a blown-up version of the floor plan from the listing, then spread it out on the dining table under a sheet of tracing paper. Eamon leans forward, elbows on the table, while I rough out the existing rectangular outline of the house, then sketch in the interior walls I want to keep.

"So here's the house now, right? We're going to add about fifteen feet to the back of the garage, which will make a nice big utility room and an office for you, like you wanted. Then we're going to right-angle back in again here, so the kitchen, dining room, and the bedroom next to it only get about five feet added on. But meanwhile, we've made a ten-foot-deep terrace at the back that spans all the way across those rooms, and it mirrors the porch at the front, see?"

He nods, so I slide the marker back to create the second new addition, so that the plan of the house takes on a flattened U-shape. "And then, for symmetry, this southernmost bedroom gets blown out, too, and that becomes the master bedroom. That'll free up some space to enlarge these other bedrooms and add two more full baths. And meanwhile, we open up this wall between that giant living room and the dining area. That way, it will feel a lot more open than it does right now."

The spaces spark to life in my mind's eye as I draw them. The design is perfect for what he wants. The house will be generous but not ostentatious, with ample-size, practical rooms: every square foot will be truly used. I toss the marker down, exhilarated. "There. Does that make sense?"

He stares at the sketch, and for one horrible second I think the look on his face is incomprehension. Then, slowly, he smooths his palm across the drawing, the way he had the pine paneling earlier today. "It's . . . amazing. I knew I loved the place, but I can't believe how quickly you could visualize all of those changes. Your ideas are awesome. How did you just . . . do that?"

I'm glowing from his praise, but a man as accomplished as Eamon will respect candor more than modesty. " 'Cause I'm great at my job," I say. "This is the right solution for this house."

His eyes widen at the intensity in my voice. "You're right. I love all of this," he says, gesturing at the drawing. He studies it for a long moment, then grabs the Sharpie. "Except . . . what do you think about putting that hall bathroom here, instead?"

—

Three hours later, we have the floor plan, the kitchen layout, and the outdoor spaces pretty much hammered out. He's asked me to help with furnishing the house as well, which means a healthy commission on top of my architectural fees.

"So," Eamon says, fishing in his takeout container for the last piece of sesame chicken, "now you get to tell me what it's all going to cost me." He clicks his chopsticks together in anticipation.

The fact that he's smiling means he thinks he's got this covered. He has no idea. Well, if he can't handle it then I will walk away from the job. I've learned the hard way not to waste time chasing my own tail, hunting for phantom solutions to meet the prices clients *think* things should cost.

When I give him the range I have in mind, he makes a face like a gargoyle.

"Are you serious? You giving me solid-gold toilets or something? I don't roll like that, Mahler."

"I'm not trying to get you on *Cribs,*" I promise. "This project is a *lot* of work. I'm not going to waste your money, but I'm not going to cut any corners, either. I'll draw up a formal budget so you can see how it breaks down, and we can identify what to prioritize and what to value-engineer. Besides," I add, unable to keep from teasing him, "you already told me you wanted to spend a lot of money on this house."

He gives a burst of laughter. "Why did I ever say that to you? You've already exceeded my expectations." He picks up my marker, taps it sharply against the table. "All right. Let's stick to the lower end of that, but I'm still game. What do we have to do to get started?"

"Well, we still have to wait for your offer to be accepted and for the inspection to come back clean; then there's the financing to go through, and the title paperwork . . ."

"They're going to accept the offer, and the financing will be quick," he says, flipping the marker between his fingers. "We'll get the inspection done this week, and I'm sure there's a way to get the title search expedited. I don't see why I shouldn't be closed on it within a month."

"So you're really ready to go full speed ahead with this? Two days ago you were just starting to think about looking at neighborhoods."

"I know. But I've been in this weird holding pattern for months now, waiting to get started on the next part of my life. Being back here these past couple days, checking out the city with you guys, I'm psyched to get started with life here. And once I find something I want, I tend to just . . ." He makes a slicing motion with his hand: a buzz saw, true and inexorable.

I already know this about him. He wanted me like that—until he didn't. I can only hope he doesn't lose interest in the house as abruptly and inexplicably as he did in me.

"Especially after the crash," he adds, almost to himself. His right hand is absently rubbing the side of his injured thigh; I wonder if he even realizes he's doing it.

"Okay," I say. "I'm ready if you are. What happens next is, I prepare drawings for the building department to approve. While they're reviewing those, I'll put together all the specs on materials and fixtures, so we can get bids for the construction work. Once the BRD green-lights us and we've got our contractor, we'll be ready to start knocking stuff down. But before any of *that*," I add, smiling, "I have to give you a contract, and you have to write me a check."

His head jerks backward. "I have to pay you? Are you sure? I can get you *excellent* deals on swimming equipment."

"Useless," I say primly. "I've already told you I'm a kick-boxer."

He flashes his teeth at me. "All right, Mahler. Get me that contract, and then we'll talk."

While Eamon heads out to meet some friends for drinks, I lock myself in my office to work on the contract. I know he's going to want it as soon as possible, because it will make him feel one step closer to being settled, so it's in my best interest to oblige him. I have a feeling it will be the first of many times I work late to oblige Eamon—and I intend to see that I am compensated accordingly. Three hours later, the single biggest check I've ever been paid in my life is tucked in my back jeans pocket, as if I get them all the time.

—

When I dig my phone out of my bag so I can share my news with Noah, a missed call from his number reproaches me. I was so wrapped up with work that I completely forgot about our phone appointment. And according to his (justifiably irritated) message, he's heading out to dinner with his co-workers, so he's not going to be able to talk. I won't get to hear his voice till tomorrow night now, and it's totally my own fault.

After I leave Noah a groveling voice mail, the next person I have to call is my stepfather, John. I remember trying to explain my family situation to Anne-Marie, Noah's mother, not long after he and I had started dating: she kept trying to understand it in relation to her own Martha Stewart existence, where everything has a neatly printed little label that makes simple, logical sense.

"So your stepfather was your mother's second husband, is that right?"

"Well, no," I said. "My mother never married my father, and he's not a part of my life at all. She never married John, either, for that matter."

Her face took on an expression of understanding pity. "I see. Did John not want to be"—she lowered her voice—"legally responsible for you?" In her mind, southwest Virginia was the kind of place where men shirked their family duties in favor of whiskey drinkin', and unwed mothers maintained a booming cottage industry of unwanted welfare babies.

"Oh no, he did," I said. "He asked her to marry him at least once a month. She was convinced it would ruin their relationship."

The thought of a single mother rejecting a marriage proposal was plainly a stumper for Anne-Marie. "So he essentially *was* your father . . ."

I shook my head again. I knew it was pointless to try to make her grasp the nuances, but for some reason I wasn't willing to let her jam my stubborn square-peg childhood into one of her tidy round holes. "John didn't come into our lives until I was nine, and it took another year before my mom let him move in with us. I love him dearly, but he's not quite the same as a father."

John thinks of me as a daughter, though, I know. He and I are closer than he is with his own daughter, Janet, who's twelve years older. Which is probably because I am almost exactly like him.

The only thing John has ever loved as much as he loved my mother was building things. I'm convinced that, if he'd ever gone to college, he could have become one of the leading engineers of his generation, putting his brilliant mechanical mind to use developing wind energy or designing spaceship wings. He says he never had the money to go to school, and while I know that's true, I don't think it would have stopped him if he had actually wanted to go; the only thing he truly lacked was ambition. He loved those wild, rolling green hills too much ever to want to leave. So he builds things close to home; which, in Floyd County, means fixing things as much as anything else. Tractors, retaining walls, split-rail fences. The 120-year-old farmhouse my great-great-grandfather built, which was about to fall down around my mother's and my ears by the time we met John.

He rebuilt that house from the inside out, with me trailing behind him at every step. Watching as he reconstructed the decorative wood trim on our front porch from scratch, using the one remaining fragment of it as a model. Crawling behind him into the attic while he repaired the roof beams there. From him I learned how to check level and plumb, how to repair old plaster with a flawless skim coat, how to strip a hundred years of clotted paint off a piece of molding until you get down to the pure, smooth form beneath.

To this day contractors are astonished at the depth of my knowledge about construction; they don't expect it from architects in general and they *certainly* don't expect it from a woman. John cackles with delight every time I tell him one of these stories; as uninterested as he was in advancing his own career, he could not be a more enthusiastic cheerleader for my own accomplishments. He is going to be beside himself when he hears about the project for Eamon.

"Hello?" he rumbles when he picks up the phone. John is perhaps the only person left alive who still relies on a rotary landline phone for his communication needs. I got him set up with a cell several years ago, but he always forgets to turn it on or else leaves it at home entirely.

"Hi, John," I say. My smile illuminates my voice like a lightbulb.

"Ree-Ree!" he bellows. He and Danny are the only people on earth allowed to call me that. "What's going on, girl?"

I tell him my news, not sparing any detail. Of course, he wants to know everything about the house, so I describe it to him as best I can, with promises to send my site photos later. I know he will pore over the photos, patiently waiting for them to load on his gerbil-powered dial-up connection. He will also Google Eamon, and call me back tomorrow to share his most interesting findings. John hates email but, having spent his entire life in a county of less than fifteen thousand people, is fascinated by the Internet's ability to offer up an unimaginable wealth of information about millions of total strangers. And Eamon, while not a celebrity, has been publicly documented long enough that there is a lot of content related to him: articles on swimming websites and blogs, old Olympics coverage, and a couple of breathless but infrequently updated fan sites authored by teenage girls. I know; *I've* Googled him.

"Well, I am just so proud of you, little bear," John says when I have answered every single question. His rich Virginia accent always gives me a wave of nostalgia for my home, and as if he can read my thoughts, he asks, "So when are you going to come home and visit?"

"Oh, not till Christmas, I don't think." I give him the same answer every time. I've relied on the same system since my mother died: John visits me for my birthday in February and again in the summer, and then I spend Christmas with him and my stepsister Janet's family at her home in Harrisonburg, a safe two-and-a-half-hour drive from Floyd. The only time I have to visit my hometown is for the annual Christmas Eve performance he does with his bluegrass band. "But you're still coming out for July Fourth, right?"

"Oh, sure," he says. "So what's going on with Mr. Harlow these days?" As always, he says Noah's name in a tone of broad solemnity. Ever since Noah ignored John's instruction to call him by his first name instead of Mr. Kurzweil, John has insisted on referring to Noah by his own last name. Even though Noah has long since come around to calling him John, it just tickles my stepdad to torture his future son-in-law. When I tell him about the glacier, he insists that Noah forward all of his photos so he can see the wall of blue ice.

"He's going to take me to see it on my next trip down there," I explain.

"Just as long as you two are careful!"

"Yes, John, we will be."

He snorts. "Kid, you sound like a bratty teenager again. *Yes, John. Stop worrying, John.*"

" 'Again'? When was I ever a bratty teenager?"

I was teasing, but his voice is soaked with sadness when he answers. "Ah, you weren't. You never got a chance to be, what with your mama and all. Too busy worrying about her to be shitty to us like a normal kid."

"Yeah, well, I don't think you missed much," I say, forcing a smile back into my voice.

I hear the soft gravelly sound of his chuckle. "No, I don't suppose we did."

When we hang up, it's after ten. Now that I've actually locked down Eamon's project, I'm exhausted just thinking about the amount of work it's going to be. Starting bright and early tomorrow: I had planned to spend the day working on layouts for the new expansion of the spa I finished last year, but instead I'm going to need to go back to Eamon's house to take a full set of site measurements. I have weeks of drafting his drawings ahead of me, and then, once construction starts, I'll be spending hours each week visiting the site, sourcing fixtures and finishes, designing the millwork, then, eventually, sourcing the furniture—I'm going to be working nonstop for the next nine months.

My elation over landing the job seesaws into anxiety as I realize that visiting Noah this summer is going to be almost impossible. Between now and August, I'm going to be too busy to breathe, and that is exactly the time we'd discussed that I would go back to Argentina—once in May, and once in July. And while Balm, the spa project, isn't scheduled to start demo on their new space until later in the summer, I know I'm not going to feel comfortable walking away from Eamon's job for two whole weeks right while we're in the first push of construction.

I blow a long breath out through my lips, and nudge my chair backward till I can rest my cheek on my desk. It was a gift from Noah, this desk—he noticed me drooling over it at a vintage furniture store on South Congress, and then when I came home from a business trip a few weeks later, there it was in the middle of my office, in all its Danish teak glory. I stroke my fingers across the cool, smooth wood, wishing it were the face of the person who gave it to me.

My eyes clench against the thought of how disappointed he will be if I have to miss one of my visits. This is *way* worse than the time I booked a conference on our anniversary weekend. But unless I can convince him to come up here instead, I just don't see how I can help it. He'll understand, eventually. After all, his job is the whole reason we're separated at all right now. We will get through this. But all of a sudden, the bubbling excitement I'd felt about Eamon's job has evaporated. Instead, I just feel like I swallowed a shovelful of broken gravel.

6

Monday, April 2, would have been my mother's fifty-third birthday. As it happened, she died ten days after her forty-third, but I made a conscious decision at the time never to commemorate the anniversary of her death. Every April 12, when the redbud blossoms hang like pink mist in the gray woods around the old farmhouse, John calls me, voice shaking with memories. But I'd far rather celebrate her birth instead. I have a ritual: I take the day off work and head to the plant nursery to pick out flats and flats of petunias, her favorite flowers. They come in every color you could dream of between blackberry purple and angel-wing white, but my mother loved the deep magenta ones best. She grew them everywhere she could find room: in our already crowded flower beds, in splintery whiskey barrel planters on our tiny porch, in the old plank boxes that listed from our windowsills.

I think Danny was surprised, the first time I celebrated my mother's birthday after I moved in with him. Not, obviously, that I marked the day, but that there wasn't a visible outpouring of emotion. As if her birthday were the Valentine's Day of bereavement—the one day a year when you're obligated to make a really big deal out of something you take for granted the rest of the time.

She died toward the end of my junior year of college, and after her funeral I went back to school immediately, to finish up the semester. My friends were convinced I was on the verge of a meltdown; I remember their quietly watchful faces, waiting for an explosion of grief that never came. Nicole sat me down on our lumpy green futon one evening, with the kind of well-meaning arrogance that only a twenty-one-year-old could muster, to tell me she was worried that I wasn't "letting my pain out." As if it was an infection that would heal up all tidy and new once the pus was released.

Instead, it's like groundwater. Pooling underneath my skin, seeping to the surface here and there, now and then. Endlessly replenished. Easy to forget about, until it startles me with the depth of it. The usual suspects—cancer movies, weddings. And then there are the times it catches me completely off guard, like once, when I fished a mat of long, golden-brown hair out of my shower drain and suddenly remembered her, trying to make a joke of her baldness, defiant in a hot-pink bobbed wig at my high school graduation. But her birthday is never one of those times; it's a day I enjoy, just keeping her quietly in the back of my mind, thinking of how much she would have loved the petunias, and the spring sunshine. Drinking them in, for her.

—

Gardening is as close as I get to meditation. Instead of chanting, I have the texture of the earth in my hands, the varied colors and textures of the plants, the rich smell of mulch. The solitude and simple repetition allow my knotted mind to uncoil like nothing else. After several hours working in the front yard, laying each plant into place, then patting the soil down over its roots and giving it a welcoming soak, I feel more relaxed than I have in weeks.

I've been spending eleven hours a day in front of my computer drafting the drawings for Eamon's renovation, but they're finally finished and ready for his review at our meeting tomorrow. It scared the crap out of me to move so far along in the design process without multiple intervening drawing reviews with the client, but he's approved most of the ideas I've put in front of him since the very first day, and his response to almost every question I've asked him so far has been some variation on "I like it, I trust you, just keep on drawing." We've been in constant communication over email while he got ready to move from Berkeley. But as of yesterday, he is officially back in Austin; he found a cute little bungalow to rent in Travis Heights, and, if I know Eamon, he is already completely unpacked.

At first it felt a little strange, having him back in my life such a long time after I'd accepted that he never would be. Especially because he's not just hovering around the periphery, he is front and center. But after the first shock of seeing his name in my inbox wore off, his current context as my client quickly submerged his previous one. I haven't forgotten, of course, but now it's more of an asterisk at the bottom of our working relationship instead of a boldface headline. Neither of us has mentioned or even alluded to our history, and that's the way I'm planning to keep it.

And meanwhile, I am giving him one hell of a house. It's about four thousand square feet laid out over a single level, divided between the four bedrooms on the southern side of the building and the living-entertaining spaces on the northern side. And, of course, the covered terrace with its own outdoor fireplace, built-in grill, and surround-sound speakers. I have already notified him that he has to invite me to a party or two once construction is finished, so I can enjoy the fruits of my labor.

I still haven't talked to Noah about visiting, though. The May trip I can manage; the July one I cannot. I've been working and reworking my outline for the construction schedule, trying to figure out a good week to go to Argentina, but nothing is budging. Especially because Eamon himself is going to be gone for most of the summer, covering the elite swim meets leading up to the world championships in Dubai at the end of August. If he and I are both out of town at the same time, the construction crew will spend the week playing bocce on his lawn. Though I'm nauseous at the thought of not seeing Noah between May and September, I just don't see how I can do it.

I'm almost finished with the plants when a shadow falls across me. I look up to find Eamon himself smiling down at me— thanks to my iPod, I never even heard him arrive. I yank the ear-buds out of my ears and shoot to my feet, face flooding with heat; I'm dressed in a ratty tank top and running shorts, sticky with sweat and dirt. My hair looks like a feather duster. And mean-while, it becomes immediately obvious that working with him in person is going to be challenging until I develop some antibodies to him. Today he's wearing faded jeans and a fitted plaid shirt in a shade of deep blue that emphasizes his smooth olive skin. *How in the hell does someone with as Irish a name as Eamon wind up with skin like that?* I think wildly. And what the hell is he doing here?

"Hi," I squeak, like a cartoon chipmunk. I take a breath to settle my voice into its usual range. "Sorry I'm such a disaster; I wasn't expecting you today!"

"But we said we were meeting today, didn't we? At one?"

I shake my head slowly. "No, that was tomorrow."

"Are you sure?"

"Positive. I wouldn't have scheduled a meeting for today. I was taking the day off."

"Damn. I don't know how I got that mixed up. I'm sorry. Let's try this again. . . . I'll see you tomorrow," he laughs, jerking a thumb toward his car as he walks backward down the driveway.

"No, don't worry about it," I call after him. "I have everything ready, so we might as well go over it. No sense in making you come back again."

"No, I interrupted your day off," he says. "I feel terrible."

I wipe my grimy hands on my shorts. "Seriously, Eamon, it's not a big deal. If you don't mind waiting for me to shower, let's just go over it now. Come on inside."

Newman trots out to greet me as soon as we step into the cool darkness of the house, twining himself around my ankles and wailing in a way that suggests he has not been fed in the last six months. "Hi, puddin'," I croon, picking him up, but he struggles until I set him on the counter, where he regards me with accusing yellow eyes. "I understand," I say, continuing our one-sided dialogue while I fish out a can of cat food and a bowl. "You're just a half-starved little creature, aren't you?"

Eamon watches from one of the stools, an amused smile tugging up one corner of his mouth. When Newman has eaten his fill, he stalks across the counter and plants himself in front of Eamon, who obligingly scratches him behind the ears.

"I'll leave you two to your bromance while I hit the shower," I say.

When I return, clean and presentable, I spread the drawings on the dining room table and systematically walk Eamon through them. The way the house exists now, what we're tearing down, what we're adding. Electrical, plumbing, HVAC. He wants to know what every single one of the symbols means. I explain to him that he doesn't need to, that, as long as he understands the concepts, the drawings themselves are only going to be useful for the contractors; but he ignores me, scowling with concentration. By the time we're finished reviewing everything, he has only minor changes—I'll be able to get the drawing set submitted for approval within a few days.

Eamon asks what contractors I'm planning to have bid the job, so I give him the rundown on the companies I have in mind.

Two are big outfits, highly efficient and highly organized, and they charge accordingly. The third is my personal favorite, Platinum Construction.

"The GC is Joe Martinez. Joe's one of the most skilled craftsmen I've ever worked with. He's fantastic at problem solving, his eye for details is flawless, and he takes a personal interest in making sure everything is done the way it's supposed to be."

"But?"

"But," I acknowledge. "He's disorganized. The other guys will have the entire job planned and budgeted and scheduled to the hilt, and they will deliver it on time or, at worst, ninety-five percent complete. Joe, on the other hand, will take thirty percent longer than he tells us—though as long as we plan for that, we should be all right. And the quality of work you get for what he charges is frankly absurd."

He taps his lips, considering. "So you'd prefer to work with Joe."

"We'll get bids from all of them, but yes, if I had my way, I'd choose Joe. I think he'll do the best job, for the least amount of money; and he knows what I expect from him. Plus I just like the guy, and I enjoy working with him."

"And he's the only one of the three who never puts up attitude at taking orders from a woman."

"Yeah," I say, surprised at his perceptiveness. "He is."

He stretches back in his chair and folds his arms behind his head. I try not to stare at the sliver of golden skin that appears between his shirt and jeans. "It's Joe's job, then."

"We should still have the other guys bid, though."

"No reason to waste their time," he says with a shrug. "I trust you. If you think he'll do the best job then he's in. Obviously don't *tell* him until he gets the bid in, but I'd just as soon simplify the whole thing."

"Wow. That was unexpectedly painless," I say candidly.

Wry amusement flickers across his face. "Can't promise I'll always be."

"I believe you," I say.

—

After he leaves, it's time for the second half of my mother's birthday celebration: ice cream and daytime television. Nutritionally and intellectually bankrupt, respectively. They were her guilty pleasures. I am two-thirds of the way through a pint of Coffee Heath Bar Crunch when Noah calls.

"Hey, sweetie!" I say, struggling to mentally extricate myself from the twisted coils of a stepbrother-stepsister romance on *The Young and the Restless*. "What are you doing calling me so early? I thought you'd be chained to your desk for another few hours, at least."

"Oh, I'm not out of work. I was just thinking about you and wanted to say hello."

Warmth spills through me—he remembered. Last year he asked me to save some of the petunias so he could help me plant them when he got through with work. "Ah, honey, thank you for remembering about today," I say. "It's been a good day. Eamon came by to go over house stuff, which wasn't supposed to happen till tomorrow, but we got a lot done so it was just as well."

There is a long, deep silence. "Wait, don't kill me but . . . what should I have remembered about today?"

Oh. "It's my mom's birthday."

"Oh, of course. Kitten, I'm sorry. I was just thinking about you 'cause I missed you, but now I'm extra glad I called. Are you . . . okay?"

I sigh. Should I be prostrate in bed cursing the heavens and drenching my pillow with tears? "Yeah. I'm fine. I'm just thinking about her a lot today."

"Ah." He pauses, uncertain of what to say next. It is a familiar hesitation: steer clear of the dark and bottomless lake, or dip in a cautious toe? He elects to stay dry. "So it sounds like work is going well?"

"It's going at warp speed," I tell him. "I'm getting stressed out by this pace, and we've barely even started. I've been cranking on the expansion for Balm, too. And Jamie, the owner, keeps hinting that she's going to have some exciting news soon, which sounds like a new project." I hesitate, dreading what I have to say next. "The worst thing is, this schedule means I'm not going to be able to visit this summer like we had talked about."

There is a long silence on the other end of the phone. "What do you mean? Not at all?"

"I'm still coming next month," I say quickly. "But the next few months after that are going to be insanity, and I'm too freaked out to drop everything and fly halfway around the world for a week."

"You're saying we wouldn't see each other for four months? That's insane."

"I know. But this is too important to me. To my future."

"To yours. Okay. But what about *our* future, Sarina?" The hurt in his voice gnaws at me, just like I knew it would.

"I know, babe, and I hate it. I've thought it over a hundred times, but I just can't see a way to do it. There's going to be too much going on."

"I get that," he says sharply. "But what I don't get is why you won't hire an assistant. Seems like that would solve the entire problem."

We've had this conversation before. Many times. "I want to, once things get under way. But I'll have to see how it goes. It's a lot of money to hire somebody, even an intern—and no, I am not going to ask somebody to work for me for free."

"So hire an architecture student from UT, and pay them twelve bucks an hour for twenty hours a week. You got a good fee on this project, you should be able to afford an intern. And then you'll be able to come visit me. And maybe you'll even get some sleep. You made yourself sick when you were finishing up Clementine; I don't want you to put yourself through that again. Find someone to help."

"That's not the only thing, though." I try to think of how to explain it so he'll understand. "I'm just scared to give up control, especially since it's a new project and a new client. . . . I'd have a hard time finding things for them to do that were unimportant enough that they could screw up."

He sighs, clearly trying to hold on to his patience. "There's got to be something they can do. Running errands, whatever. Anything will make a difference. Believe me, the business will not collapse around your ears if you're out of the country for a week."

"Maybe," I concede, but I'm unconvinced.

"Ree, I'm serious. I know this is your career, but it's our relationship, too. It's insane to think of going four months without seeing each other. I mean, if I'd known this project was going to keep you from visiting . . ."

"If you had known that, then what?"

He sighs. "Nothing." But whatever the unspoken words were, I don't think I like them.

"Well, you could always come here," I say. I know what the answer will be, but he needs to remember that this separation is mostly at his account.

"You know I can't."

"So why is it so hard for you to understand how committed I am here?" I flare.

"You are not seriously comparing a house renovation to an international corporate merger."

What? "I am comparing how important my career is to me to how important yours is to you. And it's not fair to patronize me because you're upset about this!"

"I'm not patronizing you, I'm being FACTUAL," he insists, voice rising. He huffs another irritated breath, then continues in a softer tone. "Please promise me you will find the time."

Still stinging from the comment about my "house renovation," I am disinclined to promise him anything. So I tell him I will do my best. Even though I know he hates that phrase.

I feel incomplete and out of sorts for the next few days, until our next Skype call, when the familiar glow rises inside me at the sight of his crinkle-eyed smile. He apologizes, and so do I. And I mean it. But the one thing I don't do is change my mind.

7

"Oh, honey, those are the ones. Those are some bona fide shit-kickers right there." John is studying me, arms crossed in the universal pose of evaluation, as I pace back and forth in front of the mirror in my seventh pair of cowboy boots. He decided that the first thing he wanted to do on his visit to Austin was buy each of us a new pair of boots, so, for the last hour, we have been meandering up and down the narrow leather-scented aisles of Allens, pulling boots off the shelves and testing them out. Of course, he found a pair he liked almost immediately, so mostly we've just been debating which of the pairs I've tried on so far is our favorite.

We are also killing time until the construction workers leave Eamon's job site so I can give him a tour without getting in anybody's way—or pissing anybody off. Contractors are deeply territorial creatures, as I discovered a few years before, when I unwisely brought John to check out the Albion site while Joe Martinez was there. Only had to make that mistake once.

I do a little demi-turn in front of the mirror, admiring the glossy sheen of the black-cherry leather. This pair has little gold brackets over the toe and heel—I like the badassiness of that detail.

"Yeah, I think these might be the winners," I say.

John rubs his hands together gleefully. "Alrighty, now how about a hat?"

"John! I'm going to look like Western Barbie! Let's just stick with boots."

"I meant for me," he says. "The boys are going to be *so jealous*."

"The boys" are his bandmates in his bluegrass band, the Pickers. There's a guitarist, a fiddler, a banjo player, and a mandolinist; John plays steel guitar and sings. My mother used to love to sit in with them and sing harmony, until she got too sick.

The opening notes of AC/DC's "Back in Black" roar from my handbag. It was a toss-up between that and the approaching-shark chords of *Jaws* for Eamon's signature ringtone (I enjoyed the aquatic reference), but the sheer aggressiveness of "Back in Black" won out in the end. It's been three months since he moved back to Austin, during which I have seen him or spoken to him almost every day. Even during my visit with Noah in Buenos Aires in May, I was fielding emails from Eamon while Noah was at work. We've been spending hours together, visiting showrooms, shopping for materials, and reviewing the construction progress at the weekly site meetings with Joe.

Contrary to what I'd hoped, my attraction to him has not diminished with familiarity—it's gotten stronger. And lately, I've been catching myself being short-tempered with him. Punishing him. As if it's his fault that my body temperature climbs every time I'm around him. Next week he is leaving on a work trip for six weeks—filming segments with the top American swimmers as they prepare for the national and, if they qualify, the world championships. I am eagerly anticipating the month and a half of peace of mind.

"Whatcha doing?" he says when I answer the phone. "Are you

over at the house?" He'd sounded flattered when I asked his permission to bring John by the work site. And, I was surprised to note, genuinely interested to hear what John would have to say.

When I explain where we are, his voice brightens. "Oh cool! I haven't been to Allens since I've been back in town. Maybe I'll swing over and say hi."

Shit. I'd forgotten that he lives three minutes from here. "Oh. Ah, okay," I say. "We'll be with the hats." It is far from the most gracious invitation I've ever issued, but the last thing I need is Eamon worming his way into my personal time. Especially because I suspect John is going to absolutely love him. He called me, the day after I told him I got the job, and proceeded to read me the entire contents of Eamon's Wikipedia entry. "Ree-Ree, did you know he won *five* medals last year? After breaking *thirteen* bones in a car crash? It says the only silver medal he got was when some other guy took too long on his leg of the relay!"

Oh, yes. I knew.

John is sporting a curly-brimmed brown felt Stetson when I catch up to him. With his creased, weather-scuffed skin and bristly white stubble, he looks every inch the rugged cowboy.

"Very nice," I tell him.

He turns his head to the side, scowls at himself in the mirror. "You think?" He cocks his jaw like a tough guy.

"I do. Oh, Eamon's going to stop by," I add. "I hope you don't mind. I mentioned we were here and he sort of invited himself over. He lives around the corner."

"Why would I mind? That's great!" He picks up a straw hat with a silver concha buckle on the front. "Hey, try this one on."

Shaking my head, I oblige him. He vetoes it and insists I try another, then another. Consequently I am kitted out like a rodeo contestant when Eamon walks into the store.

"Howdy, cowgirl," he says, giving me an amused once-over.

I tip my hat at him. "Howdy, yourself."

"Hi there! John Kurzweil," booms my stepdad, holding out his hand.

"Eamon Roy. I'm pleased to meet you, sir—that's a fine girl you raised there."

John beams. The fastest way to his heart is to compliment me. "All the credit goes to her mama. But it's a fine boy your folks raised, too, I hear."

My face burns as Eamon's eyebrows skip upward; he's going to think I've been singing his praises to my stepdad like a lovesick little girl.

"John's addicted to Google," I interject, and Eamon taps his temple in understanding.

"Ah. Well, thank you, that's kind of you. So what have you guys been finding? Anything good?"

John proudly points out our selections.

"Nice," Eamon says. "I love this place. I always wanted a pair of black lizard-skin boots, but I didn't feel badass enough to pull it off."

"We saw a pair like that, didn't we, Ree-Ree?" says John.

Eamon gives a delighted, boyish smile. "Really? Where?"

A minute later, he is kicking out of his gray suede Pumas so he can try on the boots. Balancing with one hand on the shelf, he wiggles one foot, then the other, into the boots and pulls his jeans down over them.

He shoots us a grin. "Well? What's the verdict?"

"Badass," says John.

I give him a carefully unenthusiastic thumbs-up. They look great on him. Everything looks great on him.

"Mahler, you are a terrible influence on me," he says as we line up at the cash register. "Every time I'm around you, you're making me spend money."

"Those were your explicit instructions," I remind him.

When we step out of the store into the sunlight, the heat hits like someone has opened the door to an oven.

"Damn, kid, I don't know how you do it," says John, wiping his forehead with his ratty bandanna. "It's hotter than a billy goat in a pepper patch out here." I've got to talk him out of visiting at the height of summer next year. I crank the A/C in the Honda, but it's barely begun to cool down by the time we pull into the driveway at the job site; I can feel sweat beading between my breasts and on my lower back.

Esteban, Joe's foreman, is just locking up the house when we arrive. He looks at me inquiringly.

"Hey, Esteban," I say to him in Spanish. "Don't worry about staying, we're just going to take a walk through."

"Who's that guy?" he asks, nodding at John. "Inspector?"

"My stepfather," I explain. "Don't tell Joe, okay?"

He winks. "You got it."

Once, not long after Noah and I had started dating, I was complaining about receiving only blank, confused stares when I tried to communicate with the Spanish-speaking construction workers. "It would be good for you to learn Spanish," he said. "It's not a hard language. I'll help you." He went out the next day and bought a set of language CDs. And, true to his word, he was a patient tutor, tirelessly quizzing me with flash cards and correcting my pronunciation. The first time I came home from work and announced that I had understood an entire extended conversation between two tile installers, he glowed with pride. "Look at that, my girl is bilingual!" he said, and kissed me.

"They've been calling me La Güera," I complained.

"Yeah," he said, tapping the end of my nose, "I bet they have."

Since then, I've had cause to be grateful for the skill almost every day I've been on the job. Grateful to Noah. And, as always, grateful *for* him.

"Wow, honey," says John when he steps into the great room of the house. "This is gonna be something else. You lucked out, my friend," he adds, nudging Eamon with his elbow.

I can feel myself beaming. I already knew the house was going to be fantastic, but it still means a lot to hear John's praise. I pull out the samples of all the materials we've chosen so far: fudgy wide-plank walnut flooring, pale gray lacquer kitchen cabinets, poured concrete for the counters, smoky blue handmade glass tiles for the backsplash. I chose the palette carefully, wanting it to be sophisticated and appropriate for a man, but not so masculine that it would feel oppressive to whatever Cowboys dancer or *Sports Illustrated* model Eamon eventually marries. Although, so far, there hasn't been so much as a hint of a girlfriend. I would have noticed.

John is unexpectedly subdued as we say goodbye to Eamon and drive back to my house. When we pull into the driveway, he is still staring out the passenger-side window.

"Well, so what do you think?" I'm not fishing for compliments; he will tell me negative observations just as readily as positive ones. I've always learned even more from those.

When he turns to me his cheeks are trembling, and his blue eyes are glossy with tears. "Your mama would be so proud of you."

As I hug his reassuringly burly frame I think, not for the first time, how much harder it's been for him than for me. Missing her. For me, moving to Austin after college was like amputating a crushed and dying limb: a clean, surgical break with my life in Virginia. But John has been pacing the same floors, and listening to rain drum the tin roof of the same empty house, for ten years. Surrounded by all those artifacts of the life that used to be theirs together, the things she used to touch every day. Sleeping in the bed he used to share with her and looking at her blank pillow, night after night. He's dated a few people over the years, the longest lasting a couple of years, but it was always kind of half-hearted. Inevitably his lady friends figured out which way the wind was blowing.

"Let's go inside," I say after a moment. "I'm starving."

He chuckles, as I knew he would. One of my more colorful childhood nicknames, due to my disproportionate capacity for food, was Gaping Maw. From the smile tickling his lips, I can see that the wave of sadness has receded. Until next time.

If my mother's guilty television pleasure was daytime soap operas, John's is Tim Gunn. He doesn't have cable at home, so whenever he comes to visit me he works his way through an entire season's worth of *Project Runway*, consumed in four-hour increments over the three or four days he's here. Though the actual craft of clothing design is unfamiliar to him, he appreciates the skill that goes into it, and the ingenuity of the designers. And he treasures Tim's trademark combination of paternal doting and blunt critique.

We are three episodes in, sprawled out on the couch with a single ice-cold slice of pizza staring us down. After the opening credits roll, Heidi Klum struts onto the runway in a short sequined number that Noah would absolutely love. When I say so, John looks skeptical.

"Doesn't look like your sort of thing, honey." He reaches for the slice of pizza and takes a contemplative bite. "Speaking of Mr. Harlow, how was your visit down there?"

"It was wonderful," I say. Though I know he was still upset by my decision not to visit later in the summer, Noah had clearly decided to let it go, and to make the most of the time we did have. He cut back on his hours in the office as much as he could, and we had a glorious week's worth of long late-night dinners, heavenly steak, and Malbec. One of these days he'll have no choice but to abandon his pet project of teaching me to differentiate between varietals, but after spending two solid weeks this year guzzling Argentinian wine, I feel *exceedingly* confident about Malbec.

"Did you get to climb around on that blue glacier like you wanted?"

I pick at a tuft of Newman's hair that's embedded itself in the sofa cushion. "Well, no . . . Noah had to work every day, so we couldn't get down to Patagonia. . . ."

John grunts. "Seems like a waste of life."

"He doesn't have a choice. And besides, he likes his job," I add, although this is not strictly true. Noah likes the intellectual challenge, and the status, and the salary, but the actual work itself often depends on obsession with infuriatingly picayune details. His talent lies in generating the abstract concepts that establish how a transaction gets structured, not arguing with the other side's lawyers about whether a sentence in the offering document needs a colon or a semicolon.

"Well, then, that's something. Is he going to keep having to go back down there?"

"Yeah, probably a couple of times a year. But he won't have to do anything like this again."

John crosses his arms over his chest. "Good. Just as long as you don't call me up a year from now and tell me you're moving to Argentina. I want to be able to see my grandkids more than once a year."

The worn cotton of his shirt is soft under my fingers when I squeeze his shoulder. Everyone else's outbursts of nosiness regarding Noah's and my future seem to revolve around getting us hitched; John has proceeded directly to grandkids. "You will, I promise. Maybe I should ship them off to you for the summers instead of sending them to camp."

This doesn't scare him; he'd like nothing better. I'm not sure how Noah would feel about his children spending a quarter of the year in the deepest heart of Appalachia, though.

Nicole told me I was a weirdo when she discovered that I'd never given any particular thought to picturing the features and personalities of my unborn children. Noah is the one who likes to do that. For me, I fail to see the point in fantasizing about who our kids will be, because I know perfectly well that they will turn out completely different than I expect. When I do think about them, all I see are images of Noah and me from childhood photos: a sweet boy with freckles, a spiky brown mop-top, and blue-green eyes sparking with sunlight, a skinny-limbed imp with messy toffee-colored braids and a devilish, gap-toothed grin.

I do have my daughter's name picked out, though. Have known it for years. She'll be named for my mother, and the hills that nurtured her: sweet little Virginia Leigh.

"I wish you would spend more time at home, kid," John says, reaching over to tug gently on my ponytail. "Except for the Christmas concerts, you haven't been home in so long. You've never even brought Mr. Harlow. You know, Dave and Ellie and everybody, they always ask about you."

"That's so kind of them."

"They'd like to see you. I'd like to see you more. I miss my girl."

I lean against him, and he wraps an arm around my shoulders. He smells cinnamony, like original-flavor Old Spice, the way he always has. "I miss you too."

"Why don't you come in the fall? You used to love the leaves so much."

At his words, I remember an amber-gold November morning when I was about eight. My mom had recruited me to help her clear up the confetti of leaves that spangled our lawn, so we spent a good two hours raking them into droopy mounds that straggled across the yard like a regiment of drunks. She approached the first mound with a garbage bag at the ready, but then she paused. And then, with a whoop, she threw herself down into the soft, yielding pile, seized two handfuls of leaves, and flung them into the air. I shrieked and did the same. We repeated the performance in one pile after another, wiggling in the leaves and tossing them all around us. I remember the rich, dusty smell of the leaves, the way they crunched in my fists. And I remember her face, glazed with sunlight, laughing up into the sky.

"I can't," I whisper to John. "I'm sorry."

—

A few days later, I am watering my petunias in the slightly less scorching air that settles in after sundown—and feeling guilty for not gardening with a more drought-friendly plant—when I get a call from my client Jamie, the owner of Balm spa.

"Sarina Sarina guess what?!?" she gasps when I pick up the phone.

"Jamie Jamie WHAT?!?" I gasp back. I have always thought she is a little excitable for someone who makes her living relaxing other people.

"It's done—it's final—I have investors!"

"Holy crap, that's fantastic news! Congratulations!" I turn off the hose and sit down on the dry, prickly grass so I can concentrate on what she's telling me.

She goes on to explain that they are close to signing leases on two new locations, in Dallas and Houston. "I want you to go up there, check out the spaces, take photos. Do whatever it is that you do. The investors want to get proposals from a couple other architects as well, but whatever. You'll rock their worlds. Just go do your thing."

"Jamie! That's amazing! Are you trying to take this thing national?"

"That's the plan, chica! First we conquer Texas, then New Orleans, then Atlanta . . . then we break out of the region and start opening in all the big daddy cities. And believe me, I won't forget that you knew me when."

I am flabbergasted. For once, she's got every right to be as breathless as she sounds. I'd figured she was doing well after she bought the space next door to her current location in order to expand, but investors, two new locations, a nationwide business plan—this is big news. For me as well as her. This is a whopper of a commission: getting hired as project architect for a fast-growing spa chain is going to be the job that finally turns me from a one-woman operation into a bona fide company. I'm going to need *staff*. I picture a serious-faced young woman, at an overloaded desk in an actual office space, pleading into her phone: "I need these drawings plotted on twenty-four by thirty-six, ASAP. My boss has a meeting with the client in two hours."

My boss.

I *really* like the sound of that.

8

Being naked under a hotel robe is one of life's finer pleasures. The unaccustomed weight of the dense, fluffy cotton on your body, the subtle naughtiness of having nothing on underneath a garment that can be removed with a single strong tug.

Not that there's anyone around to tug my robe off right now. I'm lolling on my bed at Jamie's investor's Dallas hotel, in the middle of a two-day trip to photograph and measure her new spa spaces here and in Houston. Noah was supposed to Skype me at 10:30, but he's late. I've been dying all day to fill him in on the new Balm site, which is even better than I'd hoped when Jamie told me about it a few weeks back, but so far all I've done since dinner is give John a webcam tour of my swanky hotel room and paint my toes—bright grass green, the signature color of Balm's logo.

Finally, at 11:12, I hear the familiar *beep-boop* noise of the Skype call coming through on my computer. Noah is propped against the leather headboard of his bed in Buenos Aires, eyes blurry with fatigue. I hate seeing him so tired all the time. "Ree, where *are* you?" He squints over my shoulder at the unfamiliar surroundings.

"I'm in Dallas. For the site visit? For Balm?"

"Oh, right. I guess I thought you would just come home afterward," he says vaguely.

"No, 'cause I'm going to Houston tomorrow to look at *that* site," I say. "Remember?"

Plainly, he doesn't. I smother my irritation and continue. "Well, anyway, the Dallas site is going to be amazing."

"Yeah?" He raises his eyebrows encouragingly, which I think of as his "architecture face"—the unconvincing expression of interest that he gets whenever I try to talk to him about the technical aspects of my job. He genuinely wants to be interested, I know he does. But my descriptions of spaces, floor plans, even sketches are meaningless to him, because he can't visualize what the finished result will look like. Once something is built, he is proud and impressed; he has an endearing habit of bringing his friends and co-workers to Albion and Clementine to show off what I do for a living (apparently having an architect for a girlfriend is considered cool and artsy in his circle). But anything less than a finished product just bores him.

With that in mind, I keep my narration brief, concentrating on the aspects I know he will relate to, like the location.

"Wow. She can afford McKinney Avenue?" he says.

"Yeah, they want hip, but visible. The Houston location is in the same kind of neighborhood. These new sites need to be nice, but keep the feel of the original, and they've got to reflect the brand she's developing. High-end but natural, herbal, all that stuff."

"Right. You always smell like mint from that shampoo that she comps you. I miss that smell," he says.

"I'll send you a bottle," I promise. "Actually," I add, my smile slipping sideways, "maybe I should send you a bottle of the lotion, too."

It takes him a second to get it. Then he slides me a slow, dirty grin. "Damn straight you should."

"Thank god I finally get to see you in a few weeks," I say. "I don't think you should make any plans for while you're here; I'm not letting you out of my bedroom."

He scratches his head. "Actually, I was thinking we could head up to Mom and Dad's place at Horseshoe Bay for the weekend. We can have the place to ourselves for a couple days, then they'll come up on the Friday evening. How does that sound?"

It sounds . . . like not quite the way I wanted to spend the few short days of his visit. Noah's parents are lovely and sweet and have never been less than welcoming. His mother in particular has always made an effort toward me: it's an instinct shared by several ladies of a motherish age whom I've known over the years. But her kindness has never altered the basic fact that she and I have little in common besides her son. She is as demure and decorous as her Wedgwood china service.

At our first meeting, she nervously inquired whether my tiny diamond nose piercing had some particular significance. I explained that its only "particular significance" came from having been eighteen years old, visiting New York's Lower East Side for the first time, and trying to impress my poser artist boyfriend with my willingness to do adventurous things to my body. I didn't say it to shock her, I was just answering the question honestly; but after that it became apparent that I would need to Stepfordize myself a little in Noah's parents' company. It drains me of energy along with color. But Noah hasn't seen his parents since last Christmas, so it wouldn't be fair of me to deny him their company on this visit. No matter how much I might want to.

—

By the end of August, Austin hasn't had a respite from the blistering heat in weeks, leaving me and everyone else cranky and short-tempered. Nicole, housebound with an insomniac infant, has been too hassled and stressed to hang out, and Danny just passed the nine-month anniversary of his celibacy initiative. When I asked him if he'd start to take on the smooth contours of a Ken doll below the waist if he managed to make it a full year, his only response was to ostentatiously rub one eye with his middle finger. And Eamon, who's been traveling constantly for the last month and a half, has been torturing me with requests for near-daily updates on the construction progress, complete with site photos and Skype conferences.

However, I've been taking grim satisfaction in the knowledge that I was right about visiting Noah. When I'm not working on Eamon's project, I'm up to my eyeballs in work for Balm—both the new construction at the Austin location and developing my ideas for Dallas and Houston. According to Jamie, the investors want to see presentations at the end of September. I have to give them enough of a taste to sell my designs, but not so much that I hand them a completed project. And although, as the architect for the original Balm space, I know it's my job to lose, I still want to knock the presentation out of the park. That means not just hitting them with shock and awe and a bunch of pretty drawings, but knowing the answer to every question they're going to ask, before they ask it. Which means lots of late nights fueled by coffee.

But today, in one more hour, I am on vacation. Noah is coming home tomorrow for the long Labor Day weekend, and I'm so excited to see him that I haven't been able to concentrate for days. I have cleared most of today so I can devote it to cleaning, grooming, sprucing. Both my house and my person. The last thing I have to do before I'm in the clear is meet Eamon to walk through his house. He just got back from Dubai last night, but he's been so anxious to see the progress that I'm surprised he didn't have me there at six o'clock in the morning. I've been both dreading and looking forward to his return; dreading it, I suppose, because I *am* looking forward to it.

When I arrive, he's leaning against one of the columns on the front porch, his long legs crossed at the ankle. He breaks into a grin as soon as he spots me, and, helplessly, I feel an answering spark of happiness flare inside me. He is offensively tan, and he looks so damn good I want to bite him. Meanwhile, I'm sweating like a whore in church, as John would say. Back home, this time of year is when we'd start getting those first crisp days that promised cooler air to follow, but that won't happen in Austin for weeks. I brush my bangs off my damp forehead and surreptitiously flutter my T-shirt in a vain attempt to dry off my skin.

"Where you been, Roy?" I say when I reach the porch. Casually. Like I haven't missed him at all.

Two seconds later, I'm engulfed in a hug. For a second I freeze, afraid to put my hands on any part of him, as if he will somehow sense how attracted to him I am. I settle for the backs of his arms. Even those feel good, though; there's no doubt he's filled out in the last few years. In the good way, not the donut way. Fuck.

"Hi," he says happily, obliviously, when he releases me.

"Um, hi," I say, struggling. "How the hell are you so tan? You're Irish, for god's sake. It's indecent. Show some respect for your heritage."

He grins. "My mom's Lebanese. A few days in the sun and I get unpopular at airport security."

That explains it; I've never met anybody Irish who came in a shade darker than moonglow. Suddenly, I remember the tan line at his hips, years ago. Remember skimming my thumbs over it. Fuuuuck.

"Must be nice," I mutter.

"I like your skin," he says.

"Oh. Uh, thanks." *Stop complimenting me. Stop being happy to see me. Stop making me wonder if you still think I'm pretty.* "By the way, why are you standing out here waiting for me? I would have thought you'd be inside already. Actually, I would have thought you'd have been here at six in the morning."

He scratches his chin with studied nonchalance. "I stopped by last night before I went home."

I shake my head and open the door.

It actually turns out to be a good thing that he couldn't restrain himself from stopping by yesterday; he's had time to process the initial surprise and excitement. But there's no doubt he's pleased—the crew has made a lot of progress since he left town, thanks to my relentless whip cracking. Construction is, so far, right on schedule.

"So what're you up to this weekend?" he asks as we walk back to our cars. "Anything good?"

"Noah's coming tomorrow!" I tell him, beaming. Less than twenty-four hours now.

"That's right." He leans one elbow on the side of his Jeep (a newer, cleaner version of the one he had in college). "Do you have anything special planned?"

I explain to him about Noah's parents' place.

"That sounds like fun. You'll be back for the Labor Day barbecue, though, right?"

I shake my head. Danny has been planning the party for weeks, and it kills me to miss it. "Wish we could, but we're planning on spending that day up there. Maybe we'll catch the tail end if we're lucky."

"Damn. You're missing a hell of a party," he says.

"Ugh, don't rub it in," I groan, and immediately feel disloyal to Noah for even alluding to the fact that Horseshoe Bay isn't my first choice.

"Do you not get along with his family?"

"No, no, I do. They're wonderful people. Just . . . different. You know what I mean?"

"I do know," he says. "My ex's dad is the offensive coordinator for the New York Giants." I must be giving him an ". . . and?" face, because he continues. "Mine is an insurance salesman. And my mom's an Arabic translator for the State Department. Oh, and then there was the fact that tan or no tan, I was still never going to be black, so . . . yeah."

I offer him a solemn fist bump.

"Well, have fun. We'll miss you," he says, and climbs into the Jeep.

I'm still musing over his story as I drive home. The thought of anyone's parents not enthusiastically welcoming Eamon into their family is frankly a little ludicrous. And the fact that it so plainly still bothers him is, well . . . it's almost enough to make me jealous, if I were a jealous kind of girl.

—

That night, I lie awake, imagining my reunion with Noah. I am so sex-starved that I'm going to have a hard time keeping my hands off him until we're home from the airport. I picture us, stumbling into the house like people do in romantic comedies, bumping into furniture, shedding clothes without stopping to look at what we've uncovered. He hustles me up the stairs and we collapse, laughing and breathless, on the bed. My imagination runs through round one and—what the hell, it is a fantasy—round two, but for once, I don't reach for my vibrator; I'm saving myself for the touch of an actual human being. *Finally.* He has historically been squeamish about having sex in his parents' house, but under the circumstances he is just going to have to learn to cope.

As I slip toward sleep, I embark upon round number three. It's late at night, and I'm combing the sex tangles out of my hair in front of the bathroom mirror when he comes up behind me. He slips his arms around my waist and pulls me back against him;

then he brushes my hair away from my shoulder so he can kiss me there. I remember the way his lips clung to my skin, the warmth of his chest against my naked back, the way—

Fuck! I snap upright in bed, heart pumping. That wasn't a fantasy, it was a memory. Of *Eamon*. Burning with shame, I cover my face with my hands, even though I'm alone in my room in the dark. I remember reading in *Cosmo* once that lots of guys think about other women when they're having sex with their girlfriends; apparently it's like a highlight reel of all their favorite encounters that plays in front of their eyes whenever they get busy with someone. I have never done this and I promise myself now that I never will—but pulling up a memory of Eamon when I am trying to think about Noah feels almost as bad. There's no way around the fact that I had an intense physical chemistry with Eamon that Noah and I have never quite matched. But if you gave me the choice between vanilla sex with Noah and head-spinning sex with Eamon, I would choose Noah every single time, because he would have love in his face and in his hands. And he'd be there, giving me the one unburned bacon strip, the next morning.

9

On the way to the airport, I am a handful of mismatched rhythms. My fingers drum the steering wheel in time to the Jackson 5. Too enthusiastically, my feet press the gas, then the brake, then the gas again. My pulse skids through me, picking up speed as I pass the sign for the terminal.

When I pull up to the sidewalk, Noah is asleep on a bench, his brown head buried in the arms folded over his small leather duffel. A cheerful plastic-wrapped bouquet of red and yellow daisies waits by his side. I sit down next to him on the bench. He starts awake with a sharp inhale, rubs his hand over his face before he notices me. Then I get that wonderful crow-footed smile.

When he wraps me in a hug, I press a kiss to my favorite spot, that vulnerable little spot on the side of his neck, right below his hairline. I close my eyes and enjoy the happiness washing over me. I've been waiting so long for it, and it feels so good.

"I missed you so much," he whispers.

"Me too," I tell him, hugging him tighter. Drinking in the feel of him against me, after all this time. "This *sucks*."

"Only a few months left," he says, pulling away and dragging himself to his feet. "Let's go home. I've slept five hours in the last two days, and I'm about to fall over."

He falls asleep again in the car on the way back to my place. At a long stoplight, I study him—purple shadows stain the skin under his eyes, his cheekbones are more prominent than usual, and his jaw is rough with that unexpectedly reddish stubble that I love. It makes him look sort of rakish. I've never seen his hair brushing the back of his collar before, either, but I like it. I smile, knowing he won't listen to me when I tell him he should keep it that way.

Once we pull into the driveway, he wakes up exactly long enough to stumble up the walkway and collapse, fully clothed, onto my bed. I lie down next to him for a few minutes, watching his quiet breathing, but he doesn't stir. I climb out of bed, pull the door closed silently, and head downstairs to my office. So much for my daydreams of being ravished.

—

The plan was supposed to be that we would leave in the afternoon for Noah's parents' house, but as the hours tick past and he doesn't surface, I decide he needs rest more than anything else. He just got done traveling for fifteen hours; the drive to Horseshoe Bay can wait till tomorrow morning.

In the early-evening light, I can see that he hasn't moved since I left him, not even to crawl under the covers; his shadowed form looks like metal shavings bunched together on the magnet of the bed. I want to make him more comfortable, but I don't want to take the risk of waking him when he needs sleep so badly, so I just back silently out of the room. At the last second, though, Newman darts through the closing door and leaps onto the bed, landing with the force of a cinder block next to Noah's feet.

"Newman!" I hiss and pluck him off the bed, but Noah is already feeling groggily around for his BlackBerry.

"Babe," he mumbles, "have you seen my phone?"

"I have it, and I'm not giving it back to you."

He grunts, but he's smiling when he flops back onto the bed.

"And for god's sake, take off your clothes," I say. "In fact," I add with a smile, "why don't I help you with that?" I deposit both Newman and the BlackBerry safely out of the room and shut the door.

Noah lurches to his feet and into the bathroom. "Don't you dare come near me," he calls over his shoulder. "The last time I brushed my teeth was in the Southern Hemisphere."

He reappears a few minutes later with a towel around his waist. Mmmm. I've always loved how untidy his hair looks when it's wet. I reach my arms up to him. His skin is damp and sweet and cool to the touch, but his mouth is warm.

We kiss. And kiss, and kiss, and kiss. He painstakingly kisses his way down my throat, my breasts, my belly.

"Thank god," I murmur as, after what feels like an absolute lifetime of kissing, he starts to pull off my jeans. The world-peace jeans, which he hasn't even remarked upon.

He glares up at me. "Are you in some sort of hurry here?"

"Damn straight," I answer, wiggling my hips. "Good god, man, get on with it."

I expect him to laugh, but hurt flickers across his face. "I haven't seen you in four months. I wanted to take my time and enjoy being with you."

Shit shit shit. I forgot his stupid ex told him he took too long to move things along in bed. Although, right at this moment . . . "I'm sorry, sweetie, I didn't mean to criticize you. We've just been waiting so long, I guess I wanted instant gratification. Um, literally," I add, running my hands over his arms encouragingly.

He is still frowning. "I wanted it to feel special."

And I wanted to get laid, my brain screams. Why does this have to be *special*? "It *is* special. I'm so happy to be with you," I say. "C'mere."

He reluctantly lets me pull him back up to me, and a minute

later we are finally having sex. Whether from lack of practice or lingering crankiness on Noah's part, it isn't the best it's ever been, but it's been so damn long that I barely even notice. We've got five more days to get back to how things are supposed to be.

—

We are snoozing in that last deep blue light of dusk, his head on my chest, when he looks up at me.

"I almost forgot," he says. "I brought you something." He clicks on my bedside lamp, then fishes around in his duffel until he retrieves a long, flat turquoise box with "Tiffany" stamped in black lettering on the top. "I hope you like it."

Inside the box is a silver chain attached to a small pendant in the shape of a heart, encrusted with what I assume are tiny diamonds. A minuscule key charm dangles from the top of the heart. When I lift the pendant, the shimmering chain spills through my fingers; the metal is cool against my skin. It's a lovely, generous gift that any woman in her right senses would adore. And I realize, stomach shriveling with guilt, that I don't like it at all.

Noah is watching me hopefully, so I lean forward to kiss him. "I love it," I lie. "It's beautiful. That was so sweet of you to remember how much I love silver, thank you."

He gives me a you're-so-cute smile. "Sweetheart, that's not silver. It's platinum."

I guess I should have known that, somehow. "Oh. Well, it's lovely."

"I'm so glad you like it," he says. "My co-worker helped me pick it out. I wanted to find the perfect thing for you." He rests his forehead against mine and cups my cheek. "I love you, Ree. I can't wait until I'm home for good and we can just be together again. And then we can get married and finally get started on our lives together."

It is the first time he's ever addressed marriage so directly. We've talked about it, of course, but always as something that would happen in the vague, general future, not as something imminent. We weren't in a hurry; with his divorce still fading into the past, and me quitting my old job to go out on my own, he understood that I wanted to get a little more settled before we took that next step. And now, I realize, we're actually there. He is going to propose in the next couple of months, I am sure of it. I want this to happen; I should be ecstatic. I should be melting with tenderness. Instead, the only thing I feel is panic.

I kick it into a box and shove it to the back of my mind. This is what I need. This is where I've wanted to be headed since he showed me what a real relationship was like. "I love you too," I whisper. And I mean it; I have never doubted it before and I don't doubt it now. "I love you," I repeat, for both of us.

—

Noah rousts me out of bed at 7:30 the next morning, wearing the straw cowboy hat John insisted on buying me from Allens, and he looks so goddamn cute in it that I pounce on him.

We are packed and on the road forty-seven minutes later. There's a hurricane making landfall over Galveston that's projected to drench its way northwest tomorrow, so we want to try to enjoy as much sunshine as we can before it hits. After fourteen more hours of sleep, Noah is in a great mood, loudly singing along with Garth Brooks on the radio, faking a deep Texas twang he's never had. I join in with him on the choruses.

As soon as we arrive, we dump our bags in his bedroom and head down to the dock. The house itself is an unconvincing attempt at Old World Spanish elegance, so I always try to spend as little time inside it as possible. But on the dock, I can lie right next to the water. With bold disregard for possible splinters, we spread towels right onto the wooden planks, and I lie back with my head on Noah's stomach. He pulls my hair out of its ponytail and combs his fingers through it, again and again. I feel the sun soaking into my skin and listen to the waves slopping against the shore of the lake and, for a while, everything is absolutely, beautifully perfect.

—

Noah's parents arrive early the next evening, along with the hurricane clouds. We catch them up on our respective lives over an Argentine-inspired dinner at their kitchen table. I can't imagine how tired of grass-fed beef poor Noah must be by now, and even I am hitting the wall with Malbec.

"So, work must be busy, huh?" his father, Peter, says to me between bites of fillet. "Heard you were so busy you couldn't make it to Buenos Aires earlier this summer."

"Yeah, unfortunately, it's been nutty the past few months. But cracking the whip in June made sure I could take these days now, so that's good."

Peter chews silently, withholding comment.

"Sarina's business is really growing," Noah volunteers. There is no tint of reproach or qualification in his voice, and I love him for that.

"That's wonderful," says his mother, Anne-Marie. "What sorts of projects are you working on?"

I fill her in on everything I've got cooking, especially the proposal for Balm, which is just a few weeks away.

To my gratification, Anne-Marie sounds genuinely impressed. "So when will you start work on the new spa locations?"

"It's not a hundred percent certain until I actually present to the investors, but I know the owner wants me for the job. Which is amazing—it's enough work that I'll need to hire a couple people to help me, so I'll be an official small business owner. With staff!" I can't keep the pride and anticipation out of my voice, and Noah hears it and smiles.

"Good for you, honey! That's fantastic. If you don't mind me asking, though, how's that going to work in the future?" asks Peter.

"In the future?" I repeat.

"When you have little ones," he continues. "You can't be working so much when you have a little baby to take care of." He spears another piece of steak and pops it into his mouth—my signal to speak.

I open my mouth to answer and realize that I literally have no idea how to respond to this. Foolishly, I close it again and try to recover from my shock. What could *possibly* have led him to believe that this was an appropriate comment to make?

"Well, she works from home, Peter," says Anne-Marie, as though my temporary inability to speak has somehow also rendered me invisible. "Obviously not as many hours, but she could do some work part-time. Couldn't you, dear?" She turns to me, pleased at having solved this wicket before it even got sticky.

"I might be able to do that, yes," I manage, as the power of speech returns. Sure. I might be able to do it if I didn't mind steering away from every commission that would demand more of my time than I could manage to squeeze in between diaper changes and nursing sessions. And, of course, if I didn't mind throwing away everything I've been working for the last thirteen years to build, and am just now on the verge of starting to achieve. But other than that.

Incredulous, I glance at Noah, who is staring attentively at his fork.

"Well sure, that sounds doable," says Peter. "Good to hear you've thought about it. Just as long as my grandkids don't get passed off to some daycare to be raised. I don't believe in that."

"Dad," says Noah in a low, tight tone I've never heard before.

"What? It's ridiculous. People shouldn't have children if they're not going to raise them themselves. You don't agree with me?"

"I do, but . . ."

"But nothing. That's the way it should be. Your cousin Stacy went right back to work a couple months after she had her baby, and she missed the first steps, first word, everything. It's appalling." He clunks his wineglass down on the table to show the matter is closed. Anne-Marie delicately rests her fork and knife on the rim of her plate, as if needing to free her hands for combat. Noah is staring at his lap, frowning. *Why is he leaving me to fend them off all by myself?*

I take a deep breath. *Tread carefully, these are your future in-laws.* "Well, I do think this conversation is a bit premature. We're still a few years away from that, so we have some time to figure it out."

"Really, a few years?" says Anne-Marie softly, shooting a glance at Noah. "We were so hoping we'd hear some good news within the next year or so." She sounds disappointed, not accusing. But where is she getting this from? Am I the last person in the room to find out that I'm supposed to be knocked up by this time next year?

My brain is buzzing with static. The panic I felt the other night, when Noah gave me the necklace, is back in full force.

"A year? No, I don't think . . ."

"Well, be careful you don't put it off for too long," warns Peter. "Don't want to risk running into problems, you know."

"Dad!" mutters Noah, slapping a hand over his eyes.

"He's right, Noah," says Anne-Marie. "We got very lucky that Caitlyn was just fine."

Noah's sister, fifteen years younger than he is, is fondly acknowledged within the family to have been a "blessed surprise." But Caitlyn notwithstanding, I have absolutely no interest in discussing my own biological clock with my in-laws. "I appreciate the concern, and I'm sorry to have to disappoint you, but no, no grandchildren for a little while yet," I say firmly.

Anne-Marie settles one impeccably maintained hand over mine. "You don't have to apologize, dear. I'm sure you can understand, we're just eager, that's all."

"Of course I understand," I say, and push my chair back from the table. "Unfortunately, I'm afraid something from the meal must not be agreeing with me at the moment. I think I better go ahead upstairs and turn in for the night."

"Oh no, can I get you anything?" says Anne-Marie, gracefully pretending to buy it.

"Thank you, but I think I just need to lie down for a while. Sweetie, you should stay here," I tell Noah, who is halfway out of his chair.

"No, I'll get you settled. Mom, Dad, good night, we'll see you in the morning."

Inside our bedroom, the window is open, and wind from the advancing storm is beating waves onto the shore so hard that it sounds like the ocean. Noah closes the door behind us, then takes both of my hands in his.

"Kitten, I'm so sorry about that."

With one hand, I pull him over to the bed. We stretch out, facing each other, and he strokes the side of my face, over and over, as we talk.

"First of all," I say, "where did that come from? We aren't even officially engaged yet, and they're talking about timelines and child rearing. What have you been saying to them?"

He sighs. "I told them I was going to propose to you soon, and that I hoped we'd be able to plan the wedding for fairly soon after that. They just got a little carried away."

"And did you tell them we were going to try to get pregnant right away?"

"No. I mean, I would love that, but I would never assume it. We'll figure out the right time."

Holy shit. "You'd really want to try right away?"

"If you were up for it, yes." He is studying my face like it's an unfamiliar map. "I've wanted a family for so long. Letting go of that future was the hardest thing about my divorce, but I hoped I would meet someone else who was another chance at that. And then there you were. We've had a lot of good reasons to wait, but I don't want to wait anymore. Once I'm back, there *is* no reason."

"You've just been waiting for me?" I say in a tiny voice.

"I've been happy to wait for you," he says, tugging me in tight. "But being away from you has made me realize that it's time to take the next step."

"But, Noah," I say, pulling back to look at him, "all that stuff your dad was saying. Why weren't you standing up for me? I expect that your parents will have opinions about how we raise our kids, but they shouldn't expect that we'll go along with whatever they tell us. I need you to make it clear to them that we will make our own decisions."

He doesn't answer right away, just strokes my hair. "Well," he says finally, "Dad can be overbearing, but he means well."

"I know he does, but he doesn't get to tell me I have to quit my job once I give birth. You need to make him understand that he does not get to boss me around."

"No, he doesn't. But I have to say," Noah continues, "I agree with him on this particular thing."

I jerk upright so quickly my eyes black over. "In what way, specifically, do you agree with him?"

My voice is calm, but he knows me well enough to proceed with extreme caution. His eyes fixate on the corner of the window as he carefully chooses his words. "I think . . . well, I think it would be the best thing if you stayed home with the kids until they were old enough to go to school, instead of us sending them to daycare."

I stare at him for a moment while I absorb this. "You mean in the abstract, in an ideal-world sort of situation? Or are you saying that is what you would want me, specifically, to do?"

He rubs his fingers back and forth over his collarbone. "Isn't it what *you* would want to do, too?"

Troubled, I shake my head. "No. It's not. Working for myself means I'd be able to keep a flexible schedule, and I've always figured I'd cut back on my hours a bit, but I can't see myself working less than thirty hours a week . . . anything less than that and I'd be pretty out of the mix."

"But, kitten . . . once we have kids, it's not about being 'in the mix' anymore. It's about raising a couple of tiny people, spending time with them, taking care of them. We both have to accept that our priorities are going to shift."

"I know that. But I want to do both. It's hard, but it's possible; plenty of people do it. Nicole does it."

"People do it because they don't have a choice," he points out.

"People like *my* mother?"

As I watch him struggle to respond, I almost, *almost,* feel bad. Dragging my dead mother into an argument is using heavy artillery; my dead lower-middle-class *single* mother is an atomic bomb. But my point is valid and he knows it.

"I would never put down your mom, or the work she did to support you. It goes without saying that she did a tremendous job. Especially in less-than-ideal circumstances."

I cross my arms over my chest. "Raising a kid on a diner waitress's salary with no help from the dickhead who abandoned you—that is less-than-ideal, yes."

He strokes a soothing hand along my forearm. "But sweetheart, that's my point. She worked so, so hard for you because she *had* to. You are in a situation where you don't."

"But I *want* to," I say again. "My work isn't going to stop being important to me once I have a child."

"I think you'll find the child is *more* important to you," he says gently. "Listen, becoming a parent means you have to make sacrifices. That was a big part of why I went into corporate law instead of working in the public sector. I wanted to be a prosecutor, but I knew I'd never be able to support a family the way I wanted. So I made a deal with the devil."

"You never told me that," I whisper.

He strokes his knuckles down my neck. "I was trying not to hit you over the head with the kid thing. Didn't want to be the needy divorced guy. But yeah, that was a major reason. And part of it was so that my future wife wouldn't need to work."

I kiss him softly. "That is an amazingly generous sacrifice. And I love you for it. But as it turns out, your future wife would *prefer* to work."

"But why? When it can make such a difference in those first few years? I have so many incredible memories of special stuff my mom did with me. She might not have had time for it if she'd been working. Just say you did stay home—it's not like you'd never work again. It would only be for a few years, until the kids were in school. And what Mom said is true: you could still do some stuff on the side—"

"*Stuff on the side?*" I repeat, my voice squeaking skyward. "Noah! Are you kidding me? I'm trying to build a business! A real business, with employees, and a name, and a presence in my industry. That is the *entire point* of why I left my old job at MaKA. But I guess since the most important thing I'm ever going to achieve in my life is being a *mommy*, I should have just stayed there till I was knocked up, and then quit after my maternity leave, like everybody else."

The mattress vibrates as he drops his arm to his side. "Jesus, Sarina, why do you always have to be so—"

"So *what?*" I fume, daring him.

"So sarcastic! Disparaging! I hate fighting with you to begin with, but you make it ten times worse with these snarky comments."

This isn't the first time he's called me out for this. Noah is an infuriatingly cautious, levelheaded arguer. He spent two years in marriage counseling with his ex-wife, learning how to fight constructively. It didn't stop them from eventually throwing in the towel, but it did make him evangelical about the right way to have an argument in a relationship. Statements like "I feel that you . . ." are acceptable; sarcasm, my mother tongue, is not.

"Okay," I mutter. "I'm sorry. I just can't believe you said that. I have not been working sixty hours a week for the last three years so I could do some 'stuff on the side.' I did not put myself through the hell of the licensing process so I could do some 'stuff on the side.' I do not write a fat fucking check every month for liability insurance so—"

He raises a hand to cut me off mid-lecture. "Okay! Point taken. It was a poor choice of words. I don't want to fight about it anymore. Let's just table the discussion for now . . . we have a while to figure it out." I stare at him, unconvinced, so he smoothes a hand over my arm again. "Please, honey."

I let him pull me back down beside him, and he curls behind me, face in my neck. "We will figure this out," he whispers.

I sigh, and try to let the frustration out with it. I'm sure we'll come up with a solution that makes us both happy; we always have in the past. I just can't believe this could all potentially be happening *so soon.*

—

The storm stalls out over central Texas for the next day and a half, dumping eleven inches of rain as it gradually downgrades from a

Category 1 hurricane to a nameless tropical depression. By the end of the second day, I've actually started hoping that the ever-increasing water level of the lake will threaten to flood, forcing us out of the house and back to Austin. With the exception of the migraine I fake and the protracted "conference call" I take in our bedroom, complaining to Nicole while I hide under the covers to muffle my voice, I haven't had a minute to myself since we got here. I ask Noah if he'd mind heading home early tomorrow, instead of at the end of the day like we'd planned. So we can spend some time with just the two of us.

"But if we go home early tomorrow, it's not going to be just the two of us," he points out. "Isn't Danny having some big barbecue? Your house is going to be full of people."

"Maybe we can go somewhere else, then. Spend the day on a blanket at Barton Springs."

"We can do that here. The weather's finally supposed to clear; we can lie on the dock all day."

With your parents, I think. *Maybe they can interrogate me about the guest list for our still-to-be-proposed wedding.* But I agree to stay. It just feels too petty to push the issue.

When I check my phone before bed, I notice a new voice mail. The missed call log shows Eamon's number.

Hey, just checking to see what time you're coming back tomorrow, says his warm voice. *I think Danny's planning on firing up the grill around two. Hope you're having a good weekend. And try not to feed Drano to the in-laws. You're not going to be an effective architect if you're in jail.*

Noah walks into the room, drying his face with a towel. "What are you smiling at?"

"Nothing," I say reflexively. As soon as I delete the message, I wish I hadn't. I fall asleep wondering exactly how guilty I should feel about that.

10

Though I manage to avoid stumbling into any more of my future in-laws' punji traps, Noah and I don't leave Horseshoe Bay till well after dark, thereby ensuring that Danny's party will be drained to the dregs by the time we arrive back in Austin. The drive home passes in near silence. My nerves are worn raw from the effort of being on my best, parental-appropriate behavior for three never-ending days. Coming home to Danny's smartassery is going to be like sinking sore muscles into a warm bath.

By the time I park the car, Noah is giving off a strong whiff of "We need to talk," but I'm simply not up for it right now. I'm determined that this weekend end on a good note. Somehow.

"I wonder if there's anything left of Danny's party," I say preemptively and bolt out of the car and up the front walk. Noah follows tiredly behind me. Before I even get the door open, a burst of masculine laughter drifts up from the back terrace. They must be sitting around on the chaises after the barbecue, milking the warm summer night for every last drop of weekend. A few beers with Danny and the boys will go a long way to restoring my good humor after a weekend with the Harlows.

To my surprise, it's only Danny and Jay stretched out on the chaises, though the archipelago of empties surrounding them attests to the fact that they had quite a crowd. A faint aroma of kerosene still lingers in the air. I feel a twist of disappointment that Eamon's already left.

"Ree-Ree!" cries Danny when I pull open the sliding door, saluting me with a raised Corona bottle. "You're home! Did you have a good time with the fam?"

"It was wonderful," I lie. "Super-relaxing."

"We were bummed to miss the party," says Noah. "Looks like it was a good one."

"Neighbors only called to complain once this time, though," says Danny.

"*There* you are," comes Eamon's voice from the open doorway behind us. "I'd just about given up on you."

I turn to find him carrying a handful of beers by the necks, the bottles already beaded with condensate. He's wearing a white T-shirt and his gorgeous smile, and I have never been happier to see him.

"Dude, I'd just about given up on those *beers*. Guys, join us for a drink?" says Jay, holding out his hand for the bottle Eamon passes across to him, but Noah shakes his head.

"Thanks, Jay, but we're pretty whipped and just want to head to bed," he says.

I touch his shoulder. "Actually I think I'll stay up with the guys for a drink or two, honey, but you should go on ahead if you're beat."

I can tell that he wants to go but decides against it. "No, that's okay; I'll stay up for a bit."

"Corona?" Eamon offers, and Noah plucks one out of his hands. "I'm Eamon, by the way," he adds, setting down the beers and wiping his hand on his jeans so he can extend it to Noah.

Noah does his best cool-attorney handshake. "Hey! Sarina's

told me all about your project. I'm Noah. Nice to meet you." He doesn't acknowledge that there's anywhere else on earth he might have heard of Eamon from.

"Well come on, pull up a chair," says Jay, and I sink gratefully onto the open chaise next to Eamon. Noah sits down at the foot of it and pulls my legs into his lap.

"So, crappy weekend to be at the lake house, huh?" Eamon says to me and Noah. "Tell me you at least got in a few spins on the Jet Ski before the rain hit."

"Ugh," Noah says. "Those things are obnoxious. My parents are more yacht-type people."

The comment lands in the middle of the conversation with a dull thud. I cringe mentally—Danny likes Noah, but he has an unforgiving memory for the occasional pretentious remark. He will dine out on this one for months. ("Ree-Ree, we're heading over to the Salt Lick for barbecue, but I know you're more of a yacht-type person, so I wasn't sure if you'd want to tag along. . . .")

"Noah's parents are older," I say. "So, noisy fast things aren't really their cup of tea."

Eventually the conversation turns to work; Danny and Jay need to hire a new manager for Albion, and everyone they've seen so far is woefully underqualified.

"That reminds me," Noah tells me, "my mom was mentioning that Caitlyn's looking for a job again."

"Oh no, what happened to her internship at the Met?" I ask. His sister (the "surprise" child) graduated from Hopkins this spring with top honors in art history and had landed one of the extremely prestigious internships at the Metropolitan Museum in New York.

He scrunches his nose. "It ended. It was only a summer internship; the yearlong program they offer is for a financially disadvantaged candidate."

"What a drag," murmurs Eamon. Noah frowns slightly, trying to figure out if he's being sarcastic. Which I'd bet Newman's tailless black bottom he is.

"Yeah. One of those affirmative action things, I guess. There's no way that other intern was more qualified than her."

Eamon clucks his tongue. "Who was it, somebody from some state school or something?"

I do not like where I think this is going. But Noah chomps down hard on the bait. "I doubt that. Caitlyn just worked so damn hard, she deserved that opportunity."

"We're so lucky we didn't have to worry about grades, Dan," yawns Eamon, stretching back in his chaise. "Just show up and swim fast."

"Jackass," snorts Danny, who has told me in the past that Eamon had the highest GPA of anyone on their team, and won the university's student-athlete award two of his four years.

"Seriously," says Noah, "you athletes have it made. Show up, swim fast, get laid."

"Dude, so many chicks," Eamon drawls reminiscently, sinking deeper into the dumb-jock caricature by the second. I am itching to smack him. "Not as many as the football players, though," he muses. "No greater glory than playing for the 'Horns." He nudges Danny with his foot. "Why didn't we play football instead of swimming?"

"Well, aside from the fact that gays and football go together like chocolate and garlic, I have an aversion to getting my head stepped on," Danny says. "And you're too skinny."

Eamon erupts with indignation. "Oh, come on! Brady and Romo and those guys, they're not that big, they're only like two thirty . . ."

"And you're two ten after a Salt Lick bender," says Danny.

Suddenly I spot an opportunity to find out something I have always wanted to know.

"By the way," I say, "since you *are* such a die-hard Longhorn, how come you left? They train postgrad swimmers there, don't they?"

"It was a girl," Danny pronounces.

"No, it was because the coach at the Cal club was a better fit for what I was trying to do with my training at that point," says Eamon.

"But also, there was a girl," Danny says.

"And, yes, the girl I was dating at the time was training at Cal," Eamon concedes.

Envy spikes through me. I know exactly which ex-girlfriend he is talking about—it has to be the girl he started dating a couple months after we slept together. The girl he actually fell for. Hannah Gordon: untouchably dominant in butterfly, I believe, just like him. A perfect match.

"How gallant of you," I say drily, taking refuge in irony although my heart is hammering with remembered hurt. "I hope she appreciated you."

"Most of the time," he says. He takes a long swallow of beer, clearly not wanting to discuss it further.

"Except for when you punched out that racist douchebag Gardner," says Jay.

Eamon wrenches the bottle from his lips. "Jay, you had to bring that up?"

"It was topically relevant," sniffs Jay.

This is one story I've never heard. "What happened?"

Eamon sighs. "He made a comment about her. He didn't know we were together when he said it. He figured it out after I split his lip open," he adds flatly.

"Jesus Christ, Eamon."

"Yeah. That's the only time in my life I've ever hit anybody, but fuck did he deserve it." He shakes his head at the memory.

"But she . . . didn't agree?"

"She prefers to fight her own battles. And she's right."

The admiration in his voice simultaneously impresses me and makes me sad. "So what happened with her?"

"Ree, don't be nosy," Noah admonishes.

"Same thing that always happens, I guess. We weren't right for each other."

I immediately wonder if he still has feelings for her. If that's why he's been single these last few months—because he isn't over her, and is trying to find a way to get her back into his life. The thought of it is like a sliver of glass being driven under my fingernail.

"They're still good friends though," says Danny. "Isn't he just sickeningly well adjusted?"

Eamon slaps his Corona bottle on the concrete deck with a sharp clink. "Guys, I'd really appreciate it if we could stop rehashing my relationship history. Do you think that would be all right with you?"

Danny goes "rreeeeeerr" like an offended cat, but he lets it go. "By the way, though, I've always thought Gardner knew you were dating her," he says after a moment.

Eamon sits upright and plants his elbows on his knees. "Are you serious?"

"He was always a weaselly little punk. It's exactly the sort of thing he would do to try to mess with you. Just to get you off your game for that meet. I bet he thought it was his best shot to take you out. I always thought you should get another tattoo," Danny adds. "Bull's-eye, right here." He taps the hollow between Eamon's shoulder blades.

"You have a tattoo?" asks Noah, half-laughing. I cringe; Noah thinks tattoos are stupid, but it's unusually rude of him to mock a near stranger for it. And just when Eamon had given up baiting him.

Eamon doesn't say a word, just raises his right forearm, fingers curled over his palm, to show the mark.

"Oh. Cool," says Noah, refusing to be impressed. As if it's some lame barbed-wire tattoo.

"By the way, dude, I *was* thinking of getting another one," Eamon says to Danny. "Since I'm back in Austin, what about a big Longhorn right across the top of my chest?"

I groan mentally. Not this again. Danny claps and shouts with laughter. "Yes! The horns can go right under your collarbones."

"Exactly." Eamon smiles at Noah beatifically, folding his thumb over his two middle fingers in the UT salute. "Hook 'em!" He turns to me. "What about you, Ree? What tattoo would you get?"

I'm momentarily distracted by his use of my nickname, which sounds unexpectedly intimate coming from him, and Noah seizes the opportunity to speak. "Sarina would never get a tattoo."

Eamon gives a lazy half smile. "Why don't you let *her* answer?" His tone is mild, but the words are unmistakably protective. Noah's hands tighten ever so slightly where they rest on my calves.

"Noah's right," I say. "I've seen some beautiful ones, but my problem is that I'd want it to be hidden most of the time, and all the parts of me that stay covered are the most vulnerable to gravity and ice cream."

Jay laughs. "She's got a point, Ame. Maybe you should reconsider the size of the Longhorn. You're not going to look like this forever."

Eamon gives a cocky shrug.

During the lull in conversation, Noah yawns and gently removes my legs from his lap. "All right, I think I'm going to pack it in. Babe, you about ready?" He holds his hand out to me.

I catch his hand and press a kiss to it. "I'm going to stay up for a few more minutes. Got some work stuff to talk to Eamon about."

The minute the door closes behind him, I round on Eamon. Right now I don't even care that he's my client; he was way out of line with how he was baiting Noah, and he's mistaken if he thinks I won't call him out on it.

"What the hell is the matter with you? Why were you being such a dick to Noah?"

Danny and Jay immediately begin ostentatiously conversing with each other at top volume.

Not only does Eamon not attempt to feign innocence but he tucks his chin back as though my show of anger is somehow surprising to him. "Because *he* was being a dick," he answers evenly. "And it annoyed me."

My temper surges at his arrogance. "Yeah, he made a couple of tactless remarks, but he wasn't being intentionally malicious. *You* sure as hell were."

"I opened the door, but he strolled right on through. Besides, he had no idea I was messing with him."

I cross my arms over my chest. "No, I don't think he did. But *I* did, and I was sitting there feeling angry and tense and embarrassed while you made fun of him, so the only person you were punishing was me."

His self-satisfied smirk evaporates instantly. "You're right. I didn't think of it that way. I'm sorry."

"I just don't understand why you would do something like that. You respect me, right?"

"You know I do. You don't have to ask me that."

"Okay, so even if you don't like my boyfriend, you ought to at least respect the fact that I care about him."

"You're right. And I apologize," he says seriously. "I got irritated by the sh— by the things he was saying, and I forgot who he was in the scheme of things."

"Yeah. You did." I creak to my feet, all the exhaustion from the last few days settling deep in my limbs like an extra load of gravity. As I wave good night to Danny and Jay, I catch them exchanging a look, but I'm too tired to even hazard a guess as to what it might mean.

—

Noah's BlackBerry alarm shatters our sleep way, way too early the next day. As we stumble out to the car for the drive to the airport, the raw morning is gray and so overheated that my clothes are feeling too heavy before I even reach the car. There isn't much to say on the way there; this last snippet of time together is polluted with the knowledge that it's going to be another three months or so before we see each other. He puts on John's cowboy hat again to make me smile, but we both know it's a fail.

I try not to cry. I know me crying will only make leaving more painful for him. But when I burrow against him outside the check-in area, I crumple.

"Sweetheart," he whispers into my hair, "I'll be home so soon. You know it will go faster than we think it will."

I nod into his shoulder and squeeze him tighter.

"I'll call you when I get home tonight," he says, and kisses me one more time. Then the sliding glass doors shut behind him with a whoosh of air, and he's gone.

11

In my job, there are two kinds of moments that I live for. One, of course, is the satisfaction of walking into a completed project and seeing the tangible landscape of my ideas. It never fails to thrill me the way the flow of the space, the harmony of the shapes and textures, somehow transitions so cohesively from my mind's eye to the physical realm, exactly as I had envisioned.

But long before that point, there's the eureka. That moment near the beginning of the design process when, in the midst of all the searching, testing, not-quite-there ideas, my brain reaches something that I know instantaneously is right. And then, it's like a flame ignites in my chest, and I draw and draw and draw until I have it all sketched out on paper and I can see with my eyes that the idea inside my brain will work as well as I thought it would.

The focal piece of my design for the original Balm spa was the living wall. Right when you step into the lobby of the spa, behind the teak reception desk, stands a twelve-foot-wide column of brilliant green lemon balm plants, stretching all the way from the floor to the double-height ceiling. Inspired by the herbal blends that go into Balm's products and massage oils, the wall offers clients a prelude to the sense-soothing experience they're about to enjoy in the treatment rooms beyond. And in addition to suffusing the lobby with their minty-lemony fragrance, the lushly clumped plants help to purify the air, absorbing carbon dioxide and chemicals and releasing oxygen in exchange. It's the perfect architectural feature for a high-end natural spa . . . if I do say so myself.

Dallas and Houston are getting a living wall in each treatment room. While enjoying a hot stone massage or oxygen facial, clients will breathe in the tangy scent of lemon balm and listen to the lulling sound of the leaves brushing against each other in the air from the nearby HVAC vents. The design will tie the new spas even more closely to the very plants that are the heart of Balm's brand identity (and even the bright color of the logo). As soon as I thought of it, I knew this was the solution for the new spaces— the challenge has been figuring out the implementation.

The living wall in Austin was straightforward—the huge windows provide all the sunlight the plants need, and the water is supplied by one self-contained irrigation system. But in the windowless treatment rooms of the other locations, I have had to figure out a way to provide other sources of light that will keep the plants thriving. I've also been researching ways to maximize sustainability by using the building's gray water—the wastewater from sinks, showers, dishwashers, and so forth—to irrigate the living walls. I now know way, way more than I ever wanted about red and blue light wave absorption and Texas's gray water regulations, but it's worth it.

The presentation is at the end of September, in a little less than two weeks. John, Danny, and Nicole all thought the design was fantastic. Though when I gave him and Nic a dry run of my presentation, Danny pointed out that between the living walls, special lighting, gray water system, and upscale materials I am specifying, it looked like it would be awfully expensive.

"It will be," I told him. "But they want a high-end space. You can't get that look without spending some money."

"True," he said, folding his lower lip between thumb and forefinger, "but it might not be a bad idea to highlight some areas within the design where they could cut costs if they wanted to."

Nicole's orange curls wiggled as she shook her head. "That happens later in the process," she explained. "Ree has to knock their socks off with her ideas, and then once they start getting bids from contractors, they can figure out where to scale back. If they want to at all. But she can't show them something budget right off the bat."

Danny spread his hands. "I'm just telling you what would be going through my head if I were the client. Yes, you want to impress an upscale clientele, but that doesn't mean they have an unlimited budget. Just maybe spend a little time roughing out a lower-cost version."

But there *is* no lower-cost version. This isn't a bar or restaurant, where you can cut corners on materials because the whole place is going to be in the dark most of the time. It has to feel sensual, luxurious. And the living walls are all-or-nothing; the design loses all its power if you water it down to just a couple of really nice planters. Jamie doesn't need me for that.

—

But she does, apparently, need me for nonsense.

She called me yesterday with a frantic last-minute request for my presence at a viewing of a house she is suddenly interested in buying. A viewing that was already scheduled for exactly one hour before I had to be on the road to Palm Springs for Jay and Dominic's wedding. A viewing for a brand-new house that she has already stated she has no interest in renovating. And no, it was out of the question for the Realtor to push the appointment any earlier, or for Jamie to wait until Monday, when I was back; Thursday at 2:30 it must be, or the baby Jesus would weep. And so here I am at 3:52, cross-eyed with impatience, counting down the remaining eight minutes until I have no choice but to firmly inform her that I truly, absolutely, must leave *right now* or I will almost certainly miss my flight.

I haven't even dared to glance at my phone. It's been buzzing like a hornet with texts from Danny; Nicole; her husband, Chris; and Eamon, all of whom are sitting outside right now in Eamon's car, anxious to be on the road. In order to avoid an irritating two-hour layover in Dallas, we're road-tripping the three and a half hours there in the Jeep, then jumping on a direct flight to Palm Springs. Only my confidence in Eamon's ability to lay waste to northbound Interstate 35 has kept me here this late; I hate the thought of skipping out on a client, no matter how necessary it might be.

Finally, at 3:56, Jamie pauses in her detailed inspection of the powder room linen closet, flicks her tan, chicken-bone wrist to show the dial of her watch, and smiles. "By the way, doll, you should giddy on out if you need to—I don't want you to miss your flight."

Dismissed! I practically curtsy, I'm so relieved. I throw an air kiss at her scented cheek and make tracks out of the house. Eamon's silver Jeep is waiting across the street, and when he spots me he leans on the horn.

"Mahler! You said three-thirty; it's almost four! Get your ass in this car!"

The window behind him slides down and Nicole's disembodied head appears. Except for her dimples and her pinup-girl lipstick, she is almost invisible behind her special Palm Springs accessories—a huge, floppy-brimmed hat and seventies-style bug-eye sunglasses. "Ree, we're going to miss our flight!" she yells. "Let's get on the road!"

"I'm so sorry!" I gasp, as I reach the car. "I thought she'd never stop talking." I throw my bag in the back, climb in next to

Nicole, and toss my sandals over my shoulder onto the heap of luggage.

Danny cranes around from shotgun to give me a kiss. "All right, are we ready to go?"

"Yes! Onward!" I scuff my bare feet happily on the upholstery of the floor.

Eamon fires up the car, cranks the Al Green, and guns it for the highway. Nicole and Danny both start rattling at me at once. We are giddy with excitement at peeling out of the city on a Thursday afternoon road trip, headed for fun. I haven't been so excited for a long drive since my seventh-grade overnight field trip to Washington, D.C.; I spent the whole six-hour bus ride covertly staring at the boy I had a crush on, hoping the conversation in the back of the bus would lead to a game of spin the bottle. Come to think of it, I realize as I sneak a glance at Eamon in the driver's seat, this isn't all that different.

He apologized again, the last time I saw him, for the way he behaved a couple weeks ago when Noah visited. By then, I was just anxious to forget it; I'd rather forget that entire weekend. I miss Noah now, badly. But I also realized, in the first few days after he left, that the sense of calm I suddenly felt was just the absence of the stress that had bunched in my shoulders over the course of his visit. I haven't been able to shake a lingering sense of disappointment in the way he handled that conversation with his parents—or, I guess really, the way he failed to handle it. I've been pissed at Noah before; until now, I've never felt like he let me down. But with that, he did.

———

Once we're roaring along the interstate, Chris reaches into the bag at his feet and hands around beers. It feels deliciously naughty to be drinking here, and as it grows darker outside, it's like we are cocooned inside the car, growing tipsier and looser as the hours pass. We've rehashed every ridiculous story from our overlapping high schools and colleges, and I've been laughing till my stomach hurts.

"Okay, boys and girls," Danny announces finally. "Time for a round of I Never!"

We all groan in unison. I remember when I first started college, everybody was obsessed with those purity tests that, in a mere five hundred questions, would quantify your level of sexual experience and, by association, sophistication. My score dropped from ninety to about seventy after my freshman year, then worked its way down a few more ticks during the first couple years after college, but after I started dating Noah it just flatlined. I think for most people, once you reach a certain threshold, you're unlikely ever to go crashing beyond it. My threshold does not generally win me a lot of bragging rights in contests such as these.

"Oh, you love it," Danny insists. "Come on, I'll start with an easy one. I've never had sex."

Eyes rolling, we all take swigs of our beers.

"Eamon needs a drink," yells Nicole, who forgot months ago that she hated him and is now giving Danny a run for his money in the fan club department. She dives into Chris's bag in search of something nonalcoholic, but he's only brought beer.

"I've got water in my backpack, if you can reach it," Eamon says, so she clamors ass-in-the-air over the seat, retrieves a bottle of water, and hands it forward. Eamon uncaps it and takes an enthusiastic glug. It occurs to me that participating in a game of I Never with a client—who holds a small but historic place on my own personal sex roster—is on the short list of the world's worst ideas. I can most definitely live without ever hearing the highlights of Eamon's sexual history, or filling him in on mine.

"Okay, clockwise—Ree, you're next!" says Danny.

And there goes my chance to avoid this whole disaster. If I demur now, Nicole and Danny will yell at me for being a wet blanket, even though they both know perfectly well how legitimate my reasons for not wanting to participate are. So, at the dignified age of thirty-one, I cave to peer pressure. "Ummmm, I never slept with somebody of my own gender. Or the opposite gender in your case, Danny."

He shakes his head emphatically. "Gold star gay and proud of it!"

"My turn!" says Chris. "I never had sex outside." Everybody drinks to this one, including Eamon. I note with guilty fascination that he also drinks to sex in a moving vehicle, sex in a restaurant bathroom, and sex in a locker room, but *not* sex in a pool.

"No way, man," he laughs when questioned on it by Danny. "You do not do that in a pool that somebody else has to swim in."

"Speak for yourself," mutters Danny, tipping back his beer bottle yet again.

Then it's Eamon's turn. He takes a swig from his water bottle and levels a pointed stare at Danny. "I never had sex on the Plate Tectonics couch."

"The what?" I ask, over Danny's shout of laughter.

"We had this couch in our suite in college," Eamon explains, his smile lingering around his words. "I don't even know where the hell it came from—"

"It was already there by the time I got there," interjects Danny, shaking his head.

"It was this gnarly old gray sectional that all of our friends had to sleep on when they came to visit—and also, that *I* had to sleep on every time you sexiled me—"

Danny studies the ceiling of the car in feigned innocence.

"The bitch of it was, the sections were tiny. And there was no way of securing them together. So you'd go to sleep and then wake up two hours later to find that the pieces had slid apart and your ass was hanging halfway down the middle of the couch. You'd push it back together again, and then an hour later it would be your elbow. God, that thing was awful."

"So how did you manage to have sex on it, then?" asks Nicole.

"Athleticism and sheer mental fortitude," Eamon responds.

—

By the time we arrive at the Ace Hotel in Palm Springs, which is home base for the wedding weekend, I've learned far more about all of them than I ever expected to—or ever needed to, for that matter. Yawning, we check in and shuffle off to our rooms: Eamon is next door to Danny and me, and on the ground floor below us are Nic and Chris. While I inspect the room, Danny flings himself on one of the beds and spreads his long limbs like a starfish. I make a beeline for the striped flannel robes hanging on the wall and toss one on while I get ready for bed.

"It must be good to get to see so much of Eamon again," I venture, my back to Danny.

"Yeah. I haven't seen him this relaxed since college. He got the crap kicked out of him for six years up there in San Fran."

"How so?"

"His coach, Howard, is a psychopath. Total Doc Brown type," Danny explains. "He operates by mind games and mental torture. 'Well, if I thought you could do x, I'd tell you to do y, but I know you can't do it,' and so forth. Reverse psychology. Inventing sadistic drills no one's ever heard of before. Always pushing his athletes harder and harder and harder." He joins me by the sink and continues. "So Ame rolls up there when he finishes school, and Howard's like, 'Everything you've done till now is wrong, it's a miracle you've done as well as you have, and if you want a prayer of doing anything significant in this sport from now on you have to do exactly what I tell you and only that.' "

He sounds awful. "Jesus."

"Yeah but it *worked*," Danny reminds me, leaning close to the mirror to remove his contact lenses.

"That surprises me," I muse. "Eamon doesn't exactly strike me as the most tractable human being."

Danny snorts. "No, but he wanted to succeed more than anything, and he knew everything Howard demanded was for a reason. There were a couple guys on Howard's team who might have been as talented as Ame, but nobody else had the mental strength to get up from each challenge just looking for the next one. And nobody else could have come back from those injuries."

I concentrate on squeezing toothpaste onto the brush in a perfect parallel line. "What was the list again?"

"Concussion, cracked ribs, collapsed lung, broken arm," Danny recites as he rubs soap onto a washcloth and begins scrubbing his face. "Dislocated hip, compound fracture of his femur, torn ligament in his knee. Basically the entire right side of his body got crushed." He lowers the washcloth. "Oh, and one of his broken ribs knocked a hole in one of his arteries and almost killed him."

I'm frozen, toothbrush halfway to my mouth. "Oh my god."

"Yeah," says Danny. "It was really, really nasty."

"I can't imagine," I whisper.

"Nobody could. Anybody else would have taken that as a cue for an early retirement; meanwhile Eamon's like, 'So anyway, about the Olympics?' "

I'm still mulling over Danny's words as I climb into bed a few minutes later. I'd never realized exactly how hard Eamon had worked to achieve what he did; I can't imagine being incessantly pushed to the point of exhaustion over a period of years and coming out of it triumphant. He must have a will like granite. And yet most of the time it's concealed beneath that quick humor and that radiant, easygoing charm. I grin in the dark, remembering the Plate Tectonics story. Athleticism and mental fortitude, indeed.

12

Relentlessly bright sunlight bores through my eyelids before seven the next morning, so that getting any more sleep looks as likely as spontaneously sprouting a new cup size.

"Hey, Danny, I'm going to get some breakfast and wander around a little," I say softly. "Wanna come?"

He jerks upright in his bed, fixes me with a disgusted look, and peels off the T-shirt he'd slept in. With an operatic sigh, he collapses back onto the mattress, bunching the T-shirt over his face. Only his pointy white chin remains exposed to the sunlight.

I should have known it was a doomed effort; mornings and alcohol throw Danny's complex electrolyte balance firmly onto the queen setting. "All right, princess," I say, and step onto the covered outdoor walkway that connects the hotel's rooms. From our second-floor location, I have an excellent view of the grounds: the low-slung beige stucco buildings punctuated with bright orange doors, the beautiful native plantings, glowing lime and chartreuse in the bright desert sunlight. Just beyond the buildings rears a cluster of mountains, their treeless, gravelly surfaces marbled with crisp blue shadows. The total absence of humidity in the air renders every edge and contour unusually sharp.

Noah would love it here. I text a few photos to him, and then before I even put my phone away, he calls me.

"Hi, honey!" I say, voice bright with pleasure. "I'm so glad you called."

"Yeah, it's a slow morning, so I figured I'd grab you while I could. The hotel looks amazing. I'm so bummed to miss this."

"Me too," I say, even though the secret, and terrible, truth is that I'm not. Noah and Nicole have been a mutual admiration society since day one, but he never quite relaxes around Danny and Jay and Dom, especially when they dial themselves up to eleven at big parties like this. I think they make him feel stuffy. Which makes *me* feel like I have to throttle back on my usual rambunctiousness, out of solidarity. So, I am guiltily glad that this weekend I will be at liberty to party like a lunatic.

I skim my hand along the metal railing of the walkway. "Maybe we can come back sometime when it's just the two of us."

"It's a plan," he says. "Speaking of that, I've been thinking. I think it was a bad call for us to spend that whole weekend with my parents. Bad call by me, I mean. We should have spent more time by ourselves."

"Ah, hon, you know I love your parents."

"I do know. And they love you. I just feel bad about the way they ambushed you. About grandkids. Ever since his hip replacement, my dad's really been feeling his age, and . . ."

And he thought his sense of mortality made it appropriate to discuss the future of my reproductive system, I think, but I don't want to start a fight. Not when Noah's trying to apologize. "No, I get it."

"It's actually *because* they love you that they care," he says wryly. "They would not be encouraging me to procreate with somebody they didn't want in their family, believe me."

I laugh. "Thanks . . . I think?"

"But I talked to them and asked them to cool it on that particular topic. And they will. Mom said to tell you, she thought maybe she'd drive down to visit sometime soon, and you guys could do a little wedding dress shopping. Make a girls' day out of it. Manicures, high tea, the whole nine. What do you think?"

"Wow," I say, surprised at how much the idea appeals to me. "That sounds *lovely*. I think the last time I had a manicure, the Jonas Brothers were still together. I've got no idea what kind of dress I want, though."

"Come on, I thought you girls lived for that stuff! Princess for a day and everything?"

I have an appalling vision of myself stuffed into a cotton candy explosion of white tulle, bangs crushed under a pageant queen tiara. "No . . . no princess fantasies here. But I'd love to spend some time with your mom."

"Great, sweetie, I'll tell her. And listen, about the other stuff . . . we'll figure it out. I trust us." There's another trick from his marriage counseling days—referring obliquely to our argument instead of using a specific phrase that might inflame a calm conversation.

"I trust us too," I promise. And it's the truth. But somehow, I still feel a little unsettled. I've been thinking about it a lot in the two weeks since his visit, and I haven't yet uncovered any viable ways for us to compromise. The issue is intractably black and white: working just a few hours a week would be pointless with my career, so either I'll work—or I won't. And somebody's going to be unhappy about it.

Nicole's response, when I told her about the argument, was shock that Noah and I had never discussed the issue before. But having established early on that we both wanted a family, we'd never yet bothered to discuss the nitty-gritty of how it would work. I guess we'd both been guilty of assumptions. Mine being that anybody who knows me well would expect me to want to keep working while I raise my children.

And John, of course, took it from a more personal angle. "You tell Mr. Harlow that Leigh Mahler was the finest mother I have ever seen," he bellowed into the phone. "And if he thinks he's going to marry her daughter, then he better be right damn grateful for that!"

I did not, in fact, relay John's message to Noah, but I still quite firmly agree with it. Maybe we didn't spend as much time together as I would have liked to when I was little, but I have plenty of memories like Noah was talking about. And none of my hours building Lego castles and pillow forts with my babysitters ever gave me the impression I was anything less than the center of my mother's world.

I just need Noah here, to talk through it with me. After eight months apart, I feel more disconnected from him than I ever expected to. More than anything, I want to have this separation behind us.

—

The day passes quickly, on a stream of greetings and last-minute tasks to help Jay and Dominic get ready for the welcome dinner for all the guests arriving from out of town. At the end of the night, those of us in the younger contingent find ourselves clustered around the outdoor fireplace on the hotel's terrace, making s'mores and gradually emptying bottles of wine. I look around affectionately at the circle of firelit faces and burrow back into my chaise lounge. A dreamy lassitude overtakes me, born of the delicious food, the wine, the firelight, and the company of my friends. I tip my head back to study the stars, brilliant against the darkness above the firelight. I've been living in a big, dusty city for so long that I'd almost forgotten what they look like.

After a while, Eamon's form, silhouetted against the orange glow of the fire, looms into my field of view. "Hey," he says. "It's chilly out here, you must be cold." He shucks his soft leather jacket and tucks it around me. "How's that?"

I hadn't noticed until he asked, but I *have* been getting chilly in my light summer dress. The jacket is still warm from his body. "Better. Except I can't move my arms." I wiggle my crossed arms underneath the jacket to demonstrate.

He plants his hands on his hips. "All right, if you're going to be difficult, get up."

"What?" I squeak.

"Get up!"

"Why?"

He plucks off the jacket, grabs me by the wrists, and hoists me upward, ignoring my shriek of protest. Setting me gently out of the way, he lies down on the chaise himself and beckons to me to lie down on top of him.

I hesitate until I see the expression on his face, which is a bald I-dare-you, so I lift my chin and sit carefully down between his legs. He holds the jacket up backward for me to slide my arms into, then settles me back against his chest, arms around my waist.

"Better?" he rumbles into my ear.

"Much better." He's as warm and solid as concrete in the sun. The only thing making me uncomfortable now is my awareness of him. I struggle to remind myself that he's just a friend, a client in fact, and that this shouldn't feel any different from the countless times I've snuggled companionably with Danny; but it isn't Danny's chest I'm resting against, or Danny's scent that's mingling deliciously with the scent of woodsmoke in my nostrils.

"I don't know when the last time was that I saw so many stars," he says after a moment. "I'd practically forgotten they were there."

"I was just thinking that," I say. "I haven't seen stars like this since the last time I was home."

"Remind me what part of Virginia?"

"A little town called Floyd, not too far from Blacksburg."

"I admire your confidence that I actually know where Blacksburg is."

I laugh. "Come on, didn't you know anyone who went to Virginia Tech? It's all the way down the Blue Ridge, in the mountains."

"In the sticks," he corrects me, ignoring the elbow I dig into his ribs.

"It's beautiful, though," I say.

"You miss it?"

It's the kind of question that I can answer simply, and move the conversation back to shallower water. But for some reason, I don't. With Eamon, I always wanted to give the true answer instead of just the easy one. "Yeah. Home is . . . hard for me. Virginia reminds me a lot of my mom. Mostly I try to avoid spending time there."

"I'm so sorry, Ree," he says softly. "Does John still live there?"

"Yeah. In the same house. Which is part of why it's so hard to be there. Honestly I don't know how he could stand it, after she died. If it were me I would have sold the place, along with all her stuff, but I guess it made him feel closer to her. I just wish that he'd been able to move on."

"It sounds like he didn't want to."

"No. He didn't." I roll the soft leather of one jacket sleeve between my thumb and forefinger. "I remember when I told Nicole that she had died, she said, 'May her memory be a blessing.' And I know what it means, but I don't know if her memory ever has been a blessing to either one of us. For me, it just hurts. And for John, it's like . . . it's like he's trapped. Too *much* memory."

"She must have been amazing," Eamon says, and suddenly I feel like I have a cactus in my throat. "What was she like?"

I swallow hard. "She was a goofball. Loved to laugh. She was always this happy free spirit, even when she was sick. She looked a bit like Stevie Nicks, and she was obsessed with her. Obsessed. Apparently she was all set to name me Rhiannon, but her friends talked her out of it."

"Count your blessings," he says. "Wish *my* parents hadn't been so hung up on wacky Gaelic names. The other two got normal ones, but damn, did I draw the short straw. That *E* just annihilates people."

"How *are* your brothers?"

"Kieran is still the dutiful oldest son; he's married with two insanely cute little girls. They live half an hour from my parents. And Colin's in New York, teaching Islamic art at NYU and dating psychotic women."

"That's an intense hobby."

"You have no idea. If you put Colin into a room full of women he knew nothing about, I guarantee you he would walk right up to the nuttiest one of all. He can sniff them out . . . he's like a goddamn truffle pig. 'Hello there,'" he drawls over my laughter, "'I sense that you have jealousy issues and severe problems with boundaries. I'm Colin Roy, and I'd like to take you to dinner.'"

"Poor guy," I giggle.

"He does it to himself! He doesn't know a warning sign when it hits him in the face. His last girlfriend was so paranoid that she accused him of cheating on her with one of his undergrads. And when he denied it—because he wasn't *doing* it—she stole the passwords to his Gmail and his university account so she could see for herself."

Eamon's outrage on his brother's behalf is endearing. "It sounds like you're closest to Colin."

"Yeah. Especially the last couple of years," he adds. "He was driving the night of the crash, and I know he blames himself, even though it wasn't his fault. I think he thinks if he'd seen the other driver sooner, he could have gotten out of the way."

"Wasn't it a drunk driver?"

He shifts position on the chaise seat. "Kid texting on his phone. Literally sailed right through a red light, into us. And happened to be driving a Suburban."

"Jesus," I breathe. I hesitate for a moment, then continue. "It really was unbelievable, what you did. I mean, that kind of rehabilitation would be grueling for anyone, but for an athlete, it must have been absolute hell."

"It was," he says quietly. "The pain I could deal with, but not being able to swim, it was like . . . not being able to breathe. I'd never had a problem with injuries before, so I had nothing to prepare me for it. I'd lie in bed, imagining I was racing the hundred fly, counting out the strokes, and when I got to the turn, I would *kick*—kick like I was pushing off, you know, and the pain would just stab—but I couldn't stop doing it. I would mentally run through all of my events, start, turn, and finish, over and over and over until I was exhausted. I was so scared that my body would forget what to do."

Somehow I'm certain that very few other people know about that. I drop my hands to his forearms and squeeze gently.

As silence stretches out between us, I can feel the pace of his heartbeat accelerate against my back. "I dream about it occasionally. The crash. I'm in the car, talking to Col, and I look out the window and see it, and I put my foot down, like there's a gas pedal I can step on, but the car doesn't move, and I know I'm trapped. I watch it come toward me, and then, right before it hits, I wake up. Which isn't even how it happened," he adds. "We were moving, not stopped. And I never saw it come toward us, I just looked up and saw this black grille with the Chevy logo and then—" He smacks his fist into his palm, makes a soft explosive noise.

I shudder.

"The worst part is," he continues, voice lighter, "I got to ride in a helicopter and I wasn't even conscious for it."

"That sucks! I know, I'm dying to ride in a helicopter too. But you, though, I'm sure you could find a way. Just go on some reality show—"

"*Amazing Race of the Washed-Up Pro Athletes?*"

"Exactly, or *The Bachelor*. They're constantly going on helicopter rides on *The Bachelor*."

"Yeah, but then I'd have a bunch of nervous-gigglers shoving their boobs in my face."

"Oh, come on, that doesn't sound so bad!"

"No, thank you. I've had enough"—he seems to be searching for something to say that won't offend my nonexistent delicate sensibilities—"just . . . enough. Of that. I like *Amazing Race* better."

"You're probably right," I concede. "They can determine your starting rankings based on how much weight everyone has gained since retiring. You must be up to two thirty by now!"

"You're obnoxious," he mutters, but his voice is laced with humor. We talk for a long time, then eventually lapse into silence again. At some point I must doze off, because when he whispers my name, I open my eyes to discover the stars have faded, and the silhouette of the mountains is just visible against a cobalt sky.

"Oh shit, I fell asleep!" I say, struggling to extricate myself from him.

He drops a hand on my forearm. "It's okay, I did too. But we should probably go in now, huh?" His hair is mussed adorably, his eyes drowsy and soft. The effect on me is totally unlike the sisterly amusement with which I regard Danny when he's groggy and fuzzy in the morning.

"Yeah. I need to get some real sleep or I'll be useless tomorrow." I teeter reluctantly to my feet, stiff from the awkward confines of the chaise. "At least we're not the only ones," I add, nodding across the ring of chairs to where a few scattered, shapeless bodies are sleeping off the effects of too much celebration.

We shuffle upstairs together and draw to a stop outside the paired doors to our rooms, where I hand him back his jacket. He is so close I can smell the lingering scent of woodsmoke, and the sweet tang of wine on his breath.

"Well . . . g'night," he says after a moment, a small, inscrutable smile curling his lips.

"Night, Eamon," I whisper.

13

Amber late-afternoon sunlight slants low over the arid mountains as we take our seats to watch Jay and Dominic get married. Since Noah has indicated that a proposal is looming on the horizon, I try to pay extra attention to the details of the wedding—the setup, the décor—but it's all foreign to me. The guys' retro sixties Rat Pack vibe is fun, but I haven't the faintest idea what I'd want, let alone what Noah would. My second X chromosome must be missing a couple of lines of HTML.

At the ceremony, there are no attendants, no unity candles, no pontificating from the officiant about the meaning of marriage. Everybody here knows that there couldn't be a purer example of commitment and family than the two people standing at the front of the lawn, their faces washed with love and sunset light. As Jay and Dominic recite their vows, hand in hand, Dominic says something under his breath that makes Jay duck his head with laughter. I wonder what it was; if it was something the rest of us would even understand, or if it was just some inside joke between the two of them that will one day get referenced on an anniversary card. As I watch them, I imagine what it will be like to share that moment with Noah. Pledging to love and support each other for the rest of our lives. I am almost, almost ready to do that.

Just not yet. Not . . . *quite* yet.

—

By the time we spill into the reception space, music is already pouring through the room, bouncing off the glass walls and polished concrete floor. I fidget in my seat throughout dinner, impatient for the dancing. There's a handful of rude, hilarious toasts, a touching one from Dominic's elderly father, then the cake; and then finally Jay, flushed and laughing, sticks his hands in the air. "All right, people," he announces, around cheeks still stuffed with red velvet cake, "time to get this party started."

With an elated shout, Nicole and I bolt from the table like racehorses out of the gate. Giggling, we clasp hands and rush the dance floor, just as the opening beats of Bell Biv DeVoe's "Poison" flash across the room. We're surrounded almost instantly by laughing guests, all of us bumping and bouncing in a heedless crush. After a few minutes, I catch Eamon's eye from across the room—he's been captured by a middle-aged cousin of Dominic's and is good-naturedly letting her use him as a stripper pole. I wink at him and receive an imploring look in return. I shake my head, grinning, to let him know he's on his own, and head off to the bar to get a refill on my wine.

Two hours later, I have a wine stain on my dress, a missing earring, and stubbed toes from three separate dance floor collisions. My attempt at a chignon disintegrated almost immediately, and my bangs are straggling across my forehead. The crowd has gradually thinned out, leaving only my group of friends and a few other die-hards.

I watch Eamon dancing with Jay's glamorous sister, Penelope, and as he laughs appreciatively at something she says, lowering his dark head to hear her better, I feel a stab of irritation. She smiles up at him adoringly, and the irritation blooms into annoyance. The alcohol must be making me cranky; it could not possibly be less of my business who Eamon Roy flirts with. Or takes back to his hotel room. But all of a sudden, it's like somebody has pulled an invisible plug, and my enjoyment of the evening disappears down the drain with a sad little slurp.

"I think it might be time to pack it in," I shout to Nicole, who nods, yawning, and reaches behind her for Chris's hand. Together we find Jay and Dominic to wish them good night. As we make our way across the patio to our rooms, late-night revelers, including more than a few wedding guests, are splashing in the glowing pool, their laughter echoing around the courtyard.

When I reach the door to my room, my memory flicks back to the dark, quiet early morning, standing here with Eamon. Not tonight, though; he was still with Jay's sister when I left the reception. I don't think he even noticed me go. I let myself into the room and toss my handbag on my bed. Somehow, the slam of the door behind me is very satisfying indeed.

—

On the way home, everyone is too tired for I Never (even if there were anything left to share); Nicole, Chris, and Danny all pass out in the backseat as soon as we get settled in the Jeep for the final leg of the journey. Eamon and I talk softly while he drives. As the last miles to Austin wind down, end-of-weekend gloom settles heavily over me. I find myself, for the first time in my life, wishing for traffic, a flat tire, a final stop for gas; anything to postpone the comedown of arriving home. Anything, if I'm being honest with myself, to postpone having to say good night to Eamon.

He drops Nicole and Chris off first, even though they live closer to his neighborhood than Danny and I do.

"I don't want the weekend to be over," he says as we coast quietly over the dark, empty streets.

"Me neither," I agree. I wonder if he is talking about anything more than just the weekend itself. I know I am.

"You know," he says, and I can hear the tiny pause before he continues, "I'm really sorry I never called you."

I don't even pretend not to know what he is talking about. I can't believe he is bringing this up now, within earshot of Danny, who may or may not be completely asleep—but nothing in the world could make me tell him that we should probably talk about it later. Or that we really don't need to talk about it at all.

Instead I swallow, and ask him why he's apologizing.

He flicks his eyes to me, then back to the road. "It was a shitty thing to do, just disappearing like that. I should have let you know what was going on."

I feel myself tense with curiosity and dread at the same time, but I make myself sound nonchalant. As if I hadn't agonized over this very thing for literally months after it happened. "Why? What *was* going on?"

"I was seeing somebody. Not exclusively—I mean, I didn't cheat on her with you. Although I'm sure she wouldn't have been happy to hear about you. But it was getting more serious. And then I met you, and I really liked you, and it freaked me out 'cause suddenly I wasn't sure I wanted what I thought I wanted. Which was not a comfortable feeling for me at all. I guess when I was twenty-one I couldn't articulate any of that, so I just vanished."

I'm quiet for a while as I absorb this. Oddly, it makes a twisted sort of sense, and I feel the last stubborn knot of hurt over his rejection unravel inside me. "It's okay," I say. "If I were held accountable for everything I did in my dating life before I was about twenty-seven, I'd be in serious trouble."

He laughs. "Yeah. But still. I'm not suggesting that you actually cared what I did at the time, because you shouldn't have. I've just been thinking about it, and I wanted to tell you."

"Well . . . thanks." We share a shy smile. I don't correct his assertion that I didn't care about his blow-off; I wonder if he wants me to. But there's something else I want to know. "Out of curiosity, what was it that you wanted, or thought you wanted?"

"My ex, Hannah," he says, and I remember the bitter jealousy I felt when I first figured out who she was. An image flashes into my brain: her powerful arms, halfway through a stroke, arcing over the water with astonishing grace and speed. No wonder he wanted her.

"Right," I say. "The girl you moved to California for."

He shoots me a sideways look. "The girl who was *part* of the reason why I moved to California," he corrects pointedly, but he's smiling.

"Yeah, that one," I tease.

"I probably would have gone anyway," he continues. "Junior year of college I finished just off qualifying time in all of my events at Olympic trials, and I was . . . not interested in doing that again. I knew I needed a new coach, and it was maybe sixty/forty between Cal and SwimMAC in Charlotte."

"But she tipped the balance."

"Yeah, she did. Except for that one day," he adds softly.

Which one day? *Our* day? "Which day?" I ask. Pretending to be only mildly curious.

"*That* day," he confirms. "After you fell asleep, I lay there with my mind racing, trying to figure out what the hell to do. I liked Hannah, which is what I was supposed to do, but suddenly I liked you. A lot. And I wanted to move to Cal . . . but sometime between eight and nine in the morning I actually thought, *What if I stayed here?* And then I panicked. I was so freaked out that I had even thought about deviating from my plan that I literally just bolted. And then I didn't know how to explain to you why I bolted . . . so I just didn't say anything at all."

"I wish you had," I say. This much I can admit to him. "I did wonder what the hell had happened."

He shakes his head. "I know. I still can't believe I did that. But, in my twisted mind, I was doing the right thing. I wanted to see you again so badly, but I had this stupid heroic thing where I didn't want to lead you on if I wasn't going to be staying in Austin. And I was scared that if I kept seeing you, I'd start wanting to stay, and I knew it wasn't right for my career. So, I just avoided the whole problem. By avoiding you."

I can't help but laugh at the irony. All those months I spent agonizing over what I did wrong, when apparently the only problem was that I was too appealing.

"Well, it worked out right for you," I say, without bitterness. "On both fronts."

"Cal was the right choice," he says. "There's no way I could have gone as far as I did without Howard. And Hannah . . . I guess that relationship was what both of us needed at the time. Things kind of fell apart after I got hurt, though. We were together for so long that everyone figured we were going to get married, including us . . . except when the shit hit the fan, we realized we weren't actually very good for each other." He glances at me before continuing. "I think sometimes you get so used to being with someone that it's just a habit, not something that really makes you happy."

"Yeah." I stare out my window at the passing houses, wondering what the people inside with lights on are doing. Putting the kids to bed, watching *Daily Show* reruns, making love. Quiet, Sunday-night things. All of a sudden, I am aching with loneliness.

I ought to call Noah as soon as I get home, but instead I dawdle. I play with Newman. I unpack my clothes. I sort week-old clean laundry, carefully pairing my socks and folding my underwear in an uncharacteristic flirtation with organization. But I can't stop replaying the conversation with Eamon in my head.

I don't know how to feel about what he told me. On the one hand, it's good to know, finally, that I hadn't imagined how he'd felt about me. It's better than good.

But on the other hand, it doesn't change anything. He still left Austin, still chose Hannah, still made all the decisions that made sense instead of the ones that didn't. And I still fell in love with Noah. What-ifs are pointless; we're here now. He is my client, and my friend, and that's all he'll ever be. No matter how much I like the sound of his voice on a dark, sleepy car ride, late at night.

—

Throughout the next morning, we all take turns emailing our photos from the wedding weekend. There are some gorgeous ones of Dominic and Jay, capturing the joy and hilarity and romance of their weekend, and of course lots of shots of beautiful Nicole. And there's one that twists my gut like a pretzel: Eamon at our table at the reception, eyes closed, rippling with laughter, and me next to him, face buried in his shoulder as I convulse with mirth. His hand is curved affectionately around the back of my head. If Noah ever saw this photo, he would have a couple very legitimate questions to ask me. And yet, I can't delete it. I just leave it sitting in my inbox, dangerous as a grenade with a shaky pin.

Nicole calls me later that afternoon, as I am working on sketches for the built-in cabinetry in Eamon's office. I have started doing all of the drawings for his millwork by hand, instead of on the computer, after he told me he thought my hand-drafted work was beautiful.

"So, Miss Sarina, what was that all about?"

"What was what all about?" I ask, biting my pencil as I study the drawing. The proportions of the bays of shelving don't feel quite right.

"You. You didn't take your eyes off Eamon Roy all weekend."

I feel a flash of irritation, even though—or, probably, because—the frequency with which he appeared in my photos from the weekend attests to the fact that she's right. "Well, there are worse things to look at, aren't there?"

"There are," she agrees. "Did you see the implants on that aunt of Dominic's?"

"Oh my god," I laugh. "Talk about nondairy creamer!"

"Now the other interesting thing I noticed, as I was noticing things," she says, "is that Eamon couldn't seem to keep his eyes off *you*."

"False, Nicole. He spent the whole reception dancing with Jay's sister."

"He's a flirt. But to my knowledge—and I do in fact have this knowledge—he didn't hook up with her. And the only person he snuggled with on a chaise lounge for hours was you."

"We're friends. It wasn't sexy snuggling."

"He *also* did not hook up," she continues relentlessly, "with that random blond cousin who practically had to be strapped down to keep her from attacking him."

"Well that's no surprise . . . women probably throw themselves at him all the time. If he slept with every one who was halfway attractive he'd be worn to a nub by now."

"Fine. But my *point* is, he could have slept with any of several different women this weekend, and he didn't. I don't know any single guys who would pass up a perfectly good opportunity to get laid unless they had their eye on someone else," she announces.

"Oh Jesus, Nicole. Maybe he only dates models."

"That cousin was *hot*."

"I don't know, maybe he's not into banging strangers?" I suggest with an exasperated sigh. "Why don't you just *ask* him why he didn't sleep with anybody?"

"I don't need to ask him, because I can tell," she says smugly. "He has a thing for you."

"He does not. That's ridiculous. Where the hell is this coming from, by the way? Chris sent me that photo he took of us at the reception, with some incomprehensible message about 'rocking my boat.' Why have you two suddenly decided there is something illicit going on with Eamon and me? Is this what married people do when there's no good TV?"

"So you would have no problem showing that photo to Noah. You wouldn't feel weird about it at all."

Goddamnit. She's got me, and she knows it. "Okay, yes, I would feel a little weird about Noah seeing that picture," I admit. "Especially given that Noah didn't like him when they met. Listen, I like Eamon very much, and yes, I find him attractive. You'd have to be in a coma not to. But nobody has a thing for anybody."

"Does Noah know that you two slept together?"

"Back when dinosaurs roamed the earth? No, he does not. There was no reason to tell him, because it is a nonissue."

The long silence at the other end of the phone betokens profound skepticism.

"What do you want me to say, Nicole?" I demand.

"Nothing. Clearly I shouldn't have said anything, 'cause now you're pissed at me. I just thought I picked up on something between you guys. I know things haven't been great with Noah lately, and obviously there's always been a connection between you and Ame, so . . ."

"So nothing. Okay, Nic? Nothing to see here. Move along."

We chat for a moment more, then get off the phone. I'm relieved to have successfully distracted her from the issue of Eamon, though I know if I give her the slightest opening at any point in the future, she will be on it like a terrier digging for a buried bone.

Because despite what I said to her, Nicole is not the kind of person who enjoys inventing drama out of thin air—the far more horrifying truth is that she is uncannily perceptive. Nagging me about marrying Noah has been her pet project for years; the fact that she has abruptly veered off course in favor of nagging me about Eamon worries me.

So what exactly is it that's going on with me? I slap my pencil down on my desk, knowing I won't be able to concentrate on my work until I've cleared out my head. I change into running clothes, crank up my workout mix until the music is mainlining into my brain, and slam the front door behind me. The scorch of the sunlight on my air-conditioned skin fuels my skittery mood.

So I have a crush on him. That much is blindingly obvious. I think about him constantly. As I move through my days, I've been catching myself making little mental notes of things to tell him later, jokes or stories he would appreciate. I've been listening to Phoenix incessantly for weeks, because he loves Phoenix. It's stupid, and girlish, and more than a little embarrassing, but there it is. I have a big old crush on my friend and client. I shake my head in disgust. I ought to be able to keep myself from mindlessly responding to him; I mean, how old am I, sixteen?

Now, to address Nicole's second charge, that he is interested in me—she's wrong, that much I'm sure of. I've known men like this before, who indiscriminately charm anyone and everyone who crosses their path—male, female, gay, or straight. I mean, even my freaking *cat* is in love with him. His attention doesn't mean anything more than that he likes me as a human. He calls me by my last name like one of his locker room buddies, for god's sake. It just happens to be my misfortune that I'm a sucker for his smile and his smartassed sense of humor.

But how the hell am I going to get through the next six months without embarrassing myself? I hate the thought of morphing into a simpering teenager every time I see him or speak to him, not to mention the toll it will take on my peace of mind. Growling, I turn onto an uphill road and sprint up it until I am gasping. When the wave of endorphins hits me, calm settles over me and I know what to do: I'm just going to ride it out. The novelty is bound to wear off sometime. In the meantime, I'm going to behave like the adult I am, and enjoy his companionship without getting all Taylor Swift about it. I refuse to be at the mercy of my own dopamine.

14

Propelled by a queasy gumbo of nerves, manners, and sheer paranoia, I arrive for the Balm presentation almost forty-five minutes
early. Which, unfortunately, leaves me with almost forty-five minutes to study the crisply pressed receptionist for the venture capital firm providing part of the financing. I had ranked it a major
victory that I was able to remove all the cat hair from my blazer
and the smears of plaster dust from my favorite black riding
boots, but perhaps I ought to consider looking into an actual
business suit for future presentations to corporate clients. There is
one thing that makes me feel more at ease, though—this place
reeks of money. The finishes are top-notch; the receptionist's desk
and the wall behind her are clad in book-matched slabs of Cala-
catta marble. These will be people who understand the price tag
of a high-end build-out.

As I wait, a man appears around the corner behind the receptionist's station, carrying a black leather laptop case with an air
of busy self-importance. He looks overstretched and fashionably
malnourished, with patchy blond hair and stridently rectangular
black-framed glasses. Even aside from the fact that he is a physical embodiment of the postmodern-architect cliché, he looks

vaguely familiar to me. His eyes narrow when he notices me; he recognizes me, too. But where do I know him from?

He approaches me, frowning. "You used to work at MaKA." It is an accusation, not a question, and that places him right away—he was Stephanie's boyfriend.

My ex-boss, Stephanie Madison, was one of the two principals at my former firm, and one of the two people on earth whom I held in the absolute highest regard (the other, of course, being my stepfather). She recruited me out of RISD—her own alma mater, as well—and during the five years I worked for her, she took such pains to mentor me that Noah was convinced she was grooming me to join the company as a third partner down the road.

If John gave me the foundation of my skills, teaching me about construction and proportion and balance, it was Stephanie who turned me from a kid with an architecture degree into an honest to-god architect. I learned so much from her that, when Danny and Jay approached me about designing the restaurant they wanted to launch, I didn't hesitate before deciding to strike out on my own.

Which, it turned out, was the ultimate betrayal. I remember telling a steel-faced Stephanie, my voice more apologetic than it should have been, that it wasn't like I was trying to poach clients of MaKA's—the restaurant owners were friends of mine.

"That's not the point," she snapped. "I'm disgusted that this is the way you're repaying everything I've done for you. I would have expected more loyalty than this."

"But, I'm not going to one of our competitors—"

"No. You just sucked up everything I had to teach you and then cut loose the first chance you got."

Nothing I said would alter her opinion. I was an ungrateful brat who had taken advantage of her and betrayed her trust. It was miserable—I didn't realize how much I'd been counting on her support and friendship until they were revoked. And to this day, I still wish I hadn't decided I was too independent to accept Noah's offer to help me plan a better strategy for my departure. I hadn't seen or spoken to Stephanie since I left MaKA, but lately I'd been wondering if her grudge might have subsided enough for me to get in touch with her again.

Apparently I have my answer. The guy currently surveying me with the same measure of pained contempt that Newman reserves for the diet cat food I periodically try to feed him, is Roger Harris, Stephanie's boyfriend. *Scratch that—Stephanie's husband,* I think, darting a look at his left hand. I pin a friendly smile on my face.

"Yes, I did. Sarina Mahler. You're Roger, right?"

He nods tightly. "You're pitching the Balm job?" he asks, injecting a broad tone of disbelief into his voice.

"Of course I am," I say. "I designed the flagship."

"Hmm. Interesting that they decided to request other proposals for the new locations."

I shrug. "Not really. It makes sense that Jamie's investors might want to explore a couple of other options. But it ultimately comes down to the right fit on personality and aesthetic. As I'm sure you know," I add, with a beatific smile. *Which means you and your hipster glasses don't have a prayer in hell of landing this job, you patronizing asshat.*

"Indeed," he says, and glances over my shoulder toward the door.

I want to ask about Stephanie but hate the thought of betraying weakness. I'm sure she wouldn't, if the positions were reversed. But then again, when was the last time I regretted taking the high road? "Give Stephanie my best," I say, and though for a minute I expect him to find some way to snub my good wishes, he gives me a faint smile.

"I will."

"Well, good luck." I extend my hand.

He shakes it briskly. "You too." He gives me a curt nod and clips off toward the elevators.

Well. So, Roger Harris is pitching this job. For the first time, it sinks in that there actually are other architects trying to land a commission that I've considered mine since I learned of its existence. Probably two or three other firms. No doubt at least one other that I'm familiar with, besides Roger's company. Curiosity tickles at me as I wonder what the other designs look like—what if there's something else besides mine that's actually good? What if it's *really* good?

I take a deep breath to slow the anxiety rising like floodwater inside me. I could not ask for better positioning to get this job. Not only am I already a known and trusted commodity to the owner of the company, but there is absolutely no doubt that my original design for Balm helped the company grow as quickly and successfully as it has. No matter how great the products and services are, people wouldn't be flocking there if it were located in a crummy dark hole in the wall. Online reviews of the spa—and I have read every one of them—almost always mention the beautiful space.

Calm restored, I entertain myself for the next few minutes by fantasizing about the office space I'm going to rent once I land the job. My two trusty employees and I certainly won't have enough room to operate in the overstuffed room at Danny's house. Maybe a loft space in the warehouse district? A little gritty, a little industrial, maybe even—

"Miss Mahler? They're ready for you."

I throw the receptionist a dazzling smile, even though she has absolutely no say in the decision that's going to be made in that room around the corner.

"Thanks." I square my shoulders and toss my ponytail behind me.

And here we go.

—

From there on out, it's easy. I stride into the conference room as if the job is already mine. From the moment I start talking, the investors—a middle-aged African American woman named Diane, who is the managing director from the VC firm, and a leftover dot-com millionaire named Amit—are intent and focused, holding my eye contact and scribbling occasional thoughts on their notepads. Jamie, for whom this represents a tantalizing preview of the heights her company is climbing to, is nodding like a bobblehead after a pothole.

"So," I say as I conclude my last presentation slide, "does anybody have any questions?"

And they do. Which is good. How does the gray water system work? How much is it likely to cost? Are there tax credits available for this sort of green design? Will the air-cleaning properties of the plants allow them to install a lighter-duty HVAC system? Everything they ask me, I'm ready for, and they are visibly impressed at the thoroughness of my responses. By the time Diane finally rises to thank me for coming in, there's not a doubt in my mind that I've got the job.

As I'm unlocking the Honda a few minutes later, I catch sight of my reflection in the window. I'd never realized exactly how badly my trusty old interview jacket was fitting me these days; it literally looks as though I borrowed it from another person. Someone with the fuller breasts and narrower shoulders I had before seven years of muay thai whittled my body into its present shape. I peel off the jacket and arc it into a nearby trash can. It's official: my first purchase with my Balm retainer is going to be a killer new suit.

—

"How did it go?" John demands when I call him that afternoon. "Did you kick butt?" Hearing his voice is like sinking into a chair long worn to my shape.

"I won't know for a while . . . they have to talk amongst themselves and make a decision."

"But did you *kick butt?*" he repeats.

Pride shoves at me, nudging open my reserve. "Well, far be it from me to toot my own horn, but . . ."

"You kicked butt!" he crows. Suddenly there's a massive crash, like a wrecking ball slammed through the wall of his bedroom. "John? John! What happened? Are you okay?" Seconds stretch past in silence. My heart hammers faster and faster as he does not respond. Then, from very far away, I can hear a long, muttered stanza of curses. "John!" I yell. "Please tell me that you're okay!"

There's a scratching noise, then some more curses, then he finally reappears. "Ree-Ree? You still there?"

"Of course I am. What the hell happened to you?"

"Knocked my damn chair over," he grumbles. "I was so excited, I leaned the damn thing too far back and it just went over."

"Are you okay? Nothing broken?" I've been worrying about a hip fracture for years.

"Nah, just a bruised keister," he says. Then the chuckles start trickling out of him. "Oh, I bet you would have laughed real good if you'd seen me, girl. Feet went right up in the air."

His laughter infects me. "People say 'head over heels,' but it sounds like you went more heels over head, huh?"

"I sure did," he says. "So when do you find out about this job, then?"

"I'm not sure. Could be a couple weeks, I guess."

"So, you'll have time to come home for a weekend before you have to start kicking butt officially, then!"

I trace my index finger across the satiny surface of my desk. "I'm sorry, I can't right now. But maybe I could look at changing my ticket for Christmas to add a couple extra days. Maybe Noah could even fly out, too, after he sees his folks. How about that?"

He grunts. "That's not for another three months."

"I know. And I'd love to see you. I just . . . you know how it is for me. It hurts too much."

"Honey girl, it always hurts. It always will. Maybe it will hurt a little less if you start spending some more time around here. Maybe it would help. You can't just avoid your home forever . . . it's been ten years now. Maybe it would help you, you know, heal."

"Yeah, like you're the one to talk about healing," I snap, and instantly hate myself. "Ugh, John, I'm sorry."

"No, that was fair," he says quietly. "Listen, you do what you can. I'm just a selfish old man, and I miss you."

The sadness in his voice tugs at my throat. "Tell you what. Why don't I start with Christmas, and go from there? I miss you too."

Mollified, he agrees. I'm dreading the extra time at home, but if it will make him happy, I'll endure it. I don't have any hopes about "healing," though. Every year, my trip home is like scraping a scab off an open wound, smudging blood on the surrounding skin. There's no reason on earth a longer visit would make a difference; the only thing it's going to do is make it worse.

15

The bridal store I chose for the shopping expedition with Noah's mother, Unbridaled, is where I helped Nicole pick out her own dress a few years ago. I had been a little nervous that Anne-Marie would try to steer me toward a more traditional establishment, but when I sent her the name and address she just texted back *Sounds great* with a bride emoji and a smiley face. Anne-Marie, I have discovered, is an emoji addict.

"This is going to be so fun!" she says as we walk into the store, slipping a companionable arm around my waist.

Shelly, the sales attendant, asks for the date of my wedding. "Oh, um, it's not scheduled yet," I stammer. "But I think maybe we'll get engaged next year. . . . I don't know." The more I try to explain, the stupider I feel.

"I've seen the ring," says Anne-Marie smoothly. "It's exquisite."

Holy shit, a ring? I gape at her, trying to figure out if she is just saving face for me or if, just possibly, there really *is* a ring. Noah would definitely have sought her opinion on it, if there were. And I know he would want to surprise me. But then again, he would've at least asked me to point him in the right direction— wouldn't he?

"Well then, let's get started, shall we?" says Shelly, beckoning us deeper into the space.

Although the place is familiar, being here for myself has a whole different feeling to it. Before, it was somebody else's wedding; now, any one of these creamy heaps of silk and tulle and sparkles could be for me.

"Have you thought about what sort of style you have in mind?" asks Shelly.

Darting an apologetic look at Anne-Marie, I shake my head. "Not really. Just . . . not puffy."

"Not puffy. We can do that!" Shelly gives me a professional once-over and then nods crisply. "I think I'm getting some ideas."

She shows Anne-Marie and me to a waiting area while she pulls a few gowns from the racks, then pops her head out from behind the curtain of the room where she's stashed them. "Showtime, missy. Come on in—you're going to need my help getting these on."

I barely get a look at the first dress before she hoists it over my head, but I register some creamy tulle and a black velvet sash. An unexpected frisson of excitement ripples through me as I feel the cool silk lining slide into place over my skin. She pinches the spare fabric in the bodice into place with a pair of clamps, ties the sash, then pushes the curtain aside so I can show Anne-Marie.

"Over here," says Shelly, herding me toward a small raised platform in front of a beveled three-way mirror. I step up, she settles the skirt of the dress around me, and finally I get a good look at myself.

And the first thing I do is laugh. It is just such an indescribably bizarre sensation—me, in a wedding dress. Because this isn't just a dress, this is a dress with a capital *D:* a full, gathered skirt sweeps the floor in a smooth bell, with a longer overlaid train swooping out behind me like a deflated parachute. The heavy boning of the bodice sculpts my torso into a Disney princess silhouette, and the jaunty velvet sash defines my waist in a way that makes me vow to reconsider my standing policy on girly dresses.

Bemused, I turn to Anne-Marie for feedback. "Well?"

She twists her lips in evaluation. "It's pretty. But I have to say, it does look fairly . . . puffy."

Shelly is already reaching for the sash to untie me. "You know, I have to try it," she explains. "Every time a bride walks in here with a notion of what she doesn't want, I put her in it first, just to be sure. You wouldn't believe how many people wind up falling for exactly what they swore they didn't want."

Anne-Marie smiles. "Very sensible. But my Sarina's a girl who knows her own mind."

"So," says Shelly as she goes to work extricating me from the puffy dress, "your mom seems lovely. Are you her only daughter?"

"Oh, that's not my mother," I explain. "She's my boy-friend's—my future mother-in-law."

"How sweet!" says Shelly. "That's great that she's doing this with you. Are you planning to shop with your mom, too? Or is yours as bossy as mine is?" she asks conspiratorially as she lifts another dress off the hanger.

I force myself to laugh. "Too bossy," I say, and hold my arms up for the straps. I just can't deal with the awkward apology and the pity. Not on this particular occasion.

Anne-Marie declares the second dress too wimpy. The third one looks like it belongs on a flower child at a fancy drum circle; the fourth is meant for Jessica Rabbit. "Maybe I spoke too soon," whispers Shelly in the dressing room. "Your mother-in-law's not exactly shy with her opinions, either!"

But the funny thing is, Anne-Marie is right on the money. She tips her head to one side as she studies me in the fifth dress, a so-phisticated lace sheath. Then she lifts her slim shoulders briefly and makes a noise that sounds unexpectedly similar to "meh."

"It's very pretty, but it just doesn't look like *you*," she says. "Do you mind if I take a look around?"

"Go for it," I tell her. I'm just a wee bit buzzed from the Prosecco Shelly has been feeding me, and Anne-Marie has good taste, and we're here—so why the hell not?

A few minutes later, she returns to the dressing area with an armful of dresses and a determined expression on her face.

"All right, let's see how we did!" says Shelly, graciously burying any trace of irritation at having her territory trampled.

The first of Anne-Marie's dresses is a total surprise: the same princess silhouette as the first dress, the same jaunty sash, but rendered in a heavy handmade lace and a flirty knee-length shape. I never would have dreamed of a cropped dress, but the effect is darling: flirtatious, feminine, but not taking itself overly seriously. I catch myself grinning as Shelly pins a dashing little birdcage veil onto my hair.

"This is adorable," I say.

Anne-Marie's warm smile reminds me so much of her son that my heart glows.

Her other selections are just as good. All of a sudden I don't feel like a little girl playing dress-up, I feel like myself, trying on dresses that I might possibly get married in. At some point in the not-so-incredibly-distant future. But while they're all lovely, I'm not getting any chest-fluttery "this is The One" type feelings; I'm just having fun trying out all the different possibilities.

And then Shelly puts me into the next-to-last dress, and I flutter.

I know, courtesy of *Project Runway*, that it is an updated Grecian-inspired style, with filmy chiffon layers that drape softly over the curve of my hips and ripple down to the floor. The deep sweetheart neckline flatters my modest bust, and gathered cap sleeves soften the squareness of my shoulders. It is not white or ivory but the palest, palest gray, and it was made for me.

"Wow," I breathe. For the first time, I feel like a *bride*.

Anne-Marie presses her fingers to her lips, tears shimmering in her eyes. "Wow," she echoes. "You are a vision." We smile tremulously at each other in the mirror for a long moment.

"Well, ladies," says Shelly. "Consensus at last."

I laugh, relieved to let the intense moment go. "Yeah, I think so!" I smooth the gossamer silk over my waist lovingly. I don't want to take it off. "Anne-Marie, could you take a photo so I can show my stepdad?"

"Of course, sweetheart." She reaches for her phone and snaps a couple of photos.

When I emerge from the dressing room, Shelly hands me a thick letterpress card featuring the store's cute retro logo, and the style name and price of the dress written in her swirly handwriting underneath. "Wynne," it's called. The dress I am going to marry Noah in.

—

Over lunch at Albion an hour later, I almost work up the nerve to ask Anne-Marie if she was bluffing about the engagement ring. Almost. Instead, I keep sneaking glances at my left hand, trying to imagine it with something sparkling back at me. What if I don't like it? What if it's *too* sparkly? I adjust the heart pendant at my collarbone and remind myself that the style of the damn thing doesn't ultimately matter one bit, it's the depth of the feeling that goes with it.

"You know," says Anne-Marie after a delicate sip from her wineglass—she holds it by the stem, the way you're supposed to but no one else I know actually does—"I had forgotten how lovely this restaurant is. It's been a couple years since I've seen it, but it still looks so elegant."

"Thank you so much."

"Really," she says, studying the custom walnut-and-smoked-mirror installation behind the maître d' station. "You have a special talent, and I admire that."

"That means a lot to me," I say sincerely. "And thank you so much for coming down to do this with me. This has been lovely. I'm *so* glad you suggested it."

"I am too," she says. "I really am. I've always wanted to know you better, but I wasn't sure *you* did."

"Oh . . . I—"

She waves aside my apology. "No, no, no. Don't apologize. I can't imagine what it's like for you, not having your mom around. And I didn't want to push, or have you think I was trying to make myself more important in your life than I ought to be."

"Thank you for being so considerate," I say. "But I think it will be nice . . . to have a mother-in-law."

Her smile reminds me of Noah, again. "And I want you to know, I'm sorry for the way we leaped on you the last time you visited. I hope you can forgive us. We're just excited for the future, excited to have you in our family. And we are so very gratified to see Noah so happy. You will understand—*one day,*" she emphasizes, with self-deprecating charm that makes me smile, "the pleasure that comes from seeing your child's joy."

"I bring him joy?" The thought is unexpectedly humbling.

"Of course you do, dear. His first wife . . ." Her voice trails away on a sigh. "She disappointed him so badly."

"How so?" The essence of what Noah had told me was that he and his ex, whom he had met in the Peace Corps, had simply married young and then gradually drifted apart. I'd always assumed there was a little more to it than that, but he was too much of a gentleman ever to badmouth her or blame her for their breakup, so I never got another angle on it.

Anne-Marie twitches up one side of her nose noncommittally. "I think she wanted him to stay exactly who he was when he was twenty-three. Idealistic and hell-bent on saving the world. Not that saving the world isn't a noble goal, but she couldn't accept anything else as worthy. Certainly not earning a decent living. She was the type who preferred to be broke all the time just to prove something to the world."

"Bit of a martyr complex?"

"And how. The first Christmas he was working at Bowman Gise, he bought her a couple of beautiful cashmere sweaters. He thought they would be nice for her to have, instead of all her thrift-store stuff. And she turned it into a lecture about materialistic culture and the evils of capitalism."

I lift my napkin in my hands and snap it threateningly.

"My thoughts exactly," says Anne-Marie. "She wasn't a bad girl, she just didn't appreciate him for who he is. She thought she was marrying someone exactly like herself, and she got disillusioned when he grew up."

"I am selfishly glad she did," I say.

"As you should be!" she says, clinking her glass against mine. "I am, too, at the end of the day. I will never forget the first real talk we had, after he had been seeing you for a little while. He said, 'Mom, she makes me feel like she needs me. And it's *nice* to be needed.'"

"That sounds like me four years ago, yes," I admit.

"No, even now," she says, laying a reassuring hand on my wrist. "Needing someone is part of loving them. And I can see how much you love him. It was all in your face today, when you looked at yourself in that beautiful dress. You were seeing yourself walking down the aisle to him."

—

The next day is the annual Round Top Antiques Fair, about an hour's drive south of Austin: a sprawling maze of sales booths set up by vendors hawking everything from yard-sale junk to valuable antiques, all of it piled up for display under the glaring sun. Texas being Texas and Austin being weird, there's a delicious flavor of nuttiness to many of the offerings, which I'm certain doesn't exist anywhere else in the world. It's the in-between that Eamon and I are hoping to find. When I mentioned that I was heading to Round Top in hopes of scoring some bargain goodies for his house, his face lit up with curiosity.

"This is where you found that cowboy art for Clementine, right? Do you mind if I come?"

Of course I didn't mind. It would make more sense for him to come with me and see things in person than to send me approvals based on camera phone photos. And, of course, the fact that it was his suggestion absolved me of guilt for enjoying his company.

We hit the road early, to beat the heat. As much as anyone ever does beat the heat in Austin in September. While Eamon drives, I run down our shopping list. So far we've established a late-mid-century modern feel for his house, with luxurious, masculine materials like walnut and cowhide, and touches of seventies brass and smoked glass here and there to brighten it up. Round Top is a treasure trove for smaller, inexpensive pieces like lamps, side tables, and artwork, so I'm confident that we'll score some great stuff.

When we arrive, we park in the long grass near the fair entrance and dive in. I haven't seen him so excited since the day we found his house—I feel like I've escorted a six-year-old into F.A.O. Schwarz. My idea was to start with a few vendors I know will be up his alley and then wander at will, but he insists on proceeding methodically through the aisles, stopping at every single booth, so that we leave literally no Lucite-framed Rocky poster or giant painted giraffe statue unturned.

After a few hours of prowling, I am starving and call for a time-out so we can eat. The shade of the food barn is a blissful respite for my sun-dazzled eyes. We load up on pulled pork sand-wiches, jalapeño corn bread, and barbecue baked beans, and I sink gratefully down on the bench with my precarious plate and a cold Blue Moon and dig in. Bliss. My first sandwich disappears in instants, and as I start on the second I catch Eamon watching me, an amused smile tugging at his lips.

I pause, sandwich in midair. "What?"

"You just *decimated* that sandwich."

I point the sandwich at him threateningly. "Don't tell me you're one of those creeps who expect women to be prissy eaters. I know the girls on your team weren't clocking world records on garden salads with dressing on the side."

"No," he agrees, "but the girls on my team could probably bench-press your entire body weight."

Oh, so I'm a weakling? Because I'm not as strong as his pre-cious ex the Butterfly Queen? I'd like to see *her* try to land a high roundhouse kick on somebody's neck. "Screw you. I do muay thai three days a week, so don't make out like I'm some kind of swizzle stick." I take another huge bite to punctuate my point.

"Perish the thought," he murmurs.

We devour the rest of our baked beans and corn bread in si-lence. Without apparent effort, he finishes nearly double the amount of the food on my own plate, after which he watches me, arms crossed, until I'm done.

"What is it now?" I demand, through my last bite of beans.

He runs a finger down my nose. "You're sunburned."

As he carries his tray to the trash, I take a long moment to enjoy the view of his retreating back, then catch the pair of teen-age girls at the table next to us doing the same thing. They wear identical looks of avid interest, like Newman when he scents a freshly opened can of Iams. God help me, is that what my face looks like when I look at him? No wonder Nicole gave me a hard time.

By the time we load the last of our finds into the Jeep, it's almost dark. My bangs have acquired a texture I believe beauty editors refer to as "beachy," and my skin is overcooked in its marinade of sweat and sunscreen. As we collapse into our seats, Eamon holds out his hand for a high five. "Wow, what a haul. Nice job, swizzle stick."

"Oh, you wouldn't dare."

He waggles his fingers. "Come on, don't leave me hanging here."

"No. I'm not going to validate you for calling me that," I tell him.

Suddenly his face contorts with confused discomfort, and he fishes a hand in between the car seat and his ass. He pulls out an invisible dangling object and holds it up for my inspection, eyes wide with innocence. "Look, Sarina! It's your sense of humor! Do you want it back?"

Chest vibrating with suppressed laughter, I pluck it from his fingers and hold it up, as if uncertain. "Wait, where does this go? I feel like I should swallow it, but I'm not really sure I want to swallow something that's been in your—"

His laughter drowns out the rest of my words. Still smiling, he starts the car and we leave. Once we get back into town, he suggests a stop at Polvo's for fish tacos and queso since it's been so long since our barbecue. Belatedly, I remember that it's Saturday night. Saturday night means cocktails. And an icy beverage would sure hit the spot after a long day in the sun.

The front porch of the restaurant, with its garish mural, dangling garlands, and relentlessly corny mariachi music, is noisy with laughter and conversation. Every time I eat here, it reminds me of one of my early dates with Noah. Throughout the meal, he conversed with the waiter in flawless Spanish, at one point striking up an extended conversation with the guy. When it ended, he turned to me, smiling. "He's from Mexico City," he explained.

"Mmm," I said. "And that whole thing had nothing to do with impressing me." But instead of denying it, he just blushed. Which was adorable. "It's okay," I told him. "It's working."

Two hours and three double-tall Tito's and sodas later, Eamon and I realize he's had too many to drive, so we decide to stay for a while until we sober up. By the time he pulls into my driveway, it is 1:30 in the morning.

He puts the car in park and turns to me, smiling. "I had an awesome time today, Ree. Thanks for taking me along with you."

The car cabin is warm and dark, and sitting here with him late at night, after the most enjoyable day I can ever remember spending with a guy, is leading my mind down a dangerous path. I have to get the hell out of here.

"Me too—we found some awesome stuff," I say, reaching for the door. "Nice job on your first Round Top."

I watch till the lights of his car disappear around the corner, then exhale a slow breath. This is not good. This is not good at all. Despite my resolution to put a bullet in my crush, I've been using his project as a way to indulge my craving to be near him, and, instead of burning out, it's just getting stronger. I have to find a way to distance myself. Only problem is, it's the last thing in the world that I actually want to do.

16

I try. I really do. I promise myself that I will not initiate contact with him unless it's legitimately necessary for the project, and, over the next few weeks, I stick to it. Which ultimately doesn't have much of an effect, because he calls me or emails me or texts me several times a day. Sometimes it relates to the house; sometimes it doesn't. He calls me to settle a dispute with a friend about Georges St-Pierre's weight class. He sends me links to some clothes he is thinking of getting his two small nieces as a gift. (I think they're adorable, sporty instead of saccharine, but what do I know?)

"Eamon, I've never met your nieces," I remind him. "And I have no idea how your sister-in-law likes to dress them. Why don't you ask your mother?"

"But *you're* a girl," he says, as though this should explain everything.

One Saturday in the middle of October, Nicole and I head to South Congress for brunch and shopping. A slight crispness in the air is the first hint of cool weather that we've had since March, so all the boutiques have set out their limited selections of cold-weather clothing in an attempt to seduce us warm-climate dwellers with fantasies of woolly autumnal layering. Two jackets and one studded belt later, we head down the street to my favorite SoCo shop, Uncommon Objects. Two parts pirate treasure chest and one part grandma's attic, it's a big, jumbled space packed literally to the rafters with art, vintage tableware, and miscellaneous knickknacks of the most useless and fascinating kind. Sort of like all of Round Top condensed into one slightly overwhelming space.

As we meander the aisles, a tall, chunky brass lamp catches my eye—it would look perfect in Eamon's office and I know he will love it. I email him a photo and continue browsing.

"How's Eamon's job going, by the way?" Nicole says as I put the lamp down at the register a few minutes later.

I eyeball her suspiciously, but her face is perfectly neutral. She hasn't abandoned her pet theory for a minute, but she's not going to antagonize me by getting into it again.

"It's great," I reply. "Joe's been making good progress, and we've almost filled up the guest room at Ame's rental with furniture." Using the nickname that his closest friends call him gives me a guilty little frisson of pleasure, and I'm sure Nicole is going to call me out on it. Miraculously, it slips past her radar.

"And what about Balm, what have you heard from them?"

"Nothing yet," I tell her, trying to sound unconcerned even though the unusual silence from Jamie is beginning to worry me. But, of course, she isn't fooled.

"Don't worry," she says. "It's a great design, and I've seen you present. There's no way they won't hire you."

"I thought so, too, but they brought in some big guns to submit proposals." I fill her in on my run-in with Roger Harris from my MaKA days.

"Roger Harris is a pretentious twit," she says. "What the heck does he know about luxury spas? They must just be working

through their official channels or something. You know everything takes three times as long when you have to do it by commit-
tee."

When we reach the car, she unlocks the trunk so we can load
our treasures inside. "Oh, hey, I've been meaning to ask you, isn't
Round Top coming up soon? I've got a corner in the living room
that's just begging for a wild mustang sculpture."

I turn to her in dismay. "Oh crap, honey, it's over. It ended last
weekend."

She dumps her shopping bag into the trunk with a plop. "You
mean you went already? Without me?"

"Yeah. I'm sorry, love. All those times you came with me I
thought you were just humoring me. I didn't realize you were actually into it."

"Well, it was more about spending time with you and less
about the mustang sculptures, but yeah. So you just went by yourself?"

"No, I took Eamon. We found a bunch of stuff for his house."

She cocks her head to one side, deliberately. "Oh really!"

Here we go. With two little words, the gloves are off. "Yes."

"I can see it would have been way too much work for you to
email him photos of stuff, like you did just now," she says under-
standingly.

"You're very astute, Nicole. It was much more efficient for
him to come with me and see things in person, instead of sitting
in Austin with his phone lighting up every ten minutes."

"Certainly. And did he enjoy himself?"

"He was happy as a pig in shit. He is a born thrifter."

"Adorable! And did you enjoy *yourself*?"

"I always enjoy Round Top," I say sweetly.

"It *sounds* like fun!" she squeals. "Gosh, the two of you hanging out together all day, cruising the field in search of goodies . . .
eating tailgate barbecue, swapping stories, taking turns cracking

each other up—it almost sounds like what I remember a great date being like, back when I was still single and kicking!"

"I know, we thought so too! That probably explains why we wound up screwing in the back of the Jeep before we drove home!"

A middle-aged guy passing on the sidewalk does a double take.

Nicole pulls a fascinated face. "Excellent! As good as you remembered?"

"Even better! Except, he's so tall, the conditions were a little awkward, you know?"

She wags her finger at me, a smile of pure evil breaking across her face. "Oh, see, I just busted you, missy. That little detail right there tells me you actually thought about what it *would* be like."

I can feel every inch of the massive blush that floods my face. "You know that you're terrifying, right?" I mutter.

She beams. "It is my mission in life. To terrify my friends."

I wait for her to return to the attack, but having forced me to admit to the Jeep fantasy, she's apparently decided she has broken me sufficiently for the moment. I give her two weeks at the outside before she brings it up again.

—

The following Thursday, Eamon doesn't show up for our weekly site meeting, which is highly unusual. He is radio silent on text and email. After lunch I give in to concern and try him on his cell. After it rings a few times, he answers, voice soggy.

"Hey!" I say, unreasonably glad as always to hear his voice. "What's the matter, you hungover?"

He groans. "I wish. I'm sick as hell. I think I've got the flu."

Men are such drama queens when they don't feel good. "Sack up, Roy. Pop a DayQuil and you'll be back in business. We missed you at the site meeting this morning."

"I've already taken everything in my medicine cabinet. I'm serious, Mahler, I feel awful."

"What's the matter? Is it a stomach flu, or original flavor?"

"Original," he replies. "I'm not snotty, but I feel all feverish, and everything *aches*." His voice grows a little petulant, and I can't repress a smile.

"Oh, come on," I say. "Where's that championship spirit? You recovered from a massive car crash, and a little flu's kicking your ass? Don't tell me you're getting soft in your old age."

"I don't want to talk to you anymore," he complains. "If you think of it, call me later to make sure I haven't died."

I'm still smiling as I tuck the Honda into a parking space outside Balm, where I'm due for a quick drive-by visit. To make sure everything is humming along smoothly, I like to drop by each of my job sites unannounced a few times a week, in addition to the regularly scheduled site meeting (when, impressively, the site somehow never fails to be a buzzing hive of activity).

Joe Martinez, however, has worked with me for too long to be surprised or alarmed when I materialize in front of him without warning.

"Hello, Sarina," he says. "Everything looking good today?"

And it is. I'm pleased. During demo, they figured out that, with a little creative redistribution of some plumbing pipes from the floor above, we'll be able to add an extra seven inches to the height of the new treatment rooms. It's going to make a big difference in those small spaces. Over the cacophony of hammering, we talk through a couple of other minor updates he has for me, and then I'm ready to head back home.

"Oh, by the way," says Joe, holding a piece of dangling electrical cable aside so that I can pass, "who was that guy who was here earlier?"

"What guy?"

He shrugs. "I don't know. Came by himself and took a bunch of photos."

This sounds ominous. "Was it a building inspector?"

"Nah, too fancy. Tall, skinny. Nerdy glasses."

Oh no. I know exactly who it was.

And there's only one reason I can think of why he would have been here.

I feel like I just got kicked in the chest by a Clydesdale. My eyes drift around the room, settling on one of Joe's workers, who is shifting some stacks of steel wall studs into a corner, out of the way of traffic. Reaching down, lifting them up. Reaching down, lifting them up.

"What's wrong?" says Joe. "You're staring at Ivan like he kicked your dog."

I pull my eyes away from his worker. "Bad news, Joe. That tall skinny guy was bad news. Nothing to do with you," I add, as he frowns. "Just very bad news for me."

—

They gave the job to Roger Harris. I cannot even begin to wrap my brain around it. How could his design possibly have been better? I know Roger's work—it's functional, tasteful, perfectly decent work. But it isn't *great*. It isn't striking, or original, or creative, it's just . . . adequate. And this is what they want for the future of their brand? Adequate?

I hiss out a frustrated sigh and collapse on the grass. I didn't feel like going home after Joe's accidental revelation, so I headed to my favorite spot in Austin—the shady, grassy hillside overlooking the Barton Springs Pool. Down in the pool, kids are splashing and shrieking in the chilly, sunlit water; if I were in a better mood, I'd sit on the pool deck and dangle my legs in. But that would require me to be pleasant to the people around me, and right now I don't think I'm capable of that.

Roger Harris. Ugh. Why? I cast my mind back to the presentation, trying to identify any misstep I could have made, any question I answered weakly, but there's nothing—the design was excellent, and I presented it well. I walked out of there with the same feeling I used to get when I knew I'd aced a presentation in college—and I'd never once been wrong before. So why didn't this go my way?

Jamie's voice, when she answers the phone, is squeaky with guilt. "Hi, Sarina!"

"Hi, Jamie. How are things going?"

"Oh, you know, busy," she peeps. "The addition is looking great! Joe told me about the ceiling in the treatment rooms, so I went ahead and approved that change order. Totally worth it!"

"Yeah, we were pleased when we figured that out. Listen, I hate to be a pest, but I'm just wondering if there's been any decision regarding the contract for Dallas and Houston. Are there any questions I can answer for the investment team, anything like that?"

"Oh gosh," she says, sounding so uncomfortable that I almost feel bad for her. "Thank you for asking, but you know what—unfortunately, as much as we all loved your proposal, we've decided to go with somebody else. It was such a difficult decision, I can't even tell you. I was pulling for you all the way, but at the end of the day I wasn't alone in making the decision, so . . ."

I breathe in through clenched teeth, resisting the urge to demand to know exactly *when* she was planning on sharing this information with me. "Okay. Well, thank you for telling me" (eventually), "and thank you for giving me the opportunity to submit the proposal."

"Oh, honey, of course," she says, abruptly letting go of her stilted professional manner. "Believe me, I reeeeeaaallly wanted it

to be you. Loved your ideas, loved the green walls, loved it all.
Loved it, loved it, loved it."

"Well . . . then, do you mind if I ask why you decided to go
with the other architect?"

She sighs. "Money. If it was just about the design, it was you
all the way. But the cost . . . just your rough estimate that you included was thirty percent higher than the next person's; and after
we gave the proposals to a GC outfit that one of the investors
knows, they roughed it out even higher."

"Well, but," I say, carefully modulating my voice so that I
don't sound like a whining child, "we could value-engineer it with
the GC. I had always envisioned that we would do that."

"I know, and I asked him about that, but he said the cost of
the design was just too high. He said it wasn't only materials or
finishes; apparently just the base cost of installing the gray water
system, and all the irrigation and specialty lighting for the plants,
was a huge number that wasn't going to go anywhere."

I pop my mouth open to argue that we didn't have to irrigate
with gray water, it could be just regular plumbing lines, but the
futility of it hits me in the face like a two-by-four. This is no longer a possibility; they have hired someone else. Who was on my
job site, taking photos and notes on *my* work, so that he can rep-
licate the details *I* designed because he's not creative enough to
come up with his own.

"Okay," I say, the fight going out of me like air out of a balloon. "I understand."

"I really am just gutted, Sarina," Jamie insists. "The guy we
hired, he's all right, but he's not great. But he *is* experienced, and
the investors liked that too."

"Well, now *I'm* a little more experienced," I say, unable to
keep a slight tinge of bitterness out of my voice.

She clucks. "It *stinks*. But for what it's worth, I recommend
you to everyone, doll. Everyone. My friend's husband is looking

to open a retail store downtown somewhere. It's not much of a budget, but it might be interesting . . ."

"Thanks, Jamie, I appreciate that," I say sincerely. "Listen, I should get going, but thank you again for the opportunity—and I'll see you tomorrow at the meeting at the site."

She signs off, audibly relieved to have the discussion over. I slump back on the grass, simmering with frustration and disappointment. Gradually, the late-afternoon sun shifts downward in the sky, and the families in the pool begin to pack up and head home for dinner. I should do the same, but I'm waiting to give Danny time to leave for work; I hate that he was right about the expense of my proposal, and I don't want to deal with talking to him about it. Just as I am thinking about making a move, my phone rings—Noah.

"It's good to hear your voice," I tell him.

"I know. You too, kitten. Wish I weren't so slammed lately. But what's up with you, why do you sound so down?" He always pays such good attention to my mood on the phone—sort of a necessary survival skill when dealing with a long-distance relationship, I suppose.

I fill him in on Jamie's news. "And Danny was right about the cost of it," I admit. "I am kicking myself so fucking hard for blowing off his advice. He owns two businesses in the hospitality industry, but I figured that I knew better than him what the investors' priorities would be. And now . . . all those late nights, all that effort, all that time . . . for nothing."

"Ah, honey, that *sucks*," Noah says. "I know how much you wanted this. But who knows, maybe this retail job that Jamie mentioned will turn into something."

"Yeah, well, Jamie swore up and down that I had the spa job in the bag, but it didn't exactly turn out that way, did it? Ugh, whatever. It's not even that," I say. "Even if this guy calls about his store, and even if he hires me, she already said there's no budget.

I'm never going to get anywhere if I keep doing jobs with no budget." Viciously, I rip a handful of grass and toss it away from me down the hill.

"I thought your house reno had a pretty decent budget on it."

"Eamon's? It does, for residential. And if I can get press from it, maybe I'll get some hits. We'll see. I just wanted this Balm job so *badly* because it would have boosted me into real business territory. Enough work to hire some staff, and a solid flow of money for the next couple of years—I wouldn't still be bouncing from one no-budget project to the next."

"But that's not a big deal, though," he says reassuringly. "It's not like we'll need your income when we're married. And I know you're disappointed to lose this job, but maybe it's just as well if you stick to smaller jobs for now. I don't think you'll want to be working this much while we're trying to raise young kids, you know?"

I blink a couple of times, literally shocked into silence. I watch a little gray swallow flutter out of the tree branch above my head, into the sky. And then I do something I haven't done since my penultimate breakup with the philandering guitarist, and had never dreamed I would ever do again. I hang up on him.

17

The next morning, I spend the two-hour site meeting for the Balm expansion smiling into Jamie's guilty, anxious face and pretending that I'm not still seething with bitterness. Throughout the meeting, she makes such an obvious point of praising my work on both the original space and the expansion that I am embarrassed for both of us. As we are packing up to leave, I sense her hovering, building up steam to apologize yet again, which isn't going to be anything other than awkward; so I make good on the only acceptable option, and bolt.

On my way home, I decide to check on Eamon. The phone rings through to voice mail, so I figure he's sleeping, but a few minutes later he calls me back.

"How's the invalid?" I ask, trying not to sound concerned.

"Still feel like hell. Whatever this is, it's persistent." He sounds like someone left him in the washer overnight.

I am overwhelmed by a rare attack of nurturing instinct. "I'm right down the road from that Whole Foods on Lamar—want me to pick up some soup for you and bring it by?"

"Ah, really? I'd love some soup. . . . I don't think I've eaten anything since yesterday morning."

"Then you must be mostly dead. I'll be there in half an hour."

When he answers the door, his skin is the same tentative off-white as the walls of his rental house, except for the peppery stubble shadowing his cheeks. My pathetic heart goes *squish* like a wet sponge.

"Free delivery with purchase!" I announce, brandishing my grocery bag. I breeze past him and begin unloading the bag on his kitchen counter. "I brought you chicken noodle and some sort of curried potato stuff . . . I thought the spice might help fumigate the virus," I explain with a sideways smile. "And ice cream, just in case."

"This is awesome," he says, surveying the feast. "Thanks, bud." My nostrils flare as I realize he has just addressed me with a term usually reserved for young boys and puppies. *Yes, Nicole, this man is quite simply quivering with lust.*

We load up our bowls and sit down at the kitchen table to eat. But between his flu and my bad mood, neither of us seems to feel much like talking.

"Hey," he says after a few minutes of unaccustomed silence, "everything okay? You seem down."

I haven't wanted to talk about it with my stepdad or Nicole, because they are both too loyal to be impartial; and I haven't talked about it with Danny because I haven't yet forgiven him for being right. But unexpectedly, Eamon is exactly the right person. I tell him all of it. And he listens. He even makes me go out to my car to get my laptop so I can show him the renderings.

"The worst part is," I say, staring glumly at the gray water diagram I'd labored over, "I'm just so pissed at myself. I was so far up my own ass with this stupid green wall design—I was so convinced it was the right thing. And Danny *warned* me that they might think it was too expensive to build, and he was right, and it cost me the whole fucking project." I snap the laptop closed with unnecessary force.

"It's a great design, Ree," he says. "You weren't wrong about that."

"No, but I should have showed them an alternate. I remember thinking, *What, am I just going to throw a couple planters in there?* But you know what, if I'd just pursued that idea, I could have come up with some other way to use the plantings architecturally, just on a smaller scale."

He doesn't have any reassurances in response to this, which I appreciate. There's nothing grosser than the feeling of somebody telling you you didn't do anything wrong when you know perfectly well that you did.

"So what happens now?" he asks, crossing his arms over his chest.

"What do you mean? It's over."

He leans back in his chair and stretches his legs alongside the table. "Can you resubmit another version?"

"They gave the job to somebody else."

"Have they actually paid a retainer?"

"Probably. I don't know."

"So email your client and tell her you're working on another version of your concept that will be more in line with their budget."

"Ame, I don't want to look desperate!"

"One man's desperate is another man's persistent, Sarina," he says, smiling. "And persistence pays off."

I stab at the coagulated soup with my spoon. "Believe me, if there were a point to persisting, I would persist. I would persist till every last cow came home. But they have a schedule to stick to, so unfortunately, I think I just fucked this one up.

"Oh. And you wanna know what Noah said?" I add, barreling onward, although I am fairly certain this is where the conversation should stop. But I am angry, and hurt, and both of those things make me a little bit reckless. "*Noah* said it didn't really matter that I lost the job. 'Cause when we get married, we're not going to need my income. Especially since I'm ultimately going to be a stay-at-home mom anyway . . . it doesn't matter whether I grow my business or not."

There is a long pause. "He *said* that to you?" Eamon says finally, and I can only describe the expression on his face as a sneer. And suddenly I am ashamed of myself. I shared Noah's condescending remarks because I was craving validation for my response to them; and now that I have it, I just feel petty for having aired our dirty laundry with someone who has no business knowing about it.

So I backpedal. "It came out worse than he meant it. I mean, what he said was true. About the money."

But Eamon doesn't respond. Jaw knotted, he grabs the half-eaten bowls of soup and dumps them into the sink with a crash. I gnaw nervously at a hangnail while various crashes and bangs issue from behind me. When he returns a few moments later, his face is clear and he is carrying the two pints of ice cream and a pair of spoons.

"Screw the soup," he says. "Let's get to business."

We tuck into the ice cream for a few minutes, until I notice him shifting uncomfortably in his seat. "Ame, do you want to get back in bed?"

His grin would offend every saint in Christendom. "I'm sorry, did you just invite yourself into bed with me?"

"Ass. I was only talking about you—you look achy. Have you taken any ibuprofen lately?"

He shakes his head, still smiling. "No, I'm probably due for a couple. But I do kind of want to lie down. . . . Come keep me company?"

We retreat to his bedroom, where the still life of medicine bottles, half-drunk water glasses, and abandoned tissues on the night table and floor attests to the fact that he's spent the past couple of days in bed. "Sick bay," he says with a sweeping gesture.

Covertly, I study the room, taking illicit pleasure in being there even though it's on strictly innocent terms. The space is airy and bright, dominated by a huge, low bed dressed in invitingly rumpled white linens. Framed vintage concert posters he's never bothered to hang up—Stevie Wonder, Bill Withers—lean against the wall. A David Sedaris book is splayed facedown on the night table, just a few chapters in.

He flops onto the bed with a tired sigh, shakes a couple Advil into his palm, and tosses them back with a glug of water. "You coming?" he asks, shucking his hoodie and patting the space next to him.

I hesitate for an instant—sure, he is sick, but this is still not especially appropriate. Then, with a mental shrug, I climb in next to him.

We spend all afternoon in bed, watching one movie after another and eating ice cream straight out of the carton. He insists that everything we watch be something he's seen before, so I won't feel obligated to pause it when he intermittently falls asleep. But it doesn't matter, because when he does drift off, the last thing I pay attention to is the movie; my fingers ache to touch his hair, his face, the sleek curve of his biceps just below the sleeve of his T-shirt. I'm fascinated by the structure of his masculine hands, the beauty of his profile against the white pillow. I would be perfectly happy to spend the rest of the weekend like this—the chance to spend so much time with him alone and the piercing sweetness of lying next to him while he sleeps are unexpected pleasures that I never want to relinquish. But the sun tracks relentlessly across the sky, and eventually the room grows dark.

Around nine o'clock, I return from a stealthy trip to the bathroom to find him awake, groggy and blinking in the light from his bedside lamp. "I woke up and you were gone—I thought you'd left without saying goodbye," he says accusatorily.

"Nope, just a pee break," I say, circling the bed and perching on the edge beside him. "But I should get going and let you get a good long sleep."

His eyes are fathomless in the dim light. "Do you have somewhere to be?"

I should lie. I should lie. "Not really."

"Then why don't you stay over? It's nice to have your company."

I summon the feeblest of excuses. "But I don't have anything with me . . ."

He jerks his chin to my left. "My T-shirts and stuff are in that dresser . . . help yourself. And there's a clean toothbrush in the medicine cabinet."

And suddenly I think of Noah and how much he hurt me, and the fact that, even after he promised me we'd work together to sort out the issue of kids, he still just assumed I'd do what he wants. And then through a convoluted and self-serving mathematical equation inside my head, Noah hurting me somehow equates to me being entitled to spend the night sleeping in a bed next to the only man I've ever wanted more than him.

In for a penny, I think, as I select a T-shirt and a pair of boxers and pad across to the bathroom. For some reason it feels more intimate to be in Eamon's bathroom, hunting for the spare toothbrush between bottles of his shaving cream and antichlorine shampoo, than it did to be actually lying in his bed. I find myself searching for signs of female presence, but there's not so much as a stray tampon. Sternly I remind myself that I have no legitimate reason to feel pleased.

He scrolls through the on-demand listings as I climb in beside him and fluff the pillows behind me. "Well, what do you feel like watching? I'm sure there's something else in here I won't be disappointed if I pass out in the middle of. Oh! Here we go! *Snakes on a Plane.* You will laugh your ass off. *This* I will stay awake for."

It turns out to be every bit as deliciously bad as he's promised. After twenty minutes, we are literally crying with laughter as we vie to outdo each other with jokes at the movie's expense. By the time the credits roll, I am exhausted from laughing so hard.

"I can barely keep my eyes open, but that was worth it," says Eamon as he reaches for the bedside lamp.

My shoulders vibrate as a residual giggle escapes me. "I don't know how I lived for so long without seeing that."

A sharp click from the lamp, and the room is plunged into darkness. I feel him shifting next to me as he mashes his pillow into a tight ball. "G'night, Ree. I'm really glad you came over."

"Me too." Moving as little as possible, I stretch out on my side, facing him. Carefully I position myself at what I judge to be platonic-sleepover distance, but not so far that I can't still feel the warmth emanating from his body. I tuck one arm under my pillow, bend the other in front of me, and close my eyes, listening to him breathe in the darkness.

—

The first thing I notice when I wake is the neat slices of sunlight, marching across the blank wall opposite the bed in the pattern of the half-drawn blinds. The second thing I notice is that I am wrapped around Eamon like a favorite blanket. Though I don't remember moving, we have curled together during the night; my cheek is cradled on his chest, and one of my arms stretches across him, fingers tucked under his ribs. My legs are nestled between and against his. He appears not to have found this objectionable, because both heavy arms are wrapped around me, holding me in place. It is utterly inappropriate, and absolutely delicious.

I lie still for a long minute, barely breathing. I have to move, I *will* move, just as soon as I memorize everything about this. The scent of his skin, the texture of his stubbled neck from an inch away, the solid warmth of his chest beneath me, the weight of his arms around me, the delicious roughness of his legs against my smooth ones. I remind myself that he's sick, and he's sound asleep. I have no idea how we got like this, but when he wakes up he's going to be as embarrassed as I bloody well ought to be. Until then, though, I am going to enjoy just a couple more seconds of this.

And then, as I cautiously release the breath I have been holding, his voice rumbles richly under my ear. "Morning."

Reluctantly, I raise my head. His eyes are melted chocolate, with no trace of fever in sight, and the intimacy of his sleepy smile makes warmth puddle in every corner of my body.

"Morning," I whisper back. I start to pull away from him, mortified by the liberties I've taken in my sleep, but he tightens his arms to keep me in place.

"This is ever so nice," he observes, skimming one hand lazily up my back.

"How are you feeling?" I ask, skin tingling from his touch. Why isn't he letting go of me?

"Much better," he says softly. "You cured me."

"Are you sure it was me?" I manage. "I think it was the curried potato soup."

"Nope . . . it was definitely you." His hand slips up to cup the back of my neck, and suddenly my heart is banging so hard against my ribs that I'm sure he can feel it.

Before I can say anything else, he gently tugs my head downward, and kisses me. It's a sweet, undemanding kiss, but it's the tenderness that shatters me. Dimly I think it must be a friend kiss, a thank-you-for-nursing-me-back-from-the-flu kiss, 'cause it's impossible for it to be a *real* kiss—but then it goes on, too long to be a thank-you. Too long to be friend-ish.

Also decidedly not friend-ish is the hand he skims underneath my shirt, stroking the skin on my back, or the noise I make when he sucks gently at my lower lip. He pulls back for an instant, so I peek at him from under my eyelashes, and am rewarded with another sleepy, cat-in-the-cream smile.

"Clearly you're good for me—I'm feeling better and better every minute," he whispers, and kisses me again, more intensely this time. Eamon, who I've been daydreaming about for weeks. Is kissing me.

Gorgeously.

God help me. I remember him being a great kisser, but this is unbelievable. Head whirling with incredulous delight, I devour him, sliding a hand into his soft hair. He makes a rich, curling growl of satisfaction deep in his throat and pulls me harder against him. Then, as I shift my head to kiss him even deeper, my necklace clinks softly. The necklace Noah gave me. Right before he told me he wanted to marry me.

"Oh my god! What the hell am I doing?" I gasp, levering myself away from Eamon with trembling elbows.

He knows better than to answer, just watches me with steady brown eyes.

"I have to go. I'm sorry," I say, rolling away from him and flinging back the covers.

He grabs my hand before I can flee to the bathroom with my clothes. "Whoa, come back here. Where are you going?"

I stare down at our joined hands. "This is crazy. We can't do this. I should never have stayed over; what a terrible idea."

"I think it was an excellent idea," he says, grinning boyishly. "In fact I think you should come back here so we can continue celebrating my restored health." He slides his hand up my forearm, and for an instant I think how easy it would be to stuff a pillow over my conscience and lie back down next to him. In ten minutes I'd be making love to him, his lovely skin bare under my hands. But then what?

"Eamon, I have a boyfriend. This can't happen again."

"Yeah, I don't give a shit about him. He's wrong for you anyway."

I blink, speechless at his offhand dismissal of my four years of history with another man. "What could *possibly* make you think you have the right to say that to me?"

"Well," he drawls, "I like-like you. As more than a friend. If we were playing spin the bottle, I'd be hoping the bottle would point to you."

For once, I am not in the mood for his teasing. "Give me a fucking break."

"I'm serious," he says, smile fading. "You're adorable and sexy and hilarious and I can't stop thinking about you." He watches me for a moment as this sinks in, then continues. "I know I had a chance with you years ago, and I won't say I screwed it up, 'cause I think you understand why I couldn't be with you then. But I want that chance now. I want you to be with me."

Wordlessly, I close my eyes. After all this time, I absolutely *cannot* believe he is here, saying these things to me now, offering me exactly what I had once wanted so badly.

And now I can't take it.

I can sense him watching me, but I can't bring myself to look at him again; I'm too scared of what might happen if I do.

"Come on, Mahler, talk to me," he says. "You're freaking me out."

"This is insane," I whisper. "I don't even know where this is coming from."

"Yes you do," he says softly. "It had to be obvious that I was into you." With his left hand, he reaches over my shoulder, his fingertips sparking against the skin of my neck, and scoops my hair forward. His knuckles graze my collarbone as he lets it spill over his palm. "And I don't think I'm crazy for thinking you're into me, too. Come here and kiss me again."

I close my eyes to try to process what I'm feeling. Which is that I am aching for him, all the way down to my bones. It is more complex than the physical desire. All I want to do is wrap my arms around his neck and spend the rest of the day making love to him, looking at him, touching him, laughing with him. Today, and as many other days as I can get. I want it so badly that I'm almost ready to do it now, and deal with Noah, and the consequences, later. Kind, loving, loyal Noah, who I've spent the last four years building a life with, apparently doesn't mean a thing to me when Eamon Roy tells me he wants me. The realization makes my chest constrict with panic, and it is this more than anything that makes me say no.

I make my voice firm, decisive. "I can't."

"Why not?" he says, unfazed.

He knows exactly why not, but I remind him anyway, to drive the point home to both of us. "Because I'm with Noah. Things are . . . tough right now with him gone, but I love him, and I want it to work between us. I need it to."

"Good old Noah. I have to tell you, I really don't get it," he muses, rubbing his thumb across the tender skin on the inside of my elbow.

"What is it that you don't get?" I snit, trying to use anger to marshal my shattered defenses, but he ignores my tone and considers the question.

"What he adds to your life," he says finally. "Why you're with him. I think he's a condescending asshole, frankly. What kind of dickhead tells his girlfriend her job doesn't matter because he makes more money than she does?" He pauses and studies me for a moment before continuing. "You're not in love with him."

"Of course I am," I sputter, queasy at how hollow the words sound. How hollow they feel. "And by the way, he thought *you* were an arrogant prick. I find myself suddenly beginning to agree."

He shakes his head. "You're not in love with him," he says

again. "The way you kissed me just now, that was not a woman who's in love with somebody else."

"I never said I wasn't attracted to you," I mutter grudgingly. "But I shouldn't have kissed you. It was a mistake."

"I think you're hiding behind him," he says.

"Okay, we're done." I jerk my arm free of his grasp. "The last thing I need is psychotherapy from one of my clients." Childishly, I slam the bathroom door and crank the sink faucet on full blast to drown out his response, but he follows me and yanks the door open.

"You're kidding me, right? With the 'client' stuff? After all this, *that's* what I am to you?" He leans against the doorjamb with his arms crossed, scowling.

I scowl back at him from over my toothbrush, then turn my back to spit with as much angry dignity as I can muster. "Of course not! Obviously we're friends. But even if I weren't with Noah, the fact that I work for you would be a damn good reason to avoid getting involved."

"So according to you, you and I are friends and former lovers who, in a temporary lapse in judgment, briefly indulged our mutual physical attraction, which will never happen again."

"I don't know if I would go so far as to call us former lovers, but otherwise, that's exactly right," I say.

"Okay, so, if we weren't lovers, then what do you call it when you spend all night making love with someone?"

"Well if it only happens *once,* then usually they call that a one-night stand, Eamon."

He recoils as if I had slapped him, but I refuse to feel guilty at the hurt that's stamped on his face.

"That's all it was to you?" he says quietly.

"No. But I spent eight years thinking that's all it was to *you,* so forgive me if I haven't adjusted my thinking yet. I can't give you another chance, not now. I'm already with someone else. You and

I are never going to be more than friends." Even as I say the words, grief stabs at me, but I don't back down. "Now, please get out of here so I can change."

"That seems like an excellent reason to stay," he murmurs.

I stab my finger toward the bedroom. "OUT!"

He rolls his eyes ostentatiously but shoves away from the door, leaving me alone. I take longer than necessary to dress, and, when I finally emerge, the bedroom is empty. I find him in the kitchen, rummaging in his fridge for ingredients for one of his disgusting power smoothies.

I have no interest in continuing our discussion, so I stand a safe distance away, in the dining area. "Hey, I'm going to take off," I call, jerking my thumb toward the driveway. "Gotta get home. I'm glad you're feeling better."

"Me too," he says, flipping open the door to his freezer. "Thanks for keeping me company." Without looking at me, he rattles some frozen blueberries into the blender.

For some reason his reserve annoys me. I just spent ten minutes telling him I want nothing to do with him—why am I disappointed that he's decided not to push it? "No problem," I say. "I had fun—" The growl of the blender drowns out the rest of my words. He looked me right in the eyes when he pressed the button.

"Are you serious?" I yell when the motor stops. Noah would *never* pull a trick like that.

"We were done talking. You made that clear."

I don't even bother to swallow my sound of disgust. "God, you can be an asshole."

He tips the blender jug over a drinking glass and slaps the bottom of it, dislodging a mudslide of purple sludge. "Not the first time I've heard it," he says, giving the jug another resounding thump.

"Good," I call without looking at him, as I stomp toward the door. "At least you're consistent." And then, because apparently

Eamon turns me into someone who behaves like this, I slam his front door behind me so hard it rattles.

Fuck, fuck, fuck, fuck, fuck. What am I *doing?* That infuriating scrap just now aside, my schoolgirl infatuation with Eamon has clearly ballooned into something much more serious. What unsettles me most about the whole encounter is not actually the kiss—although my entire body blooms with heat every time I replay it in my mind—but the dense mix of emotions I felt the night before, watching him sleep. Tenderness, protectiveness, desire, affection, and an aching longing to be able to act on those feelings. For him to return them. And then the joy when he told me that, maybe just a little bit, he did.

18

To my relief, Danny isn't home when I get back to the house; right now all I want to do is go for a run to clear my head. As I find the familiar rhythm, my feet striking the sidewalk and springing off in smooth, steady opposition, the panic and tension drain out of me, leaving behind a messy residue of confusion. My thoughts keep snagging on one particular comment Eamon made, about how it should have been obvious that he was into me. Because he's right—it should have been.

I've been lying to myself for weeks: acting like it's no big deal that we can't go two hours without emailing or texting each other; insisting to Nicole that our trip to Round Top and the three-hour Polvo's marathon that followed didn't feel like a date. Pretending that he hasn't been treating me like much more than a friend, because admitting that he was would have meant finding a way to make him stop. When, in fact, all I wanted was more.

Emotional infidelity. It sounds like the topic of an *Oprah* episode—her guest, a woman who's formed a too-close friendship with a male co-worker but keeps telling herself it's okay because "Well, he understands that I'm married, so nothing's going to happen . . ." Except that, in my case, it did. I indulged myself and rationalized myself all the way into Eamon's *bed*, and then still somehow managed to feel surprised when the tension between us ignited.

I'm ashamed and disappointed in myself. Maybe some people would adopt a more laissez-faire attitude toward a little kissing in the middle of an intercontinental relationship, but not me. And certainly not Noah.

Because it wasn't just any kiss. I've been replaying it in my mind the way you hit repeat on a new favorite song. His hands on my skin, his lips teasing mine—it was dazzling. And it wasn't just any guy, it was Eamon. Eamon, who I already fell head over heels for once, back when I was twenty-three. Eamon, who knows better than anybody what it's like to have a goal that you're burning for, because his goal had him practicing butterfly turns in a hospital bed with half the bones in his body broken. Eamon, who I'd rather help roller-paint his ceiling than do just about anything else with *anyone*.

Why, why, *why* couldn't he have decided he wanted a relationship when I wasn't already in one? All those years ago, when there was nothing I wanted more than to be with him? Instead of now, when I've invested four years with somebody else, somebody amazing. Somebody who deserves better than to be replaced like a busted laptop with out-of-date software.

—

A few hours later, I am stretched out on the couch watching a satisfyingly violent zombie movie when Danny stops by on his way out to work.

"Hey, love, what time do you think you'll make an appearance tonight? I'm going to be at Clemmie."

I grunt. "Think I'm staying in tonight, actually."

He blows a raspberry. "Sheesh, what is the matter with you people? I just talked to Ame, he was cranky as hell. Said he wasn't over his flu. Don't tell me he got you sick after you braved his plague-infested household."

Eamon is cranky? Well, golly, that makes two of us. "Nah, I'm just not really in the mood to go out. I'll see you tomorrow."

After he's gone, I can't stop thinking about his parting words. A few hours ago Eamon kissed me, then announced that, now that he's finally gotten around to wanting a relationship with me, he'd really like it a lot if I dumped my boyfriend of four years to be with him. Thus offhandedly obliterating my peace of mind for the foreseeable future. And *he* is cranky? Is he for real?

Before I have a chance to think better of it, I am dialing his number.

He answers, sounding surprised and happy to hear from me. Maybe even, if I'm not reading too much into it, a little hopeful. I abruptly lose all desire to read him the riot act; more than anything, I just feel sad.

"I want to know something," I say quietly, fingering Noah's diamond heart pendant where it rests between my collarbones.

"What's that?"

"Why now? Why did you have to decide you wanted this now, when I'm already with someone? I wanted this so much eight years ago. I liked you *so* much. But you weren't interested then."

"I was, Ree, I told you that. It was just the wrong time."

"It didn't have to be. For me it wasn't. *You* decided that it was. And you decided somebody else was a better option than me."

"Trust me, it was the wrong time. Even if we'd found a way to be together, you would have been miserable. We met when I was in light training, but the rest of the time, I was a robot. Swim, eat, sleep, that's all I did. That's all I cared about. It was all I *could* care about, if I was going to achieve what I wanted to. The only reason Hannah could deal with it was that she was doing the exact same thing. She wanted it as badly as I did, so we could co-exist in that narrow little world. You would have hated it. You would have hated *me*."

"I just wish you'd given us a chance," I tell him, even though I recognize the truth in what he's saying.

"I'm asking for it now." His voice is a low, sexy rumble.

"But now it's impossible. Noah and I have a great relationship. We're planning on getting married. And you're acting like he's nothing, like you and I can just pick up where we left off? It's crazy, Eamon." I press the pendant harder against my skin.

"It's not crazy. This isn't picking up where we left off; this is a thousand times better. We're both grown-ups, and I have all the time in the world to spend with you. And as for Noah, if your relationship was that great, you'd be married already."

My temper flares right up again. "What a stupid thing to say."

"Really? You've been together what, five years?"

"Four. But we weren't ready—"

"You both weren't ready, or you, Sarina, weren't ready?"

"Both of us," I say, even as I think back to Noah's face the night that he gave me the necklace. His sweet, hopeful face, and my plummeting stomach.

"And it doesn't bother him that after four years you still live with a roommate, instead of with him?"

"I like my independence."

"That didn't answer the question. Does it bother him?"

I am silent, stubbornly.

"So it does bother him, but he's decided not to make an issue out of it because it's not worth fighting over."

"What is your point with all this?"

"My point is that I don't buy that your relationship is this amazing thing that you can't give up. You keep telling me how committed to him you are, but I don't see it in your actions. You've postponed living together, you've postponed getting married. . . . I think you've been stalling because deep down you don't really want a life with him. It's time to be honest with yourself about what you want."

"Commitment means choices as well as actions, Eamon." My voice is trembling. "I've chosen to be with him for four years, and I'm choosing it again. It's not going to happen with you and me."

No matter how deeply it digs at me to say it.

—

The next morning, overwhelmed by a wave of missing him—and, also, overwhelmed with contrition—I call Noah. I hate that we've let things between us get so disconnected. If distance is the test of a strong relationship, then we are failing. He is utterly absorbed in his work, and I have been utterly absorbed in mine, in Eamon's project—and in Eamon. I need to revitalize our connection, to remind myself how good we've been together, right from the very beginning.

I open my laptop on my desk, the desk he gave me, so I can try him on Skype first. I need to see him, even if the image is hiccupy. I get lucky; the call connects and he appears on my computer screen, smiling like it's Christmas morning. The rush of pleasure that floods me at the sight of his face reassures me. This is Noah; Noah, who I love. All this stuff with Eamon is nothing—we will be fine. I just have to make it a couple more months.

"Hey, kitten!" he says. "Listen, I'm so sorry for what I said the other day. I was trying to make you feel better, and I—"

"No, *I'm* sorry," I say quickly. "I shouldn't have hung up on you like that, it was childish."

He waves a hand. "I deserved it. So, what're you up to?"

"Not much. I missed you. Just wanted to see your face."

"I miss you too, honey. Whatcha been doing this weekend, anything fun?"

Guilt churns in my belly. I cast about for something, anything, to tell him. "Not a whole lot . . . I watched *Snakes on a Plane*. Did you ever see that? It's freaking hilarious."

He makes a face like I do when somebody tells me I should try organ meat. "Yeah. I saw it on—no joke—a plane. It was terrible."

"Of course it was. Hilariously terrible!" I grin, waiting for him to agree with me, but he just shrugs.

"If you say so."

I refuse to read too much into the fact that he doesn't share my opinion of one Samuel L. Jackson horror-comedy. *Except that he doesn't really share my sense of humor in general*, I suddenly think. How had I never noticed that before?

"What about you, did you get some time off from work yesterday?" I prompt him.

"Yeah, actually. Diego, the lead partner down here, invited a few of us out to his country house for the day. He's got a nice family; his three-year-old was about the cutest thing I've ever seen. She kept hiding behind her mother's legs and peeking out at me when she thought I wasn't looking." He is mentioning the little girl on purpose, I know.

I smile, waiting for the sense of calm, happy inevitability I used to feel whenever I thought about starting a family with Noah. But it doesn't come. I press my hands onto the surface of the desk, and my fingertips leave little smears of dampness.

"I really wish you were here," I say abruptly.

He hears the strain in my voice and frowns. "Me too. You sound upset. Is everything okay with work? Aside from the Balm thing."

Well. Yes, and no. "I'm fine—work is going well. I just really miss you. I'm sorry, I know I sound like a broken record," I say. Suddenly I'm on the verge of crying.

"Ah, honey, I know. I hate it too. Is there any way you can take off enough time to come down here?" he says.

"I can't afford to take another trip right now. Jay's wedding was not cheap."

"Don't worry about that—I'll cover it for you."

Out of nowhere, irritation flashes. "I don't want you to. I want to pay for myself, Noah, I'm a grown-up."

His mouth hangs open. "But you just told me you couldn't afford it."

I press my palms over my face. "I know. I mean, I technically have the money, I just—"

"Sarina, I acknowledge that you're a grown-up. But you're a grown-up who has a budget. Please let me do this for you—I can't let money stop you from coming. And anyway, I was talking about work. Can you take the time?"

I demur without even thinking about it. "I'm right in the thick of it on Eamon's project," I explain, but he interrupts me.

"You've been in the thick of it since March. You can't even leave town for four days? Fly down on Friday and back on Monday. What's the point of working for yourself if you can't take time off when you want to?"

He's absolutely right. Shame scalds me as I recognize the real reason I'm hedging is a reflexive desire to avoid being away from Eamon. But after yesterday, it's obvious that being away from Eamon is the best thing I could possibly do.

—

We decide that I'll come down two weekends from now. Ostensibly, this is to avoid the worst of the last-minute airfare charges, but it also conceals from Eamon the fact that this is a panicked flight back to the arms of the man that I'm supposedly in love with. I skate through the next few days on a sense of giddy relief—the decision to visit Noah has gotten me my equilibrium back, and so far I've been successful in refusing to think about Eamon or the kiss. Things between us have been friendly but neutral all week, neither of us so much as alluding to what happened. But I wait until the Thursday site meeting to mention the trip to Argentina, because I want to watch his reaction.

It is the first time I've seen him since we kissed. I knew better than to think my attraction to him would disappear on command—it certainly hasn't before—but I wasn't prepared for the way it's been amplified. I cannot stop staring at his slim, curving lips, remembering how incredible they felt against mine. I'm hypersensitive to every nuance of his interaction with me. Though he doesn't step one toe over the line I etched out between us, he nonetheless manages to make sure I understand that he wants to.

I wait till the end of the meeting to deliver my news. "Oh, by the way," I say breezily, as if I had merely forgotten to mention it until now, "next weekend is my trip to Buenos Aires. I'll be reachable via email on my phone; the only time I won't be available is while I'm on the plane. But I'll have my laptop with me, too."

Joe gives me a silent thumbs-up, but Eamon kicks at a stray hunk of drywall lying near his foot. "You never mentioned you were going to Buenos Aires."

I make an apologetic noise. "Oh, didn't I? I'm sorry about that, I thought I had. It's not much of a trip; just a quick zip down to visit Noah. I'll be back by next Tuesday. And as I said, I'll be on my phone most of the time."

He nods—there's nothing he can object to in this. But his jaw is tight and something is sparking in his dark eyes. "Well, I hope you have a great time," he says with finely tuned sarcasm.

"Thanks." I drop my notepad into my bag, pretending not to notice. But inside, I am buzzing. He is unmistakably jealous. And, though I'm ashamed to acknowledge it, I love that he is.

19

The shrilling of my phone jogs me awake early Sunday morning. Noah.

"Hey, babe. Everything okay?" I say groggily, pushing myself up on my elbows in bed.

"Nope, not at all," he says, voice like a whip, and I freeze in horror. Somehow, I don't know how, he has found out about the kiss. And I have absolutely no excuse for what I did. Wilting with shame, I wait for him to continue.

"The fucking clients have decided to push up the closing by two weeks. We were already under the gun, but now we are going to have to work literally around the clock to get everything finished in time. And you know what that means."

I am so shocked that his anger is not directed at me that for a moment all I can do is sag back on the bed, limp with relief.

"Sarina?"

"What?"

He huffs an impatient sigh. "It means I'm going to be working nonstop from here on out. Including next weekend."

Next weekend, when we were supposed to be rejuvenating our struggling relationship. Which he doesn't even know is struggling as badly as it is.

"Well, I don't mind. I'll be there when you come home from work."

"I don't think there's any point in you coming anymore." His voice is as bitter as coffee grounds. "It would have been worth it if I could have actually spent the weekend with you, but if I'm just going to be at the office the whole time—it's a waste of time and money."

Tears prick at my eyes. "Are you sure? I just want to see you so badly," I say, trying to keep the panic out of my voice. Somehow seeing him next weekend has become the magic charm that will restore our relationship to health; if I can't hold him and make love to him, I will be doomed to two more months of unease and uncertainty.

But he says no, as I knew he would. He's right; it makes no sense whatsoever for me to go. I know this. But it doesn't make me any less disappointed.

And what upsets me even more is that somewhere in there, underneath the disappointment that I won't get to see Noah, there's relief.

—

I'm wide awake, staring at my ceiling, when I hear Danny get home from work at 2:49 in the morning. I have been waiting for him. I can't go another day without talking to somebody about what's going on, and as Eamon's good friend, he is uniquely qualified to offer insight.

"Danny, I want to bunk with you tonight," I announce.

He glances up from his laptop with a smile. "Come on in, love. Just don't let that cat in; I will only share my bed with humans."

"I always wondered what your minimum standard was." I dig a spot for myself under his blankets and neglected laundry.

"Nice one," he comments without looking at me. "I knew you'd been spending too much time with Eamon Roy."

After a few more minutes, he shuts the computer with a snap, brushes his teeth, and joins me under the covers. We snuggle companionably, side by side. Nerves keep me quiet until I realize he's about to fall asleep, so I just start letting it all spill out of me.

For some reason, first, I fill him in on my day with Anne-Marie a couple weeks back: her kindness, her unexpectedly on-point suggestions, the gray dress I knew instantly was The One. The details on Noah's first marriage. And then finally I work my way around to her comment, the one about me imagining myself walking down the aisle to Noah in the dress.

"That's awesome, Ree Ree. She *should* be excited for him to marry you. Anyone should."

"But that's the thing, though," I say, in a voice so thin I can barely hear myself. "She was imagining it . . . but *I* wasn't."

"Okay . . . but that's not a big deal, right? So you weren't thinking about that exact thing right then—"

I ball his sheets in my sweaty palms. "No, I mean . . . I wasn't thinking about it at all, Danny. I was having a fun girls' day with Anne-Marie, and trying not to miss my mom too much, and thinking about how I couldn't wait to send John the photo of me in the dress. I didn't even realize it until she said that later on, but I spent the whole time kind of just feeling all wedding-y and parent-y and verklempt, and I wasn't—I wasn't really thinking that much about Noah."

He's silent for a moment. Then comes the long *hmmm,* which is ostensibly noncommittal in tone yet is unmistakable Danny-speak for "Houston, we have a problem."

"I knooooow," I whisper. "I don't know what's going on with me. I love him, I truly, truly love him, but it's like every time I try to think about getting married, my mind just goes blank."

"Hmmm."

"And that's not even the worst part," I admit, dreading what his response to the Eamon half of the situation will be.

When I finish the story, he claps his palm to his forehead and says, in an elaborately patient voice, "Okay, clearly there must be something I'm missing. I've been waiting for you two idiots to pull it together for months now. So can you please explain to me what the hell you're doing here in bed with *me*?"

"Aren't you going to yell at me for cheating on Noah? I deserve it."

"Of course you do. But it's already done. And I don't think you would have done it at all if you were happy with him," he adds, more gently.

"I *am* happy."

Danny gives a skeptical grunt. "You used to be. But you haven't been for months, Ree-Ree. Not really."

I sigh. "The distance has been harder than I expected. Much harder."

"Are you sure that's all it is?"

"Yes," I say, because I can't bear to admit aloud that I'm not. "We have some stuff to figure out, but once he's back, we will."

He doesn't *hmmm* again, but I can still hear him thinking it.

"What do you think about us?" I say quietly after a moment. "Me and Noah. I don't mean right now, I mean the whole thing. Before he left."

He takes his time to answer, which means he understands what I am asking him, and he understands why. "I think Noah is a great guy," he says. "Even if he is a yacht-type person." He waits for me to chuckle in acknowledgment before he continues. "You guys always seemed happy, so I never really thought to question it. I mean, the guy clearly adores you. But seeing you with Ame, it's like . . . you come more alive. You're you, just . . . brighter. I've never seen Noah bring that out in you."

"Eamon has that effect on everyone. Even Newman."

"Yeah, and as his friend, it's annoying as shit, let me tell you. But we're talking about *you*. Listen, I'm not the one inside your relationship, or inside your friends-who-urgently-want-benefits thing with Ame. All I can do is tell you what I see from the outside. But to me it looks like you two kids are crazy about each other. So, make of that what you will."

After that, he falls asleep. But I stay awake, thinking. I think about what Eamon said, about me postponing commitment to Noah because I don't truly want it. I know it's not as simple as that . . . and yet. I've always scoffed at women who embroidered elaborate wedding plans before they were even engaged, picking locations and colors and first-dance songs. I took pride in my ungirlie disinterest in all of those trappings of the Wedding Industrial Complex. But now, in the soft darkness with Danny breathing beside me, I wonder if there was more to it than that.

—

I am nursing my third cup of coffee on Monday afternoon when my phone explodes with "Back in Black." I am so tired—specifically from a terrible night's sleep directly attributable to the person who is calling me—that I don't think I am mentally prepared to talk to him right now. I let the phone ring for two seconds, then two more.

That is your client, I scold myself. *It's your own problem if you can't conduct yourself professionally.*

With a deep sigh, I pick up the phone.

The call is brief. He just has a couple of questions about the house. He's been cooler to me since I told him about my trip to Argentina, and, while I should be relieved, the truth is I'm disappointed. It's awfully good to hear his voice.

"Oh hey," he says, as he's about to get off the call, "I can't remember, are you leaving for Argentina Thursday or Friday?"

My eyes flick to the framed picture of me and Noah that sits on my desk. We were at the top of the Eiffel Tower, all of Paris spread out beneath us. My hair was whipping into his face and he caught a hank of it between his teeth, like a pirate with a dagger. I remember thinking, as I beamed into the camera he pointed down at us, *This is how it's supposed to be.*

"Actually, I'm not going anymore."

He waits a beat before replying. "No?" The single syllable is polite, neutral, utterly devoid of intonation. And yet I understand what he is asking as clearly as if he had spoken every word.

"Yeah, Noah had to cancel. His client decided to push up the closing date of their deal, so they're all scrambling to meet the deadline. I'd barely have gotten to spend any time with him, so it wasn't worth it to go all the way down there." *It had nothing to do with you. My relationship is on solid ground. We are not breaking up.*

"That's too bad. Is his job always this intense?" *Does he always blow you off for work?*

"Not usually—this rotation is just extra-tough. Once he's home, the hours won't be nearly as bad. But at least with the deal closing sooner, he'll be home sooner." *Once he gets home, he'll have time for me again. We will shore up the foundation of our relationship, and you will not be able to make any more cracks in it.*

"Good, I'm glad to hear that." *I don't believe you, but I'm not going to push you on it. Not right now. But we are not through with this yet.*

20

After my mom first got sick, when I was eleven years old, I became obsessed with the concept of premonitions. I was convinced that the universe held clues to the future, if only I could figure out how to read them. I became acutely attuned to every cry tossed into the wind by a crow gliding over our house, every movement of the winter-bare branches of the dogwood tree outside my bedroom window. I would observe the phenomena of my daily life, watching for a moment seemingly ordinary, yet imbued with warning of misfortune to come.

But the warning never came. Our lives unraveled slowly; they had already started to fray before we even knew it, before the lump was big enough for her to find (actually, John found it—he told me so, many years later and several beers in, still wondering what if he'd noticed it sooner). And at the end, I didn't need a premonition to tell me she was dying.

I doubt that, even if I had been watching, there would have been any warnings to analyze on the day that I find out about John. It's a sunny, innocent afternoon in early November, the day I was supposed to be flying down to Buenos Aires to see Noah, but instead I am with Eamon, shopping for his sofa in one of the high-end furniture stores downtown. My cell starts ringing, deep in the recesses of my bag, and, fumbling, I almost don't catch it in time. Then I see my stepsister Janet's name on the screen, and my hand starts shaking so hard I can barely hold the phone.

"Sarina?" As soon as I hear her voice, I know it's bad. *Please no, not yet.* John is supposed to live to be a hundred; that was the unspoken deal. Fear is turpentine in my mouth.

"What's happened?" I whisper.

"He's—he's dying," she blurts. She starts babbling, something about a massive brain tumor, just discovered, no symptoms, and bleeding, but I can barely hear her over the roaring in my ears. The phone slips from my sweat-slick fingers and clatters on the wood floor of the showroom, where I stare at it like it's a backwoods copperhead. I will not pick it up. I cannot bear to go on hearing the things that Janet is saying to me, which cannot possibly be true.

Dimly I feel Eamon's arm go around my waist and guide me into a chair. His voice telling me to breathe, breathe. After a minute I realize Eamon is holding the phone to my face with one firm hand and Janet is still talking, saying my name, over and over again.

"Sarina. Sarina? Are you still there?"

I inhale uncertainly and take the phone back from Eamon. "Yeah. Uh. I'm sorry. What were you asking me?"

"I was asking when you can come. His doctor thinks he only has a few days."

This is impossible, and I tell her so. "But I just saw him a few months ago. He was fine. He was *great*."

"I saw him a few *weeks* ago," she says, subtly reminding me that she lives closer, sees him more often, is a better daughter. His real daughter. "The first time I noticed anything wrong was when I talked to him a couple days ago. He seemed out of it. Confused. So I drove down and took him to the hospital and they ran an

MRI. The doctor said it's been there awhile but it's growing very quickly now, and it's too advanced for them to operate. They can't relieve the bleeding"—her voice wobbles, then she forces herself to continue—"the bleeding in his brain. Please, you need to come."

"I don't understand, how can this be happening so quickly?" I can hear panic in my own voice, and little-girl disbelief. As if somehow I had forgotten that people I love are capable of dying.

"We should be grateful. He's not in any pain, he's just so disoriented, it breaks my heart."

I sob at the thought of him weak and confused, his bright blue eyes unfocused, his quick mind blunted. It's unendurable. "I'm coming," I whisper, as much to him as to her. "I'll be on the first flight home. Please . . . please tell him to hang on."

Her voice is tiny and sad. "I will. We'll see you soon."

Numbly, I hang up and set the phone in my lap. I breathe in, then out. It is an unthinkable affront that everything else in the world is exactly the same as it was two minutes ago: the sun is still shining, sifting through the branches of the trees across the street; I'm still sitting here in Urbanspace, surrounded by beautiful furniture that costs three times my monthly rent. The hip Europop music is still piping away in the background.

Eamon is squatting in front of my chair, looking up at me with worried brown eyes.

"John?" he says quietly, and I nod, feeling my face contort as I struggle not to cry. If anything could possibly make this worse, it would be having a meltdown in the middle of a store, in front of a client and a vendor I work with all the time. Not looking at him, I waver to my feet and hurry toward the door. I force myself to take deep breaths as I walk back to the Jeep, focusing on what I'll have to do to prepare for the trip.

When I reach the car I stand perfectly still next to the

passenger-side door, staring at the gold tips on my Allens boots, while I wait for Eamon to catch up to me. I think back to the day John gave them to me, four months ago. Were there any signs I missed? He has been gradually growing more forgetful over the last few years, but that didn't seem like cause for alarm, given his age; we always just joked about him having a "senior moment." How could a deadly tumor have been growing in his brain, and I never noticed anything wrong until it was too late? What about that time he fell out of his chair while we were on the phone? Was his balance failing? Why didn't I tell him to go get checked out?

I press my hands against my face, trying to push back the urge to scream and pound the car with my fists. Histrionics won't help John right now. From what Janet said, nothing will. As I try to tamp down on a rising sob, I choke.

After a moment I feel Eamon's gentle hand on my shoulder. "What happened?"

"Uh, he—he has a brain tumor," I say, not taking my eyes off my boots. I know the compassion I'll see in his face will completely unhinge me. "Apparently it's been there for a while and just hasn't caused any symptoms until now. I have to go home right away. He doesn't have long."

Eamon begins rubbing circles on my back with his hand. "There's nothing they can do?"

"She said no. My stepsister. I hate that I'm not there with him now. I should be, I'm the only thing left of my mother," I mumble. "I have to be there for both of us. I only hope I can make it there before—" My throat locks and I can't finish the sentence.

I hear him whisper, "Come here, baby," and then his arms are wrapped around me so tightly it's as if he's trying to physically absorb this ache that's spilling out of me in ugly, gulping waves. I cry until my breathing is gaspy and hitchy and my throat is hoarse from sobbing. I had forgotten the way grief can just drown you sometimes.

"It's just too soon," I croak, when I can speak. "He's only seventy. He's supposed to be there to see me get married, and spoil the hell out of my kids. He's been accumulating model buildings for years to torture them with. I can't stand him not being there for all of that. I can't handle it."

"He will be there, sweetheart," Eamon says, stroking my hair. "You'll always have him with you, just like you have your mom."

"Oh, that is such a load of shit," I snarl, pulling free of him. "Only somebody who's never lost anyone would say that. People don't hang around like ghosts after they die. I don't have Ouija board conversations with my mother where I ask her for advice and she guides me to the right answer. Believe me, I would give *anything* to feel her presence. For her to haunt me. But she's been dead for ten years and sometimes I can barely remember what her voice sounded like. I have some paintings, and some photographs, and some memories, and those are getting duller—all the time. She's *gone,* and he will be too.

"And *don't* tell me," I rage, suddenly infuriated by his helpless face, "don't you dare tell me that I should be happy that they're going to be together again, because I don't believe a word of it. And John doesn't, either. He's not lying there in that hospital bed, peacefully letting go 'cause he knows he's going to see his Leigh again, Eamon, he's just *sick,* and he's dying, and he's probably scared if he's lucid enough to know what's happening. Sick, and frightened, just like she was. And I need to be there. Fuck, why am I still standing here *talking*?" I slam the flat of my palm against the car window.

"Okay," he says. "Let's go." He unlocks the car and starts the engine.

While he drives, I call Joe, then Jamie, then Danny and Nicole, to let them know what's going on. I feel myself go numb as I answer the same questions, accept the same expressions of sympathy and concern.

After a few minutes of silence, Eamon glances at me, a little hesitant. "Do you need anything? Is Danny going to be around to look after Newman? I can cat-sit him if you need me to."

"No, it's fine, thank you; Danny said he would." I flash him a half smile. "You're just fishing for an excuse to hang out with my cat."

He returns the smile. "That might be true. Well, how about I look for flights while you get ready?"

"That's really nice of you, but you don't have to do that."

"Why not? It might save you some time. It's not like I'm doing anything important today."

Once we get to the house, he doesn't wait for me to give him permission, he just walks me inside and sets up my laptop at the dining table while I head upstairs to get ready. When I return twenty minutes later, changed and packed, he has Newman balanced in his lap as he works on the computer.

I lean over his shoulder to peer at the monitor. "What're you finding?"

"You're booked on a four-thirty to D.C. with United. You change at Dulles and get into Roanoke at eleven."

"Oh, that's perfect," I say gratefully, then pause. "Wait, what do you mean I'm booked?"

"I used my miles," he says. "I put the return flight in for next Friday, but obviously you can change that to whatever you need."

I'm floored. "Thank you, Eamon. I'll pay you back when I—"

He shakes his head. "No way. I'm just glad I could do something useful with them. We better get a move on if you're going to make that four-thirty, though," he says, gently dislodging the cat and getting to his feet.

"We?" I say.

"What, you thought I was just going to put you in a cab? Come on, let's roll." He clicks the laptop shut and loads it into its carrying case.

I blink away my surprise. "Yeah, okay. Just let me get some food out for Newman," I say, heading toward the laundry room.

"I already fed him," he calls after me. "Why do you think he was sitting on my lap instead of yelling at me?"

I glance at Newman, who is sitting on the banquette, washing his belly with one leg over his head, like a tubby ballerina. Eamon drops my duffel onto his shoulder and jingles his keys suggestively. Suddenly I feel like I'm about to cry again.

He steps toward me, cups the back of my neck, and places a gentle kiss on my forehead. "Hey. Tell Newman you'll see him in a few days, and then we gotta go, girl."

Inhaling sharply against the tears, I do as he tells me. Twenty minutes later we are pulling up to the departures concourse. When the car rolls to a stop at the curb, I turn to him.

"I'm sorry I yelled at you before; I know you were just trying to make me feel better."

He waves away my apology. "No, you were right. I didn't know what I was talking about."

"But you were just being kind; I shouldn't have screamed at you."

"You don't have to apologize," he says. "Now, hurry up before you miss your flight."

"Thank you so much for doing this," I say softly.

He touches his knuckles briefly to my cheek. "I wish there were more I could do to help. Have a safe trip. And give me a call when you land so I know you got there okay."

I dig up a smile. "Okay, I will." On impulse, I lean over and kiss him softly, just once. Then I hoist my bags over my shoulder and shut the car door behind me before he has a chance to react.

—

At the gate, I flop down in an almost-empty row of seats, passive-aggressively dumping my bags on one side of me and my jacket on the other. While I wait for the plane to board, I call Noah to give him the news, but, as usual, I just get his voice mail. I hang up without leaving a message. I know it's not his fault—he's working—but I still feel a mounting sense of frustration. It's one thing to have to wait for a late-night callback to discuss the events of an ordinary day, but when the news is that somebody I love is dying, I don't think it's unreasonable to want to be able to talk to him right away.

Suddenly furious, I call him back. "Hey, Noah," I tell his voice mail, "just calling to let you know that I just found out that John is dying, and I'm heading to Virginia. Sorry to leave such a bummer message on your voice mail, but that seems to be the extent of our communication these days, so, there you are. Call me when you get the message, but if I don't answer, it's 'cause I'm on a plane." I click off and stare out the window, watching as one silver jet after another arrows up into the sky. The message will make him feel terrible, and he doesn't deserve it. He has no way of knowing how badly I need him right now. *As opposed to all the other times he didn't pick up when I only* sort of *needed him,* I think, and sigh.

When I board the plane, I hunt in vain for my seat before realizing Eamon has put me in first class. I let the flight attendant shepherd me to my spot, where I burrow into the extra-wide seat. I pick up my iPod and swirl through it to the bluegrass mix that I hardly ever listen to; never listen to, in fact, unless I'm feeling homesick, or it's rainy and cold in Austin. One thing often begets the other. And today the sweet jingling of fiddle and banjo in my ears is taking me home again.

My life in Austin is so distant, in space and in time, from my life in Virginia that it feels like it exists independent of everything that came before—except for the one time a year when I come back for the Christmas concert. John is the last real link left to those first twenty-three years. I can't process the idea that he's dying; he's been the most constant presence throughout my life, aging slowly, almost imperceptibly, solid and immutable as Stonehenge. I cannot bear to imagine what my life would—will—feel like with him gone.

What if I don't get there in time to say goodbye? The doctor said he had a few days, but what if he gets suddenly worse? At one point my mother's doctor thought she'd have six months left; she was gone in less than three. I clutch my armrests and breathe in and out, willing myself to stay calm.

Just before I switch my phone off for the flight, I get a text from Eamon. *Don't worry: he'll wait for you.* I concentrate hard on that thought, willing it to be true, as the ground drops and the plane soars into the air.

21

When I arrive in Roanoke, the airport is still and empty, the only signs of life a janitor vacuuming the carpet and the groggy-eyed attendant who gives me my rental car. As I pull onto the highway I crack the window so the rush of cold night air will keep me awake, then I call Eamon, as I promised I would. I don't even have the heart to return the contrite, frantic message Noah left me while I was on the plane; it's Eamon's voice I want to hear.

He answers right away. "Hey. Are you there?"

"Yeah. I'm here."

"Any update?"

"When I talked to my stepsister at the layover, she said he was about the same; he's been sleeping a lot but he's had moments of being awake and fairly lucid. So that's good. I'm going to crash in Salem where the V.A. hospital is, and head there first thing tomorrow. They wouldn't let me in to see him tonight."

"Well, it sounds like it's good news overall, though. I'm glad."

"Yeah, me too." I'm quiet for a moment. "Eamon . . ." Between the late hour and the memory of his kindness, my voice sounds like a caress, even to my own ears.

"Yeah?" I can tell he hears it too.

"Thank you for today."

"You're welcome." There's a long pause. "I wish I could be there with you."

I didn't realize how much I was wishing the same thing until he says it. I open my mouth to tell him so, but just exhale a sigh. Whatever this is between us, it frightens me. I feel like a skittish cat, inching closer to some unknown shadow and then timidly shying away.

"Thanks," I say finally, and then say good night.

Later, in the hotel bed, I lie stiffly on my back, desperately pushing back sleep. I have the impulse to pray, but knowing John's opinion of those who only bother to talk to God in moments of direst need, I don't. Instead I just listen to the bluegrass music he loves so much, humming along with the melodies as if hearing my own voice in the darkness will make me feel less alone. As if the presence of the music in my ears will somehow, somehow buoy him up from a few miles away. I fall asleep with mandolin and steel guitar notes coursing through my veins.

———

There's a relentless noise drilling into my sleep, buzzing again and again and again. My phone alarm. I swat it without opening my eyes, but after a minute, it rings again. Then my heart crashes against my ribs and my eyes snap open. It's still black inside the hotel room; this is not my alarm. It's a call.

And I know what it means.

When I pick up, Janet is sobbing so hard that she can't speak.

Without a word, I hang up the phone. I drag on my jeans and the thick wool jacket I only ever need in Virginia, and white-knuckle my way to the hospital. The vapor of my breath catches the streetlights as I hurry inside from the parking lot. The woman at the front desk does not want to let me in, as it is still only 6:08 A.M., and visiting hours must be maintained at all costs.

"Please," I say to her. "I won't disturb anyone. Please let me see him."

She heaves a sigh and jerks her head to the left. "Room 216."

Navigating the tunnel-like fluorescent corridors with their linoleum flooring and vague medicinal smell prompts long-buried memories of my mother's illness, but I choke them down and focus on finding John's room. When I walk in, Janet is slumped like a sandbag in a chair next to his bed, holding his hand between hers. Her face is raw and swollen with tears.

My eyes scrape over to him, large and unmoving in the hospital bed. I know, I know, and yet, I can't help looking for the rise and fall of his chest. But the sheets are still.

"What happened?" My voice is an ugly croak in the silence. "I thought you said he was doing a little better."

"He was," she says.

"Then what happened?" I ask.

She gives a defeated little flutter of her hand. "He was just asleep . . . and then he was gone. The doctor said something about the bleeding, and brain function, and . . . I don't know. I don't know," she repeats. "They were sure he would last another couple of days."

"When?" I whisper.

"Just an hour ago. Maybe less. I didn't even know what time it was until I went to call you."

"Did he wake up at all?" I ask, and she shakes her head.

"But yesterday, every time he woke up, I told him you loved him, and you were on your way. He knew you were coming as fast as you could. I guess he just couldn't"—she struggles past tears—"he couldn't hold on."

I want to ask her something. I don't know what I want the answer to be, but I have to ask her anyway. "Did he . . . did he mention my mother at all?"

She gnaws at the side of her lower lip, not taking her eyes off her lap. "Well . . . no. But you have to understand, Sarina," she continues in a rush, "it was so hard for him to speak at all."

I swallow. Death is not the way they show it in the movies, with the dying person holding on just long enough for one last embrace, some final words of love or absolution.

"So, uh . . . the nurse told me they need to have the room back," she says. "Would you like me to leave you alone with him for a little while?"

I nod dumbly. I still can't believe this is a question she is asking, that I have to answer. I do not understand how this room, this night, this emptiness, has become a part of my life.

She leans over, presses a kiss to his hand, and wobbles to her feet. She looks at him again, face crumpling, then wipes her hand across her eyes. "Okay," she whispers. "I'll be down in the cafeteria. Come find me when you're ready."

—

I've never been any good at clearing my mind, the way you're supposed to do for meditation. During my short-lived experiment with yoga (Noah's idea), I would lie on the mat at the end of the class, when you're supposed to be feeling all serene and purified, and my mind would still be racing a million miles an hour, thinking about work, my friends, a student loan bill I had forgotten to mail. But sitting there with John, in that dim, airless room, my brain quiets down until all I am thinking about is what I want to say to him. I don't actually say it, because I don't want to hear the sound of my voice wavering in the empty air; I just close my eyes and, holding his hand, I think it.

I tell him what a wonderful parent he was, and how badly I'm going to miss him. I thank him for giving me my craft, my sense of humor, my love of music, my stubbornness. I thank him for coming into my mother's and my life, giving us love that we didn't even know we needed—in particular, her. Sweet, free-spirited Leigh, who gave her heart to the wrong person at twenty-two, and never expected to find love after that, especially with a young kid in the picture. I thank him for giving her twelve years of happiness, for taking care of her all through her illness, for loving her like gold. For loving me like sunlight. I tell him I love him, again and again, and again.

And then I say it out loud, after all. Wherever my silent thought might be going isn't enough; I need more. With my voice, I tell John I love him, and I imagine the sound waves blossoming out from my throat, shivering through the air, bouncing against the walls and the window, and beyond. Clear and strong, vibrating out to wherever he is. As if maybe he hasn't gone too far yet, and maybe, just maybe, I can still catch him.

There's a tentative knock at the door. A young orderly with bushy red hair pokes his head into the room.

"Miss? I'm so sorry to disturb you, but we're going to need to get the room ready for another patient. We have a lounge down the hallway, if you'd like . . ."

I shake my head. I fight against gravity to stand, pushing my feet down onto the floor. I kiss John's raspy cheek, feeling his whiskers scratch my lips. For the last time.

On a chair in the corner of the room are John's things— personal effects, I believe they call them in situations such as these. The paint-stained jeans he always referred to as dungarees, and one of his favorite wool plaid work shirts. They are folded into a perfectly symmetrical square: Janet must have been desperate to impose order on the one thing in the room she could control.

I gather the shirt in my hands and press it to my face. His scent envelops me: sawdust, gasoline, cinnamon. I try to summon the embrace of his arms around me, but there's only the stagnant air and a brief stutter from the gray overhead light. "I love you with all my heart," I whisper. Then, without looking back at him, I scoop up my jacket and walk out of the room.

—

Janet is waiting for me in the cafeteria so we can discuss "the arrangements." Even though she's only twelve years older than I am, for some reason it strikes me how much she embodies the Everymom—the kind creases at the corners of her eyes, the soft padding of never-lost-the-baby-weight around her midsection. There is even something vaguely reassuring about her optimistically hair-sprayed bangs and limp spiral perm.

She steps toward me uncertainly. She is comfortable to hug.

I hear her sniff once, deeply. "Okay, let's get this over with," she says, and leads the way to a small table by the window.

She draws a large, rumpled manila envelope from her mom handbag and sets it on the Formica tabletop between us. The word "Dad" is written on the upper right corner in her round cursive. From it she pulls a page titled "In case of death," which I find bleakly amusing—it sounds as if death is something that may possibly, but only under certain circumstances, come to pass. The necessities are quickly dispensed with: not being a spiritual man, John had explicitly requested a cremation without a funeral or service. Janet and I agree to organize a wake for him at the Country Store, where his bluegrass band performed every Friday night. I offer to call the Pickers to come and play, and she smiles.

"Yeah, I know he'd like that."

She clears her throat before reaching again into her manila envelope. "Um, he's made the will pretty straightforward." She worries her lip briefly before continuing. "He's just split his savings and investments between the two of us. He named me executor—

I'm sure because it will be easier for me to do from a couple of hours away, as opposed to you—so I'll take care of getting all of that sorted out. I'll send you copies of everything."

I wave my hand dismissively. I may not be close to Janet, but she is honest to the bone; even without seeing any paperwork I know she will give me my share down to the penny.

She digs at the kinks at the base of her neck with one hand and continues without taking her eyes off her papers. "Also, he's left you pretty much everything *in* the house, it looks like. I mean, it was your house. *Is* your house." She is clearly desperate for me to understand that she doesn't resent this, but she would have no reason to; nothing in that house is valuable, and almost all of it dates from his life with my mother, by which time Janet was already living out on her own. The only things I imagine she'd want would be his photo albums, keepsakes, sketchbooks. I'll set aside half of all of those things to give to her.

"Well, let's divvy up his things between us. And let me know if you see any other stuff that you want. I don't know what the hell I'm going to do with it all," I say. "Donate it, I guess."

"He wasn't much of a pack rat," she says. Visibly adjusting to speaking of him as part of the past. Something that was, but isn't anymore.

"No, but my mother was, and he never threw out a single thing of hers." They are both in the past now.

She looks up at me. "Would you like a hand? With all the sorting and packing?"

I open my mouth to say no—a lifelong habit of trying not to be a bother—but instead I say yes. I would love that. And thank you.

She squeezes my forearm. "I thought maybe you would."

"But don't you have to get home to the boys?"

"Hal is with them. I'll have to get back to work after a few days, but I can stay for a while and make some headway on it."

I am unprepared for her kindness. "Thank you, Janet. I really appreciate that. And please, keep anything you want to. Truly."

"Well, let's figure out what else there is to do, and get the heck out of here." Her smile transforms her face into something beautiful and familiar. She is *John's daughter*. From now on, that is always going to matter more than it ever has before.

—

For the rest of the morning, we do easy things that make sense. While Janet drives to Walmart to pick up moving boxes and packing materials, I call the Country Store to arrange for the wake in four days' time. I call the real estate agent that Janet recommended, to find out what I need to do to list the house, which has technically belonged to me since my mother died. Then I call John's friends. As I explain, over and over, what has happened, I can hear my Appalachian accent, which has faded somewhat with time and distance, slipping back into my voice like dye into water. For the next few days, I'm no longer an architect from Austin, I'm just John Kurzweil's stepdaughter. Leigh Mahler's girl. At some point, Noah calls. Then Eamon, half an hour later. I send both of them to voice mail.

Eventually, I can't put it off any longer—I have to go to the house. Janet has been there since noon, setting up zones for all the stuff: my keepers, her keepers, donations, and garbage. As soon as I leave behind the strip malls and stoplights of Roanoke for the winding road down to Floyd, the sight of those sweeping green hillsides is like a fist inside my chest, tugging at the sinews holding my heart and lungs in place. John had asked me to come back here and visit him, so many times. And for every single one of them I had an excuse. I know he understood that it hurt me to be here, but I could have done it, for his sake. I should have done it.

The knowledge that I didn't burns through me like battery acid. I can't imagine a time when I will ever forgive myself for that.

As the car follows the curving gray ribbon of road toward my home, the pull of memory becomes so strong it rivals gravity. The way the woods open onto a meadow, here. That pond at the base of that muddy field, there. The black and brown cows grazing near the water's edge, flicking their tails lazily around their craggy hip bones. This is where I come from. Where I was a child. Where I was part of a family. And after this is over, I'll never see this place again.

—

The farmhouse I grew up in clings to the top of a hillside, at the end of a long, rutted lane that I always dreaded having to drive in the dark. My stomach flops over at the sight of John's battle-worn old truck, parked out front, red Virginia mud still spattered over the wheel wells from the last time he navigated the driveway in the rain. At the thump of my car door, his golden retriever, Maggie, trots out from behind the house, her plumy tail swishing in welcome. Janet's planning to take her home with her when she goes back to Harrisonburg. The truck's going to his best friend, Dave. That's what we're here to do—pack away, redistribute all the leftovers of his life.

Since I only see it once a year, I'm never prepared for how utterly unchanged the house is. The whiskey barrels on the porch, still overgrown with petunias withered by a recent frost (John plants—no, John *planted*—them too). The wide-plank pine floors, smooth with age, that still creak in the exact same spots that they've creaked for at least the last thirty years. I'd tried at one point to convince John to make some sort of a change and paint the shutters a different color—dark blue instead of dark green—but he'd just shrugged.

Inside, my mother is everywhere. There are not many photos of her, but her personality and her memory are still impressed upon every room in the house as clearly as a handprint in concrete. Her artwork covers the walls, her books line the shelves, and her thrift store treasures clutter the surface of every table—all of them chosen for the same quirky beauty she loved to find in the world. We never directly spoke about it, but I know why John couldn't bear to part with any of it—it would have felt like throwing a part of her away.

I find Janet at work in the kitchen, emptying out the cabinets. I dump my coat and bags on the Windsor bench in the hallway, like I used to do every day when I got home from school, and join her. We talk intermittently as we work—her family, my job—but both of us skate around mentioning John directly. At one point she asks me if my boyfriend will be able to get time off to attend the wake. Without even thinking about it, I tell her no. I've been avoiding calling Noah back; I need to let him know what has happened, but the truth is I'm dreading talking to him. Trying to pretend that I feel comforted and sustained by him from five thousand miles away. Right now, I just want to focus on getting this house cleared up so I can head back home.

By the end of the day, we have finished sorting most of the first floor. My shoulders and back are tight and aching by the time I climb the swaybacked stairs to the upper hallway. The door to John's room is closed, for which I am grateful. Janet must not be able to face it, either, because instead of sleeping there, she set up a nest for herself on the couch downstairs.

I cross the hall to the room where I slept as a child. It looks exactly the same: the low, sloping ceiling; the bookcase crammed with peeling paperbacks; the bewitching watercolor portrait my mother painted for me of Anne of Green Gables, my childhood idol. It even smells the same, just like the rest of the house does: stale woodsmoke and old paper and a hint of the Murphy's oil soap we always used to clean the floors. With a tired sigh, I sink down on the creaky twin mattress and pull the scratchy wool blankets over my shoulders. Beyond the open window, the branches of the dogwood tree are black against the moonlit sky. My throat is throbbing with the urge to cry, but I don't give in; I'm already tired of crying, and it's only been two days. I have four more to get through, just in Virginia. And then all of the days back home. I remember how this goes.

Before I fall asleep, I reach for my phone and reread Eamon's last message. *Give me an update when you can. Thinking of you. Wish so much that I could be there.* Before I can think twice, I tell him what I was too scared to say to him the night before: *Wish you were here too.*

22

Birdsong wakes me, easing me into the day almost apologetically. It's just after sunrise and the air is damp and cool, sweetly redolent of dry leaves and woodsmoke. Mist clings to the treetops in the valley beyond the house. The trees are glowing with autumn color, still subdued in the early-morning light, and the lines of the rolling hills, tumbling westward like waves, flood me with affection for my home. Strange to think that the suburban tundra where Eamon grew up is even part of the same state.

I scrub the grit from my eyes and rub my forehead, trying to ease the band of tension that's already tightening there. My heart pirouettes slowly in my chest as I reach for my phone to check what, if anything, Eamon has written in response to my text from last night. But instead of a message from him, there's a send error waiting for me on the screen. Apparently the virtues of the Blue Ridge don't extend to cell reception—my message never got sent. In the bald light of morning, I'm feeling much less courageous. I delete it from my outbox without resending.

—

The next three days meld together into one long blur of packing and sorting, sorting and packing. Janet and I take turns running carloads of donations to the Salvation Army in Christianburg when one of us needs to get out of the house for an hour. Despite my best intentions, the "Sarina" pile in the living room has been growing steadily. I thought I'd only find a few things that I'd want to keep, but I guess I underestimated how many physical objects in this house would have memories clinging to them. Memories I'm frightened I will lose.

Like the tattered patchwork throw cushions that my mother made during one of her sporadic flirtations with sewing—the foam filling is lumpy with age, and they don't work with a single damn thing in my house back home, but I can't let them go. The same story with the goofy hand-painted wooden chicken statue that used to have pride of place on top of the kitchen cabinets, and the battered steel thermos that John used to take with him to job sites. Always filled with a toxic sludge of coffee so strong I could never understand how his feet stayed planted on the ground after he drank it.

And then, before we realize it, we're done. The house is totally cleared out except for the few pieces of furniture I want to leave behind to stage the place for sale—although I know part of it is that I simply can't bear the thought of seeing those rooms utterly vacant and cold. The final thing to get through is the wake, which I have been dreading. The last few days have been, strangely, like a vacation from my grief; with hard work to throw myself into, I haven't had time to sink into it. Packing up John's house has become a project that's almost disconnected from his death. But the wake is going to wreck me. All of his lifelong friends together, sharing stories, making music. I'm going to drown.

The ache in my chest as I drive into town that evening does not bode well. Janet is driving with her husband and kids, who have come down from Harrisonburg for the wake. So I'm by myself, watching the last of the color fade from the early-darkening autumn sky as I drive. I guess when I was packing back in Austin, I must have been refusing to acknowledge that I might have to attend some sort of occasion such as this, because all I packed was jeans; so I'm wearing an old Stevie Nicksesque gypsy skirt of my mother's that I found in a closet, with my Fryes hiding underneath. The fifteen-year-old elastic in the skirt's waistband is shot, so I improvised with safety pins. One of them is digging me in the belly right now.

By the time I reach town, there are no parking spots left anywhere near the Country Store; I have to park at the back of the courthouse lot two blocks away. As I walk, I pass the tidy clapboard house where my high school boyfriend's parents still live. On their porch, a forlorn jack-o'-lantern lists drunkenly to one side. Not unlike the actual boyfriend, the last few times I saw him.

I can hear the rush of noise even before I reach the door to the Country Store; I invited about forty people, but it sounds as if more than twice that number are inside. It sounds as crowded as it is for the usual Friday night concerts. No sooner do I step through the door than I'm swept into a hug from Ellie, the wife of the Pickers' banjo player, John's closest friend, Dave.

"Oh, child, we're going to miss him so much," she says, pulling me against her spare frame. I feel tears like darts behind my eyelids. Was that even a full minute?

"Yeah," I say unsteadily, and she pulls back to look at me, hands on my shoulders.

"Lord, I can never get over how much you look like your mama. Leigh, the spitting image. Isn't that so, Susan?" she adds, addressing another friend of John's who has come to greet me.

I have heard this a thousand times, since even before my mother died. When people would say it to the two of us, she would grin proudly, wrap her arm around my shoulders, and hip-bump me. Then she would deliver her favorite smartass response:

"Yep, I figured out the key to human cloning. She's something, huh?" Everyone always laughed, even if they'd heard the joke before. She was like that. Impossible to resist. Not unlike Eamon in that respect, it suddenly occurs to me. They would have adored each other.

"Oh yes. Same green eyes and everything," says Susan, cupping my cheek.

I drag in a ragged breath, wondering what the ever-loving hell possesses people to say things like that at times like this. Ellie hooks me by the elbow, steers me over to the refreshment table, and presses a mug of spiked cider into my hand with an understanding smile.

"Drink up, my sweet. I promise, it'll help you get through it."

I tip the mug back and down the cider in three long gulps.

—

After a while, I stop trying to hold back the tears. They just keep coming. With every joke, every toast, every piercingly sweet bluegrass tune, John's Dobro parts deliberately left empty. As I look around the familiar pine-planked room, glowing with light and music, I'm so saturated with love and sorrow that I can barely breathe.

By the time I say good night to the last of the guests, my head is throbbing from so much crying. I am shivering on the sidewalk with Janet and her family, trying to delay the moment when I have to go back to the empty house alone.

"Well, that was lovely," I say.

Janet tucks her hands up inside her coat sleeves. "It was. I'm sure he's outraged that he missed it."

"Yeah, it doesn't seem fair to the man, does it, to go and throw him a fantastic party after he can't be there to attend?" I say this, pretending to participate in the fiction that John is, somewhere, drolly put out at being prevented from attending his wake by the minor inconvenience of his own death.

Janet laughs and glances down at her younger son as he does a Pez-dispenser yawn, belatedly remembering to cover his mouth with his hand. She sets a gentle hand on his head. "Well, we better get going. Have to get this crew back home tonight, and it's a pretty long drive. Will you be all right at the house by yourself?"

I make a dismissive gesture. "Of course. Go. Get these boys home before they pass out standing up."

"You know," she says, glancing at her husband, who nods, "we'd love to have you with us for the holidays if you don't have any other plans, of course. Just 'cause Dad is gone doesn't mean you're not still part of our family."

It's like someone wrapped a blanket around my shoulders. "Thank you, Janet. That means a lot to me. I was going to spend Thanksgiving with my boyfriend's family in Dallas, but it would be really nice to be with you guys for Christmas. I think I will."

We share a smile for a moment, then she pulls me in for a hug. "Don't be a stranger, girl."

"I won't. And thank you again for all the help with the house. I couldn't have done it without you."

There is a loud chorus of goodbyes from the boys, and then they pile into their car. The older boy carefully scoots John's dog, Maggie, into the backseat before climbing in after her. The back window is a flurry of waving hands and wagging tail until the car drops out of sight beyond the streetlights.

As I make my way back to the parking lot, the wind scuttles dried leaves across my path, and the sight suddenly fills me with sadness. This will be the last time I'll ever see this street, which I drove or walked on nearly every day of the first eighteen years of my life—tomorrow morning I am starting the long drive back to Austin, with all the last earthly remnants of John's and Leigh's lives heaped in the back of a rented moving van. This was the last time I'll see all of those kind people at the Country Store tonight. Though I've avoided this place for years, it's unexpectedly painful to accept that I'll never have a reason to come back here again. My last reason is gone. From now on it will only exist for me in memories and photographs. And in the occasional homeward turn of my voice, when I get too sleepy. Or too sad.

—

When I unlock the door of the house—for the last time—I immediately begin turning all the lights on. They're supposed to make me less lonely, but somehow they make it worse. Sighing, I turn most of them off again. But the silence is terrible. I turn my iPod's tiny speaker on, set it on the kitchen counter, and open the bottle of wine I found in the cereal cabinet. Inside the refrigerator, only a misshapen lump of cheddar and a few strips of bacon huddle together on the top shelf. I toss them into a pot with some grits—John's favorite dish. I saved them for tonight on purpose; it felt like the right thing.

There is something I have been putting off doing. On our first day of cleaning, I found a big cardboard box, its sides sagging with age, with the words "MY GIRLS" written on top in John's distinctive all-caps handwriting. The flaps on the top were heavily creased, as if they had been opened and refolded many times. From the weight of it, I could tell it contained papers. And I was pretty sure I needed to be by myself to see them.

When I was a kid, my favorite spot in my room was the dormer window that pops through the sloping roofline opposite my bed. John built a window seat for me that spans the width of the niche, and I spent untold hours there, sketching, with my knees bent in front of me and my back resting against the wall. As I got a little older, it became my hideaway for long phone calls with my high school boyfriend. I can still see the lines where I wrote our names together over and over again, practicing my architectural lettering. Predictably, I had to erase it later. But the marks never fully faded.

I heave John's box onto the window seat and angle my desk lamp so that it throws a beam of light across my lap. As soon as I open the box, I smile. They are file folders. Each of them with a year written on the tab, beginning with the year Janet was born. I pull out the ones that date from the years before he met my mother, and set those aside so I can mail them to Janet when I get home. Then, hands trembling, I pull out the folder from the year Leigh Mahler hired him to do some work on her dilapidated old farmhouse.

The wine is bad, and slightly skunky (John was a beer drinker), but the level in the bottle drops steadily as I thumb through the papers, one folder at a time. It is a treasure trove I could never have imagined. There are little scraps from my childhood that had long since sifted out of my memory—sketches, cards, proudly excited postcards from my class trips to Washington and Charlottesville.

But the real jewels are the things that relate to my mom, most of which I've never seen before. Photographs, letters, silly notes they wrote to each other. Poems with rhymes so deliberately stupid that I can almost hear her chiming with laughter as he read them aloud to her. I lose track of time completely as I pore through the box, only taking my eyes away from it to add another item to Janet's pile.

The year I was a junior in high school was a particularly good one for photographs. A regional newspaper decided to do a feature on the burgeoning Floyd bluegrass scene, so they brought a photographer down to shoot one of the Pickers' Friday night concerts. Somehow John must have gotten ahold of the photographer's film and developed some of the best shots. There's one in particular that catches my attention: John and my mother are dancing, and he's pulling her toward him by their clasped hands. She's laughing up into his face as he smiles down at her. At that moment in her life, she had one breast and one jagged scar. Radiation had permanently reddened the skin on her chest and made it difficult for her to raise her right arm. But you would never know it to see the joy that is glowing out of both of them. I've never even seen the photo before, but it is so purely *them* that it feels familiar.

The folders from the more recent years are, somehow, more difficult than I expected. Unbeknownst to me, John had been printing out my emails, especially the ones that related to my work. He had magazine clippings in here, from features on bars and hotels I'd worked on at my old job. There are a couple articles I'd sent him from local Austin blogs that reviewed Albion and Clementine. He even—and I don't know how the hell he figured out how to do it, but he did—he even wrote a Yelp review for Balm, about how pretty the space was. And then, for posterity, he printed the page with all the reviews.

I drop the Yelp page on the box and bow my head as a fresh round of tears swamps me. When it subsides, I smear the moisture off my cheeks and reach for the last folder—this year. It's full of Janet's boys' school photos, emails from her about their progress at piano lessons and baseball. A card they wrote him for his birthday—"Dere Grandpa." A few random emails from me; the postcards I mailed him from Argentina. And then, the floor plan of Eamon's house.

It's so disorienting to be sitting there in my little nook, in Virginia, studying the pattern of those lines I've known by heart for months now, those lines that are guiding a house back home in Austin. But it's not just any house. It's Eamon's.

And then it's like a doorknob I didn't even know I'd been holding in my hand just suddenly turns, and I realize. That photograph of John and my mother felt so familiar because it reminded

me of another one. The one of me and Eamon, at Jay's wedding
reception. Me with my face buried in his shoulder, him with his
head thrown back, both of us helpless with laughter. I'd made
some joke and then he'd flipped it back on me; and I don't even
remember what it was now, but I remember that moment of being
lost in laughter with him and just . . . sparkling with joy.

All of a sudden it is so perfectly clear that I'm in love with
him, that I can't understand how I didn't know it before now. He
means everything to me—absolutely everything. Even these last
few, terrible days, he's been my first thought in the morning, my
last thought at night. Eamon—not Noah.

I think back to the night Noah gave me the necklace, telling
me he wanted to spend the rest of his life with me; and I think
about our talks about kids, about our future. And I feel so hollow
that I'm ashamed. I never intended to mislead him. Every word I
said, I meant at the time; but now I don't understand how I could
ever have thought that what I felt for him was enough. Because
this, this is making my head spin. Emotion is churning inside me
like boiling water.

I have to break up with Noah. Right away. And when I get
home, Eamon will get the chance he asked for. If he still wants it.
I hope—and I think—he does.

—

The old farmhouse sits on the side of a mountain, looking west
across a broad valley, with the waves of the Blue Ridge in the distance. I used to stare at those mountains from the kitchen window
and wonder what lay on the other side. Of course I knew—it was
just West Virginia, followed by Kentucky—but sometimes I'd
send my mind out farther than that, to the unknown, mysterious
west. The land of the dusty cowboy tunes the Pickers would
sometimes mix in with their bluegrass; the land of big sky, stretch-

ing huge and endless over the flat horizon. When John and my mom and I would go on our weekend driving excursions, I used to beg to head southwest, into Tennessee, far enough that it would be flat, that it would actually feel like a different part of the country. But to my dissatisfaction, none of our road trips ever took us to the other side of those mountains.

I remember this as I realize that, for the first time in my life, I'm going to drive over and beyond them. I've made the trip a dozen times before by airplane, but flying isn't the same; this time I'll be driving across the vast expanse of everything in between Virginia and Texas. My two homes.

—

I did not sleep last night. I didn't even want to; I just wanted to think. I thought about how many times during my first six months with Noah I had wished I could pick up the phone to tell my mother about something wonderful he had said or done. Something generous or loving or sweet. Because I finally understood what she had tried to explain to me so many times when I was eye-deep in the morass of my high school relationship, or my college one: kindness only mattered when it came naturally. Not when it was handed out with my vagina as the reward, or my forgiveness for some selfish transgression.

And I thought about how, maybe, the wonder of that had kept me from realizing there could be even more.

And then this morning, strung out on coffee and fatigue, I called Noah. The call went to his voice mail. I decide to try once more before I hit the road, but with the same result. I stare at his contact page on my phone, with my favorite photo of his crinkle-eyed smile. I click it off with a sigh.

And then, that's it.

The van is packed, the place is spotless; there is literally not one thing left to do here except leave. The house, empty of everything except a few pieces of furniture, is so silent that the sound of my breath seems to echo. I push up from my spot on the bottom step of the staircase, and rest my hand on the well-worn wood of the newel post that supports the banister. I already know the shape of it, the texture, by heart, but I relearn it now. I walk to the front door, open it, and lock it behind me. Tears blur my eyes as I walk to the van, and I swipe them away and start the engine. The van bounces down the driveway, lurching from side to side on the uneven terrain. When I reach the bottom of the hill, I pause. Then, with a deep breath, I turn left, toward the highway.

23

By the end of my first day on the road, I've decided that if we ever *had* made it as far as the flat part of Tennessee when I was a kid, I would have been pretty damn disappointed. By the time Route 81 leaves behind the long spine of the Appalachians and turns due west, the terrain bears the same featureless appearance that stretches of interstate almost everywhere in the country share. It might have been anticlimactic once; now, I'm just glad to be on my way home.

That night, I call Eamon from a roadside motel outside Nashville. I think about what it will be like to talk to him, now that I Know. Will he sound different? Will *I* sound different? It feels utterly unbelievable to me that I am on the verge of a relationship with him, so many years after I'd relegated my feelings for him to some sort of childish self-delusion. Except now it'll be better than it could ever have been before. This is not me idolizing the idea of him; this time I am in love with the real thing.

When he answers, his voice is warm as sweet Virginia cider. He asks me if I want to talk about it, or if I'd rather not; but as always with him, I want to. Even though every muscle in my body is screaming with the need to sleep. I tell him everything: Janet's phone call in the middle of the night; making it to the hospital too late; packing up the house; the wake. I lose track of time as I lie there in the overbleached motel sheets, staring at the ugly white popcorn ceiling, cellphone hot against my face as the batteries drain down. I realize, as I talk, that the last six days have been so surreal, so foreign in every way from my normal existence, that I hadn't yet accepted them as part of the narrative of my life. It all just felt like a bizarre performance, featuring someone else in the role of Sarina, while the real me waited in the audience until I could go back to Texas, where everything would be normal again. But telling it to Eamon makes it real. And permanent.

—

Noah calls the next evening, while I am on the road, just east of Memphis. I pull off at the nearest exit and park in the lot of an Exxon, dread heavy inside me like a cinder block. The only time he called yesterday was a ten-minute break between meetings; not enough time for a conversation like this.

"Hey, sweetheart," he says. I can hear an occasional car horn in the background; he likes to walk home from work, even though he's entitled to take a car service; it helps him unwind from the frustrations of his day.

"Where are you, can you talk?"

"Yeah, I just left the office. I'm so sorry I couldn't call you back before this; you wouldn't believe how insane it is around here with this stupid deal. Anyway, how are you doing? I've barely gotten to talk to you. Are you still in Virginia?"

"No, I . . . I'm in Tennessee. I'm driving back." I pause, heart clanging so fast I feel almost out of breath. How the hell am I supposed to open my mouth and say these words that will crush him so badly? "Noah, listen . . . I'm so incredibly sorry to dump this on you over the phone, but it can't wait until we see each other. I've been doing a lot of thinking, and . . . we need to break up."

There is a long, confused pause. "Sarina, what the hell is going on? What are you talking about?"

"I'm sorry, I know it's coming out of nowhere. But I've been thinking about it a lot, and I just . . . This isn't working."

"Wait. I'm still not understanding. *Are you actually breaking up with me?*"

I watch a woman hurry across the parking lot, clothes and skin gray under the glaring lights of the gas station canopy. "I am. I'm so sorry."

He gives an incredulous stutter. "Ree, I know it's been tough with me away for so long, but I'm going to be back in a month and a half. Whatever's bothering you, we can work it out together."

I shake my head sadly even though he can't see me. "That's the thing, though. I don't think we can. I've thought about everything. Everything that's between us. And I just don't think it's going to work."

"What? *Why?*"

"I just . . . these last couple months . . . I've been feeling like things weren't quite right. For a long time I thought it was just the distance, but I think it's more than that. I think we're just not right for each other."

"This is insane," he says. "This is the first time I've heard that you even felt anything was wrong, and you're telling me it's over?"

"Things have not been great for a while. You can't tell me you didn't feel that. But when was the last time we talked long enough to have a conversation about our problems?" I point out.

He sighs. "I know. And I'm sorry. I should have tried harder to make time for you. But I took it for granted that you understood. I just kept thinking that once we made it through this separation, we'd get back on track. I can't believe I didn't realize what a mistake I was making. Especially now, with you losing John. Please, can you try to forgive me for that?"

It's typical of him not to make excuses for himself; one of the things I've always admired about him is his ability to admit when he's wrong. "Honestly, it's not even that. I wish it were that easy to fix."

"So what can I do? How can I fix it?" His voice is frantic with frustration, and the sound chokes my throat with grief. This is a man who already lost one marriage, and now here I am destroying his plans for another. The one he thought was the *right* one.

And yet, I wouldn't be doing him any favors by camouflaging the heart of the problem. "I . . . I don't think you can fix it," I whisper. "I'm just not in love with you the way I should be. I thought I was, but . . . I was wrong."

"I— Wow. I'm literally speechless. Because unfortunately," he continues bitterly, "I wasn't wrong about being in love with *you*. I was planning to *propose* to you when I got home, do you know that? Right at the goddamn airport! I already bought the ring! My god, Sarina, I want you to be my *wife*."

Oh god help me, he does have a ring. Was planning the proposal. I am a monster. "I know. I know you do. And I understand what a tremendous honor and a gift that is. But I think . . . that's one of the things that made me realize. When I thought about it, I didn't feel right, I felt anxious. Which is not how I should be feeling."

"But why? You never seemed anxious before about us getting married. I thought you wanted that. You *told* me you wanted that."

"I thought I did," I say, hating myself. "I truly thought I did."

"You sure acted like you did. My mother even bought you that dress."

Somehow, this is a bigger shock than the ring. "She *did*? Oh god."

"Yeah. The day after she visited you, she went home and ordered it. It's supposed to be ready next month, so she was going to give it to you for Christmas."

"Noah, I'm so sorry. Please tell Anne-Marie I'll pay her back for the dress, I—"

"Stop. Stop talking. Just . . . stop. Look, can we at least not make a final decision on this until I'm home? Give us a chance to get back on solid ground, together. I know you said it's more than the distance, but I don't think you'd be feeling this way if we hadn't had this separation."

I pick at a loose piece of vinyl on the steering wheel as I consider this. What would have happened if Noah had been in Austin these past ten months? If I'd been spending time with him, making love to him, instead of listening to his tired voice from the other side of the equator? "I think it would have taken longer to realize," I say slowly, "but I think we would have ended up in the same place."

"But why? What went wrong? Things were so good between us until I left."

"Things were good. And there's not anything obvious I can point to that went wrong, it just . . . it stopped feeling right."

"Is this because of the thing about kids? And your job?"

"Well . . . that's part of the reason, yeah."

"So why wouldn't you talk to me before you decided to end things?" he demands. "If the alternative is losing you, I will do whatever you want."

"Because I'm not trying to force your hand." I think back to our argument. No matter how many times I tried to brush aside my unease by telling myself we'd find a compromise on the issue, there was one stubborn nugget of hurt that wouldn't budge. "I realized the reason that whole thing upset me so much was it—it made me feel like you didn't even *know* me."

He is silent for a long time. "So, you're breaking up with me because I can't read your mind."

It's really bad if *he* is being sarcastic. I rest my head on the bony steering wheel and close my eyes. "That isn't what I meant, and I think you know it. That is a huge, huge thing not to under-stand about the person you're with."

"But I could just as easily say that about you, and about my feelings on it," he says.

"And if you think that, then it kind of proves my point," I whisper.

He sighs. "Listen, I don't mean this to put down your feelings, but is it possible this has something to do with losing John? It's been less than a week since he passed. You didn't even call me back for the first two days afterward, and now you're calling me up and telling me we're over. You're pretty unsettled emotionally right now."

"I understand why you'd say that," I say, "but the truth is, this whole week, with everything going on . . . it actually clarified for me that we're not right together. I should have felt close to you, even though you couldn't be here. But it just felt all wrong."

"So you're telling me there is nothing I can do to fix this? That you don't want to try to work things out?"

It would be so easy to take it back. To tell him we'll try. To wait and see. Except I know perfectly well it wouldn't make any difference. "No. I'm so sorry."

"You're flushing four years down the drain, just like that?" His voice quivers with hurt.

My silence answers his question.

After a long minute, he speaks again. "Is there somebody else?" he asks in a flat voice.

I am prepared for this. Whatever happens with Eamon, there's no reason to tell Noah about it; it would only hurt him more, and I'm ending the relationship no matter what. So I lie. "There's no one else," I say, amazed I can manage such a whopper with a steady voice.

"Okay," he says, believing me, which makes me feel a hun-dred times worse. Silence stretches long as he struggles to absorb what I've done to him. "I just don't understand. How can this be happening?" His voice is so broken that my throat constricts.

"I'm so sorry," I whisper again, barely able to speak. "I hope we'll be friends, after a while."

"Unlikely," he says. "Well, I guess that's it, then."

"Just for now. Please take good care of yourself, okay?"

"You too," he says, voice wobbling. "Have a safe drive home."

"I will," I say. "Okay." I search for something else to say, to keep the words dripping out of my mouth so each moment that passes doesn't have to mean the end, but then I realize: He's already gone.

Still clutching the phone as if it's a physical link to him, I put my head down on the steering wheel and let the tears go, wailing like an animal. I imagine him resuming his walk through the warm spring night, letting himself into his silent apartment, dropping his keys into their tray on the table by the door. I'm aching, thinking of how much he must be hurting, halfway around the world, and the urge to call him back is overwhelming. But I know, *I know* this was right.

Exhausted, I start the car again and make my way to the Super 8 across from the gas station. For once in my life, I'm not even hungry for dinner; I just lie in a ball in the middle of the bed, unable to think about anything but Noah and how badly I've hurt him. Because at least that's better than thinking of that dark, empty house on the hillside. Or screaming and pounding my fists on the floor like a toddler because neither of the people who lived there is alive to reassure me that crushing the heart of a good, kind man was somehow the right thing to do.

My room is black, except for the rim of light seeping in around the stiff nylon blackout curtain. Now and then I hear the boom of a car door and a scrap of conversation as strangers park outside and make their way to their rooms, scuffing their feet on the concrete sidewalk. I've never felt so desolate and alone.

Not knowing whether I'm trying to ease Noah's pain or my own, I text him. *I'm so, so, so sorry.* I wonder if he's already deleted my name from his phone contacts, so the message will show up as a note from a vaguely familiar-looking but anonymous number. Either way, he doesn't respond.

I'm almost asleep when I realize I never called Eamon today, and I feel a flood of pure need. I have the impulse to punish myself by going to sleep without speaking to him; it's barely been a few hours since I ended things with Noah, and I feel guilty and mean putting in a call to one of the biggest reasons why. But I do it anyway.

The sound of his voice is as soothing as a mug of hot chocolate. He senses right away that I'm upset, so he makes me laugh with stories from when he and his brothers were kids. With only a tiny hint from me, he texts me a photo of the three of them. I stare at it hungrily. Kieran, a rounder-cheeked version of Eamon, is squinting into the camera, bored and pained the way only a seventeen-year-old can look. Colin has a narrow face and heavy glasses, and the beginnings of the kind of bone structure that could drive even a sane woman to paranoia. And Eamon, all of twelve at the time, is already taller than Colin, beaming unselfconsciously around a bristling mouthful of braces.

"You *were* skinny," I laugh, because I can't exactly admit that I'm swooning. "And geez, your poor ginger dad is outnumbered."

"Kieran's girls are reddish-blond. Dad says he's finally getting back at Mom after a generation of genetic dominance."

Eventually, the conversation works its way around to music.

"That's the only thing I hate about road trips," Eamon says. "Being at the mercy of the local radio stations and their six favorite songs."

"Actually, I made a driving mix before I left Floyd. Lots of Angry Country Girl road ballads about kicking that no-good man to the curb and hitting the dusty old highway."

To my surprise, he doesn't laugh. "Does that mean you're kicking *your* man to the curb?"

The question is lightly phrased, but he's not really joking, and he's caught me completely by surprise. My heart bumps from side to side in my chest as one second of silence passes, then another. As soon as I tell him about Noah, all the cards will be on the table. I'll be offering him my heart, to do with as he will. To brush aside again, if he wants to. Eamon places a premium on what is hardest to achieve; what if his interest evaporates as soon as I lose my off-limits status? I need a little time to figure out how to handle this.

"I didn't mean that," I falter.

"Oh," he says softly. "I was thinking it was about time."

In an instant all the blood pulsing through my body is heavier, warmer.

"You can tell me I'm completely out of line," he continues, "but I think you should do that sooner rather than later." It is not a request. He expects me to. But he lets it go, for now.

—

For the next push of the trip, my plan is to get as far as Dallas and stop for the night there, so that I only have a few hours left to go on the final leg the day after. When I finally pass the WELCOME TO TEXAS sign at the state line, with its familiar Lone Star flag, a huge grin breaks across my face. But even though the engine is roaring beneath me as the van devours the miles, it still doesn't feel like I'm getting any closer to Austin.

Eventually I even get tired of my road mix. Somewhere in northeast Texas, my restless shuffling through the radio turns up a local college station. The night DJ is clearly in a mellow mood, as he's playing slow, quiet sixties classics and murmuring sleepily into his microphone between songs. The opening chords of my favorite Simon and Garfunkel song sift through the darkness, and I smile and turn it up. Simon and Garfunkel always remind me of childhood, perched on the cramped backseat of John's ancient pickup truck on our wanderings across the Virginia countryside, listening to him and my mother sing along with the beautiful, beloved songs. He would sing the melody, my mom chiming in with the higher harmony, as I do now, voice confident with long familiarity. "Home," the chorus goes, "where my love lies waiting silently for me . . ."

The song continues, but the words are stalled in my throat. *Eamon. Home.* The promise of seeing him has been drawing me home these last few days, sure as the moon draws the tide.

Suddenly, the idea of stopping for the night is intolerable; all I want to do is crawl into his bed and fall asleep with my arms around him. I'm currently incapable of addressing any of the ramifications of that fact, but there's no question of going home without seeing him. I need to be with him.

He probably will have gone to bed by the time I get there, but he won't be surprised to see me, he'll just give me that heart-melting smile, and open the door to welcome me in. He'll curl his long frame around me, anchor me with an arm over my waist, and this unbearable sadness will start to seep away, just a little. And then in the morning I'll tell him about Noah, and for the first time, there won't be any barriers between us. I know I'm the only one who's fallen in love here, and maybe I'll always be all alone out on that limb, but I can't find enough pride to care anymore.

I pull into his driveway at 2:19 A.M., bleary-eyed with exhaustion but also more relieved than I've ever felt in my life. I hop down from the van, not able to go another minute without pressing my face against his skin.

I'm halfway to his front door when, belatedly, I notice there is another car besides the Jeep parked in the driveway. A sassy little red convertible Miata, with a One Direction sticker slapped un-apologetically on the bumper. A girl's car. At two o'clock in the morning.

Something in the region of my stomach twists viciously, and I stop in the middle of the driveway, buffeted by confusion.

He has a girl over? I've been vibrating with need for him for the last seventy-two hours, and he is—with somebody else?

I cup my forehead, struggling to fight through the wave of nausea back to reason. The thought flutters down like a leaf from above: he and I are not actually in a relationship. As far as he knows, I'm still dating someone else. He hasn't yet been made party to my eleventh-hour revelation.

I know it's true. Of course I do. But acknowledging it doesn't stop jealousy from splintering inside me as my mind conjures a stomach-turning vision of him tangled in his big, white bed with a faceless blonde, his broad back rising as he settles himself above her. What if I hadn't noticed the other car, if I'd gone bounding cluelessly up to his door, expecting to be welcomed with open arms? How does it always go in the movies—guy comes to answer the doorbell, extemporaneously draped in his blanket; Other Woman approaches behind him, concerned, her bare shoulders poking out of the sheet she's wrapped around herself—"Ame, is everything all right?"

Oh, don't mind me, I'm just the idiot who couldn't wait to tell him she was in love with him. Please, carry on.

I picture his discomfort, his dismay, his mingled pity and em-barrassment on my behalf. The face of a good guy stuck in an awkward spot. I hurry back to the van, so scorched with hurt and humiliation I want to peel off my own skin. For all I know, he's been seeing this girl the entire time I've been indulging in day-dreams that he and I were finally going to be together. Maybe there are even others. Eamon, with his rings tattoo and his comet tail of accomplishments, can have anyone and everyone that he wants. Sure, he likes me, but clearly I'm not the only one he likes. And I can't stand not to be.

The first time I met Noah's friends, a few weeks into our relationship, his voice was bright with pride when he introduced me as his girlfriend. Affection curved his fingers against the small of my back. A few days later, he invited himself along to one of my after-work happy hours, for no other reason than he wanted to meet the co-workers he'd heard so many stories about. And as I relayed all of this to Nicole one day over brunch, fizzing like the bubbles in my mimosa, something in her smile told me: I should never have been surprised. This was how it was supposed to be. This was what I *deserved*. Not excuses and mixed signals and "Let's just keep things light." And suddenly, I was mortified by what I had tolerated for so long.

Noah may not be a part of my life any longer, but I will not go back to that place again.

I make the drive to my house on autopilot. There isn't even a light on for me. *So much for that "Home is where Eamon is" nonsense,* I think bitterly as I thump the van into park. Home is where *I* am, where I make it. *And where Newman is,* I amend, as he yawns reproachfully at me from the middle of my bed. At least I've learned one lesson—never to adopt romantic song lyrics for personal significance. Right now the only person waiting silently for me is my fucking cat.

24

For the first four seconds after my alarm explodes in my ears the next morning, everything feels normal. Newman is a warm ball behind my knees, and my body aches with the kind of fatigue that comes from having put it through the wringer at muay thai the day before. Then I remember.

I pull the covers over my face as it all seeps back in, pain pooling in my chest. It's not any less raw in the daylight. I'm home, but John is still gone. And I'm in love with Eamon, who right now is probably getting ready for round three with the Miata girl. He can't sleep in unless he's sick or hungover, I remember, taking pathetic pleasure in knowing such an intimate thing about him. I wonder if that rule still holds when he's been up half the night having sex.

"Ugh, *stop,*" I say aloud. But I can't stop thinking about it, wondering where he met her and what she looks like, this stupid girl who's fucking him on that big, welcoming bed I thought I belonged in.

After I eat, I recruit a grumbling Danny to help me move the Virginia stuff inside. His objections fade once he gets an eyeful of the artwork, though.

"These are more of your mom's?" he asks, gently lifting the Anne of Green Gables portrait from against a stack of boxes.

"Most of them are."

"She was incredibly talented, Ree," he says softly. "Runs in the family, clearly."

It's funny how, when you're upset, the thing that yanks you from holding it together to bawling uncontrollably is a display of compassion from another human being. My face crumples, and the next thing I know, I'm clinging to Danny's solid chest like it's a buoy in the ocean and sobbing into his T-shirt, breath shuddering in and out.

"Oh, sweetie," he sighs, and wraps his arms around me. "Do you want to talk about it?"

I don't want to talk about it. I just want to cry, because it hurts, and crying makes it hurt a little bit less. Danny holds me until the sobs fade to sniffles and I can sort of breathe again.

"I wish there was something I could do to make you feel better," he says after a while.

"It's . . . it's not just that," I confess, and I tell him about the red Miata. When I finish the story, he's frowning.

"So you never told him how you feel? Or that you broke up with Noah?"

"Thank god, no," I say. "I managed to avoid making that much of a fool of myself."

He hooks one hand over the open van door and drums his fingers on the metal. "I think you ought to tell him, love. He asked you to break up with Noah so you could be with him."

"He didn't ask me to, he told me to. And anyway, I don't even know what that means anymore," I say, reaching into the van for the Anne painting. "For all I know 'be with me' means 'be available to have sex with me.'"

Danny grabs an armload of boxes and follows me into the house. "Give me a break. You know him better than that."

"Really? It's not maligning his character to say he might only be interested in something casual. It's just not what I want."

"Right, and I'm telling you it's not what he wants, either." He plops the boxes on the kitchen counter for emphasis. "The boy's a serial monogamist, and he's really into you."

"He's into Red Miata too." *Literally*, I think, and have to resist the urge to gag.

"Look, here is the thing about Eamon," Danny says, then hesitates. "He is such a good soul. He is a fluffy little angel on fluffy angel wings. *Except* for the fact that he's always kind of had a tendency to think with his dick."

My eyebrows shoot up to my hairline. "Danny! *Not* helping!"

"Just listen to me. When he's with someone, there's nobody more loyal. He's never cheated, and I'd bet my ass he never will. But when there's nobody he's made a promise to, well . . ."

"At what point does this clarify my situation?"

"Okay. Take when you met him, for example. He was dating Hannah at the time."

"He actually just *finally* told me that," I grumble. "But he said they weren't exclusive."

"And they weren't," Danny continues as we walk back to the van. "But it was mostly because they lived in two different states, not because they really wanted to be dating other people. At least, she didn't. But even given that, and the fact that he knew damn well he was leaving Austin soon, *and* the fact that you were my roommate, he still went after you."

I clutch my forehead. "So in the current scenario, I am Hannah, and Miata Girl, whoever the hell she is, is me? This is not making me feel better. In fact I'm feeling a hell of a lot of sympathy for Hannah here."

"Nobody is anybody. I'm just telling you he doesn't always think through when to sleep with somebody and when he should keep it in his pants. It doesn't mean he's an operator; it just means he's stupid. Trust me, if I don't know who this girl is, she's nobody important. Why don't you give him the chance to tell you you're the one that he wants? Ooo-hoo-hoo?" He does a little Olivia Newton-John dance move until I glare him into submission.

"Because he won't. If you care about someone this much, you're not going to be sleeping with somebody else at the same time. You wouldn't want to. Especially not while the person you care about is out there in the middle of the night somewhere, and they're hurting and they *need you.*" I swipe angrily at another tear.

If he doesn't care that much about me, I don't *want* to need him. I'm not going to spend my time pining for someone who's never fully there. I did that too many times before. With Eamon, I simply couldn't bear it. And I honestly don't think I can take any more pain right now.

—

Eamon calls me a couple hours later, as I'm unpacking the painted chicken statue from back home.

"Hey, Ree." The intimacy of his voice sets my teeth on edge—how dare he sound so glad to talk to me, when he was with somebody else just a few hours ago? I mean, Christ, has he even changed his sheets? "Where are you right now? When will you be back in town?"

"I'm home," I say shortly. "I got in late last night."

"Oh," he says, sounding taken aback at my tone. "I thought you'd decided to crash for the night along the way."

"Nope, I wound up just coming home." *With one brief but informative stop.*

"Well . . . I know this is a long shot, but do you think you'd feel up to coming out today? I've got tickets to ACL, and Phoenix is playing . . ."

And there it is. Tired as I am, I would love to go stand in a muddy, crowded field with Eamon and eat food truck tacos and watch Phoenix. I would *love* to. But I can't settle for a place in the rotation, not with the way I feel about him.

"No," I say. "I'm exhausted and I just want to chill out here, and get ready for the week."

"That makes sense," he says. "Then how about I bring you some takeout later?"

He has the implacable confidence of a man who has never failed to get a single thing he wanted, and the notion of my own feelings being regarded as so devoid of mystery fuels my hurt and resentment like a kerosene bath. Never mind that I am aching to see him; the fact that it doesn't occur to him that I might blow him off infuriates me.

"No thanks. And I've got a ton of work to get caught up on, so I really have to run."

"No problem," he says, audibly confused by my abruptness. "I'll just see you Thursday at the meeting, then. I'm glad you made it home safe."

When I hang up, only a long-standing policy against destroying expensive objects keeps me from hurling my phone across the room.

—

After an unusually rewarding sparring session at muay thai, I fill the rest of the empty day with settling back in and getting caught up on work. I clean my office, filing samples and wedging magazines into my overcrowded bookshelves; then I organize the landslide of papers on my desk into regimented stacks. I thump the chunky crystal paperweight that Anne-Marie gave me for Christmas two years ago on top of the pile of active stuff for Eamon's job, and banish both to the far left corner.

It occurred to me, when I scrolled past one of her old emoji-peppered texts earlier, that I will probably never talk to Anne-Marie again. Six weeks ago she was welcoming me into her family, and now I have to reimburse her for the wedding dress I will never wear to marry her son. I emailed her this morning, abjectly apologizing, and couldn't repress a deranged little flicker of hope that she would respond with some small word of kindness—*If you really feel that way, then it was never meant to be.* But I'm sure she's as disappointed in me as she was in his ex-wife. God knows she has reason to be.

The last thing I do is replace the photo of Noah and me in Paris, which has held pride of place next to my draftsman's lamp for years, with a picture of John that I dug out from his memory box. I haven't heard from Noah since our conversation the other night, which doesn't surprise me—he's too proud to keep trying to talk his way out of a breakup. What does surprise me is how badly I miss him. When I check my email before bed, I see his name in my chat contacts, with the little green dot that means he's online. All I have to do is click on his name and write something. And then he will write something back. And then maybe, just for a minute, I will feel a little less alone. I want to tell him, again, how sorry I am, but I know it's meaningless. He doesn't want me to be sorry, he wants me to love him. Just like I want Eamon to love me.

—

Surprisingly, I barely hear from Eamon all week. I am relieved, until it occurs to me that he is undoubtedly respecting my heavy workload—the one thing I wasn't lying to him about—and, furthermore, being considerate of the fact that I have just lost a family member. Mercifully, at the site meeting on Thursday, Joe runs through the project status quickly and efficiently. Throughout the meeting, I sense Eamon watching me, so I avoid his eyes. But he catches up to me as I'm about to get into my car.

"Hey, wait up a minute. I've been wanting to talk to you."

My heart spins. "What about?"

He jams his hands into his jeans pockets. "Just wanted to check in on you. How've you been doing?"

He means because of John. Of course. "Okay, I guess. It helps to be back at work. I've got his favorite thermos with me now," I add with a half smile, waving it in one hand.

He studies the sturdy shape of it and smiles. "Yeah, that looks like him." After a pause, he continues. "And how's Noah?" His voice is neutral as paint primer.

Noah is miserable, I think. *Due in large part to you.* This is my opportunity to tell him what happened—not even the why and how, but to succinctly let him know, as I would if it were anyone else asking the question, that my relationship with the person he is inquiring about is over. And yet, I don't. I don't even want to open that can of worms, don't want him to suspect that he had something to do with it. Don't want him to start asking me out on dates for nights when he isn't already busy screwing the owner of the red Miata.

"He's fine," I say. "He'll be back in a little over a month."

He nods. "That will be good."

"Yeah," I say, although I know it will be anything but good. Though Noah has been silent so far, I think once he's home he will probably want to see me, to talk about things in person. It is going to be painful for both of us. I know I'll be tempted to give things another try, just to take his pain away—but I can't give in to it. Not when I know it would only be kicking this can a little farther on down the road.

That afternoon, my client Jamie's friend with the retail store does, in fact, call to ask about working with me, and he does, in fact, have no budget. But I'm so grateful for something to work on besides Eamon's house and the Balm expansion that I lowball my contract so he can afford me. When I call Jamie to thank her for the referral, I inquire—out of both politeness and morbid curiosity—how things are going with the plans for Dallas and Houston.

"Not so great," she confesses glumly. "This guy we hired is a bit of a prima donna. He keeps getting hung up on 'architectural purity.' I keep telling him, 'Yes, but people have to use this space, and work in this space, and I have to make money in this space,' but he just spins his wheels over all these details that don't matter to me. Like, there's a row of huge columns that runs along the north wall in the Dallas space, and he can't stand the sight of them. So instead of just encasing each one individually, he wants to run a clean sheetrock wall all the way across the front of them."

I remember those columns. They were cool old concrete pillars, and I'd wanted to leave them exposed. "But wouldn't that take away like eighteen inches of depth from the treatment rooms?"

"Why yes, madam, it would. And when I pointed that out to him, he acted like I was some clueless yokel. 'Well, if you insist, we can do it,'" she intones, mimicking Roger's pretentious drawl, "'but the aesthetics are not optimal.' Well excuse me, princess, but shrinking my treatment rooms by a foot and a half is not optimal, either, so wrap the damn columns. Ugh! He gets on my nerves!"

Yep, that sounds about right for Roger Harris. "That sucks."

"Girl, I really wish we had hired you. This guy—not only is he a diva but his best ideas are just recycled from what you did at

Cesar Chavez. Ah well," she sighs, "you win some and you lose some. We'll get back on track. I'm just glad you nailed this store job—you deserve it."

"Thanks again, Jamie. I hope things get better with your planning," I say, and it's the truth. Just because I was crushed not to get the job doesn't mean I'm pleased to hear things aren't going well for her. I'm not *surprised,* but I'm not glad, either.

—

The rest of November evaporates before I even know it. As I always have when my life gets shaken out of my control, I seek comfort in routine. Get up, coffee, run, more coffee, work, lunch, work, dinner. Muay thai Tuesdays, Thursdays, Sundays. Dinner at Albion on Fridays; boozing at Clementine on Saturdays. I go on a binge of making plans with all of the friends I haven't seen in a while; if I stay busy enough, maybe I won't notice the emptiness where John's funny little emails and notes should be. The silence where his weekly phone calls should be.

At one point, my Realtor calls from Virginia to advise me that I have an offer just below asking price on the house. Without hesitating, I direct her to accept it and move to contract. Technically I could keep the house if I wanted—it's been in our family for ages, so all I'd be responsible for is the property taxes, which for one year are only slightly more than I pay to Danny in rent each month. I could probably even lease it out for a modest amount. But keeping it would be foolish and sentimental; I need a nineteenth-century farmhouse in southwest Virginia like I need a broken spine. And I can use the money from the sale to invest in a better website, some real business cards, maybe even a PR person to try to drum up some more business. Selling the house is the only thing that makes sense. Which does nothing in the world to stop me from sobbing until my throat aches the night I send back the signed contract.

—

For my first few years in Austin, I used to spend Thanksgiving at Danny's parents' place in the suburbs, until things got serious with Noah. However, since I am quite certainly no longer invited to the Harlow family dinner, Danny's folks are saddled with me again. Yesterday's mail included a small envelope in luxuriously heavy cotton paper with the initials "A.H.S." embossed on the flap—the H larger, the way it's done on proper monograms. The only thing inside was the check I had sent Anne-Marie for the wedding-dress-that-wasn't. No note, just the money. Rejected along with my apology and my regret.

As soon as I arrive at Danny's parents' place, and his mother wraps me in a hug that lasts a good couple of seconds longer than usual, I know he's told them about me losing John. They're going to be on Bereavement Watch all weekend, ready to spring into action at the slightest sign of a sniffle. What sort of action, I don't know—and I'm sure they don't, either—but a quick look around at their sympathetic faces confirms that they are all on red alert. It's going to be the spring of my junior year all over again.

To show everyone that I am, actually, completely fine, I throw myself into holiday heartiness, making a nuisance of myself in Danny's mother's overheated kitchen until she banishes me to the living room. Danny's dad and I play armchair quarterback throughout the endless stream of football on TV. As we scrape our chairs under the table for dinner, I utter a mental plea that nobody will initiate a round of Things We Are Thankful For—while there is no doubt that I have a great deal to be thankful for, I'm not really in the mood to celebrate it these days.

Instead, though, Danny's dad takes his wife's and his daughter's hands. The rest of us follow suit, glancing at each other in silent surprise; a formal grace isn't usually their family's style.

"Well, since we're all gathered together here, I figured I might as well say a few words," Danny's dad begins solemnly. He pauses for a moment to gather his thoughts. Then his face cracks in a smile. "Rub-a-dub-dub, thanks for the grub!"

I hear Danny's quiet, urgent "Dad!" and then everyone else's laughter goes blurry around me as I stumble blindly from the table and toward the front door. I fold down onto the stoop, bury my head in the warm darkness between my knees, and rock back and forth. But the tears won't stop, even when Danny sits down next to me and silently wraps his arm around my shoulders.

It was John's grace. One of his silly jokes that he would deliver at the dinner table before our holiday meals, always with the same sly, shit-eating grin. The first few times, my mother tried shaming him with a stern glare, but he would just grin right back at her until her lips started twitching, and after a minute she'd give up the fight, her shoulders shaking with laughter.

"Ree-Ree, I'm sorry," whispers Danny. "I told him about that so long ago, he must have forgotten it came from John."

"It's not your fault," I sob. "I just miss him so much. I miss them both so much."

Danny shifts slightly so he can get both arms around me. We sit like that for a long time, until he finally pulls away.

"Hey, you're shivering," he says gently. "You ready to come inside?"

"In a minute."

He nods, straightens, and walks back inside, pulling the door shut softly behind him so I'm alone again.

This is one of the shittiest parts of grief, right here. The absolute futility of it. The way that no matter how much you feel, there's nowhere for it to go. It's not like a noise you can dial down or turn off—it just squeezes you. And when it's squeezing, all you can do is cry from the pain. And then wipe your stupid face and keep walking. Nothing changes. Nothing suddenly heals. You never actually get to feel *better*—you just get to stop crying. I don't know how one force of emotion can be at once so sharp, so ragged with splintered edges that pierce and rip, and yet also so blunt and blank and immutable.

I suck the cool air into my lungs and tug my sweatshirt tighter around me. I'm not quite ready to endure Danny's family's pity and embarrassment. But I need to try to ease away this desolation.

Halfheartedly, I cycle through the contacts in my phone, but all of my friends are going to be with their families, gorging themselves on pie and falling asleep on the couch. I pause at Eamon's name. He's at home, in Virginia. Eating the turkey he told me his mother always manages to overcook, and the baklava she laboriously makes for her boys every time they come home.

I try to imagine his parents' house—a split-level in a modest neighborhood, with twenty-year-old wall-to-wall carpeting and a brick fireplace that doesn't quite draw properly. Does his bedroom still look exactly the way it did when he left for college? I picture a wall festooned with his teenage achievements, national and NCAA medals pinned to the drywall with humble thumbtacks. A couple pieces of art he snagged from a flea market, maybe some photos from their family trip to Lebanon when he was seventeen. I doubt there's a single detail he's ever shared about himself that I don't remember.

I can't call Eamon. Nothing says "inappropriate romantic feelings" like a phone call on a sentimental family holiday. I think back to a few weeks ago, when we were constantly in touch, all day, every day; to that last night on my trip home, when I was arguing about the all-time best Stevie Wonder song with him late at night in a Super 8 motel room, with a dopey, infatuated smile on my face. Before my rude awakening arrived in the form of an entry-level sports car.

I know who I want to call. I'm sure he's been in the office all day—in Argentina, it's just another Thursday. But I can't call him, either.

My ex-boyfriend from college would call me, for months after he'd tossed away my heart like a deflated kickball, whenever he was lonely and feeling sorry for himself. He would ramble on about his problems with his family, and I would listen and sympathize and proffer advice that he never, ever listened to. He would tell me how good it was to hear my voice, and how much he missed me; a few times, we met up for drinks and wound up making out on his sofa while Billie Holiday played softly in the background. Until eventually I figured out that he had absolutely no interest in a relationship with me; all he wanted was attention in the intervals when there was nobody better in the picture. I'm not going to play that game with Noah.

Sighing, I shove myself to my feet and go back inside. Everyone in the living room wears an identical expression of nervous concern.

"I'm sorry to run out on dinner like that, you guys. I hope you all went ahead and ate?"

Danny's dad flips off the noise of the football game, immediately making me wish he'd left it on. "Of course we waited. Sweetheart, I apologize for my tactlessness—I forgot that that particular gem was a favorite of your stepdad's."

I tell him no apology is needed. Instead of reconvening at the dining table—the holiday mood being effectively shattered—we decide to eat in the living room, plates balanced on our laps. They try to distract me with stories and laughter, and I'm happy to let them. It is perfectly pleasant, but despite their generous hospitality I feel more like an outsider than I ever have before at their home. When I go to Janet's for Christmas in a few weeks, it will feel the same, I know. I wonder if I will ever have a family to belong to again.

25

It used to be that the holiday season, with its relentless avalanche of commercials featuring kindly grandparents and tender mom-and-daughter moments, drove me to wrap myself in a brittle cocoon of rage until the first week of January. But when Danny, Jay, and I opened Albion three Decembers ago, I discovered a far more effective means of fighting back against the beast: throwing a kickass party. And we've been doing it every year since.

We've spent the last week frantically whipping together the details, and, as the last few hours slip past before the guests begin to arrive, my skin starts humming with excitement. I am unaccustomedly fancy in teetery stilettos and a clingy black shirtdress ("Quit tugging at it, dumbass, it's supposed to be that tight" was Nicole's helpful contribution). Eamon is going to be at the party; I have to look good, as a point of pride.

Guests start pouring in as soon as the clock hits 8:00, and for a while I forget to look out for him as I get caught up in the swirl of greetings and conversation. A few of Danny's other Longhorn buddies arrive, including a blond giant named Brody, who gives me a frankly appraising smile that I fleetingly wish I were in a mental state to respond to. When Eamon still hasn't arrived by 9:30, I grab Danny as he zooms past to check if he's heard from him, but he just flashes no-idea hands, not even pausing in his stride. Then, a few minutes later, I finally spot him, half a head above everyone else, elegant in a tailored suit, picking his way through the crowd. Carefully leading a beautiful African American girl by the hand.

From her imposing height and defined upper back, I know her right away for another swimmer. As I gape at her, I realize I remember her from TV, that she was a member of the Olympic team. And, of course, his ex-girlfriend. *The* ex-girlfriend, the one he left Austin for. The one he picked over me . . . Hannah. Why is she even in town? Was I right that he wanted them to get back together? My jaw tightens with resentment.

Danny materializes next to me and touches my arm, frowning with concern. "Love, you okay?"

There's no point attempting to fool him. "Who is that?" I snap.

"That's his ex, Hannah," he confirms. "They broke up a couple years ago, but . . ." His voice trails off uncertainly.

"But he doesn't always think through when to sleep with somebody, and when he should keep it in his pants," I recite grimly.

I watch them stop to greet Jay and Dominic, chatting animatedly. They don't look like two people who are broken up. Granted, they're not groping each other, but there's an unmistakable air of comfortable affection between them. And she is a *knockout:* her lean figure is poured into a turquoise sheath dress that shows off her toned limbs and wenge-brown skin. She carries herself with the kind of effortless grace that I could never fake, even if I knew how, the kind of grace that characterizes Eamon's every movement. Together they look like royalty.

Well, what is that old cliché? The best defense is a good offense? I square my shoulders and head toward them, pasting a welcoming smile on my face. I manage to give Eamon a cool, perfunctory cheek kiss, though my fingers tighten reflexively on his arm as my lips touch his skin. I fight down a wave of heat as I inhale the scent of his freshly washed hair, and extend a friendly hand to Hannah.

"Hi, I'm Eamon's architect, Sarina," I say, trying not to gape at her. She is even more striking up close, with pronounced cheekbones and luminous eyes the color of sherry. Unlike some tall women, she doesn't try to minimize her height; she's rocking glossy black pumps that put her unapologetically over six feet.

"Of course! So nice to meet you, Sarina. I'm Hannah," she says. Her smile, like her handshake, is warm and self-assured. "Eamon tells me you designed this restaurant as well? You did a wonderful job; it's beautiful."

"Thank you! So, are you visiting from out of town?"

"I am, yeah. I live in Berkeley, but I figured I was due for a visit. Ame's been trying to get me to come for months."

Oh, he has, has he? I don't trust myself to look at him, so I just hitch my smile a little higher. "Has he taken you to see the house yet?"

"No, now that you mention it, he hasn't!" She swats him playfully. "What's the matter with you? Why haven't you taken me to see the house?"

He holds up a warding hand. "There isn't much to see," he explains. "It's just a construction site."

Though I know he's right—construction sites are never interesting to anyone except the architects responsible for them—his dismissiveness still stings. After all, he owes every last nail gun and sawhorse of that construction to me.

"Oh, I don't know, I bet Hannah would at least like to see the site. She can admire the hole in the ground where the pool is going to go." I turn to her, smiling. "Thanks to this project, I now know the exact dimensions of a short-course pool."

She gives a cute little hop. "Yeah, I can't wait to see it! Let's go tomorrow, Ame." I can't tell if she's just curious, or if she's eager to see the home where she will eventually be living. She's so beautiful that I feel like a dandelion next to the blazing glory of a tiger lily. Faced with the caliber of woman he will give his heart to, I feel foolish all over again for ever having thought he could be serious about me.

Eamon smiles at her with long-standing, affectionate indulgence. I know that smile; Noah used to give me that smile every time I got hungry two hours after a meal. It only took three weeks of dating me before he started stocking his glove compartment with Clif bars to ward off my hunger attacks. I miss having somebody to look out for me in those wonderful, knowing little ways.

—

Around one in the morning, I'm in the bathroom, mouth agape in the awkward rictus of lipstick application, when Hannah walks in. A flash of memory hits me from nowhere—didn't Eamon have an I Never story about sex in a public bathroom? Odds have to be good that that was with Hannah. My imagination quickly sketches a few details: their intertwined hands, pressed against the wall; his mouth against her arched throat. Jealousy slams into me like a rough wave at the beach, almost knocking me off my feet.

"Sarina, this is such a fun party," she says from inside the stall, innocently unaware of the storm of white-hot envy that's seething inside me. "I'm having a blast."

"I'm so pleased," I say from behind gritted teeth, struggling to regain my equilibrium as I put my lipstick away with shaking hands. But as she keeps talking, babbling about the food and the cocktails, I can't help being amused that the elegant Hannah Gordon is not above chatting midstream with a near stranger. She's undoubtedly spent way too much time in locker rooms to have any modesty left—I bet she's also the girl standing in the communal dressing room at Loehmann's in nothing but a thong, dispensing kindly advice on fit between her own costume changes.

"I don't really want to leave, but Ame's been a cranky little brat all night, and I can't deal with him anymore," she says, exiting the stall and coming to wash her hands at the counter next to me. "Though I guess I could just send him home in a cab," she adds, hiking a conspiratorial eyebrow at me in the mirror. "Maybe then I'd actually get Brody Gilsik to come near me."

My surprise must be splashed all over my face, because she stops toweling her hands and stares at me. "Oh, you didn't think . . . oh! Noooo, no, no, no. There's nothing going on with us. We were together for a long time, but we're just friends now." She narrows her eyes and cocks her head to the side, rather like a tall and beautiful bird. "Oh no. That boy is such an ass."

"What?"

"He didn't tell you that I was going to be visiting this weekend? Or that he was bringing me to the party?"

I cross my arms over my waist. "Not a word."

She flicks open her handbag and digs around for her own lipstick. "Oh, for god's sake. I hope you don't mind that he told me, but I got the recap on your whole situation with your boyfriend. Ame won't admit it, but it's obviously driving him insane. So, he brought me to this party to give you some of your own medicine."

"You really think so?"

"No doubt about it. I think he wanted to see how you'd react. He wanted to see if he could make you jealous. And instead of being a bitch to me all night like he would if it were him, you've been ignoring him. Which of course is killing him. And he deserves it, the little shit," she adds, exasperation and affection mingled in her voice. I feel another twist of jealousy, that she's known him long enough and well enough to blow him off with an epithet I usually reserve for my misbehaving cat.

I digest this in silence as she smoothly swipes a deep plum stain onto her mouth. "Is it driving him insane because he likes me, or because he can't stand not to win?" I hate throwing myself on her mercy like this—the girl he picked, who knows him so much better than I do—but I can't seem to help it. Apparently I need her help figuring out what's going on here.

"He *really* hates to lose," she concedes, snapping the lipstick shut, "but if he weren't into you he wouldn't care. I slept with another one of our teammates right after we broke up, and he didn't bat one pretty eyelash. That's how I knew it was really over." Her tone is matter-of-fact, not bitter, and I'm grateful to her for her self-deprecating honesty.

"Well, it worked," I admit, repaying her in kind. "I've been jealous as hell of you all night."

She shakes her head ruefully. "He's a total pain in the ass sometimes, but he's all heart. You just have to call him on his bullshit."

I want to ask why they broke up, if he still means so much to her, but the door bangs open, admitting two drunk, giggling girls wobbling on platform heels, and the blast of music shatters the confessional mood.

"Well, shall we?" I say, gesturing to the door.

She dips a curtsy, then swings the heavy door open as if it were made of cardboard. She might not be able to land a high roundhouse kick, but the girl could damn sure hold her own in a fistfight.

City code forces the party to shut down an hour later, but Danny, undeterred, announces an after-party at our house for the truly dedicated. Which, of course, means only the usual suspects: Nicole, Chris, Jay, and Dominic.

"Ame, Hannah, what's your status?" demands Danny, waving a bottle of Albion's house red in each hand.

They exchange an awkward look. "I'm pretty pooped, so

Brody's going to give me a ride back to you guys' place," says Hannah. I take in the gorgeous specimen standing behind her— somehow I have the distinct feeling that she's not going back to Eamon's tonight. Damn, the girl works fast.

"Mm-hmm," says Danny.

"So, I guess I'll head over to Casa James for a while," says Eamon. I feel a little bubble of mingled pleasure and anxiety. Did Hannah say something to him?

"Mm-hmm," says Danny again. "Well, whoever's coming, let's roll out. The party bus is leaving."

However, once we get home, it turns out that the other four have lost their mojo on the ride over; they stay for one last toast to Albion before heading back to their respective homes. After they leave, Eamon, Danny, and I keep drinking, finishing the first bottle of wine and ambitiously opening another. I pace myself, having learned from painful experience the effect of too much red wine on my system, but Danny, aglow with holiday bonhomie, is sucking down the alcohol like water. Eventually he totters to his feet, one hand clamped onto the table and the other pressed uncertainly to his stomach.

"Uh-oh," he moans. "You guys are kind of"—he makes a vague circular motion in the air with his index finger—"swirly."

"That's one thing I've never been called before," mutters Eamon as he rises and circles the table toward Danny. "Come on, man, better let me help you."

"Fuck off," grunts Danny, but he doesn't resist as Eamon tugs his arm over his shoulders and maneuvers him toward the stairs. I don't envy him the task; Danny is almost as big as Eamon is, and if he stops moving under his own volition it could get a little hairy on the stairs. I decide to follow behind in case of emergency.

Eamon glances at me over Danny's shoulder and shakes his head. "I've got him, Ree. Besides, if we go down, I don't exactly think you're stopping us."

He has a point. I return to my seat and wait, cringing at one point when I hear a shattering bang from upstairs. Before I can get up to see what's wrong, Eamon's voice calls down to me.

"It's okay, Ree. Collateral damage."

He's grinning when he reappears. "Well, he's down for the count."

"What the hell was that noise?"

"He tripped over a lamp cord I didn't see. He's fine. The lamp, not so much."

"Poor Danny," I say, shaking my head affectionately. "I have never met someone so big who's such a failure at holding his booze. Was he always this bad?"

Eamon pulls a disgusted face. "Appalling. Every time we had a party, we used to set up an over-under on what time Danny would pass out, and how many drinks it would take to get him there. I usually won," he adds, all teeth.

"Of course you did."

"But, hey, no reason to pack it in, right? The night is young." He tops off our wineglasses and settles back on the banquette, stretching his long legs out across the seat.

"No reason at all," I say.

He clinks his glass gently against mine. "Sláinte, Miss Mahler," he drawls in what can only be his grandfather's broad Irish accent.

My heart flips like a doomed fish.

26

I've always been convinced that time actually slows down in the middle hours of the night; that the minute hand creeps around the hours of three and four and five just a little more slowly, before speeding up again to blaze recklessly through the period between six and nine. As Eamon and I sit there, talking late into the night, with the homey glow of the Christmas tree the only light in the house, the wine sends tendrils of dreamy warmth curling through my body. I'm flushed from the pleasure of spending so much time with him after my self-imposed moratorium.

Which appears, against the odds, to have worked; despite what Hannah said about him being jealous of Noah, he's been perfectly happy just to sit with me and talk. Who knows, maybe he's gotten serious with Red Miata? I ought to be glad. This late at night, though, when every object around me somehow seems a little softer and more transparent, I'm not capable of pretending that I am.

After a long time, a lull falls in our conversation. The kind of peaceful, natural lull that comes in any good talk. The kind of lull where, if it's late at night, you get to your feet, and stretch, and announce that you are bound for bed.

Neither of us moves. He looks rumpled and half-asleep over

on the banquette; the only sign he's still awake is his right hand, which is idly twisting his wineglass on the table, making the brilliant liquid swirl in the goblet. Heat blooms through me as I watch the flex of his fingers and wrist. I imagine pulling the glass from his hand, leaning forward, tracing the pattern of his tattoo with my tongue.

I'd stopped noticing my Christmas mix playing softly in the background, but when I hear Nat King Cole croon "Chestnuts roasting on an open fire" for the third time, I get to my feet. "Enough holiday cheer for one night," I announce, scrolling through my music library for something to suit my soft and sleepy mood.

"How about some Otis Redding?" suggests Eamon, and, as the slow, bluesy strains fill the room, he joins me by the counter. "Dance with me?"

With a smile, I cross my wrists at the back of his neck, still holding my half-empty wineglass in one hand. Since I abandoned Nicole's stilettos hours ago, he seems even taller than usual, but we fit together just fine, drifting drowsily in time to the smoky music. Gradually, though, my languor dissipates, replaced with pulsing awareness of his body against mine, the warmth of his hands on my back, the masculine scent of his skin. I look up to find that his eyes have gone black, and, I think, his breath is coming a little fast. Maybe I was wrong that he's not interested in me anymore. God, I hope I was wrong.

I swallow jerkily and drag my eyes away from his. Suddenly desperate for a distraction, I go to take a sip of my wine, but at the exact second that I raise the glass to my lips, I step awkwardly forward and slide my foot into the side of his, nearly tripping. Most of the contents of my glass slosh over the front of my dress.

"Shit," I mutter, embarrassment searing my cheeks. Avoiding his eyes, I set the glass down and turn to reach for a paper towel, but suddenly his hand is on my wrist, stopping me.

The bottom drops out of my stomach at the look in his dark eyes. "Let me," he whispers, and, as I stand transfixed, he reaches out to wipe away a trailing droplet of wine from my skin with the side of his finger. He brings his finger to his mouth and sucks the wine away, never taking his eyes off mine. At that point I stop breathing.

He pulls my hips against him, and then slowly, slowly, he leans toward me. My eyes drift shut and my lips part in anticipation, but suddenly I feel his hot mouth on the wine-slick skin exposed at the neckline of my dress. I gasp with shock, my hands tightening on his arms, but he doesn't release me, just continues relentlessly stroking the upper curves of my breasts with his lips and tongue.

And if I thought I wanted him before, then, my god, I am burning now. Hungrily I pull him even tighter against me, fingers biting into his hips, and arch backward to encourage him. He growls at my response and begins undoing the buttons at the top of my dress.

"Eamon," I gasp, and at this he finally raises his head.

"God, I want you so much," he whispers harshly, and kisses me at last.

My arms wind around his neck and I'm on my tiptoes, craning upward to absorb him and his wine-flavored mouth.

With my weight supported by the counter behind me, I lift one leg and wind it around the back of his; in another heartbeat one of his hands is scalding a path up the outside of my raised thigh, skimming my skirt along with it. Blindly I reach out to undo the buttons of his shirt, sighing with deep satisfaction as I slide my hands inside. His skin is warm and sleek over the honed contours of his chest and belly, and as I smooth my palms up across his powerful shoulders, he impatiently shrugs out of the shirt.

His hand settles on my thigh again, only now he rotates it until his thumb strokes slowly, deliberately, against the aching core of me. Helplessly, I groan out his name.

"Fuck," he gasps. "Come here."

He sets his hands underneath me and carries me, legs around his waist, to the dining table. "Is everything okay with you?" I whisper.

"Yeah, yeah, you?"

"Yeah, just please, hurry." I bite mindlessly at his neck as I feel him skimming off my underwear. The taste of his skin goes straight to my head.

And then, from halfway across the house, the toilet flushes. Incredibly, laughably, the sound of Danny getting up from bed to piss is what jerks me back to myself, to an awareness of what exactly I'm doing and who I am doing it with, and at what cost. He already crushed me once. If I make love to him now I'll never stop wanting him again; my pride won't mean anything compared to what I feel for him. Fear breaks over me like a thunderclap.

"Shit, Eamon, stop, please stop," I plead.

He pauses, hands on his belt buckle. "What?" His face is confused, disoriented.

"We have to stop, I can't do this."

"Sarina." He snaps splayed palms at the air. "Why?"

I open my mouth, take a breath, only to blow it out again on a sigh. How in the hell am I possibly supposed to explain to him? I don't even know where to begin.

He plants his fists on either side of me and leans in close. I close my eyes to hide from his nearness, like a coward, and he capitalizes on this by kissing me again. I put my hands out reflexively to push him away, but the minute I touch his smooth skin, my fingers curl into him instead. He presses his advantage, torturing me with a light, teasing kiss, rubbing and brushing my lips

264 – BETHANY CHASE

with his until I am desperate for the full weight of his mouth. *It's just dopamine,* I tell myself frantically, but my body is suffused with the feel of him, and my hands just drag him closer.

God help me, I have never in my life wanted anything more than I want him right now, but I have to put an end to this. I pull away again.

"Please let me go," I say quietly. "I can't."

He rests his forehead against mine, chest heaving. "*Why* are you still hanging on to him?" he demands, thinking, of course, that my hesitation is because of Noah. "You're not in love with him. You belong with me. I don't know how you can't see that."

I stare at my lap, unable to answer him.

"What is it about him, Sarina? You have to explain to me, because I honestly don't understand." His voice is urgent, relentless. "You didn't even seem like yourself around him, that time he was here. You were so tense. How is that the way you're supposed to feel around someone you've been with for four years? I don't think he makes you laugh. I don't think he makes you happy, period. And I *know* he doesn't turn you on the way I do," he whispers, lips a half inch from mine. "God, baby, you're melting in my hands."

Suddenly, anger scatters the haze from my brain. "This is not a fucking contest, Eamon," I snap. "Is that all this is about? You wanted me because I was already with somebody, and you liked the challenge of making me admit I want you more? It's really not about me at all, is it? It's just about beating him."

"No! No, not at *all.*" He shakes his head in emphatic denial, but I'm certain that I'm right. That may not be the only reason he wants me, but it's definitely in there. It's who he is. Does everything he values in his life only come as a result of besting somebody else? Feeling nauseous, I slide off the table, button my dress, and gather my discarded underwear without looking at him.

"Please just go," I whisper.

He catches my arm as I pass him. His face is stricken. "Baby, it's not like that, I swear to you. I know what that feels like, and that's not where I'm coming from. I hate that you would think that of me."

"Save it," I mutter, jerking my arm free. "I'm going to bed; you can let yourself out." And without a backward glance, I hurry upstairs, into my room, and close the door. I picture him putting his wine-stained shirt back on, and his shoes, then straightening, standing indecisively for a moment in the darkened hallway. One by one, I count the seconds that he's still there. I could still open my door, call him to me, and let it all slide away—my fear, his motivations.

I hold my breath as I hear his quiet footfalls approach the staircase, and pause for a long moment. Then, just as quietly, he moves away again. Finally I hear the soft click of the front door closing.

—

When I head to the kitchen for a refill on my coffee the next morning, Danny is sitting at the counter, pressing his fingers into his head as if that alone is keeping it on straight. "As God is my witness, I'm never drinking again."

"Demon Baby?"

He winces, green-faced. Demon Baby is our term for the unholy bastard child conceived of too much alcohol: a malicious roil in the depths of the abdomen that typically doesn't surface until the following morning, when it's too late to do any good by throwing up.

I feel irresistibly compelled to tell Danny about what happened with Eamon. It's lame, and a cop-out, to pester the mutual friend between you and the object of your affection for insight, but apparently I am lame, and a cop-out. And besides, the need to talk about Eamon is burning in my throat. I make a production out of pouring us fresh mugs of coffee, carefully avoiding looking at the dining table.

"So, I almost slept with Eamon last night," I announce as I stir in my sugar, "but I couldn't go through with it. Panicked at the last minute. Honestly, I think it's best in the long run." Oh boy. Even to my own ears, I sound like I'm trying to convince myself.

If I was expecting any show of sympathy from Danny's corner, I am sorely disappointed. He raises his head and regards me with bleary blue eyes. "Then you're a fool. You wasted four whole years of your life on Noah, but you keep yapping about how you're scared of getting hurt by Eamon. And meanwhile he's worth twice what Noah was. I thought you had figured that out."

I slap his coffee mug down so hard it sloshes. "Fantastic! A lecture on taking risks, from a man who's so scared of failure he stopped having sex. Let me know when you decide whether you're the pot or the kettle." I stalk over to my office and slam the door.

He scuffs softly at the door a few minutes later and enters, the picture of boozy contrition. "I'm sorry I barked at you, sugarplum. It's just frustrating to see you spinning your wheels over this vague possibility that you might get hurt."

"Vague possibility?" I repeat. "Did you forget the part about him fucking some other girl while I was driving back from Virginia?"

He bats my question away like a housefly. "You never asked him what was up with that. I guarantee he would have dropkicked what's-her-tits into Lake Travis if you'd asked him to. Did you even tell him you'd broken up with Noah?"

Without looking at him, I spin my drawing pen inside its cap.

"Hmmm," he says, and I dart a glance at him. One eyebrow is pitched at such an angle I briefly wonder if it's possible to sprain it. "Seriously, Ree-Ree? You know I love you, but I hear it's mighty hard to breathe with your head in your ass."

—

By the end of the day, I've accomplished roughly a third of what I should have, because I can't stop thinking about Eamon. He hasn't contacted me, undoubtedly figuring that he's given me more than enough to stew over for a while. Either that, or he's busy showing the house I made for him to his gorgeous ex-girlfriend who can bench-press my entire body weight.

We're supposed to be driving to San Antonio tomorrow, to check out the inventory of this mid-century furniture and lighting dealer down there; and I need to have a conversation with him before we set out on the trip. I just need to talk to him, seriously and candidly, about what's going on between us; he has to understand that I'm not interested in being a plaything, and I won't jeopardize my professional life over sexual attraction. I picture myself saying these things to him, calm and self-assured; him nodding seriously.

"You're right," he'll say. "It won't be nearly as fun"—wry smile—"but it's smarter this way." And then I'll be safe. He respects me—he won't push it. I don't think. But just to make sure I don't give in to temptation, from now on I'll have to avoid being alone with him, and I'll have to stop noticing every maddening, sexy detail about him, and forget how delicious he is to kiss, and touch, and be touched by.

Oh, and I'll have to stop loving him. But no big deal. One thing at a time.

27

When Eamon arrives for the San Antonio trip the next morning, he looks good enough to eat: cuffs of his fitted plaid button-down rolled up over his forearms, open top button showing off the hollow at the base of his throat. For an instant, I remember the heat of his mouth on my skin, the impatient glide of his hand up my thigh.

As I walk to the passenger side of the Jeep and climb in, I quickly run through the bullet points of the speech I have prepared. Our professional relationship. Unwilling to jeopardize it over sexual attraction.

But no sooner am I seated, reaching to buckle my seat belt, than he leans over, pulls the seat belt out of my hand, and kisses me.

I force myself to pull away. "Wait, Eamon, I . . ." I can't finish my sentence, because there's no objection I could offer, nothing I could say with any conviction, that would convince him I actually want him to stop.

He clearly senses this, because instead of releasing me, he cups the back of my head with one hand and scatters soft, drifting kisses across my cheekbone, my jaw, the spot just below my ear. "I haven't stopped thinking about you since the other night," he says between kisses. "The way you feel, and the way you taste. I need to taste you some more."

His words and his touch are utterly intoxicating, but he is deploying them with the ease of experience. This is not emotion, this is seduction. Without warning, the hurt I've been trying to stifle since my return from Virginia flares brightly, and I jerk free of him. "Forget it, Eamon," I snap. "I am not interested in a fling with you. Can we please just go, and never talk about this again?"

His brown eyes are startled and hurt. "Whoa, wait a minute. A fling? Where are you getting this? What did I do to make you think that? Ree, talk to me." He tugs my hands away from my lap and begins massaging my palms with his thumbs.

I give an impatient huff. "I just—the other night was a mistake. Please, for the sake of our professional relationship, don't pursue this. It isn't worth it." I avoid his eyes, staring instead at my hands in his, palm-up and vulnerable.

And then he drops them. "Oh, I'm sorry," he says acidly. "For some stupid reason I thought it *was* worth it. Maybe the fact that I've been crazy about you for fucking months, waiting for you to stop wasting your time with that pretentious douchebag you call a boyfriend."

"Hey!" I yell, stung by his casual contempt for Noah, but he barrels right over me.

"And the fact that I was damn sure you had feelings for me, too, if I could just get you to admit it. But apparently I was wrong, so to preserve our *professional relationship,* I'll never mention it again."

"Spare me," I snarl. "If you really had feelings for me, you wouldn't—" I stop, teetering on the edge of admitting I went to his house that night. The night I thought I was coming home to him.

"I wouldn't what? Sarina, look at me. I wouldn't what?"

Reluctantly I lift my head to look at him. His eyes are blazing, his jaw clenched.

"I wouldn't *what*?"

I struggle to come up with something to say, to provide even the flimsiest footbridge over the chasm of humiliation I've just opened beneath my feet. But there's nothing else I can think of, no lie I can tell.

"You wouldn't have been fucking some other girl the night I got home from Virginia," I say finally. Somehow, it's a relief to lay it out in the open.

Shock sparks in his face, but to his credit, he doesn't try to deny it. "Oh, so I was supposed to be celibate this whole time?" he snaps. "The last time we had talked, I asked you point-blank if you were going to leave your boyfriend, and you said no. But I was supposed to just pine away for you until such hypothetical time as you changed your mind?"

"Well . . . no, but—"

"Then why are you so *pissed* at me? And how do you even know about that, anyway?"

"Because I came to your house!" The words come tumbling out of me, out of control, like marbles bouncing down the stairs. "I'd been driving for three days straight, by myself, talking to you for hours every night, missing you so much my teeth ached; I couldn't wait to see you, and I thought you felt the same way. And when I got into town I drove straight to your house instead of going home, because all I wanted to do was crawl in bed with you and put my arms around you and fall asleep. And then I got there, and there was some bimbo's car parked in your driveway because *obviously* I was the last fucking thing on your mind." Noah's admonishments about giving rein to my acid tongue during arguments are ringing in the back of my head, but I don't care, I'm too hurt and too angry.

"So why am I *pissed* at you?" I repeat, pounding my thigh with my fist as I land on the word. "Because I feel like the biggest fucking fool on the planet. I leaned on you so much when John died; knowing that you were thinking about me meant so fucking much to me—I actually started believing you cared about me like I did about you. The night before I left Virginia, I realized I had to break up with Noah because he doesn't mean anything close to what you do. But when I got here, stupidly thinking you'd be waiting for me with open arms, you were with somebody else. That, Eamon, is why I am pissed."

For a long moment I stare at him, trembling and out of breath.

He stares back. "That's why you were so cold to me that day you got home."

"Yes. Because I don't mean anything more to you than whatever random you'd been banging a few hours earlier."

"I don't know how you can be so wrong about that," he rasps, and grabs my head to kiss me, his lips velvety and warm. Nothing in my life has ever felt so natural or so good. And though it scares the living hell out of me, I don't know if I have ever needed anything as badly as I need him. I open my eyes briefly as we kiss, and the view of him—dark lashes, cheekbone, sideburn—sends a rush of lust and tenderness spiking through me.

We are both panting by the time we break apart. He shakes his head in mingled disbelief and frustration.

"Baby, of course I wanted to see you. More than anything. But you'd given me no reason to think you felt the same way. I missed you so much while you were gone. And I wished so much that I could have been there with you, but when I told you so, all you said was 'Thanks.' I felt like an idiot." He pauses, blows out a sigh. "She didn't mean anything—that girl. Brody dragged me out that night on purpose, to meet women who weren't already taken."

"Apparently he succeeded," I snark, but without the heat of before.

One corner of his mouth kicks up. "I needed a break from getting rejected," he says softly, rubbing my lips with his thumb. "Yes, I have dated other women since that time we kissed, because every time I tried to show you how much I liked you, you just backed away. And there was no sign of Noah disappearing from the picture, so what was I supposed to do?"

I am still stuck on the earlier part of this comment. "Other women, plural?"

He growls like a tire in snow. "Sarina! You are not hearing me! I'm trying to tell you, you are the only one who matters! If you hadn't run away that day you slept over, that would have been it, done deal. We wouldn't even be having this conversation. And, by the way, it's ridiculous for you to be pissed at me for seeing other people when you *still* have an actual boyfriend."

Oh god. I can't hide behind the cardboard cutout of Noah anymore, not after this. I have to tell him.

"Um, actually, I don't."

He looks blank. "You don't what?"

"I don't have a boyfriend. Not anymore."

His smile is like the sun coming out. "What the hell! Since when?"

He is not going to like my answer. "Since November," I say quietly. "I broke up with him when I was on the road. Somewhere in Tennessee."

His jaw goes rigid, and he stares at me silently for a long minute. "Are you fucking kidding me?"

I swallow nervously. I had expected exasperation from him, but not this cold rage. "I know I should have told you," I continue in the same quiet voice, trying to pacify a wild and dangerous animal. "But after that girl, I didn't see how anything could happen between us, so it was safer just to let you believe he was still in my life . . ."

"It was safer to lie to me, you mean."

I start to correct him, insist that I didn't lie, but the look on his face dares me to finish the sentence. A lie of omission is still a lie.

"I'm sorry," I whisper.

He shakes his head and turns to stare out the driver's-side window, cheek propped on his left hand. "I can't believe it's taken you this long to have an honest conversation with me," he says finally, still not looking at me. "All this time, you let me think you were still with him. If you weren't going to tell me what happened, why even bother breaking up?"

I struggle to explain. "It's not like I consciously tried to mislead you. When you asked if I was going to leave him, I almost told you that I had, but I panicked at the last second."

"Jesus, I wish you had just told me. I've been waiting for you to leave him for so long. I don't understand, what are you so afraid of?"

"I'm afraid of *you*," I flare. "And . . . of giving too much of myself up to someone who doesn't really want it."

He turns back to me at that, and the raw hurt on his face shocks me. "Do you know what it feels like to hear that you don't trust me to treat you well? I know I was a jackass when I was twenty-one, but you can't possibly think I'd behave that way now."

"It's not that," I say. "I just didn't think you wanted the kind of relationship that I do. I want to be the only one you think about. I want to mean as much to you as you do to me, and it would hurt too much to settle for less than that. So it was better not to have anything at all."

"And you never bothered to talk to me about it," he says. "I just don't understand how you got it into your head that I couldn't be serious about you. Do you think because I'm an athlete, I run around sticking my dick in anything with a pulse?"

"No, but . . ."

"No! There is no 'but'! Except for the last couple years, I've mostly been in relationships. Hannah and I were together for five years."

"Hannah is the female version of you," I remind him. "I'm nothing like that. She's perfect for you—I don't even know why you two broke up."

His voice is sharp with exasperation. "Okay, first of all, you're wrong that you're nothing like her. Not on paper maybe, but you both have the same kind of comfort in your own skin. It was the first thing I noticed about both of you."

The compliment prickles my skin with pleasure, but he's not done yet.

"Second of all, she is *not* perfect for me. I love the hell out of her as my friend, but as my girlfriend she was exhausting."

"Why?" I feel oddly defensive on her behalf.

"Ugh, so much drama. I put up with it at first, 'cause I was young and I figured that was what girls were like. And dating another athlete in my sport was great as long as we were keeping pace with each other. But once I got hurt, and we weren't training together anymore, I realized swimming was all we had in common. My body had been smashed to shit and I was scared as fuck that I wasn't going to race again, and I just wanted *something* in my life to be easy. But she didn't know what to do with me if she couldn't compete with me. She started picking fights to fill in the gaps."

"I don't get it, though. How would she compete with you?"

"In every possible way except at actual meets. Distances, splits, medals, endorsements. Everything. And I was constantly on notice to prove myself to *her*: how much I would compromise for her. How much I loved her. It was never-ending." He levels his eyes at me, and my breath catches in my chest. "But with you, I always just felt . . . at rest. Not like motionless, I mean like . . . like it was just *right*. That's why I was pushing you to break up with Noah. It made no sense that I could feel like that about you, if you were set on a future with somebody else. I thought that was the answer."

At his words, a boulder lands on my chest. "You *thought* it was?"

He kneads the back of his neck. "This is a huge deal, Sarina. You've been lying to me for a month about a phantom boyfriend, while I've been obsessing over what I had to do to get you to leave him. And then the other night, knowing I could make you melt like that, and then having you push me away because I didn't have the *right* to, and somebody else did . . . Christ, I was so fucking jealous. And now I find out that you were just playing with me."

"Ame, no," I plead, horrified. "I never meant that. I did it because I was scared, not because I wanted to manipulate you. I was just trying to protect myself."

"And that's the other thing," he continues bleakly. "I don't know what kind of future we can have if you're convinced I'm going to hurt you. If that's how you feel, there's no way anything can get off the ground. I'm not going to start a relationship fighting an uphill battle to persuade you that I care about you."

"This is the first time I've actually believed it," I whisper. "I think I was so stuck in feeling rejected from last time, I didn't really think anything had changed. But what you said just now . . . I believe you."

"You think you do. But I need you to be sure. I can't have this conversation again."

I drop my eyes to the hands twisted in my lap. "So what now?" I ask, reaching for, and missing, a dry, ironic tone.

"Well, I don't feel much like a road trip to San Antonio anymore," he says flatly. I wince. I shouldn't be surprised, but his withdrawal is jarring nonetheless. "I think we should just take some time to think about things, and see how it goes."

The boulder on my chest grinds in deeper. "Let's take some time," I know as well as anyone, is one of that lethal handful of sentences inscribed on the tombstones of millions of relationships. Although it sounds innocent enough, somehow the "time" in question never ends happily for the party who is having the moratorium imposed upon them.

"Okay," I say, struggling to keep my voice level. How is it possible that, within ten minutes of finally finding out exactly how he feels, I am on the verge of losing him? How could I have screwed things up so badly?

I reach for the door handle and thump the car door shut behind me before I say something humiliating. I force myself to step calmly back up the front walkway, hoping desperately that he can't see my legs shaking. Trembling, I turn the lock, let myself in, and quietly close the door behind me. Maybe he'll relent; if he cares about me as much as he says he does, it has to hurt to watch me walk away. I breathe in, out, and in again as I wait for the knock. Then from outside I hear the ignition catch. Then the retreating noise of the engine. He's gone.

28

Since I got kicked out of Eamon's car instead of driving with him to San Antonio, the day looms long and empty ahead of me. I decide to spend the afternoon measuring the site of my new retail project downtown. Anything to keep me from sitting in my office moping and waiting for a message from Eamon. A message that doesn't come.

By evening, I am burning with restless energy.

Where are you hanging tonight? I text Danny.

He writes back a few minutes later. *Clementine. Thought you'd be out of town though?*

Told E about Noah. Didn't go real well.

Come over immediately. Will have hot new bartender pour shots straight down your throat.

Lord love my friends, they're always equal to the situation at hand. With the manic enthusiasm of a girl with something to prove, I blast some screechy hard rock as I shimmy into a short, sexy T-shirt dress. A quick check in the mirror satisfies me; the overall impression is of big dangly earrings and about four feet of leg, which will be just right for my purposes.

Danny is as good as his word; the minute I walk into the bar he materializes in front of me and gives me a big, bracing hug.

Without a word, he takes my hand and leads me to the chunky reclaimed-wood bar, where a shaggy-headed blond I've never seen before is pouring out a measure of vodka.

"Paul," Danny announces, "this is Sarina. She designed this bar, and she had a shitty day today, so I want you to be very, very nice to her."

Paul, who appears to be all of about twenty-three, winks one deep blue eye and whips out a trio of shot glasses. "Hi, Sarina," he says, in a rich Australian accent. "I think we can do something about that shitty day. How does Tito's strike you?"

"Strikes me just fine," I say; then we all pound the bar and knock back the shots in unison.

The rest of the night is a blur of shots, dancing, and shouted laughter. Paul and I flirt scandalously. It turns out that he is the keyboard player in a band called Leadfoot Lane—apparently I am back to musicians now. But the fact that he is also blond, blue-eyed, and on the short side just makes me like him better. Eventually, the alcohol takes hold and I stop watching for Eamon's dark head to appear in the crowd. It's about this point, after shot number four (possibly five?), that Paul leans one elbow on the bar and crooks his index finger at me.

"So Danny gave me the rest of the night off," he murmurs into my ear. "You want to head out of here?"

"Yes please," I say without hesitation.

As soon as we reach my room, he gets directly to business, pressing me against the door and hitching my dress up and off. I close my eyes, trying to unmoor my body from the restraints of my brain, but my body proves to be curiously resistant. He's touching me with skill and enthusiasm, but he feels all wrong somehow, and, as the vodka haze burns off slightly, I know why. He feels too short because he's not Eamon's height; his lips are too full compared to Eamon's; and instead of Eamon's leanly powerful physique he has the rounded, bulky muscles of a gym rat. Trying to use him to distract myself from missing Eamon is, to borrow one of John's favorite expressions, a Band-Aid on a bullet hole. Suddenly, the thought of John swamps me with such a wave of sorrow that I feel tears squeezing the backs of my eyelids.

"Oh shit, I can't do this," I say, my voice weirdly strangled. I pull away from him and stumble to the edge of my bed, my shoulders heaving as I sob. John, Eamon, even Noah—everything comes pouring in on me at once. I feel like I'm drowning in loss.

From across the room, I hear Paul clear his throat uncertainly. "Uhhh . . ."

I raise my head, not even caring that my face is streaked with tears and mascara. "It's nothing to do with you. I'm sorry. You should go."

Not waiting to be told twice, he grabs his T-shirt and backs out the door. "Um, I hope you feel better," he mutters, and closes the door behind him. I wind myself into a ball under my covers and concentrate on breathing until the sobbing eases its grip.

How could I ever have thought anyone else could be a substitute for Eamon? Sex is never going to be just sex again, because my craving for Eamon's sweet, teasing warmth is tangled around that basic physical need like a wild morning glory vine. I dig my nails into my scalp as I relive every minute of his touch the night of the party, the hunger in his face as he looked at me, his dizzying words this morning—*I'm crazy about you, I feel at rest with you.* And yet I've lost his trust. I had everything I wanted cupped in the palm of my hand, and I opened my fingers and let it blow away like dandelion seeds.

After ten restless minutes I throw back the covers and stalk to the kitchen with a grim sense of purpose. I pull down our vodka bottle from the liquor cabinet, slosh a couple more shots' worth into a glass, and swallow it in three blazing gulps. The fumes, flavored like raw rubbing alcohol, rise into my nose and make me cough until my eyes water. *That ought to about kill it,* I think triumphantly as I settle myself in bed again, but my stomach expresses its skepticism by roiling queasily. My last thought before I fall asleep is a deep sense of foreboding.

—

A few hours later I'm drawn up from sleep, like anchor chain out of the ocean, by an increasingly insistent billow of nausea. Moments later, as I'm retching miserably into the toilet while Newman watches from the safety of the bathtub, it strikes me what an utter failure the evening was. It started out promisingly enough, but instead of getting happily drunk and forgetting Eamon in the arms of a young Aussie charmer, all I achieved was some mediocre making out and a bad case of Demon Baby.

Once I've puked up every last ounce of bad judgment, I stagger back to bed and collapse with an arm over my eyes. A few minutes later, I hear Danny's soft knock at the door.

"Go away," I moan. "I can't face an interrogation right now."

"I have spiked coffee," calls his disembodied voice. Grudgingly I tell him to come in.

"Where are the other three horsemen?" I mutter, gingerly taking the mug he hands me.

"I thought you might need some tonic," he says mildly, sitting down at the foot of my bed and folding his long legs under him. "You sounded pretty miserable."

"You could hear me?"

"Are you kidding? They could hear you in Dallas. I would have come in to help you, but I figured you'd rather be alone."

"Your instincts are unerring as always."

"I'm surprised, though," he continues. "I didn't think you drank enough to make you that sick."

"I didn't, not at the bar—I pounded two more shots after Paul left because I couldn't stop thinking about Eamon."

He winces. "That good, huh?"

I close my eyes and press the warm mug against my cheek. "Worse. Something reminded me of John in the middle of things and I collapsed into a gibbering mess."

"Oh, honey."

"So, uh, give me a heads-up on the nights he's going to be working, okay? At least until he's reasonably sure I'm not going to creep up behind him with an ice pick."

"You got it. So, I take it you told Ame the truth about Noah, and he didn't take kindly to being lied to?"

Trust Danny not to pull any punches. "No. No, he sure didn't," I confirm. "Before that even came up, though, I blew up at him over that girl he slept with the night I got home."

"And he told you you were an asshole for expecting him to be celibate when you had a boyfriend yourself, to which you responded, 'Actually, about that'?"

I set the mug on my nightstand and glare at him from under my bangs. "Why do you even need to talk to me if you've already figured out exactly what happened?"

He flips his palms up helplessly. "I've known him for ten years, I know how he thinks. And I've lived with you for eight. So yes, I think I could pretty much write the script."

I cross my arms over my chest and eye him expectantly. "Go on."

"Well, judging from how miserable you are, I assume it finally got through your little concrete head that you are his number one girl—right about the time he decided he needs to figure out whether he's willing to trust you again."

"You missed the part where I'm supposed to think about whether I really do believe that he cares about me, and stop torturing him to make him convince me."

"Oh, yep, that sounds like something he would say."

I wait a beat, then another one. Finally I can't take his silence anymore. "So?"

He eyes me cautiously. "So, what? So, do I think he's a bastard? So, am I going to talk to him? Or so, what do I think he will do?"

"Just the last one," I sigh. "I don't think he's a bastard, and I'd never ask you to get in the middle of this. But I am curious what your take on it is."

He looks relieved. "Look, the problem is, you've trashed his pride. I know you think he hasn't been clear about his feelings, but as far as he's concerned, he's laid it out there for you from the get-go. And from his point of view, all you've done is"—he ticks off the points on his fingers—"push him away, get mad at him for sleeping with some other chick after you pushed him away, refuse to explain to him what you were pissed about, and then hide behind a fictitious boyfriend to keep him at arm's length while he quietly went insane with jealousy."

I cover my face with my hands. "Oh my god, I'm as bad as his ex-girlfriend."

"Hannah? No way. Not even close. Good heart on that girl, but she liked to put him through the wringer just to generate drama. That is not you."

"But I fucked it up. I made this whole *thing* drama. He's not going to want anything to do with me."

Danny ruffles my hair like a jovial dad. "Buck up, little camper. He'll come around. It might take a while, 'cause he's a stubborn bastard, but he will."

—

With Danny's bracing words in mind, I try not to be too upset that I don't hear from Eamon that day, or the next. It makes sense that he'd take a few days to think about things. Wednesday morning, my heart starts jackhammering when a new email from him arrives in my inbox, but it's only a question about the house. No subtext, no humor; nothing. Purely matter-of-fact. I answer in kind, and I don't hear from him again for the rest of the day.

By the end of the day it's obvious that this isn't going to blow over quickly. It's the longest I've gone without talking to him for months, and I miss him more than I would have thought possible. It's like all the oxygen has been sucked out of the air. By the morning of the weekly Thursday site meeting, my nerves are jangly as out-of-tune guitar strings.

I arrive at the site half an hour early, wanting the psychological advantage, as well as the opportunity to walk around to check on the progress by myself. The house is about two-thirds of the way done now, and, with most of the walls sheetrocked, it's beginning to look like a place where somebody's going to live instead of just a raw tangle of metal and plywood. But seeing the drywall in place makes a couple of screwups immediately apparent.

"Joe!" I shout, but he must not be able to hear me over the whine of his drill. I bellow his name into the hallway, and after a moment he saunters into view, wiping his dusty hands on his jeans.

"Good morning, Sarina," he drawls, imperturbable as always.

"Joe, would you like to take a look at this outlet cut and tell me what's wrong?" I say, arms folded over my chest.

"Hmm," he says noncommittally, surveying the room.

"By 'Hmm' I'm going to assume you meant 'There is only one outlet on the north wall, where there are supposed to be two of them, a hundred and twenty-six inches apart,' " I hiss. "Fix it."

"You got it, boss. Anything else?"

"Yes. Whoever thought that J-box was centered on the ceiling is either blind or lazy," I snarl, pointing at the mounting plate for the ceiling fixture. "I want it moved by the end of the day. *And* I noticed in the master bath you've got ninety-degree elbows running to the valve for the rain shower. It's no good; that water's going to slow down when it hits those corners and all he's going to get is drizzle. Take it out and do it with wide elbows like you should have in the first place. You know better than that."

Joe nods, apparently not feeling that further speech is required, and for some reason it is this that pushes me over the edge.

"I don't want to see any more sloppy work around here, Joe. I can't have it. I went out on a limb to get you this job, and if you make me look like a hack in front of this client, then I will never have you bid one of my jobs again."

He throws his hands in front of him. "Don't worry, Sarina, we'll get it taken care of. The guys will get it all fixed today."

"They better." I spin on my heel and almost slam directly into Eamon, who's been standing in the doorway unnoticed, and undoubtedly caught the entire exchange.

So much for psychological advantage. What was left of my composure splinters as the impact of his nearness crashes into me. How is it possible that, the last time I saw him, he was kissing me as if he would never get enough of me? And now he's looking at me with all the intimacy of a seatmate on a Greyhound. He is clearly fresh out of the pool; the smell of chlorine is stronger than usual, and his hair is standing up in wet dark spikes. All I want to do is sink my fingers into it, and pull him to me. I urgently scan his face, searching for a sign that he's feeling the same need, but his usually expressive features are blank.

"Good morning, Sarina," he says. "Joe. Looks like you got a head start on the meeting before I got here?"

"Just going over a few corrections," I explain unnecessarily. Pretending he didn't just catch me taking out my frustration on poor innocent Joe Martinez. "But since you're here, we might as well get started."

I don't know if Joe is deliberately punishing me for dressing him down in front of a client—I wouldn't put it past him—but the meeting drags like a legless zombie. Part of me had been hoping that spending time together would thaw the chill between Eamon and me, but instead he remains polite, affable, and brutally distant, without so much as a flicker of his usual warmth. By the time we wrap up the last item on the work list, my hands are trembling from the effort of acting normal.

"Well, I'll issue a revised paint schedule this week," I say, glancing somewhere in the vicinity of his collarbone. I can't bring myself to look at that cool, blank face for one minute more. He nods, says thank you. Then I duck into my car, and, finally, I'm away. My sense of relief lasts exactly as long as it takes to get out of sight of the house. Then the gnawing ache descends again.

—

Back at my desk, I click open my Outlook calendar. Months ago, I'd put in a projected completion date of February 26. Just under a year after he blew back into my life. I scroll forward a few weeks—there'll be a month or so of punch list items and follow-ups, during which I'll still have to talk to him all the time . . . so, April. Beginning of April. I have to get through four more months of this. It will get a little easier; everything does. That's one thing I know from experience. Maybe eventually it won't hurt so much.

And then what? He'll fade out of my life, after having been the most important thing in it. He'll call me now and then, with a question, easily answered. I'll bring a photographer in over the summer, while he's out of town, to shoot the place for my portfolio. Danny will mention him every once in a while, though he'll try to avoid it. I'll see him from time to time, at Albion, Clementine, Danny's and Jay's parties. Inevitably, at some point, there will be a girl in tow. Maybe Red Miata, maybe one of her clones. Or worse, someone like Hannah. A keeper.

Eventually I'll meet somebody else, too, who will or won't be a keeper; either way, it will be fine. I will be fine.

———

The week that follows feels empty and muffled, forcing me to realize how deeply Eamon had infiltrated every aspect of my life. I spend literally hours each day talking about and thinking about and walking through the house I've been designing with him. Pouring my time—and my heart—into it *for* him. And when I close my laptop each evening, there's no escape. I look around my own home and see reminders of him everywhere—the kitchen counter, where he cooked omelets the first weekend he visited; the dining table, where he waited while I packed to go to Virginia and say goodbye to my family. The same table, where we almost made love.

I can't even look at Danny anymore without thinking of Eamon; every time I see him, I wonder if they talked today, if he mentioned me, if Danny, unable to restrain his curiosity, has asked what's going on. What, if anything, Eamon would have answered. I feel nauseatingly jealous of Danny, for having been Eamon's friend for so long, for the fact that he always will be, that he can take that for granted.

Danny, for his part, watches me with worried blue eyes. Since the Tito's vodka incident, he hasn't attempted to draw me out with drinking or socializing, undoubtedly sensing that I have moved from the hectic, defiant phase directly into the morose and withdrawn one. Danny has nursed me through a breakup or three.

The most depressing thing, though, is that I can't even call it a breakup. *Breakup* implies we were at some point *together*. Which is the grim irony of my situation: here I am, with all the heartache

I'd been trying so hard to avoid, and absolutely nothing to show for it except a few intoxicating kisses. Aside from that one day, eight years ago now, I never felt him inside my body, never watched his face as we moved together; for all the months I spent gradually falling in love with him, there was not even one bittersweet day in which he was, just for a few hours, mine. It's supposed to be the wild, untrammeled joy of flight that makes it worth the crash, but I never even made it off the ground.

And god, I miss him. Miss his Bambi eyes and his cute little overbite and his beautiful smile, miss the familiar sound of his voice on the phone, his incessant teasing. The transparent—and completely adorable—pride that he takes in his newly acquired construction expertise. I even miss the smell of chlorine.

I've never missed anyone like this, so fiercely. My mother slipped away for months before she died; I had time to get used to the idea that I was losing her. Even John, much as I loved him, was less of a daily presence in my life than Eamon was—and now, he's just . . . gone. Except for the fact that I know he's only a few miles away, moving through his days: waking in the darkness and driving to the pool, falling asleep at night in his big white bed. Giving that smile to age-groupers, friends, gas station attendants. Nearby, but totally out of my reach.

—

It's the banner ad on my browser that gives me the idea. "Last-minute flights!" it crows. "Cancún! New Orleans! Miami! Tulsa!"

One of these things is not like the others, I think, but the idea of getting out of town for a few days is highly appealing. I can't stand the thought of moping by myself in the house all weekend again, but the prospect of attempting to socialize while enduring the sympathetic coddling of Danny or Nicole is equally intolerable. And, yes, it is rank cowardice, but I'd be ecstatic not to have to put myself through another site meeting with Eamon right now.

But where to go? I gnaw on my pen as I weigh the options. Lounging on a beach by myself sounds depressing, and, as an adoptive Texan, I cannot in good conscience set foot in Oklahoma voluntarily.

So, New Orleans. I've never been there before. And it's supposed to be lovely. And, I suddenly remember, it's where Jamie wants to open her next branch of Balm. Jamie, who is exceedingly unhappy with her current architect.

Twenty seconds later, I am punching in my credit card info.

Hey team, says my email to Joe and Eamon, *I'm going to be out of town for another job on Thursday and Friday—please go ahead without me. It's a slow week, there shouldn't be a lot to go over.*

No problem, Eamon writes back. *Touch base on Monday when you're home.* Not a flicker of interest in where I'm going or what I might be doing there. I wonder if he had to stop himself from asking—or if he just doesn't care.

—

The next afternoon, I am packing in my bedroom while Newman supervises in meat loaf position, all four paws invisible beneath him. I feel guilty leaving him in the care of his uncle again, especially because I'm going to be away yet again when I head to Janet's home in Virginia for Christmas next week. Danny is a diligent caretaker, but he doesn't actually enjoy having the cat around, and responds to all of Newman's attempts to cuddle by placing him gently but firmly on the floor.

"Just one more trip after this, and then it's all Mama, all the time," I promise him, scratching him under the chin. He purrs, but his yellow eyes remain suspicious. Then, I hear my cellphone ring, half-buried under a pillow.

My heart skitters, as it has every single time my phone has rung in the last week and three days. I changed Eamon's ringtone back from "Back in Black," just so I wouldn't always know, instantaneously, that it *wasn't* him every time somebody else called me. For some reason those three or four seconds of mystery were very important to me. So this could be him now.

And, all of a sudden, I'm sure that it is. He is calling to set things right, unable to stand the thought of me leaving for this trip with the two of us still estranged. The universal impulse to reach out to a loved one before they set foot into one of the glorified aluminum tubes known as airplanes.

But when I retrieve the phone, just before it goes to voice mail, it isn't Eamon's name flashing up on the screen. It's Noah's.

29

The human voice, sometimes, is an absolutely extraordinary thing. It's amazing how much emotion can be imparted with one soft, simple little syllable. All Noah says to me when I answer the phone is one word, but in that word I hear that he's home, and he's missed me, that he's glad to hear my voice but that it also hurts him, and that he and I are not going to be friends for a long, long time. All this from one tiny word:

"Hey."

I sink down on the bed and gather my legs under me. "Hey, Noah. I was wondering when you were going to be back home."

"Just landed a couple of hours ago."

"Wow. And this is it, right? You don't have to go back again after the holidays?"

"Nope, this is it. No more Argentina. It feels weird."

So this is the actual day that I spent so many months looking forward to—the day he'd be home for good. Except instead of waiting at the airport, scanning the crowd in the baggage claim area for his beloved brown head, I didn't even know he was coming.

"I'm so happy for you," I tell him.

"Yeah," he says distractedly. "I guess I'll settle back in after a little while. I don't have to start back at the office until after New Year's."

"Well, that's good. Did you catch up with your family yet?"

"No, I need a day or two to decompress before I head up there. I'm at home." He pauses for a moment. "It's weird here, Sarina. I didn't expect it, but the first thing that came to my mind when I walked into my apartment was you. That stupid rug, in the living room."

I remember. I helped him pick it out, at the same warehouse sale where I got mine. He insisted we get ones that looked nice together, so they wouldn't clash when they eventually wound up in the same house.

"And there's photos of you everywhere," he continues in the same flat voice. "The one of us in Iceland, and the one I took of you up at the lake last year, holding the sparklers."

I close my eyes, aching. I wouldn't trust myself to speak, even if I knew what to say. But he doesn't seem to expect me to say anything.

"Maybe this is a bad idea," he says, "but can I see you? I just need to understand, 'cause I still don't understand, and I think we need to talk about this some more."

Of course I can't say no to him. Even though I don't think meeting in person will accomplish anything other than hurting us both even more. If he wants this closure, then I owe it to him to try to provide it.

—

The afternoon sun is slanting low over the naked-limbed trees lining Town Lake as I wait for Noah to arrive at our meeting point on the pedestrian bridge. Shivering in the unusually brisk wind blowing off the water, I dig my hands deeper into the pockets of my hoodie and bounce on the balls of my feet. When I glance back toward the south, there he is, striding along the walkway. Already scowling.

He draws to a stop in front of me, not speaking, and my eyes drop uncertainly to my shoes. I want to touch him but I gave up the right. When he says my name, softly, I raise my head. Then, slowly, with such hesitance that my throat tightens with sadness, he wraps his arms around me. I close my eyes and let myself hug him back, hard. I am feeling so many things at once that, for safety's sake, I just concentrate on the scratchy wool of his jacket against my cheek.

He buries his lips in my hair and rocks me back and forth. "Ree, Ree, Ree, why are you doing this? Why are you doing this to *us*? I love you so much. I always have. I know I let you down while I was away, but I'm home now. I want to fix this. That has to count for something."

With his face so close to mine, I can smell the familiar minty scent of his toothpaste. Tears seep from my eyes, making little damp spots on his jacket. "It counts for everything," I whisper. "It's more than I deserve. I just . . . I know that I don't love you enough to make you happy. I'm so sorry."

He makes a frustrated noise. "I don't even know what that means. You love me plenty."

"But—"

"Listen. In a weird way, part of me was not completely surprised by this. You know that thing about how in every relationship, somebody loves a little more, and somebody loves a little less? I think . . . I've always loved you a little more. And I was fine with that. I was *happy* with that," he whispers intently, "because it meant I got to be with you."

I squeeze my eyes shut tighter.

"So, if you think you want to set me free to find somebody

else who will love me more, I'm telling you right now that's not what I want. I don't want somebody else. I want you."

I pull free of him, and wipe my eyes with the balls of my thumbs. I beckon him over to a picnic table, and we sit down side by side on the top, our feet lined up in a row on the bench. We sit like that for a long, long time, not speaking.

While I watch a pair of scullers glide along the surface of the lake, I ask myself, one more time, whether this is the right decision. Taking a mallet to a flawed but basically good relationship, causing such pain to someone I love. Because I do love Noah, still. More than I'd realized before I saw him here today. If Eamon had never come along, I don't think I would have realized that I was capable of loving someone more than this. But he did, and I am; and I do. And even if Eamon never decides to trust me again, Noah deserves better than to be the backup option.

I take his hand and smooth mine over it, again and again. "But the thing is, I know it's not enough, and that would make me miserable. I don't want to be the person who loves less."

"Why not? I want to take care of you, and make a home for you. We'll have a good life, sweetheart. Let me make you happy."

It is so easy to imagine how it could go. I could say yes to him right now and wipe away the pain and confusion of the last few months. Now that he's home again, surely we could rebuild everything that was good and strong between us. I would be welcomed back into his heart, into his family, and then one day I would walk toward him in that wonderful gray dress and watch his face light up with joy. And spend the rest of my life basking in the warmth of his gratitude and his love.

But the thing I can't forget is my last night on my way home to Austin. Driving halfway through the night, exhausted and brokenhearted, and aching with need—and not for this man here offering me his beautiful heart in his hands.

I smear another tear away with the side of my hand. "I'm so

sorry, but I can't. I just can't. I cannot tell you how badly I wish that I could give you a different answer, but it just . . . it just isn't enough."

He shakes his head, staring at the graffiti on the railroad bridge to the east of us. NEVER GIVE UP, it says. "I don't understand how you go from being contented and happy to not being happy enough. It's not like you've said that you just don't love me anymore."

"No." This would be easier if I didn't.

"Because you still do. I can see it."

I'm silent.

"So *why*, then? How? What happened to make you so sure that what we have is not enough?" He turns to me, face tight with emotion.

And I realize that there is only one thing that will make him understand. It will also make him hate me, but it will make him understand, and it will make him let go, and that's more important than anything *I* want.

"I developed feelings for someone else," I say quietly, staring at my knees, pressed together. "I never slept with him. There was no affair. We're not together now. But . . . my feelings were strong enough to make me realize it wasn't right to be with you anymore. I lied about it because I thought it would just hurt you more, for no reason. But I should have told you the whole truth. And I'm sorry."

I dart a glance at him; he looks like he wants to throw up.

"You said you didn't sleep with . . . this person," he says after a minute, his voice quiet and tight. "Did you do *something*?"

I should have known a lawyer would notice the specificity of what I said—and didn't say. "We kissed. Once. It was a horrible thing to do. But that's all, I swear to you."

He jerks his hand free of mine and jumps down from the bench. "Who?" The word is like a lash.

"No one you know." I lie without hesitation. If he knew the truth about this, it would torture him. He'd fill in the gaps between the things he knows and wind up inventing something even more painful and humiliating than what actually happened.

He narrows his eyes, trying to decide if I am telling the truth. Then panic rises in me as I see him starting to do the math. "It's that smug prick Eamon, isn't it?"

I shake my head, forcing myself to stay calm. "No."

"Come on, of course it is," he says, with lacerating scorn. "I noticed he was pretty chummy with you when I was home in September. But, stupidly, I trusted you. And to think I actually encouraged you to take that job in the first place!"

"It's not him," I insist, brazening it out in spite of my shame. I will lie about this as many times as I need to, to throw him off the scent.

"Then who? Somebody from kickboxing? Somebody from the restaurant?"

I hunch my shoulders inward, my self-loathing driving an instinct to physically shrink. "Please, Noah, it doesn't matter who it was."

"Fuck!" he yells. "I can't even believe this is actually me and you having this conversation right now! But you know what? I guess you're right. It doesn't matter who it was," he says, slashing the air with his hands. "I just wish you'd told me a month and a half ago, so I could have spent this whole time forgetting you instead of thinking I could convince you to give us another chance. Believe me, if I'd known you were hung up on somebody else, I *certainly* wouldn't have bothered."

And then he's walking back the way he came, away from the sunset that's shimmering on the surface of the lake. Walking away from me.

30

According to the weatherman shouting on my TV the next morning, the neon blob on his map of Texas is one of Austin's exceedingly rare winter storms, which has moved in over the city just in time for my flight to New Orleans. He's calling for half an inch of snow, which nobody where I come from would bat an eyelash at, but around here that is literally historic. As I drive to the airport, snowflakes the size of quarters begin to fall, and traffic practically stops as thousands of Texans hit their brakes in confusion. The flakes are melting as soon as they hit the surface of the road, but my lane still slows to a crawl. Molasses in January, John would say.

"Come on!" I yell, banging on the wheel. The girl in the car next to me looks at me quizzically as she takes a drag on her cigarette. When her lane moves and she pulls ahead of me, I notice a pink breast cancer awareness bumper sticker under her rear window. Good to know she's *aware* that her boobs might one day turn on her. I bet she even does the self-exams when it occurs to her. Her lungs, apparently, are on their own.

—

Usually, walking off a plane into a strange airport is like a sugar rush for me, but as my eyes sift through the strangers milling around me while I make my way toward the taxi line in New Orleans, all I feel is lonely. I give myself a stern mental shake—this is not a pleasure trip, I am here on business. Everyone gets lonely on business trips.

I haven't told Jamie what I'm planning to do—it's presumptuous, and not *entirely* dissimilar to stalking a former lover who has already told you you need to move on. But the fact that she's not happy with their choice of architect has given me an opening. And as Eamon pointed out after they rejected my first proposal, one man's desperate is another man's persistent. Or one *woman's* persistent, as the case may be. I could sure as hell do worse than to take advice on persistence from one of the world's most accomplished athletes.

If nothing comes of it, then at worst I will have wasted a few hundred dollars, and a few days of my life; but at least I will have gotten to explore a new city. And at least I will have tried. But somehow, I don't think nothing will come of it. I was arrogant about the Dallas-Houston proposal, because I knew my design was good, and I didn't think the cost would matter. Now I know better. I understand what they will be looking for when they move to select a New Orleans site, and I know what the design has to accomplish. Relaxation and pampering—assisted by Jamie's bright herbal blends—with just a hint of local flavor.

Fortified by coffee, I drop my duffel at the hotel and roll out, armed with my camera, notepad, and laser measuring tape. I don't even waste my time venturing into the heavily touristed French Quarter, or the genteel Garden District, with its graceful nineteenth-century homes—Balm isn't right for those places. Balm is a modern brand, luxurious but hip, with just a little bit of an edge. Downtown, not uptown. Jamie's first location, in Austin, was in the still-evolving East Downtown area, and the Dallas and

Houston sites are in similarly up-and-coming neighborhoods; the New Orleans site should follow suit. So, I head for the self-proclaimed SoHo of the South, the Warehouse and Arts District.

The history of the neighborhood is in fact very similar to SoHo's: a nineteenth-century industrial neighborhood whose buildings fell into abandonment as shifts in commerce rendered them obsolete, then were gradually "rediscovered" and redeveloped in more recent years. And, I discover, the architecture is similar. Lots of sprawling four- and five-story buildings with rows of tall, generous windows that promise spacious interior ceiling height.

The broker I had contacted, pretending to be the owner of an upmarket pet grooming service (what the hell, it amused me), takes me through seven available spaces, three of which have real potential, so I document all of them with photos and notes. While I wait for my room service back at the hotel, I upload the day's photos to my laptop and scroll through them.

Of the three spaces I liked, one is a corner layout, so the space is flooded with sunlight from two walls of windows. This is a good thing, but poses its own challenges because I need to provide the treatment rooms with privacy. As the evening draws on, I rough out the base floor plan and sketch a few possible layouts on top, as well as some details to finish off the space. When I'm satisfied, I study the drawings. The concept is good—I like it. But there's nothing about it that says "New Orleans" to me, really. I can't shake the feeling that I'm not quite there. It's after eleven, and I should go to bed; but, instead of getting up, I cycle through the photos again, yawning. And that's when I spot it.

In one of my photos, half-hidden behind a taller building, is a single-story brick structure, on another corner lot. It has several windows that stretch all the way from the ground to what must be the ceiling inside, and the windows themselves are beautiful— classic old industrial steel casements, with tall, slatted wooden shutters on either side. It's an odd mix of industrial architecture and New Orleans grace, and I love it. Gnawing on my thumbnail, I zoom the photo in tighter till I can make out the red lettering on the sign on the side of the building—FOR SALE.

—

By ten o'clock the next morning, I'm pretty sure I'm about to be arrested. Or, at the very least, questioned by the police. I have been lurking outside the mysterious brick building on St. Charles Avenue since a little after eight, taking notes and photos, and there isn't a doubt in my mind that everyone who sees me thinks I am casing the joint. Especially when I start shooting measurements with my laser.

I have no way to get inside; the place is locked and deserted, and the phone number on the sale sign keeps going to voice mail. But it's not even that important. I've got the overall dimensions of the building from the outside, and I can get a pretty decent look at the interior through the windows. It's empty, but the sheetrock on the ceiling and perimeter walls has been ripped off, as though somebody got most of the way through demo and then quit. If I had to guess, I'd say the buyer or developer defaulted and the place is now a short sale. I'm not sure if the Balm team would consider buying the real estate for the New Orleans location rather than renting, but, if so, this is exactly the kind of property they'd do well to pick up. Great location, bound to be a good price.

A call back from the property's broker confirms my suspicions about the sale circumstances. I jump in a taxi back to the hotel, churning with excitement. I've found exactly what I was hoping for: a terrific building that lends itself intuitively to a single defining design gesture. One of the hallmarks of historic New Orleans architecture is a townhouse with a floor plan built around a central interior courtyard, which provides a serene, secluded oasis from the city streets outside. For Balm New Orleans, the courtyard would be uniquely appropriate both to the location and to their business. If opening the roof and setting up drainage proves too expensive, I can still create the effect with operable skylights. It even gives me a low-cost and low-maintenance way to incorporate the lemon balm plants into the design. It's perfect.

Back at the hotel, I set to work. I don't know how to describe what happens to my mind when I work through a design, except to say it's like a trance: an extended period of intense concentration during which my usually cacophonous brain goes silent, except for an absolute focus on visualizing, drawing, and reworking my lines to resolve the flaws I spot as I draw. I study the design periodically, checking it for rhythm, proportion, balance, just as John taught me all those years ago. I don't notice hunger or fatigue; all I'm aware of is the black-and-white landscape taking shape in front of me. When I finally toss my pen onto the desk and stretch backward in my seat, exhausted, I am genuinely surprised to discover that it's almost nine o'clock in the evening.

I creak up from the desk and flick open the draperies. The lights of New Orleans stretch out below me in an unfamiliar pattern of orange and white, the streets dark and glossy with rain. Now that the storm of creative output has spent itself, I can physically feel the weight of everything else that I've been dragging around settling back in my shoulders. I *need* for Balm to hire me on again; I need something to throw myself into, and I need it badly. I've got to have something to distract myself from all this hurting. Work is a healthier drug than any of the other options.

—

First thing the next morning, I email the photos and the sketches from both potential sites to Jamie, with John's address bcc'd for good luck. Deliberately, I do not include the addresses. *One of these two is your New Orleans location,* I write. *And these designs are perfect for them, because I understand your brand and your goals. You should be able to afford either space. But first, you have to hire me back again.*

Forty minutes later, I have a response.

Girl, you've outdone yourself. They want to see you the first week of January.

It's been so many weeks since I felt something as basic as happiness that it takes me a second to recognize the odd bubbly sensation in my chest. But I let it froth around inside me like water in a hot tub. I did it. I fucking *did* it.

I close my eyes and imagine John doing a gleeful improvised line dance across the kitchen at the old farmhouse, sunlight soft in his white hair. I can practically hear his laughter, the scuffing sound of his feet. It makes me sob and laugh at the same time. But for the first time since I lost him, it feels *good.* Maybe this, maybe something a little like this, is what Nicole was talking about, all those years ago. *May his memory be a blessing.*

May *their* memories be a blessing.

I spend the rest of the weekend crisscrossing the city, dutifully checking out every historic house in my Lonely Planet. I do a ghost tour and a swamp tour and a riverboat cruise. I stuff myself with beignets and Cajun food. And yet, the longer I'm there, experiencing all these new and guidebook-recommended things, the more acutely homesick I become. I miss Danny, and Newman, and my own comfortable bed, and even my homey little office.

And, of course, I miss Eamon.

—

Incredibly, it's snowing again when I land on Sunday night. Austin hasn't seen snow in fifteen years, and now there have been two storms in the space of four days. I'm sure more than a few people are busily preparing for the Rapture.

The house is silent and empty when I get home; Danny's still at work and will be for hours. Even Newman, who is usually all over me like a needy girlfriend when I return from a trip, is avoiding me; I spend five minutes searching all his favorite spots before I give up on him. I flop down on my bed without turning the light on, booted feet sticking off the end. I take out my phone and stare at its dark screen.

I've been delaying the moment of turning it back on after the flight; as long as it's off, there's still the possibility that Eamon has called me and I just don't know about it yet. For all I know, he could be across town right now, wondering when I'm going to call him back. I savor this delicious image for a moment, and contemplate leaving the phone off till morning to draw out the fantasy as long as possible.

I press the on button and wait for it to boot up, hope and dread playing tug-of-war with my stomach.

No new calls.

The flicker of hope snuffs out like a poorly struck match. Alone in the silent dark, I realize how much I'd been hoping that he would contact me today. That he'd want to share his amusement at the city's snow-induced helplessness with a fellow veteran of actual winters, and he'd forget he was angry at me long enough to call. That, somehow, knowing I was physically out of town would make him miss me, enough to reach out to me and tell me he'd forgiven me. But he didn't.

But I miss *him*. So badly I can't think straight. And I can't stand the thought of going any longer without seeing him, without telling him how I feel, even if what he has to say is that I've messed things up too badly for him ever to trust me again. I have to go all in. And since waiting for him to initiate contact has yielded nothing but two weeks of solitary confusion, I'm going to have to reach out to him. If Mohammed won't go to the mountain, the mountain is going to have to come to Mohammed. Though it occurs to me the parties in this scenario are somewhat misnamed—if anyone is a mountain, it is the six and a half feet of unyielding stubbornness with whom I seem to find myself locked in a battle of wills.

I roll onto my stomach and turn the phone over and over in my hands, like a wishing stone. It's all very well and good for me to decide to reach out to him, but how exactly am I supposed to combat such a masterful application of the silent treatment? Do I need to make some kind of grand, cinematic gesture to convince him of my sincerity? A flotilla of man-appropriate flower arrangements? Skywriting? I have a brief vision of myself standing outside the house in Travis Heights in a trench coat, holding a boom box over my head.

Whatever I do, I need to do right now, before I lose my nerve. It's starting to reach into that witching hour of the night, when it's easier to do and say things you wouldn't dare in daylight. Like *I miss you. I love you. Please give me another chance.*

Shivering with nerves, I dial his number.

There's a cautious pause between when he picks up and when he says hello to me, sleepy-voiced. "Sarina?"

Longing courses through me at the rumble of his voice. "Did I wake you?"

"Well . . . yeah. What's going on?"

So much to say, but I give him the simplest answer. "I miss you."

"You had to call me at twelve-thirty on a Sunday night to tell me that?"

My bravado evaporates. "Please don't be mean to me. You've been punishing me for two weeks, and I get it, I know how much I screwed up. And I'm so sorry. We don't have to talk about things if you're not ready, I just . . . I really want to see you."

There's a long, portentous silence. "Well, I'm awake now."

Not exactly a warm welcome, but not a total shutdown, either. Not giving either of us time to think the better of it, I tell him I'll be over in twenty minutes. Then I realize I am stale and unappealing after traveling all day—will he think I'm trying to hit on him if I show up freshly showered? I decide it's worth the risk. And besides, let's be honest—I *am* trying to hit on him.

Before I leave, I stop at the laundry room to give Newman enough food to get him through till morning. I'm definitely jinxing myself, 'cause I know I'm only going to be coming back in as much time as it takes to drive to Travis Heights, get told to go fuck myself, and drive right back home again—but just in case. Wouldn't want him to get hungry.

The city is Sunday-night quiet as I make the drive; the only signs of life are the holiday lights blinking fitfully in people's yards. I smile. Even after eight years in Austin, I'm still taken aback by the sight of Santas and reindeer cheek by jowl with live oaks and agave plants. Except, for once in their lives, the desert plants are dusted with a light, tentative coating of snow. Climatic indigestion.

When I turn onto Eamon's street, my nerves return in force. If he wanted to see me, he would have let me know; instead I have invited myself over in the middle of the night for what is bound to be an unspeakably humiliating rejection.

I park in his driveway, and as I watch the blue light of the TV flickering through his front window, I remember the last time I was here. Arriving in the middle of the night after thirteen straight hours of traveling because I just needed to be with him that *badly*. Then that stupid red car, and all of the ways it threatened me.

And then I think of the photograph I found in my stepfather's memory box, in a bedroom that used to be mine, in a house that doesn't belong to me anymore.

I step onto the porch, suck in a deep breath, and knock.

31

I clench my teeth to keep from launching myself at him the moment he opens the door. He's rubbing his injured thigh tiredly, and his face is more shuttered than I have ever seen it. The only possible positive sign is that his hair is wet, as if he, too, has just gotten out of the shower. And his track pants are creased across the knees, as if they were recently unfolded. He stares at me expectantly for a moment till I give him a tentative smile.

"Can I come in?"

Unsmiling, he moves aside. He shuts the door behind me, then faces me, still rubbing his leg.

"Are you okay?" I ask. "You look like you're hurting."

"The damp weather makes my injuries ache. It's not a big deal."

I think of all the bones that cracked in his body when that truck hit him and shudder. "Is there anything I can do?" I ask, knowing that there isn't, hating that there isn't.

"No," he says flatly. "But thanks."

I play with the zipper on my sweatshirt, flicking it against my fingernail. I had started to hope that he might be thawing out a little bit, since he hadn't actually forbidden me to come over, but clearly I was wrong. I don't even have to ask him if he'd be willing to give me another chance—his feelings couldn't be any more clear. I have to get out of here before I embarrass myself any further.

"I'm sorry, I guess this was a mistake," I say. "I just couldn't stand that we hadn't spoken in so long. But, um, I'll go. I'm so sorry for lying to you. For everything. I hope you already know that I'll see the rest of your project through with professionalism." Aching and unbearably hollow, I turn and fumble with the door lock. Clumsily, I turn the latch to unlock it but only succeed in locking myself in.

He heaves a long sigh as if he's letting go of something. "Don't go," he says softly.

I hesitate, unsure I've understood correctly. "What?"

"Come here." And as I'm still standing there stupidly, trying to figure out exactly what he means by that, because he couldn't possibly mean what the actual words mean, he steps forward and encloses me in his arms.

It is like I've been welcomed into my own personal Promised Land. I fit perfectly. He rubs his cheek against the top of my head and massages the nape of my neck with gentle fingers. I inhale his familiar bleached-laundry smell and feel satisfaction and relief seep through my body. The slow, steady thump of his heart is as soothing as rain.

"Can I stay with you tonight?" I ask after a while, voice muffled against his chest. "I've missed you so badly. I just want to lie next to you and sleep."

His only answer is to press a kiss to my head, and I suddenly realize how ridiculous I must sound. "God help me," I groan, "what am I going to say next? 'Just the tip, just to see how it feels'?"

He sputters with laughter and pulls back to look at me. On his face is a dizzying mix of affection, humor, resignation, and hope. "Okay. Come on." He takes my hand and leads me back to his bedroom.

He slides unceremoniously under the covers of his big white bed and holds them up for me to join him. He nods at the bedside lamp. "Hit that light, will you?"

The last thing I want to do is darken the room so I can't see him anymore, but I reluctantly comply. I *did* tell him all I wanted to do was sleep. Not wanting to push my luck any further than I already have, I stretch out on my side facing him and whisper good night.

"Come on, Mahler," comes his voice through the dark. "You can do better than that."

My eyes ping open. "Better than what?"

"Come over here and turn over."

I obey, and seconds later I am pulled tight against him from head to heels. "That's better," he murmurs, and I silently nod, too bliss-loaded to speak. I rest my forearm over the one locked around my middle, and thread my fingers through his. I feel him tuck my hair out of the way so it won't tickle his face. I smile.

Several minutes pass as I wait to fall asleep. When I headed over here tonight, I hadn't thought beyond satisfying my need to be near him, but now, lying here with him with so much still unsettled, the last thing I feel is relaxed. Also, whatever the state of his wary mind, Eamon's body is unequivocal about the direction in which it would like to proceed, which has my blood racing through me like white water. It is the understatement of the century when, after fifteen minutes of reverberating with his every heartbeat, I tell him, "I can't sleep."

"Me neither. You might already be aware of that," he adds, humor in his voice. He pauses, then continues. "I have the strong sense that there is some sort of conversation we should be having."

"Yes."

He waits for a moment for me to speak. "Are you going to elaborate?"

"Actually, I don't really feel much like having the conversation right at this exact moment. Tomorrow definitely, just not . . . now."

Another pause, as he digests this. "Okay. Well, what *do* you want to do?"

"I want to turn on the light."

"You do?"

"Yes."

"Why?"

"So I can see you."

Obligingly, he lifts his arm from my waist so I can reach forward to his bedside lamp. This accomplished, I turn back to face him.

He is propped up on one elbow, squinting against the soft yellow light. I study him as if I've never seen him before, taking in all the planes and angles of his face, that bump I love at the bridge of his nose, the curve of the gentle smile that's tugging at his mouth. He's overdue for a haircut, and the hair behind his ears is threatening to curl. Of all the moods I've seen him in, all the sides of him I've come to know, I love him most like this: soft, sleepy, rumpled. I know I must be gazing at him with the syrupy adoration of a Labrador retriever, but I can't help it; I am brimming over with love.

He waits patiently. "Is there anything else you'd like to do?" he asks after a long minute.

I nod. "I'd like to take this off," I whisper, tugging at the hem of his T-shirt.

His lips part. "That would be fine."

Without breaking eye contact, I lean toward him, hook my thumbs under the shirt, and skim it up and off. He has a beautiful body—lean, with impossibly broad shoulders tapering to a flat, narrow waist; every muscle is sleekly defined under his light golden skin. When he was twenty-one, still outgrowing the last of his boyishness, he was already the finest thing I'd ever seen; now, he is perfection. But what I love most is that he looks like this because of who he is, because that body houses power that transmutes into speed. Form following function, the purest maxim of design.

"God damn," I whisper.

He gives me a tiny, pleased, sweetly self-conscious smile, and I fall a little deeper.

A ridged scar stretches from just below his sternum to a couple inches above his belly button. I trace it with my fingertips, and his stomach muscles jump. "What was this?"

"From the crash. Internal bleeding. Donate blood, Sarina."

I close my eyes and breathe in and out, banishing the what if before it materializes. He's here, warm in my hands. I drag my hands up and outward across his chest, thumbs grazing his collarbones, then fill my palms with the rounds of his shoulders. "What happened to the Longhorn tattoo?"

"Reconsidered the location," he breathes. "Let me know if you find a good spot for it."

"That reminds me." I glide my hands down his arms, then turn his right hand palm up. The act of setting my mouth to his tattooed wrist feels shatteringly intimate, and the expression on his face when I raise my head tells me he feels it too.

"You have no idea how long I've wanted to do that."

His smile almost raises blisters on my skin. "Let me be clear right now that you have carte blanche with my entire body."

"Yeah?"

He nods, one eyebrow raised invitingly.

"Hmmmmm." I drum my fingers on my lips, as if considering the possibilities. "So much real estate, so little—"

"Also," he interrupts, "you have carte blanche with my schedule, for the next"—he peeks at the clock—"ten and a half hours. Though I could probably reschedule that conference call," he adds, grinning.

"Well in that case, I think mostly, right now . . ." I brace my hands on his forearms and lean toward him slowly, stopping just shy of his lips.

"Don't tease," he chides me softly.

"I'm not teasing. I just love to look at you," I say.

"You can look at me later. I was more interested in what you were about to do."

"Oh, you mean kiss you?"

"Yes."

"Yes, what?"

"Kiss me!" Finally losing patience, he grabs my rear and pulls, so that I pitch forward on top of him with a shriek; and then our mouths collide and we are kissing so hungrily that my whole world shrinks to just his face, his hands, his lips. It's like nothing will ever matter again except Eamon. I'm trembling with need, but also with nerves, so before I chicken out I pull off my tank top and throw it aside. The pressure of his hands on my hips makes me pause, and he gazes up at me with serious brown eyes.

"Promise me you're not going to change your mind this time," he says quietly. There is more than a trace of remembered hurt in his voice.

"I promise," I whisper hoarsely, feeling so many things at once that I don't even know which one to say. "I—"

"It's okay," he says softly. "Later."

I want desperately to explain to him, to apologize, but a second later, he rolls us to reverse our positions, and my thoughts scatter. After that it's just a series of fleeting impressions: the silhouette of my pale hands against his olive skin; his voice, laughingly whispering "Easy there," when my nails sink into his back;

his mouth, hot and urgent, on my throat. The groan that tears out of him when he buries himself inside me. As he begins to move, eyes locked fiercely on mine, joy blazes through me, searing away the last of my fear, leaving only regret that I wasted so much time denying this. It's beyond anything I've ever felt before; he is everywhere at once, inside me, all around me, filling me up so that the only things I'm conscious of are his taste, his touch, his voice. The orgasm that shudders through me is so intense I'm certain the heat has actually fused our bodies together, like steel under a welder's torch.

Exhausted, he drops his head on my shoulder. I can't speak, just tighten my arms around him and press a kiss to the damp hair at his temple. After a while, I feel him move inside me again and the joy wells up, and, just like that, I know that I have to tell him.

"Eamon, the conversation we need to have . . ."

"It can wait," he mumbles into my neck.

"No," I say. I feel like a skydiver standing at the open hatch of an airplane, miles above the earth's surface. Leaning out into the roaring wind, fingers clinging to the edge. "I have to tell you."

He raises his head. "Tell me what?" The naked fear in his voice humbles me.

With a deep breath, I step out into thin air. "That I love you," I say simply. "This whole time, I was so afraid of getting hurt that it didn't occur to me that I could be hurting *you,* and I'm so sorry for that. But I'm not going to push you away anymore, I promise you."

He releases a long sigh and fits his hands around my jaw, kissing me with aching tenderness. "Believe me, I wouldn't let you."

—

We make love again and again, ravenously, not stopping even when bleak winter light begins to seep through the curtains. I lose track of time. Even when we are just lying together, talking, or dozing, we are tangled around each other, needing as much contact as possible.

I am half-asleep, face resting in the sweet crux of his neck and shoulder, when I feel his thumb begin doing something bewitching to my breast, and the hunger starts to rise through me yet again. A few lush kisses, and I press closer. Suddenly, he pulls away with a groan, and flops next to me on his back. His shoulders are shaking with laughter.

I am completely confused. "What?"

"Oh, Jesus," he moans, forearm over his eyes. "I want to, but I . . . I honestly don't think I can. I think my dick would fall off if I tried."

I bury my face in his shoulder and snort with laughter, which just makes both of us laugh harder.

"Don't they give out Purple Hearts for that?" I giggle. "Wounded in the line of booty?"

He laughs so hard that I bounce up and down with his body. "Oh god, I love you," he says weakly, wiping his eyes.

Joy is an earthquake inside me, until I realize he has said it in the way you might say it to anyone in a moment of particular fondness. The way I said it to Danny, when he uttered a particularly stinging assessment of my poorly endowed, cheating ex-boyfriend. Or to Nicole, when she told off our chauvinist goat of an engineering professor. I smother my disappointment and hang on to my smile.

But Eamon's face sobers a little. "I mean, I *love* you love you," he says, rubbing his thumb across my lower lip. He smiles. "Feels good to tell you."

Earthquake.

I trace my fingertips across his cheekbone, scarcely able to comprehend how I can possibly be this lucky. He turns his face and presses a kiss to my palm.

"I missed you so much these last couple weeks," he continues. "I don't know what I was trying to prove."

"You had every right to be upset with me."

He shakes his head. "I overdid it. Sometimes I overdo things, Ree. You're not Hannah, and it wasn't fair of me to lay all that on you. Next time I start acting like an asshole, just . . . tell me. Danny said you went to New Orleans while I was sulking," he adds. "What were you doing there?"

Oho! So he *did* ask about me! Even though it's in the past now, I'm still pleased. "I decided to go and find Balm their New Orleans site, and give them a preliminary concept for it. They're not happy with the architect they hired, so I figured I'd remind them who they should have chosen in the first place."

His face is bright with interest. "Yeah? And what did they say?"

"They want to see me after the holidays."

"No shit! That's fantastic!" Needing some sort of physical outlet for his excitement, he half-hugs, half-drags me until I'm sprawled on top of him, and gives me a rib-crushing hug. "That's amazing, Ree. My brilliant girl. I'm so proud of you."

"I owe it to you in part," I say, suddenly shy.

He strokes my hair back from my face. "How so?"

"I remembered when you said that one man's desperate is another man's persistent. You were right. And it did pay off."

"It usually does," he says softly, and I know he's thinking about me. "It usually does."

32

As it turns out, I don't go to my stepsister Janet's family for Christmas, though the plan is to visit her while I'm on that side of the country.

Instead, December 23 finds me stamping my feet in six inches of snow outside the yellow vaulted arrivals concourse of D.C.'s Reagan Airport while Eamon loads our bags into his brother Colin's scruffy Jeep (which is, oddly, their only discernible resemblance beyond their coloring). After a short drive, during which Colin sells his brother out by telling me all about Eamon's childhood terror of Santa, we pull into the driveway of what is, amusingly enough, a split-level exactly like the one I had pictured. It looks like a house that belongs to a perfect sitcom family.

As I sit there, staring, Eamon and Colin hustle the bags out of the car and up to the porch. When I step out of the car, Eamon is already waiting for me at the front door, silhouetted against the warm gold light spilling from inside. I walk up, slip my arms around his waist, and turn my face up for a kiss.

"Hey, baby," he says softly. "Mom's got dinner going. You ready to meet the rest of the pack?"

I nod, and we walk inside, together.

ACKNOWLEDGMENTS

The first person I need to thank, because I will never be able to thank her enough, is my agent, Meredith Kaffel. I owe so very much to her skill, her brilliance, her thoughtfulness, and her bottomless reserve of patience with me—I simply can't imagine doing this with anyone else.

A huge, bottom-of-the-heart thank-you goes to my wonderful editor, Kara Cesare, for the love she's given this book right from the beginning. It wouldn't be what it is right now were it not for her intuitive understanding of the story I wanted to tell, and her guidance in helping me enrich that story in ways I'd never thought of. I'm truly grateful to work with someone who shares my vision so completely, and pushes me to take it further. Thanks also to Nina Arazoza, Hannah Elnan, Jin Yu, Beth Pearson, Diane Hobbing for the wonderful interior design, Belina Huey for the beautiful cover, and the rest of the Ballantine team.

Another tremendous thank-you goes to my darling friend Liz Scheier. She was my first reader, my first critic, and my biggest cheerleader, and I'm not sure this book would exist without her. For that, I owe her everything. Not to mention the fact that the woman put up with me through two drafts, one agent hunt, one round of publisher submissions, and enough spastic texts and emails to exonerate her for justifiable homicide—and yet in spite of everything I'm fairly confident she still actually likes me. That right there is a damn miracle.

Next: my beloved husband, Allen. Speaking of patience with me (I'm noticing a recurring theme here), this man has a remarkable supply of it. And of everything else good. Every swoon-inducing man I ever write is going to look a lot like him in the heart area.

Other particular thanks go to Wynne Newman, Lauren Fitzgerald, Laurie Pachence, Jess Rogers, Yumi Kim, and Katie Lantzsch, who all read some chunk or draft along the way and gave me invaluable feedback on it. Also, there have been more than a few moments when I've owed any appearance of sanity to Alison Heller's wise advice and brilliant suggestions.

Very little of my Austin knowledge would have been possible without my ATX girls: Andrea Roe, Erin Williamson, and Karly Hand. Their spectacular hospitality, insight, and tolerance for bizarre follow-up questions were instrumental in helping me bring their wonderful city to life on the page.

I need to give a shout-out to my colleagues and buddies from my writers' group, the Women's Fiction Writers Association—their collective wisdom and support has been a wonderful and unexpected gift. (Especially Jennie Shaw, whose critique of my query letter was invaluable in getting Meredith to pay attention to me in the first place.)

I also need to state that the foundation of any writing ability I have was laid by the teachers of Wakefield School, which I attended from seventh through twelfth grade. The incredible education I received there taught me not just how to write but how to think.

Last but quite obviously not least: the swimmers. Thank you to the brilliant Whitney Hedgepeth of Longhorn Masters (and, of course, Atlanta '96) and heavily chlorinated man-about-town

Mike Gustafson for letting me pester them with questions. And thank you to the entire U.S. National Team for being awesome in the truest sense of the word.

And to all of my friends and family as a whole—and I specifically want to call out Allen's friends and family as part of this, because you've been every bit as wonderful as all those poor slobs who've been stuck with me since early days—thank you, so incredibly much, for your tireless support and enthusiasm throughout this entire process. I love you all.

Hi there, reader friends!

Thank you, so very much, for reading *The One That Got Away*. I hope you enjoyed reading it as much as I enjoyed writing it for you. Because I did write it for you, you see. Authors don't write in a vacuum; sharing our stories with the rest of the world is the whole reason we write them in the first place. So I would love to hear from you! Please, track me down (my contact info is below, and you should know that my website has fun freebies to read!) and tell me what you thought of the book. Tell me your own stories about home, or love, or your own One That Got Away. If what I wrote touched you in some way, or made you think about your own life, I'd truly love to hear about it.

Also, if you might be generous enough to take the time, I would be so grateful if you'd consider leaving a review of the book at any retailer or book-sharing site of your choice. You may not realize what a big help those reviews are to authors, but believe me, they are.

Last thing—in the pages beyond this, you'll find some goodies: an essay I wrote about the way the concept of home shapes our lives, and how that became the theme of the book; some fantastic, thought-provoking questions for book club discussion (seriously, these questions are so awesome that I'm dying to hear what every one of you has to say about them—I will show up at or webcam in to your book club if you'd like me to!); AND an excerpt from my upcoming novel, in which you'll get to know Eamon's older brother, Colin (and catch up with what Sarina and Eamon themselves have been up to since the end of *The One That Got Away*). Enjoy!

XOXO,

Bethany

Email me: m.bethany.chase@gmail.com

Read freebies on my website: www.bethanychase.com

Chat with me on Twitter: @MBethanyChase

See the images that inspired the book on Pinterest: www.pinterest.com/mbethanychase

Hang out with me on Instagram: instagram.com/ bethanychaseauthor

Be my friend on Facebook: www.facebook.com/ BethanyChaseAuthor

THE
ONE THAT
GOT AWAY

BETHANY CHASE

A Reader's Guide

THE PLACE WE CALL HOME

BETHANY CHASE

I just wanted to write a love story.

As an incurable romantic, I've always had a soft spot for those stories that are as warm and gooey as the center of a molten chocolate cake. My lifelong favorite, over even Elizabeth Bennet and Mr. Darcy, is the story of *Anne of Green Gables'* Anne Shirley and Gilbert Blythe. So that's what was foremost in my mind when I started working on *The One That Got Away*. But what I soon began to realize, as the book developed, is that it's equally a story about home.

Home is one of those simple ideas that gets more complicated the harder you think about it. On one hand, it's such a universal concept that, in its broadest terms, it ought to mean the same thing to everyone—a place of shelter, safety, belonging. Just the phrase "keep the home fires burning" conjures a place we can return to after wandering, where someone we love will be waiting . . . a place that will always be there. But, unthinkable as it is to ourselves as children, what happens to all of us is that our definition of home changes over time. And sometimes it changes more than once. The thing is, though, that each of our homes, and the people who share them with us, shape us in ways it takes years to fully understand.

Most of us begin with the same kind of home: Where we come from. Where we grew up. Our oldest, most fundamental place; the place we really began. It may not have been happy, but it's still our origin, and for better or worse, we can't forget it, or carve away the imprint it left upon us.

For me, this home was the ten acres in the Blue Ridge foothills where my parents built their dream house. Before then, we had been living among clinking sailboat masts and dapper white-clad midshipmen in Annapolis, Maryland, and my six-year-old self utterly failed to see what had so enchanted my mom and dad with this steep and unruly hillside in the boondocks. By the time construction was completed, though, I was as bewitched as they were. And partly because the house had been designed according to my parents' specifications, I was always aware of the way my physical environment reflected who our family was. One big bathroom for the three of us to share, but separate his-and-hers art studios for them. The spacious open-plan living/dining room, because my parents disliked the tradition of separate "formal" rooms that sat mostly unused. The immense windows along the western façade, so we were seldom out of sight of the rippling blue silhouette of the mountain range that formed our horizon, thirty miles away.

My mother took her last breath in that house. Her blinds were often open as she lay in her bed; I can only hope the beauty of the mountains eased her pain. She had bright eyes and a joyful smile, and the kind of laugh that could make friends from all the way across a room. Her warmth drew people to her like a hearth fire in January. Since I was only thirteen when she died, we were robbed of the time for me to grow to appreciate her, not just as my mom, but as the vivid, kind, charming woman I now know she was. But in the time we did have, her love taught me to value myself, and to treasure beauty, and those two things have been at the core of every good decision I've ever made.

My second home, I wasn't looking for. While I was studying

in England during my junior year of college, everything my father had been struggling with at home collapsed. When my winter break came, I had no home to go to. My mother's older sister, without question or hesitation, said, "You come here." And her house has been my go-home-to place ever since. Because of the woman whose house it is, that place represents as big a part of me as where I came from. My aunt opened both home and heart to me, and her dead sister's girl became her third daughter. With remarkable patience and more than a little tough love, she knocked a navel-gazer, overly prone to whining and stewing, into a decisive and determined adult. I owe more than I can ever convey to my exposure to her challenging, sparky intelligence.

If you're lucky, your own go-home-to place, the place you head for holidays and family weekends or just to take a break from being an adult for a couple of days, is still the same as where you come from. But for many people it's not. Parents move, divorce, die, betray. Your go-home-to place may not even be where your parents or siblings are, but it's a place that brings you comfort when you arrive there. It's the place where you know all the stories and inside jokes that get retold, and where somebody will have your favorite meal waiting for you when you arrive.

Of course, like most of you, I also have my own home now. Mine is a sunny little aerie in Brooklyn, and I share it with my husband, whose dimples are the only thing that can coax me out of bed in the morning, and our cat, who travels from sunbeam to sunbeam as each day glides by. I made it partly with pieces of my other homes: artwork my mother painted, books my aunt has given me, furniture my grandmother bought in the fifties, which is beautifully scuffed with age and with my family's use. But also, my home is made with pieces of who I am now. Artwork I drew, books my friends have written. Because I lost my mother's gardens, I cram my windowsills with flowers, and because my husband loves to cook, I grow herbs to use in our meals. This is the place where I welcome friends and family, both my own and my husband's. And every single inch of it is made of something I love.

Throughout *The One That Got Away*, Sarina is on a journey to find her home. The home she comes from is too laden with painful memories to be a welcoming place any longer, so she's left Virginia behind and made a life for herself in Austin. She's spent much of her adult life trying to find the right go-home-to place, where she truly belongs, and to build her own home at the same time. When the story opens, she believes Noah is the answer to both of those. Except, as Eamon points out, she's never taken any steps to make her home with Noah a reality; she only thinks it's her future because it looks like it should be. So what she has to find the courage to do, in spite of the risks, is to open herself up to the person she's come to realize is the one who really belongs in that future, and in that home.

This is why the home you build yourself, in many ways, is the most rewarding one of all. You can fill it, and populate it, with whatever and whoever you wish. It can be whatever you want it to be, whether it's the place you share with your partner, or your partner plus the colorful chaos of children (or the furry and malodorous chaos of pets), or just the solitary peace of your sofa, a good book and a big glass of wine. This home is the one you fill with your own family, whoever you choose them to be—but the peace is in the choosing.

QUESTIONS AND TOPICS FOR DISCUSSION

1. *The One That Got Away* starts with this arresting line: "Every woman has one. That name you Google at two o'clock in the morning." How does that opening set the tone for the novel?

2. In what ways does the author contrast Eamon and Noah? Do their personalities bring out different sides of Sarina? What makes Eamon the right choice for her?

3. In reference to Noah, Sarina thinks, *He made it so easy for me to fall in love with him.* What do you think her statement suggests about the kind of guy Noah is? What does it suggest about the way she sees him?

4. As Sarina contemplates her future with Noah, the topic of children frequently comes up. How did you react to the scene in chapter 9 when Noah's parents are questioning Sarina about how she will adjust her career to accommodate children?

5. Sarina and Noah come from very different upbringings, which have ultimately had an impact on their priorities and sensibilities. Do you think it's possible for two people from such diverse backgrounds to really be compatible?

6. How do Eamon's swimming career and car accident affect who he is as a person? Can you see the way in which these two defining parts of his life affect his decision making?

7. Why do you think Sarina is so drawn to Eamon? Is it because she never got a real chance with him when they were younger? Do you think Sarina would still end up with Eamon if Noah had always been in Austin?

8. John and Sarina have a special relationship, and yet she always found it difficult to go visit him. How do you think she handles the guilt she feels for not visiting? Is it possible to channel regret like that in a healthy way?

9. Grief and coping play important roles in Sarina's story—from her mother's early death to John's passing later in life. How do those experiences, for better or worse, shape her character?

10. When the story takes place, Sarina's mother has been gone for ten years, so hers is not a recent loss. What are some ways you see that her mother's absence impacts Sarina, both prior to the story and in terms of her actions throughout it?

11. How does Sarina grow throughout the novel? Are there any scenes in particular that really stand out as turning points for her? Why?

12. Is there a greater significance behind Sarina's entrepreneurial spirit? How does her desire to build a strong business relate to, and affect, the choices she makes in her personal life?

13. One of the main themes in this novel is the strong role that timing can play in relationships. In what ways does the author use the concept of time to illustrate how we make decisions?

14. Of all the themes touched upon in the novel—love, second chances and starting fresh, grief and coping, stability and comfort versus taking risks, creating a sense of home—which do you connect to the most? Is there a scene that makes a strong impression on you? Why?

READ ON FOR A GLIMPSE AT BETHANY CHASE'S
NEXT NOVEL, FEATURING SARINA'S BROTHER-IN-LAW
COLIN AND FRIEND HILARY!

1

A black cat got me pregnant.

For some reason, as I'm hunched like a shrimp on my toilet, staring at the plastic stick I'm clutching in one trembling hand, that is the first thing my brain seizes on. Because it's true— although the actual impregnation part was taken care of by a very beautiful human male, the series of events that led me here, one following neatly and logically after the other, began with the first time I laid eyes on that little black Manx.

His name was Newman. His owner, a gangly Jane Birkin type with ink-smudged hands and a big, wicked smile, had brought him into the clinic back in September because he'd been vomiting more than normal. "And more than normal is a lot," she'd said. "My husband says cat puke represents forty percent of our household GDP."

I liked her immediately. When I mentioned that I was new to Austin, she got a look on her face like I'd offered her a box of fresh Gourdough's donuts, and I knew I was about to become a Project: help Dr. Koretsky make friends. Which surprised me at the time— married girls don't usually like to hang out with single girls. We aren't an appreciative audience for the endless litany of "we," "us," "my husband," "the baby." That is, if they can be bothered to socialize at all; most of my married friends back in Colorado stopped going out even before they had kids. Somehow cuddling in front of Bravo became the ultimate leisure-time activity.

But Sarina was different; she was irreverent and potty-mouthed and we laughed like coked-up hyenas when we hung out together. I didn't get bored when she talked about her husband, because her stories about him cracked me up. Then, a few weeks ago, she invited me to a party they were throwing at their house at the end of January. A No Legitimate Reason party, meant to console everyone who was crashing hard into the postholiday blues. I was just excited that I'd recovered from an atomic stomach bug in time to be able to go.

I was waiting for the hallway bathroom when I heard the scrabble of claws on the inside of a nearby door, accompanied by a bitter wail. I dropped to my knees and inched the door open. A black paw shot out of the gap and swatted at the molding, trying to gain purchase to wedge the door open wider.

"Hello, *Newman*," I said.

A yellow eye glared at me through the gap. I extended my fingers to stroke his cheek, and Newman, taking advantage of my relaxed vigilance, wedged himself forward and through the door.

"Damnit!" I launched myself after him and caught him around the ribs just as he was about to round the corner toward the living room. I scooped him up in my arms to return him to his prison. Newman, immediately forgiving me for derailing his bid for freedom, placed his paws on either side of my neck and head-butted my chin, purring like an idling Harley.

Behind me, I heard the bathroom door open and the light switch off. "Don't let my brother see him loving on you like that," said a man's voice. "I don't know whether he'd be more upset to find out his wife was cheating on him, or his cat."

I turned and experienced the sensation of tripping over an unseen extension cord. The guy, who was apparently Sarina's brother-in-law, was goddamned spectacular. Dark, sleepy-lidded eyes, a pleasingly assertive nose, geological cheekbones, and long-ish, wavy black hair tucked behind his ears: he looked like Johnny Depp crossed with Julius Caesar. (Kate Moss–era Johnny, not Jack Sparrow—important distinction.) He was smiling at me, a lazy, sexy smile that crinkled the corners of his eyes.

"It's not what it looks like," I quipped. "I'm his vet."

"Oh, well in that case." He stepped closer and stretched out his fingers to scratch the cat under the chin. I was instantly jeal-ous.

"I'm Hilary, otherwise known as Dr. Koretsky," I said. "I'd shake your hand, but as you can see, I've got my hands full."

Eye crinkles. "Hey Hilary. I'm Colin."

"Eamon and Colin? Tell me you have another brother lurking somewhere around named Seamus."

"Actually, it's Kieran."

I laughed. "No it is not."

"Would I lie to you?" he said.

I cocked my head sideways to evaluate him. "I don't know you. You *might* be lying to me."

He gave me a lady-killer eyebrow. "Why don't you put my nephew back in his room, and I will go and get us some beers, and then you can get to know me."

—

I got to know him. Once supplied with drinks, we burrowed into one of the low-slung, vintage leather couches that anchored each end of the massive living room, and we pretty much didn't move all night. When I caught Sarina and Eamon making kissy fish faces at me over Colin's shoulder, I stuck my tongue out at them.

Colin took a sip of his Shiner Bock without turning around. "They're giving you shit, aren't they?"

"Yes, they are."

Still without turning, he lifted his arm and saluted them with a raised middle finger. "I'm in town for a couple more days. Do you want to meet up for dinner tomorrow?" I must have looked confused, because he continued. "That asshole will give me his car. He's my little brother, he has to do what I tell him."

Privately I thought it was a bit of a stretch for Colin to refer to his brother as "little," since Eamon is essentially a walking skyscraper, but I liked Colin's more personable scale; just south of six feet is more than enough man for someone as vertically compromised as I am. In fact, I liked everything about Colin—except the fact that he lived in New York. Brooklyn, he was careful to specify, as if I would understand the nuances of that distinction.

And back to Brooklyn he went, two days later, though I almost made him miss his flight. *HILARY YOU MUST RELEASE HIM*, said Sarina's text. *Col is not answering his phone, Eamon is pacing like an animal, and I'm going to strangle him if he doesn't stop. Tell Colin he has to get back here if he wants to get to the airport on time.*

"Listen," said Colin, one hand on my doorknob behind him, "I know we're not going to make this a thing, but if you ever feel like coming to New York, let me know, okay?"

"I will," I promised. "Same for you when you come back." I gave his chest a gentle shove. "But you have to go."

"Mm-hm," he said against my lips. Then we both heard the insistent buzz from his jeans pocket. "Okay. Going. Try to keep my nephew out of trouble." And then, with one last flash of a smile over his shoulder, he was gone.

—

And now. This. My life, clicking along as steadily as a freight car on one of the MoPac trains that rumble past the clinic all day long, slammed off its tracks in a pile of twisted steel by the impact of a Mack truck. This wasn't supposed to be mine, this consequence or this decision—this was never supposed to be me.

I dig my hands into my hair, making it flip forward in dark ribbons around my lowered face. *This is impossible,* I want to scream, but no sooner do the words bubble up than I know them for liars. All doctors, human or animal, know the inverses of statistics. The microscopic percentages everybody else likes to ignore when they make assumptions about what is or is not going to happen. I, Hilary Koretsky, am a statistic. My birth control failed. I am the 1 percent.

Except, I'm less than the 1 percent. I'm the 1 percent divided by an additional factor of hellish improbability.

I remember a lot of things about that third time we slept together: the way he caught my thigh under one arm and hitched it up against his waist; the satisfied sigh that slipped out of him when he felt the orgasm start quivering through me. The pop of his hip when he stood up to drop the condom in the trash can. His voice, swearing softly in the darkness.

"What's wrong?"

"I think . . . I think the condom broke."

"Oh shit, really?"

"Yeah. I totally didn't notice. Little too wrapped up in everything else." I could hear the apologetic smile better than I could see it.

"Well, no big deal," I said. "Unless you have a rare Micronesian bat flu that's only transmitted through sexual fluids."

"No Micronesian bat flu," he said, crawling back across the bed. He stretched out next to me and wrapped one arm over my rib cage. "You're on the Pill?"

"Yeah."

"Whew!" he said, wiping imaginary flop sweat off his forehead.

"Tell me about it," I said. "But it's all good."

And I really thought it was.

Of course, I forgot one fairly significant thing. The fact that I'd spent two whole days the week before puking everything I put into my stomach right back into this very same toilet I'm melting down on right now. Including two life-changing little tablets of Ortho Tri-Cyclen.

A native of Virginia's Shenandoah Valley, BETHANY CHASE headed to Williams College for an English degree and somehow came out the other side an interior designer. When she's not writing or designing, you can usually find her in a karaoke bar. She lives with her lovely husband and occasionally psychotic cat in Brooklyn, three flights up. This is her first novel.

ABOUT THE TYPE

This book was set in Sabon, a typeface designed by the well-known German typographer Jan Tschichold (1902–74). Sabon's design is based upon the original letter forms of sixteenth-century French type designer Claude Garamond and was created specifically to be used for three sources: foundry type for hand composition, Linotype, and Monotype. Tschichold named his typeface for the famous Frankfurt typefounder Jacques Sabon (c. 1520–80).